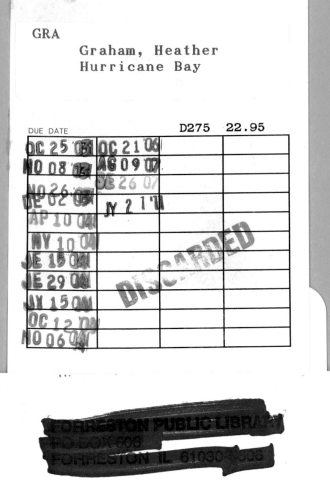

GRA

Graham, Heather
Hurricane Bay

# HURRICANE BAY

# HEATHER GRAHAM

## HURRICANE BAY

MIRA®

ISBN 1-55166-897-1

HURRICANE BAY

Visit us at www.mirabooks.com

**Printed in U.S.A.**

First Printing: April 2002
10 9 8 7 6 5 4 3 2 1

This book is dedicated with the deepest gratitude to many people.

First and foremost, Choly Zequeira. You are a saint.

Sonia Fraser, Kettia Gaspard and Fay C. Watson. Thanks for so much.

The incredible folks at St. Philip's Episcopal Church,
Reverends Eric Kahl and Jennie Lou Reid, David Karcher,
Joyce and Glenn Downing, Vida Welborne, Ron Theobald, Sylviane Sacasa,
George and Myrtice Hektner, Patrice Fike, Judy King, Julie McCready,
Ellen Sessions, Lee Turner, the Right Reverend and Holly Richards,
Manny and Laverne Diaz, John Dickason and Kris Charlton.

For the Southeast group—
especially Doris McManus, Audrey Fetscher and Rocco.

Sincere thanks also to Dr. Antonio Ucar, Max Sanchez and Omar Garcia.

And with the greatest respect and appreciation to three special
Metro-Dade policemen—Sergeant Greenberg
and Officers Mallon and Szolis of the Kendall division.

# PROLOGUE

Web loved the Florida Keys.

In fact, his old nickname, Web, had been born there. So few people knew that name. It was special and unique, to a time as well as a place, just like the islands themselves.

Like pearls cast against the ocean, the Keys meandered down from Miami in a southwest string of dazzling and opalescent beauty. The water lay on both sides of the many islands, shimmering in shades of aqua, blue, green, ever varying with the different depths. There were two ways to leave the mainland behind, Card Sound Bridge and US1, and once those routes were touched, the magic began. There was nothing in the world like sunrise on the Keys, the sun arcing into the sky in shades of crimson ecstasy, the heavens flaring with sudden light, golds as brilliant as the reds, pastels streaking from the bright colors with a soft beauty that seemed to caress the soul. Sunsets were even more heavenly, when the fiery globe of day began to fall in slow majesty, creating a new realm of color, magenta stretching fiery fingers out to the horizon, fading to threads of yellow-tinged pink and mauve, until silver and gray began to seep in and finally the orb of the sun disappeared with a last gasp of steaming gold and darkness fell.

There were few other places where darkness could be so complete.

Not, of course, on the beaten path. Not where the clubs stayed open, and the hotels and motels offered streaming lights for their clientele, and not where the laid-back Tiki bars still sent out soft beacons of welcoming, come-hither brightness. But away from civilization, where nature still prevailed, the darkness could be as complete as a stygian hole, as fearsome as a hell crawling with tiny demons, ready to eat away flesh and go deep enough to consume a human soul.

Ah, darkness. It could offer so much. Sweet secrets and sins, a place in which to hide...

And so it was at night, in the darkness, that Web waited, reflecting on the mystery, beauty and romance in the solitude of night and nature. And the task at hand.

There was an element of danger, of course.

A small element...but enough to give a little edge to the thrill.

There were those who thought of Key West as the main draw. But Web found the upper keys far more welcoming and natural. Close to the heady civilization of Miami, far enough away to offer the reefs, the sunrises and sunsets...

Not to mention shadow and darkness. An aura of mystery in which to meet *her* tonight. A surprise, of course, since she would have no idea of all he'd planned, the night, the breeze, the salty-sweet scent of the air, the beach...

Eternity.

She was so beautiful. Even more so when caught in shimmering rays of light...and shadow.

Web had planned tonight's event meticulously. Everything before her arrival had been set, and everything to follow was arranged to a *T*.

Almost.

The day had fallen into place perfectly, but now, as Web waited, the timing began to go awry. All the magic would be lost if she did not arrive soon. And this had to be the night, the night when so much would be solved, when reckoning would be met.

Web's watch ticked away the time. Minutes passed, then more minutes. Frustration, nervousness, set in.

Leave it to Sheila to be late.

It gave him time to reflect....

Every move she had ever made touched Web's heart and soul.

She had to come. And soon. Or all the detailed plans, the ebony mystique of the night, the brilliant ecstasy of dawn, would be lost.

And then...a sound.

Her car on the road.

Web switched on the portable floodlight.

The bright beam blinded her. It was like the wrath of God. Her car veering, she braked to an abrupt halt. Web calmly walked to the driver's side.

She shielded her eyes with a hand.

It might all have gone badly then. She might have had the window closed and the air on; it was cooler at night, but they were into the dead heat of summer.

But she had been driving with her windows open, luckily. It was a nice night. The air touched with coolness, a forerunner of the storm that would come in during the next day or two. The storm, of course, was part of the perfect plan.

"Who...what the *hell?*"

She had seen Web, of course.

"What in the world are you doing?"

"You agreed to meet me," he reminded her politely.

"For a minute, only a minute. And I never said I'd meet you *here,* in the frigging middle of nowhere."

She was angry and impatient at having her time taken up. Actually she was frequently impatient with anyone who wasn't in her favor at any given moment.

"It's so lovely here. I wanted you here with me, to see and appreciate just how beautiful it is here. I wanted to give you the night." Web sighed. "I take it you're not glad to see me?"

"Look, I just saw you earlier today. And I said I'd see you again, so we can talk then. *Briefly.*" Her voice had a husky growl to it that meant she was getting really aggravated. "But I never expected you to half blind me on this godforsaken road. And you are an idiot. I could have hit you."

"But you didn't."

"You could have been killed."

"Interesting thought. But to see you, and alone, it was worth the gamble."

Suddenly she actually saw Web. "Are you wearing gloves?" she asked incredulously. "It's summer."

Being Sheila, she didn't have a clue.

"It's not so hot tonight. There's a storm coming in. They haven't named it. It's not a hurricane, a tropical storm, or even a depression yet. But you can feel it. Soon rain will pound. Lightning will soar across the heavens. Thunder will sound like drums."

"Great," she said, bored. "Poetry. That really explains the gloves."

"Oh...they're just diving gloves."

"Diving gloves? With a storm coming in? You're going diving *now?*"

Web ignored her question. "I told you, I really wanted to see you. Alone."

"Great." She tossed her silky hair and looked straight ahead at the road. "You've seen me. But we aren't going to be alone. I didn't agree to any of this ridiculousness. I have to go. I haven't got time for your games."

"You're so wrong. You're going to make time. To spend the night on the beach. To watch the sunrise. To...appreciate. You have all the time in the world."

"I don't!" She frowned, growing wary.

"Yes, you do."

Her frown deepened. "You have a camera."

"For taking pictures on the beach."

"We're not taking pictures on the beach. Look, I mean it, I have to go. I don't want to run over your feet, so get out of my way."

"No, no, you don't understand. There's so much that's worth experiencing, especially before a storm. The colors...you've got to see them. You never really see what's right in front of your face. You never saw...me."

She was staring at Web, completely confused and dismissive. "Look—"

"Sheila, you *are* going to see the sunrise."

Web tossed the floodlight into her car, then reached for her. Real alarm rose in her eyes as she read something in his.

Web meant business.

She tried to hit the button to roll up the window. Too late.

"Let go! I'm leaving—now."

She hadn't expected the strength in the hands that curled around her wrists. She gunned the engine, but she'd put the car in Park.

"Dammit, what is the matter with you? You can't make me—"

"Oh, yes, I can. And guess what, Sheila? I'm going to."

Web got the door open and forced his way in, shoving her aside.

She started to scream.

But there was no one there to hear.

No one except for the mosquitoes that buzzed so annoyingly in the darkness, the night owl, the mangroves, the stars cast in the velvet sky and the sea breeze that drifted over the island.

And Web. But he didn't care. He just smiled, and within seconds, he had her silenced.

He was determined that they would share the coming of dawn.

Eventually the sun rose against the morning sky, the colors brilliant, despite the billowing clouds of the coming storm. Soon, soon...the rains would begin.

"See how absolutely beautiful?" Web asked.

Her eyes were fixed on the horizon.

"Really quite glorious," Web continued.

For once, she didn't argue. She just stared.

"You are as beautiful as the sunrise, Sheila," Web told her. "And I won't take long. I just want a picture or two."

Aim, focus, shoot...

The camera was a Polaroid. Instant gratification. He only had a few minutes to linger...to see the light, the shadows, the colors of this world.

The time had come. The scene had been set. The plan had been meticulously made.

But there was more to do, and he had to take care. The task must be completed, nothing left undone.

And so Web began.

Later the sun was full up, and Sheila...had moved on.

Anticipation filled Web's soul. Delight, glee, that each detail of the night and the dawn had come to such perfect fruition.

Now...

Patience. Web had to practice patience.

There was nothing left to do but wait...and watch as the plan unfolded.

# CHAPTER 1

Kelsey Cunningham walked into the Sea Shanty like a diminutive whirlwind.

Dane Whitelaw was stretched out on one of the lounge chairs beneath the palm-covered roof of the back patio when he saw her walk through the rows of crude wooden tables toward him.

He'd been sitting there downing draft Budweiser as if it were water, and it still hadn't dulled the brutal dilemma that pounded through his mind like a storm surge.

He'd come here, far off the main road, to sit in the breeze and watch the boats out on the gulf because it was something he often did. The norm for him. Usually, though, he didn't inhale his beer.

If he'd expected something to happen after his recent discovery, it sure as hell wasn't *her.*

The minute his eyes fell on her, he knew she just meant more trouble.

She wore designer shades, a straw hat, sandals and a brief white halter dress. She was tanned, and her hair was a light honey shade, not the kind of color caused by endless days in the sun but a natural amber. She had dressed the part for a lazy, laid-back place like this one—she was even carrying some kind of fruity, umbrella-laden drink in a plastic cup. She looked like a tourist, which maybe she was now.

She knew him right away. Well, naturally. He hadn't changed much. She, on the other hand, *had* changed. Despite that, he had known her the minute she entered his vision. And a single word had come into his mind.

*Fuck.*

What the hell was Kelsey doing here now?

She made straight for him with long, no-nonsense strides and stopped right next to his chair.

Even with the heat, she managed to smell like some kind of expensive perfume. She was well-built, smooth and sleek, nice cleavage displayed above the bodice of the casual white dress that still managed to maintain a strange look of elegance on her form. She had gained an edge of sophistication in the years that yawned between them. And she didn't seem to remember him with any affection, or that they might once have been considered friends. Still, Kelsey was a beauty. Always had been, always would be. And a torpedo of pure determination.

And, long ago now, she had determined to keep herself far away.

So what the hell was she doing here now? Today, of all damned times?

She didn't give him a chance to ask, didn't even start off with so much as a simple "Hello."

"Where's Sheila?" she asked, a sharp note of demand in her voice.

His heart slammed. The name hit him like a blow to the head.

"Sheila?" he said, forcing a quizzical frown to his lips.

"Yes, Dane, where's Sheila?"

He studied her for a long moment. "Hmm. Not, 'Hi, Dane, how are you?' Or, 'Long time no see. How are you?'"

"Don't get funny. And don't pretend you don't know what I'm talking about."

"Kid, I'm not pretending anything."

"Don't call me 'kid,' Dane."

"Sorry. You *are* still Joe's kid sister, aren't you?"

"Dane, where is Sheila? And don't tell me you haven't seen her. There are witnesses, you know."

"Witnesses to what?"

"No one has seen Sheila in a week. The last time she was seen was here, with you. And you're going to tell me exactly where she is."

He was glad of his own sunglasses. And though there were few times in his current life when he was glad of his past, this was one of them. He kept his face totally impassive.

*Because he did know what had happened to Sheila Warren, even if he didn't know exactly where she was. And in the last two hours, the one driving purpose in his own life had become finding the* exact *whereabouts of Sheila.*

Of all the damned things he didn't need, it was Kelsey Cunningham coming here now, accosting him. Looking for Sheila. As far as he knew, the two women hadn't seen each other in years.

"Sorry, kid. So she was here with me. She's here a lot. With a lot of different people. Why in God's name would I know where she is now...honey?" he asked, his voice a slow, lazy drawl, the tone purposefully insinuating. Why not? They weren't kids anymore. And the time when they'd been bonded together in sorrow was eons ago now. The last time they had met, she had been far more than cool. In fact, she'd been as frigid and brittle as ice.

Kelsey the compassionate. Sincere, earnest, a daredevil at times. Quick with laughter, swift to challenge. Full of empathy for any underdog; a pit bull against any evil, real or imagined. Once upon a time, Joe's darling of a sweet little sister.

Times changed.

"Dane, dammit, she talked to you. You were seeing her again."

Irrelevantly he noticed that she had grown into her effortless grace. And she had gained the ability to appear as cool and remote as a goddess.

He almost sat up, but didn't. He forced himself to shrug casually. "Seeing her? Well, yeah, honey, I was seeing her. In a way. Me and half the men in the southern half of the state, not to mention nearly every tourist in pants who set foot on the island."

"You asshole," she said. Her tone didn't rise, but something in her words conveyed the extent of her contempt.

"Yeah, honey, I'm an asshole. But before you go off in a tizzy about Sheila Warren, you need to accept the fact that she'd changed over the years. In fact, you pretty much need to accept the fact that she was damn close to being a prostitute."

She was silent for a moment. She didn't move, but it didn't matter. The fury she was feeling seemed to emanate from her like heat waves off black pavement.

"She was...a free spirit. But I know she was with you again and now she's missing. Someone knows something. If it's anyone, it has to be you. You talked to her, and she talked to you."

"Yes, she talked to me. And I talked to her."

"So talk to me."

He slid his glasses down his nose for a moment, studying her. "*She* talked to me nicely," he said.

"This isn't a social call."

"Right. So leave me alone."

"Since you don't seem to want to talk to me, I'll have to see to it that you talk to the police."

"Fine. The police are usually polite and courteous." He pushed his sunglasses back up his nose and folded his arms over his chest.

She was still staring down at him. He sighed and looked up at her impatiently.

"So what is it now? I can't help you. Can't you leave me alone anyway? See something you like? Hey, kid, have you changed, too? Just like Sheila? Do you want to...catch up on old times?"

Her composure was amazing. She took her time answering him.

"Do I see something I like? No, not at all. In fact, I'm amazed by how much I see I *dis*like."

"Well, then, you *have* changed, honey. So...you're not into the muscle-bound beach type anymore, huh?"

"I'm just not into assholes like you. Available? You must be joking."

He looked up at her blandly. "Is that all?"

"All? No, not quite."

She spoke softly, and, with an economy of motion, she twis. d her wrist. The fruity drink fell over his chest like a rain of sticky slime. He almost jumped up to grab her. Instinct again.

He managed to keep his place on the lounge chair. It was important that she keep thinking of him as an asshole.

Strange, he hadn't seen her in years. But still...she was a Keys kid from way back. Joe's little sister.

No, Kelsey was a hell of a lot more than that, he reminded himself. But any fleeting memory of what might have been an inescapable bond in the past was quickly doused by the lethal trauma of the present.

Even more than he had feared when he first saw her, he realized that she was trouble. Real trouble.

And he sure as hell didn't want her...

Dear God, he didn't want her going the route Sheila had gone.

Still staring down at him, she shook her head with revulsion. "An asshole and a drunk," she said. "You're covered in liquor and you don't even move."

"I imagine it's good booze. I'll just lick myself all over," he said. "Want to help?"

With one last look of disgust, she turned on her perfect little sandal-heels and started to walk away.

"Kelsey!"

Despite himself, he got to his feet, every muscle in his body quickening with tension.

"Go to the cops, Kelsey, then get the hell out of the Keys, do you hear? Go back to your hot job and your condo on the bay. Do you understand?"

She paused for a moment, then told him what he could do with himself.

"Whatever you want, Kelsey. But I mean it. Tell the cops anything you think they ought to know. Then go home."

"This *is* my home—as much as it's yours."

"The hell it is. Your home now is a cute little condo in a ritzy section of Miami, with a gate and a security guard. Now go away."

"Who the hell do you think you are?" she asked. She didn't expect an answer, but he gave her one anyway.

"I'm the man telling you that you don't belong here anymore," he said. *Especially not running around asking questions about Sheila.*

"Like I said, Dane. This *is* my home just as much as it's yours. And I *will* find Sheila."

She started walking away again, taking a circuitous route past the tables. He was tempted to go after her, shake her, tell her to get her nose out of the entire thing. FedEx her back to Miami.

Except that he would wind up getting arrested if he tried that. He was certain that if he so much as put a hand on her, she would call the cops for sure.

So he watched as she walked away through the back door of the Sea Shanty. He had to convince her to go back to Miami and get her the hell out of this. How, he wasn't sure yet.

But he would. He swore to himself with a vengeance that he would get her out of here if it was the last thing he did.

When she was gone, he clenched his teeth and shook his head, suddenly glad the beer hadn't kicked in. He walked down the sand - and shrub-covered path to the small spit of salt beach off the back of the Sea Shanty and just kept going until he was immersed. It was the quickest way he could think of to remove the drink she'd spilled on him. And the cool water was good for his head.

He'd wanted to behave completely normally after what had happened. But Kelsey arriving like a cyclone had changed all that.

Now the police were about to get involved, and sooner or later they would find Sheila Warren.

Jesus.

He had to find her first.

Kelsey walked into the right side of the duplex just off US1 in absolute disgust. She threw her purse across the small living room, watched as it landed in a wicker chair, then indulged in a moment's delicious relief as the air-conditioning surrounded her. Sea breezes be damned. It was hot as hell outside.

Pausing by the door for a moment, she let out a breath of aggravation.

"Well, that went well," she said, murmuring wryly aloud to herself. Her fault, maybe. Okay, her fault definitely. She could have started out with a, Hi, Dane, how are you? Wow, it's been ages....

But he had looked like such a beach bum lying there. And Nate, the owner of the Sea Shanty who she was actually married to for a very brief time when they were young, had said he had been drinking all afternoon. And that he'd been seeing Sheila. That they had argued. And that Dane had been strange ever since he'd moved back down from St. Augustine. That he'd taken on a case up there and someone had died strangely and...Nate hadn't really known all the particulars because Dane hadn't wanted to talk about them. So something not great had happened, and he'd come home to drink himself to death. Sheila had told her, too, that Dane had been strange. Like a guy ready to throw his life away.

When they were kids, Dane had been like the Rock of Gibraltar. He and Joe had been the leaders of the pack. Even when she had wanted to run away from life and—more than anything in the world—from Dane, she had wanted things to go well for him. It had been upsetting to hear that he had fallen into being little more than a beach bum, with no care for the world, no ambition, no concern for anyone at all—even old friends.

Sheila had been concerned about him.

But it seemed that Dane didn't give a damn about her.

Kelsey kicked off her shoes and walked into the kitchen. She opened the refrigerator door, thanking God that she'd taken the time that morning to do a little shopping for herself. Juice, soda, beer and wine. She had a choice.

The heat she'd come from made her opt for a beer. She hesitated, her fingers curling around a bottle, remembering that she'd found Dane swilling the stuff. She moved her hand, choosing a bottle of cranberry-raspberry cocktail instead. No. She wanted a beer, and the fact that Dane had turned into a slug who drank the stuff lying on a lounge chair in the shade shouldn't keep her from what she wanted.

Why the hell had he made her so mad? Right from the get-go. Okay, she'd been disturbed from the minute she'd talked to Nate, maybe unreasonably angry with Dane before she'd even headed out to speak to him. Why?

Uh-uh, she argued with herself. She wasn't going to delve into the psychiatry of that one. She hadn't seen him in years. And still, today...damn, she'd blown it, that was all. She'd meant to talk to him, get information. Everyone knew he'd been seeing Sheila again. Maybe they hadn't become a twosome, the way they had been when they were young, but apparently they'd still been close. Even Larry Miller, another friend from the early days who she worked with *and* Sheila's ex, had apparently known that, because he'd mentioned something about Sheila saying she was seeing Dane again when Kelsey had told him she was heading to Key Largo for her vacation, to spend time with Sheila.

Nate had told her that Dane and Sheila argued the last time

he'd seen her. Cindy Greeley, one of her and Sheila's best friends growing up, had told her the same.

She pulled out the Michelob, twisted off the cap, took a long swig and looked around the kitchen. "Sheila...am I crazy? Are you just being a careless and inconsiderate bitch, the way everyone seems to think? Where the hell are you?"

The air conditioner hummed in reply. No answer there. In the quiet of the early evening, the sound seemed absurdly loud.

She walked to the rear of the living room and opened the glass doors to the patio at the back of the duplex, separated by a small privacy wall from the neighboring side. Beyond stretched the standard-size pool that belonged to both occupants, surrounded by flowering plants and shrubs. The entire yard was surrounded by a rustic wood privacy fence. The backyard was beautiful and peaceful, the high point of the duplex. And actually, on the patio, she could feel a sweet, salt-touched breeze. She was startled to feel suddenly that it was good to be home. And it *was* still her home, no matter what anyone said—especially Dane.

Not that she had gone so very far. Her section of Miami was only an hour to an hour and a half away, depending on traffic. But life there seemed as different as night and day, even if the temperatures in both places were almost identical and the same flowers bloomed. A short walk from this duplex could bring her to the Atlantic, and she could look straight out from her condo patio and see the waters of Biscayne Bay, heading into the Atlantic, as well. And still, this was so different. She had felt it today at the Sea Shanty, the small-town warmth, the laid-back ease, even with the place crawling with tourists and the main objective among most of the populace being to make money off those tourists. There were other people, as well, retirees, Northerners sick of the snow, and weekenders who had fallen in love with their weekends and made Key Largo their home. She'd always wanted to see more of the world, and she'd gotten to see a lot of it now. Maybe that was why it seemed so good to feel as if she had really come home.

Once upon a time, home had been the pretty white-painted wooden house south on US1 on the ocean side of the island. No more. Her parents had sold the place years ago. They didn't come back here anymore. In fact, the house no longer existed; it had been torn down to make way for the tennis courts for one of the new hotels. It had bothered her deeply when she'd started driving around today, so much so that she wished she had told her parents she wanted the house when they offered it to her before moving to Orlando.

Too late now.

Like them, at the time she had just wanted to get out of Key Largo.

She knew, of course, that when she'd left, she'd been running away. There had been far too much of Joe here then, and she had needed a new environment. Time could do good things. Now she liked it because there was still a lot of Joe here. Just as she had liked seeing Nate at the Sea Shanty, feeling the sun and the breeze at the Tiki hut bar, knowing that a short walk in bare feet would bring her to the little patch of private beach.

The Sea Shanty was like a bastion of memory. Nate's dad had run it when they were kids. Now the place was Nate's. And when she walked in, she really had felt that sense of coming home, of memory, nostalgia and mostly good things. She had felt a sense of poignant pleasure, being there. But then she had spoken with Nate and mentioned how worried she was about Sheila. Nate had started talking, and then she had seen Dane Whitelaw, plastered and vegetating in the sun, sunglasses in place, beer at his side, the picture of total inertia.

Dane Whitelaw, of all people.

Wasting his life. She'd seen it so many times. People who used this little corner of Eden to escape all responsibility, to drown themselves in beer and couch potato themselves into early graves.

And he was lying, to boot. He had seen Sheila, talked to her...done a lot more than talked, by his own admission. Why not? They'd been off and on for years. The worst of it was that he should care, be concerned. Even Larry, whom Sheila had hurt, had been concerned, insisting that she call him if she needed anything, if Sheila needed anything, if there was anything he could do...Sheila wouldn't even need to see him. If she needed money, he would be happy to help her out. Nate had been concerned, too, shaking his head and telling her that they all worried about Sheila, but hell, what could they do? She was a grown-up.

Nate had told her, too, that Sheila often made dates with her friends—lunch, dinner, drinks, coffee, breakfast, whatever—and forgot to appear. She always had an apology, of course. Even so, Nate had seemed concerned, even as he tried to tell Kelsey that she shouldn't be. He hadn't seen Sheila in a week, and she never stayed away from the Sea Shanty that long.

Only Dane seemed indifferent. Crude. It appeared that he had come home just to drink himself into oblivion, and he didn't give a damn about Sheila or anything else.

And, of course, there was that last page in Sheila's diary, which she had found beneath the pillow on Sheila's bed. At first she had shoved the book back under the pillow, surprised that Sheila had kept a diary, then determined that a diary was private and she had no right to read it. But when Sheila hadn't appeared, she had skimmed through, and then gone to the last page.

*Have to see Dane tonight. Tell him I'm afraid.*

Private or not, she was going to read every page in the diary. Maybe she should have mentioned it to the police.

No. Not yet, anyway. Not until she knew what was in it herself. She wasn't airing Sheila's life to anyone, unless it became absolutely necessary.

There was a knock at the door. For a moment she clenched her teeth, wondering if Dane had decided to follow her back from the Sea Shanty. A man wouldn't need to be a P.I. to find out where she was staying.

And he undoubtedly knew the way to Sheila's place.

She marched barefoot to the front door, grateful that the owners of the duplex had done away with the old-time jalousie and put in solid wood doors. She looked through the peephole. Cindy Greeley, now her official next-door neighbor in the duplex where she herself was an unofficial guest, was standing on the porch with a tray of something in her hands.

Kelsey opened the door.

"Did you find out anything?" Cindy asked her.

Kelsey stepped back, letting Cindy enter. Even in her bare feet, she was almost a head taller than the other woman, five-nine compared with Cindy's petite five-two. The smaller woman was compact, with sun-bleached hair, huge blue eyes and a tiny frame. She looked as if she should be heading off to high school, but she'd always had a terrific head on her shoulders, had made it nicely through college, and now owned eighteen T-shirt and shell shops throughout the Keys that might one day make her rich.

"Did I find out anything?" Kelsey said, her tone both musing and slightly bitter. "Nope. Nothing."

"I told you," Cindy said.

"Well, wait a minute. Maybe not exactly 'nothing.' I did find out that everyone saw Sheila arguing with Dane, but no one knows where she is now. Except, of course, I'm sure someone is lying. Want to come in and have something to drink?"

Cindy gave her a quizzical look for a moment. "Kind of early for you, isn't it? You're the kid who never had anything to drink during the day. And I thought you just came from the Sea Shanty?"

"It's after five. Isn't that cocktail hour?"

"Yeah, I guess. Sorry. I didn't realize how late it was. Daylight Saving Time, you know. Seems it stays light so late. But hey, I told you to try one of those Wind-Runners over there. That should have knocked you for a loop. Didn't you get one?"

"I ordered one. But I didn't drink it."

"Why not? They're delicious."

"It spilled," Kelsey said. "Are you coming in?"

"Oh, yeah, sure. I just made quiche. Thought you might like some."

"Good, you supply the food, I've got the beer."

They walked on into the kitchen together. "I went down to the sheriff's department. Sergeant Hanson let me fill out a missing persons report, though he wasn't real thrilled about it. He didn't seem to think there was anything odd about Sheila being gone for a week. Usually all you need is forty-eight hours. Here, your remains could be mummified and everyone still thinks you'll show up when you feel like it."

"Kelsey, that's not true. It's just that..."

"That what?"

"Sheila was living...a certain lifestyle," Cindy said.

"Still, a missing persons report is important," Kelsey told Cindy. She looked pointedly at her friend. "And it's something no one else thought to do."

"Kelsey," Cindy said, taking a seat on one of the three bar stools at the kitchen counter, "I'm not sure what to say to make you feel better. You've got to realize, Sheila is always going off and not telling anyone."

"I'm worried because she was supposed to meet me. Here. We made plans. I took my vacation time."

Cindy shrugged, accepting a bottle of Michelob. "Kelsey, you haven't seen a lot of Sheila in the last few years."

"I haven't seen her at all for at least two years," Kelsey said.

Cindy spoke slowly. "So you just have to realize—you don't really know her anymore."

Kelsey shrugged, feeling the guilt that had plagued her lately over that very fact.

They'd all been friends, growing up. Slightly different in age, but friends because they were islanders, and the area had been pretty darn small back when they'd been kids. She was the youngest, Cindy was one year her senior, Sheila and Nate were the same age, two years older than Cindy. Of their little group, her brother, Joe, had been the oldest—with Dane Whitelaw just one month younger. Then there was Larry, who had been about the same age as Dane and Joe, but he had been a weekender, so he hadn't really been in the same tight-knit group. Sometimes there had been other kids in the group, as well, guys like Jorge Marti, and even Izzy Garcia.

They'd all grown so far apart over the years.

Well, except for the fact that she worked with Larry, who had been instrumental in getting her into Sherman and Cutty, the advertising and promotions firm where she worked in the conceptual design department. Then, of course, Cindy and Nate were still close friends. And maybe she hadn't really been that far away, because she had kept up with Cindy. And Nate. Despite the fact that she and Nate had been married and divorced in the blink of an eye. Oddly enough, though totally unsuited to be husband and wife, she and Nate had made it as friends. When she thought back, she was angry with herself for what she had done, marrying him. Of course, she had felt empty then, hurt and very alone. The void in her life had seemed like a bottomless pit. There had been nothing she wanted more then than to get away. And Nate...Nate had never been going anywhere. He'd loved Key Largo and known he was going to stay from the time he'd been a boy. Maybe she had thought of marriage as a means to run away. Whatever her thinking, it had been wrong, and she had done nothing but hurt Nate. Still, it seemed he had forgiven her. And he was happy. He loved his Sea Shanty. Loved fishing, diving, boating and just being in the sun. He had never talked about anything other than living his life right here.

Just as Sheila and Dane had talked about nothing but moving on.

She understood why with Sheila. And with Dane...maybe she understood him, too.

But they'd both come back.

And now she was back here, as well, especially to see Sheila. Except that Sheila had invited her down, sent her the key to the duplex and never appeared herself.

"Have you been out to see Sheila's stepfather yet?" Cindy asked cautiously.

Kelsey experienced a slight and involuntary shudder. "No," she said, her admission rueful.

"Well, neither have I," Cindy murmured. "And he's actually the man we should be asking about her."

"I'm surprised she keeps in any kind of contact with him."

"She has to. They're connected by her mother's trust fund."

"You know what?" Kelsey said, suddenly decisive. "I'm going out there right now."

"Wait a minute! Why?" Cindy asked. "We're going to have beer and quiche. Kelsey, you have to eat, you know. You can go out and see Andy Latham anytime. Go tomorrow in the daylight."

"It's still daylight now," Kelsey said. She was already at the door, slipping her sandals back on. "I suppose I really should have gone out there to see him first."

"Why? Sheila hated him, you know that. If she had plans, she'd never have shared them with him. Not that she really made too many long-term plans. I lived in the other half of the same building, and I never knew what she was doing."

"You just said she had to keep in contact with him because of her mom's trust fund. He still might know something," Kelsey said.

Cindy sighed. "Kelsey, her car is gone, so she obviously drove somewhere. Maybe you should start by looking for the car instead of with her stepdad. Though I still think you're making a mountain out of a molehill."

"Cindy, she knew I could only take so much time off. And she really wanted to see me. She was worried about something."

Cindy was silent, which made Kelsey aggravated—with herself and with everyone else. Maybe they were right. She hadn't seen Sheila in forever. A sense of guilt had brought her here, but the fact that she was feeling guilty didn't mean that Sheila had suddenly become responsible, or that she wouldn't forget her plans with Kelsey the same way she forgot plans with anyone else. Sheila might have talked to her, sounding desperate, then forgotten the plans they'd made just a few minutes later.

"Want to come with me?" she asked Cindy.

"No," Cindy said with a shudder. "And I really don't think you should go out there, either. You should wait. Get Nate or someone to go out with you. Dane would go. Dane has actually opened an investigations firm here. This is the kind of thing he does for a living. If anyone can find Sheila, it should be him. Make him go see Andy Latham with you."

Kelsey shook her head, still feeling the burn of her encounter with Dane. "Hire one drunk to go see another?"

"You don't understand about Dane," Cindy said.

"Cindy, you'd champion Dane if he'd just robbed the National Bank."

"Not true. He's just...I don't really know the story, but one of his clients was killed in St. Augustine."

"Murdered?"

"Not exactly. According to the police, it was accidental manslaughter, or something like that."

"All right, so something bad happened," Kelsey said. "Bad things happen in the world. It shouldn't have changed Dane into a vegetable. Anyway, I certainly don't want his help now. He was like a slug this afternoon. I'll be fine by myself. Andy Latham is just scuzzy, not dangerous. I'll be back soon. Throw some quiche in the refrigerator and I'll microwave it when I get back." She was at the door.

"Great dinner companion you turned out to be," Cindy called.

"Sorry."

Kelsey, glad to feel that there was something she could actually do rather than sit around and wait for Sheila, let the door close behind her and headed quickly for her car.

She was startled when the door opened in her wake and Cindy came out. "Hey!"

Kelsey paused. "Yeah?"

"Kelsey...he might have been drinking this afternoon at Nate's, but...why did you call Dane a drunk?"

"Let me see...Nate says he comes every afternoon. He'd had half a dozen beers by the time I got there. He was just sprawled out on a lounge chair when I arrived, looking like his mind had been fried for years. Nate said he's been back here for several months, and that he's opened a business so he can *look* like a solid citizen, but that his heart isn't really in it."

"That doesn't make him a drunk."

"He sure looked like one today."

"He goes to Nate's and drinks club soda most afternoons," Cindy said.

"Trust me, he was reeking of beer."

Cindy shrugged. "Okay, maybe he was drinking today. I've been known to have a few too many myself on occasion. Whatever. If you want to think he's a drunk, fine, think he's a drunk. I still think you'd be better off bringing a big drunk with military training out with you to see a scuzzbag."

"I'll be all right. I'll keep my distance."

"Honestly, Kelsey, you should wait," Cindy said.

But Kelsey was already on her way.

*"Help me, Dane."*

He could remember her words so clearly, and now, with the lowering sun bringing the onset of evening, he found himself hearing their echo over and over again.

There were things he should be doing. But he had searched the beachfront over and over again, and he had found exactly what he had expected: nothing. The "near storm," as they were calling it, an exceptionally bad spate of weather that had never actually formed into a hurricane, had come through about a week ago before petering out when it moved north and west over Homestead and the Everglades. There had been no damage to the house, but palm fronds had come down with a vengeance, and the beach had been flooded for twenty-four hours before the water receded.

His first response upon examining the photo shoved under the door had been to search, regroup, search again, then think it all out and search for a third time.

No, his first response had been shock. Then sorrow. Deep, gut-wrenching sorrow.

Then had come the knowledge that he was being framed, and that no matter how hard he searched he wouldn't find fingerprints or proof of any kind that anyone but he had been on his private beach—with Sheila.

The time for emotion was past. No, maybe it could never be past. But he sure as hell didn't have time for the luxury of pity, self or otherwise. Nor could he fly off in anger.

Now it was time to spread out further, to figure out what the hell was going on and who the hell had hated Sheila viciously enough to kill her. Who was cunning, cruel and psychotic—and held such a deep and maniacal sense of vengeance against him?

With Kelsey in town, acting like the FBI, he was going to have to move more quickly than he'd imagined. Thankfully he had friends in the right places. But since he was withholding evidence, he'd also been aware that he would have to take everything very carefully. But now...

Now it was different.

He had an almost photographic memory, which was going to stand him in good stead right now. After the initial shock of seeing the photo, he had known just where to begin, starting on the most logical path to carry him in the direction of the truth. Except that, with what he did know, the path didn't make any sense. He shouldn't be wasting time, except that sitting here had never really been wasting time.

The water and the peace that could be found on a spit of dock on a little island called Hurricane Bay were always good for rational thinking and reasoning.

And remembering.

The long summer day was ending; at last the sun was beginning to set. This was the time when the world was most beautiful. He remembered, thinking as a kid, that his dad was just crazy. They'd had no air-conditioning, but his father had pointed out that the breeze always came through. The house had seemed a shack, but his dad had pointed out that they didn't need any art on the walls, because they had the most beautiful vista anyone could ever imagine, every night. All they had to do was sit on the rustic porch and watch the sun set, watch as colors came out over the Atlantic, pinks, reds, golds, yellows. Sometimes the skies would be clear and the blue would turn slowly to strange pastels, then indigo, and then night would fall. Sometimes there would be clouds in the sky, and they would become a billowy cobalt before turning into dancing shadows against the moon. When storms came, it was just as beautiful, if different. The lightning would strike the water like bolts cast down by a furious god, and the trees would whip and bend in the wind.

Everything his father had said was true. Now he knew. Just as he knew that no meal in the world was better than fresh fish, just pulled from the sea and thrown on the grill. Odd that he would come to love this place, Hurricane Bay, when he had been so blind to its charms as a kid. Back then, he'd had no idea how great it was to own a private island.

He was glad he'd had the time to let his dad know how much he appreciated the place and had come to love it.

Sitting on the wooden dock, staring out over the water, he closed his eyes and heard her voice again.

# CHAPTER 2

*"Help me, Dane."*

Sheila's voice was an echo in his head. A ghostly reproach.

He didn't need to keep hearing it. He'd already damned himself a hundred times over.

He'd been sitting here that night, just as he was now, the last time he'd seen Sheila arrive at Hurricane Bay.

But before that...

Would things have been different if he hadn't seen her in action just that day?

He'd been at the Sea Shanty just before she had come over. He'd been drinking soda water with lime, discussing surveillance cameras with Nate. Nothing big had happened. Nate thought that maybe one of his bartenders had decided he wasn't quite making it on tips and was helping himself to the till. Dane didn't intend to work for Nate, and he had no intention of charging for the advice he gave. Sheila had been there, too. She came almost every afternoon at about five.

She never bought her own drinks.

Maybe she hadn't known he was there. Maybe she had known

and hadn't cared. Once upon a time, way back when, he and Sheila had been something of a twosome. But he had to admit, he'd never been in love with her. From the time he had been a little kid, he'd had a path in mind for himself, a plan for his life. A lot of that had come from Mr. Cunningham and Joe, but whatever the reason, his future had been the burning essence in his mind.

He hadn't wanted to wind up a fisherman in Key Largo, hoping for a catch, dodging the tourists, sucking up to the tourists, watching restaurant managers come and go.

If anything, he'd been determined he was going to own the restaurants.

And Sheila...

Well, at one time she might have loved him in her way. But she'd been just as intent on her own path. She'd wanted out. And getting out had meant more to Sheila than attaching herself to a man with no specific prospects, even if he had ambition. She'd spent her high school years sizing up the tourists and the weekenders—Floridians who usually lived fairly close to Key Largo, where they kept condos or vacation homes, and left their prestigious jobs in the city on Friday after work and returned Sunday night, ready to go back to work on Monday morning.

But he'd always thought he was her friend. They'd had their occasional thing together, even after their passionate breakup way back when. But not in the last few years. Not since he'd finished his military obligations, settled in the St. Augustine area, opened Whitelaw Investigations...and fallen in love with Kathy Malkovich.

He'd seen Sheila a few times since he'd retreated back home. Only with other friends, mostly, or sitting around the bar. She'd even shown up at his place once with Nate when they'd made a major dolphin fish haul a few weeks back and barbecued it on the grill at his place. Because of their past history, people were making more of it than it had been.

Nate had talked about Sheila's current activities, then cut himself off, remembering that she and Dane had once been more than friends. The usual guy talk had sounded too coarse, even for Nate.

So he should have known. Sheila had always been a flirt. And she was soundly of the opinion that most people fell out of love in life, and that some guys were good in bed and some guys weren't, so going to bed with a man because he could offer her something was in no way a sin. Look at the jerks most women slept with because they thought they were in love, or thought the guy was decent, she always said.

Sheila gave new meaning to the term "jaded."

That afternoon, though, just a week ago, he had really seen her in action for the first time. Seen her work her "magic" at the bar.

So he was a little jaded himself. Not exactly sunk in despair, but then again, not ready to go out and tackle the world. And when he had watched Sheila, he'd experienced some strange sensations. Relief, for one. He was thankful they'd never gotten serious or—God forbid—married each other. He felt sorrow, too, remembering the kid she had been. And he had also felt a bit of disgust, wondering what the hell she was doing. There she was, a beautiful woman, doing things she didn't need to do. She was young, with the world in front of her, and she had seemed to be on the path of self-destruction.

Her sole purpose was apparent from the minute she climbed on a bar stool next to a guy. First there had been the middle-aged Hispanic man sporting the loud jewelry. Heavy gold chains had hung around his neck, and his fingers had been bedecked with gold and diamonds. Sheila had crawled atop a chair with a cigarette, asking for a light. They'd started talking, and he'd bought her a drink, but he hadn't stayed long. There had been a woman waiting for him out on the patio. Before he'd left, however, Sheila had written something on a piece of paper and given it to him.

Then there had been the younger guy, maybe twenty-five. His cutoffs had carried a designer label, and his sandals were straight from the pages of *GQ*. His T-shirt had sported a label, as well—not just designer but *top* designer. Even if he ever got as rich as Croesus, Dane couldn't see spending that kind of money on a T-shirt.

Sheila had been studying her drink when the young guy had walked in. She must have had some kind of natural radar, because she'd turned around immediately, seen her new quarry, squashed out her cigarette and knocked another out of the pack in front of her.

They'd talked for a long time. And again Sheila had given him her number.

No one had appealed to Sheila after that. She'd noticed Dane at the back of the bar by then. She might have colored just a little, seeing him there. Then she'd tossed her long dark hair and come over.

"So...it's the long-lost home boy nursing his woes at the shanty bar, huh?"

"Hi, Sheila."

She'd lit her own cigarette then and tapped her matches on the bar.

"See, old flame, men do still find me attractive," she'd said softly.

"Sheila, you're beautiful, and you know it."

That had brought a smile to her lips. "But it isn't enough, is it?"

He remembered lifting his hands with a certain aggravation. "It depends on what you want. What the hell are you doing?"

She looked at him. "Do you remember when you liked me, Dane?"

"Sheila, I still like you. You're a friend."

That brought another smile. "You never loved me."

That seemed out of the blue. "*You* never loved *me.*"

She looked ahead. "We both wanted to get out, and here we are again. You loved *her,* though, huh? That woman in St. Augustine."

He didn't answer because she didn't allow him to, rushing back in. "What's wrong with me, Dane?"

"Sheila, there's nothing wrong with you. We just didn't have the commitment, the shared interests, the right whatever."

She shook her head, staring ahead. "I couldn't stay with Larry, either. Why not? I should have. It's like I'm always looking for...I don't know." She stared at him. "Hey, want to sleep with me?"

"Sheila—"

"Oh, yeah. I heard. You're still in mourning. I wish you weren't. I'd feel...secure if I were with you."

"Sheila, feeling secure isn't a reason to sleep with a guy. Any more than money is."

She turned to look at him with amusement. "Money is as good a reason as any. Come on, Dane, aren't you feeling just a bit of the old magic?" She reached out beneath the bar, long delicate fingers light on his thigh, then zeroing in.

Actually it was the little jump of arousal he'd felt that had stirred his temper. He'd gripped her fingers, pushing her hand aside, and risen. "No," he told her angrily—and too loudly.

"Dane, don't leave me."

"Sheila, I can't leave you if I'm not with you."

He'd turned and left the bar. Nate had seen them, of course. He hadn't known what they were saying, but since he was at the end of the bar, he must have heard the anger in Dane's voice. And damn if Cindy Greeley hadn't been there, too, that day—he hadn't seen her until then, but there she was, with Nate at the end of the bar, showing him the new T-shirts she'd designed for his bar.

He'd said hi to Cindy and gone on.

That night Sheila had shown up at his house. She'd told him not to worry, she was just stopping by, seeing what he was up to. They were still friends, right?

"Friends, Sheila," he had told her, and let her in.

At first she had been so casual.

She'd asked him about what had brought him back. He'd told

her it had just been time to come home. She hadn't believed him, but she had pretended to.

"I think, for you, everything changed with Joe."

He hadn't answered that. Instead he'd said, "Sheila, what the hell are you doing?"

"Getting by. I should marry some nice guy and settle down. Problem is, there aren't that many nice guys out there. Besides, you knew me when I was young and sweet and innocent. Okay, I was never innocent. But I *was* a little sweet."

"You were married to Larry Miller. There's a nice guy."

"A boring guy, I'm afraid. I like excitement. Or maybe every nice guy is a boring guy. I don't know. You know what, Dane? Men just don't come in the kind that I really want to keep. Actually, I may be a real voice for my sex."

"Oh?"

Sheila had laughed, and looked stunning. "Yeah. Guys are usually ratty to women. They fall in love...lust first, most of the time. They marry, they cheat."

"Not all of them. I'd say it's pretty even."

"Not on your life! Trust me. Men always seem to need someone to bolster their egos. Some guy told me once that it's just natural. You know, survival of the species. Long ago, guys had to sow their seed, just like lions, or some shit like that. Mate all they could so their DNA would go on and on. Instinctively they're still that way—except, of course, that they don't really want to procreate anymore, because on the not so instinctive side, something resembling brains kicks in and they don't want to pay child support. But some guys are innately bad, maybe not even in a way they can help. Look at all the old geezers looking for trophy wives. Sixty-, seventy-, even eighty-year-olds throwing out wives they've had for years, finding some beach bunny and patting themselves on the back for having a kid when they're members of AARP. Makes 'em macho."

"Sheila, you know, I have friends who have been left by their wives, taken to the cleaners big time by them."

"See, there you go. Defending your sex."

"I'm not trying to defend anyone. I just think that people in general aren't always so great to others. I've seen plenty of men behave like real assholes. I've seen some women who are just as cold and calculating."

"Different thing," Sheila said, waving a hand in the air. "Someone should do a study on it. As for me, well, I guess I'll just go on thinking that I'm standing up for my sex, using guys like paper cups, tossing them out as soon as they get a bit soggy." She'd looked at him then. "Dane...are you sure...I mean, sometimes, way back when, we'd get together when neither one of us had a steady thing going."

"Sheila, you've got to trust me here. I'm not what you're looking for. But I will give you a speech, which is what you need. You're beautiful. You deserve ten times more than you're giving yourself. Not to mention the fact that your lifestyle is dangerous. There are a bunch of assholes out there, not to mention the fact that these days the world is full of sexually transmitted diseases, some of which can kill you."

She'd laughed then. "Oh, great! You think I'm infectious. Dane, I'm careful as hell."

"No, you're not. If you were, you'd be looking for something more than money."

"It's not just money," she said softly.

"Then...?"

"I told you, I'm making up for all the assholes out there." She'd leaned against the pillows on the sofa then, watching him with a rueful smile. "I hear you're in deep mourning over something gone wrong. I can help. I can make you feel better. If only for a night."

He had to admit, the thought had been tempting. But Sheila

couldn't really give him anything. And there was nothing he could give her.

"No good, Sheila," he had told her softly.

And still she'd stayed. They'd had some wine, played chess. She was a good player. Then they'd had some more wine. And finally it had been really, really late, and she still hadn't gotten up to go.

"I wish you'd want me, Dane."

"Sheila..."

"What's wrong with me?" she asked for the second time that night.

"Nothing. You're beautiful. It's what's wrong with me, and the fact that I don't think we're particularly good for each other."

Then that smile. "You know what? I don't sleep with that many guys. I string them along pretty far, but...I like gifts, good food, expensive bottles of wine. I swear, Dane, I'm not diseased or anything. I'm smart and I'm careful, and more selective than it might appear. And I always carry protection. Dane, dammit, I know you're hurting, but...don't you ever just get urges, need some kind of relief? I'm perfect for you. I know you don't love me, and I don't want anything from you except to be around sometimes.... You can turn off the lights, drink yourself into a stupor, and I won't mind. And it's not like it's something you haven't done before, a place you haven't been before."

She'd made a move for him. Chess pieces had fallen to the floor. And he'd had a lot of wine, a lot of pain, a lot of guilt and self-recrimination, and a lot of longing. Sheila was beautiful. So overtly sexual she was impossible to ignore. Maybe men were nothing more than slightly evolved beasts. She hadn't been wearing a damn thing beneath her red dress, and she'd made a point of letting him know it.

"Sheila, I'm telling you, it just wouldn't be right." But there had been a guttural quality to his voice then.

"I don't care, Dane. I don't care. I just want to stay. For one night." She stood then. With definite talent, she let the red dress fall to the floor. "Call it a mercy fuck," she pleaded.

He wasn't sure he could throw her out naked. He wasn't sure he wanted to.

It hadn't occurred to him that she was scared of leaving. Chalk it up to arousal and maybe even a certain ego. Before he knew it, she was on her knees before him. Her eyes were pleading.

And Sheila was good at what she did.

They hadn't wound up in his bed, but right there, on the couch, where they'd played chess. He'd awakened feeling a dull throbbing in his head. Sex. Like eating food with no taste. Breathing in and out because the lungs did so without the commitment of the conscious mind. He didn't want to hurt Sheila. They'd both been banged up enough. He didn't want to talk, either.

Hadn't needed to.

Sheila had gotten right up, grabbed the red dress and walked to the door, pausing long enough only to look out to make sure it was light. "Thanks," she'd said, not turning back.

"Hey, my pleasure," he said lightly, hoping to make them both feel better.

Still, she hadn't looked back. That was when she had said it.

"Help me, Dane."

"I'm trying to help you, Sheila. You don't want to listen to me."

Then, still with her back to him, "You can't help it that you don't love me. I don't expect you to.... I don't love you, either... Well, as much as anyone, but...I just..."

Then she'd turned for a minute.

"I need help."

"Sheila, we can get you some help—"

She'd laughed, cutting him off. "A psychologist for my nympho tendencies?" She shook her head. "You don't understand. And I can't...explain." She had stood in his doorway just a moment longer. In the soft pink light of dawn, he thought he saw a brief look of desperation cross her face.

"I look tough, but...I'm afraid."

"Jesus, Sheila, then you've got to change your lifestyle." His outburst had brought him to his feet. "Quit picking up strangers and going off with them. Settle down with a different goal in mind, rather than striking a blow against men for all women, or whatever it is you think you're doing."

A slow smile had crossed her face. "None of you have ever known just what it was like, being me. And...as for my crusade... Oh, Dane! You just don't know how fucked up men are."

And then she'd left.

*God, she* had *needed help! He hadn't seen, hadn't known, how much.*

It was the last time he had seen her.

Alive.

And now...suddenly, even his palms were sweating. What was the killer going to do next to implicate him?

He had to get to the truth.

Andy Latham lived on the Gulf side of the key.

It was something that had always pleased Kelsey, although she wasn't sure exactly why. Key Largo wasn't big enough for her to feel any advantage of distance just because he lived on the other side of US1. But she had never liked Andy Latham, and during all the years when they had been growing up, Sheila had hated her stepfather.

He fished for a living, as many people in Key Largo did. He lived off the main road on a little piece of property that tenaciously clung to the ability to be called land, off a small street that had once been little more than mangrove swamp but had been turned into viable land with fill from the dredging for a nearby hotel harbor that had been built in the late fifties.

It wasn't more than a ten-minute drive from the duplex to

Andy Latham's house. Once upon a time it had been a pretty decent structure. Back in the fifties, contractors had known the full vengeance of storms. The home had been built well out of concrete block and stucco. It was a small house, two bedrooms, a kitchen, a living room and an open back porch that led straight to the dock and Andy's fishing boat. Kelsey knew the house fairly well because Sheila had lived in it until she had turned seventeen, when she had gotten work at a now defunct seafood restaurant. She had never asked to stay with any of her friends but first had taken a little room at the home of the restaurant owner, then gotten her own apartment on the day she turned eighteen. Kelsey could remember her folks talking about Sheila, saying that they should take her in. But there had been a hesitance in their wanting to do the good deed, and since Sheila had pointedly told Kelsey she wanted to be entirely on her own, she hadn't pushed the matter.

She wondered now if things might have been different if she had.

Even as she turned off the main road and headed southwest down the poorly kept county road that led to the few scattered houses on the street, the sun seemed to take a sharp drop toward the horizon. There were still some pinks and grays in the sky, which was good, since Latham had no outside lights on, and the front yard was dangerously overgrown with shrubbery and weeds.

So much for it being daylight.

Kelsey couldn't quite get her little Volvo into the drive, so she parked on the heavily rutted street. Getting out of the car, she wished she had changed into jeans. Twigs and high grass teased her legs as she made her way to the excuse for a front walk, and she was certain that every creepy crawly thing in the brush was making a beeline for her bare legs.

At the door, she knocked, looking at the sky. She reminded herself that she wasn't afraid of Andy Latham, he was just a scuzz.

"Yeah? What do you want?" Latham demanded, throwing open the door.

The strange thing about Andy Latham was that he wasn't a bad-looking man. He had been younger than Sheila's mother by about five years when they had married, Kelsey knew. She reckoned that made him about forty-five now. He was tall, with the lean strength of a man who spent his life occupied in physical labor. When he wasn't fishing, he worked odd construction jobs and had managed to keep his lean appearance all these years. His face was weathered, like that of many men down here who had spent years outside in the sun. He had keen hazel eyes and a full head of dark hair, only lightly dusted with gray. Tonight, he was dressed decently in jeans that appeared to be both clean and fairly new. He was wearing a polo shirt that also appeared to be clean and even pressed.

"Why, if it isn't little Kelsey, all grown up," Latham said before she could speak.

"Hi, Mr. Latham. Yes, it's Kelsey Cunningham."

"Come in, come in," he said, stepping back. Kelsey felt as if he were wearing the look of a spider who had unexpectedly come across a fly already caught it its web.

Looking past him, she could see the interior of the living room. It hadn't changed much. The old place actually had a coral rock fireplace, and the overstuffed chair in front of it was the same one that had been there as long as Kelsey could remember.

And also just as she had remembered, there were beer cans littering the floor next to it, along with wrappers and leftovers from various fast food chains. Latham had never air-conditioned the place, preferring to leave the back glass doors open to the patio all the time for the breeze. Air-conditioning cost too much money; natural air was cheaper. Many people relied on it when their houses were set in the shade of overgrown trees, taking advantage of the cooler air that came off the water. But in Latham's case, the open doors didn't seem to bring in the breeze. The smell of decaying fast food and fish seemed to permeate the house. Flies buzzed around an empty French fry wrapper.

Kelsey didn't want to set foot inside the house.

"No, no, Mr. Latham, I didn't come by to bother you. Looks like you're ready to go out."

"I am, I am, but there's always time for an old friend. Come on in. Can I get you something? Beer, or...beer or water, I guess. Aren't you looking fine, young lady. Well, I guess big city life agrees with you."

"I have a good job that I like very much," Kelsey said. "Really, I don't need to come in, I just came by to ask you about Sheila."

If she was going to talk to Latham, she was going to have to step inside, Kelsey realized, since he was already walking into the living room.

She entered cautiously, leaving the door open behind her.

Latham had to check two beer cans before finding the one that still had something in it. His back was to her as he finished off the contents and stared into the fireplace.

"Mr. Latham, I was just wondering if, by any chance, you knew where Sheila was."

He turned to face her then, hands on his hips, staring at her.

"Why? What has the little tramp done now?"

"She hasn't done anything, Mr. Latham. She was supposed to meet me down here, but she hasn't shown up since I've arrived. We were supposed to meet yesterday at lunchtime. She hasn't been home, and it seems no one has seen her in a week."

To her amazement, he started to laugh.

"She's only been missing a week, and you're worried?"

"We had plans, Mr. Latham."

He looked her up and down for a long moment. "You can call me Andy, you know. You're an adult, all grown up."

"Yes," Kelsey said politely. "But since you'll always be Sheila's stepdad to me, it's just more comfortable to call you Mr. Latham."

Kelsey didn't know why it seemed imperative to keep as close to the door as she could, but it did.

Latham started shaking his head as if he were looking at one of the craziest people on earth. Then he laughed again, a sound with no amusement. "Well, missy, I can promise you—I'm the last person Sheila would come to and report her whereabouts. Raised her when her ma up and died on me, and what the hell did I get for it? A slap in the face and a kick in the ass. She never once thanked me for keeping her after her ma died. Never realized that I hadn't adopted her, that I didn't owe her squat, that I put myself out to keep her in clothes and put food in her mouth. From the time she was ten years old, she was a little bitch, hassling me for the way I lived, knocking me for not making enough money. She hightailed it out of here the minute she could. And she only comes back when she wants money."

Despite her unease, Kelsey felt compelled to defend her friend. "If I'm not mistaken, Mr. Latham, Sheila's mother left money to you for the express purpose of raising Sheila. And I believe there are also several joint trust accounts."

"Little wise ass, aren't you, girl? The whole lot of your generation, not a bone of gratitude in you. What do you think it costs to keep a kid in school? Go to the doctor, the dentist, buy books, paper, clothes. Hell, her mother couldn't have left enough money for what Sheila has cost me. I don't give a damn whether I ever hear from her again or not."

"But she has to keep in touch with you, because of the money," Kelsey persisted.

Latham took a step toward her.

Out on the streets, she thought, he wouldn't have scared her. If she hadn't known him, he might even have appeared to be a decent looking and friendly kind of fellow. An all-around American male, the type to watch football on a Sunday afternoon, play armchair quarterback and show up for work on Monday morning to talk over the game with the guys.

Except that he smelled a little like fish.

But she did know him. She knew he had taken a belt to Sheila several times when she had lived at home.

And he made her nervous as hell.

She took a backward step toward the door.

"Look, I'm really worried about Sheila," Kelsey said. "If you do hear anything from her, anything at all, please have her get in touch with me right away."

"And where would that be, missy?" he asked. He was walking toward her again. She had the strangest sensation that if he touched her, she would somehow be marked for life. The remaining light outside had faded. The living room was lit by one weak bulb in a lamp with no shade. The pale light fell on the carcasses of mounted fish on the wall, and the head and neck of a tiny key deer with glassy eyes.

"Just tell Sheila to get ahold of me if you hear from her. She'll know where I am."

"You're staying out at her place, eh?"

"Mr. Latham, you did raise Sheila. You must have some feelings for her."

"Yeah, I hate the little bitch."

"I'm worried, and she's missing. And the police will be around to talk to you," Kelsey said, her sense of both uneasiness and indignation rising within her.

"The cops?" Latham said, then he repeated the words, his voice seeming to rise to a roar. "The cops! You called the cops on me because that little twit of a girl has gone off with some poor Joe she intends to milk for all he's worth?"

At that point he was almost upon her. Dignity and courtesy be damned, Kelsey was getting out. She turned and headed for the door. She heard him following after her. She felt his breathing.

His hand clamped down on her shoulder. She almost screamed as he spun her around. "Don't you go causing trouble for me, you hear? You mark my words—Sheila is off with some man—

a fool with money, with any luck. Getting the police involved is just going to get her into trouble. Maybe she'll even see some jail time, understand? Don't go getting the cops involved with Sheila and me. Don't you do it over that riffraff girl!"

He had powerful fingers. They were digging into her shoulder. His face was taut with tension, and his eyes had a hard yellow gleam about them.

The stench of fish wafted over her.

"Let go of my shoulder."

He smiled. The man had amazingly good teeth. Very white. It could have been a good smile, but instead it was full of menace and pleasure at the fear he was sensing in her.

"You came to my house to throw accusations in my face, little lady," he said quietly, not releasing her.

"Accusations?" Kelsey said. "I didn't accuse you of anything. I asked you if you had seen Sheila, and if you could tell her I'm looking for her if you *do* see her."

"If you didn't accuse me of anything, why are you calling the cops on me?"

His grasp had a definite biting quality. He was strong, or, at least, stronger than she was.

Cindy had been right. She shouldn't have come here. Alone. At night.

Alone at any time, she thought.

She wanted to remain calm and rational; she also wanted to scream and jerk away from him. She tried to remember all the movies she had seen, all the programs she had watched about dealing with dangerous situations. Don't show fear? Or scream like blue blazes, push away with all her strength and run like the wind?

She didn't have to make a decision. She heard the slamming of a car door and a man's voice. "Hey, what's going on there?"

Latham's hand fell from her shoulder. They both recognized the voice. Latham shook his head with disgust, his eyes moving from the newcomer back to Kelsey once again. "There he is, the big military man, ready to knock my lights out," he said. "I wasn't about to hurt you, little girl. And you want to know where Sheila is? Ask her good buddy, the half-breed coming up the walk."

She'd known from hearing him, without turning, that Dane Whitelaw had arrived. She'd been relieved.

But Latham's words gave her a chill.

She turned, Latham's words echoing in her mind. *"You want to know where Sheila is? Ask her good buddy, the half-breed coming up the walk."*

Dane was coming up the path. He wasn't looking at Kelsey; he was staring at Latham.

His hair was combed back, freshly washed, a little long at the collar, but off his face now. He was in khakis and a short-sleeved blue tailored shirt. Dane wasn't exactly a half-breed. His grandfather had been a Miccosukee Indian who had married a Swedish tourist. The two had set up shop in the Keys, died together in an automobile accident and left his father with ownership of Hurricane Bay. His dad had made a career out of the military, retired, turned to fishing off his peaceful property for an extra income, and then married Mary Smith, a woman who could claim ancestors all the way back to the Mayflower. Kelsey could just barely remember Dane's mother. She had welcomed every kid in the world into their house. She had been quick to laugh, to entertain, to love children. She had wanted twenty, she had told them once. At least a dozen little sisters and brothers for Dane. But both she and Dane's father had married late in life, and complications had set in when she'd finally gotten pregnant again just before Dane's tenth birthday. She had died months before the baby was due. Dane's father had never remarried. He had always been a wonderful man when the kids were around, but he had seldom left his own little island, except to sell his catch.

Dane Whitelaw seemed to have inherited the best to be had from his background. He had dark eyes, a chiseled face with slightly broad cheekbones, dark-wheat-colored hair that was always sun-bleached to a lighter shade, and the height and stance of a Viking. She had adored him growing up. He'd been her brother's best friend. But then Joe had been killed, and their little world had changed for everyone.

Dane reached the open doorway, still staring pointedly at Andy Latham. His dark gaze had never wavered once.

"What the hell are you doing here, Whitelaw?" Latham asked.

"I was in the neighborhood," Dane said, an obvious lie. There was nothing in the immediate neighborhood that could have drawn him.

"You're trespassing on my property."

"Don't worry. I'm getting off it." He stared at Kelsey.

She was tempted to stay just because she didn't want Dane helping her, not when he was top on her list of...well, not suspects, but highly suspicious people. And not when he had been such an ass that afternoon. Maybe she had approached him badly. But he should have cared. He should at least have frowned with worry and tried to say something good about Sheila.

Then again, maybe she just disliked Dane because of what had happened after Joe had died.

"Kelsey, were you staying?" Dane asked when she didn't move.

"No, I have a dinner engagement," she said.

She turned to walk down the overgrown path, certain this time that creepy things were touching her flesh when the overgrown brush swept over her legs.

She reached her own car. Dane was right behind her, Andy Latham still standing at his door. Dane waited until she had gotten in the driver's seat, closed her door and started the engine.

Then he walked to his own car, a Jeep with oversize tires. Necessary, she knew, for living out on Hurricane Bay. The road to the little island was private, not state or county. Dane's grandfather had built it; his father had improved it. Now Dane kept it up. It still wasn't much of a road. During a heavy rain season or after a storm, it was often underwater, sometimes so deep that the only way on or off the island was by boat.

Dane started up his car but didn't start moving until she did. She drove away with Dane just a short distance behind her.

In the rearview mirror, she could see that Latham was still standing in his doorway. Watching.

Andy Latham muttered as he watched the cars go. Then he walked back into his house, cursing his stepdaughter and her friends. In the kitchen, he reached into the refrigerator for another beer. There was a big fat palmetto bug, a winged cockroach, sitting right next to his beer, waving his antennae.

He cursed the cockroach and reached for the can, then splatted it down on the roach before the filthy creature had a chance to move.

He thought about cleaning the carcass out of the refrigerator, but it seemed like too much of a project for the moment. He hadn't really wanted another beer; he'd wanted to get going. He liked nightlife. No, he loved nightlife. Nightlife took him away from his hell of an existence and made him feel like a man. He'd been ready to go when Sheila's little buddy had shown up. Kelsey.

Drinking his beer, he decided to make a pit stop. In the mirror over the sink, he surveyed his features. Good. He was still looking pretty good. He really wasn't old at all; those kids just didn't realize it, because he had made the mistake of marrying an older woman.

Well, she'd had some money. A virtue. She'd had her faults, as well. A hell of a lot of them. Who would have thought that she considered herself a match for any man?

And worse, who would have thought she'd leave the money tied up in a trust that could only be accessed little by little, and then only by him and Sheila at the same time.

He picked up the comb sitting on the sink and ran it through his hair. The face that greeted him in the mirror pleased him. He had good features and fine eyes. His skin was tanned and creased, but women seemed to like the weathered look. He was built just fine. Not muscle-bound, but tight as piano wire. Sleek, hard-toned. He was in good physical shape. The whole package was still just fine.

Funny. Once upon a time he'd had a thing for older women. Now he liked them younger.

Yep, that Kelsey was looking darned good. Too bad he'd been saddled with Sheila. The girl had poisoned everyone against him. Hell, if it hadn't been for Sheila, he might not have known Kelsey at all as a kid. Who knows? She might have let him buy her a drink at a bar.

She might have let him do more.

He tensed, remembering the way she had looked around the house. As if he were lower than a pig.

Lower than the cockroach he had crushed in the refrigerator.

He shrugged. Imagine that. The damned thing had been in the refrigerator. Maybe that was why it had been so easy to kill. Maybe it had already been cold, shaking in its little cockroach boots, frozen right to the spot.

He looked around the bathroom.

Hell, maybe he should get a maid.

Of course, it would have to be someone who wasn't afraid of cockroaches.

He exited the bathroom, humming to himself. He started to leave the house, then paused and looked around, damning Sheila once again, thinking of the way Kelsey Cunningham had looked around his house. Fuck them both. Fuck them all. Everyone knew that Sheila took off whenever the hell she felt like it. Everyone but Kelsey, coming back here as if she were something special, raising all kinds of trouble.

Still...

He looked around his domain. Strange, once it had been clean. Sheila's mother had been good for something. She had cooked, too.

But he couldn't really remember what the place had looked

like back then. There had been food in the refrigerator, and not so many beer cans. The cockroach would have died a lot happier if he had come all those years ago.

Now the place was a dump. Nothing but fast-food wrappers and beer cans. So what if the police came? They would probably leave damn quick.

He left the house, not bothering to lock his door. No one ever came out this road. There were only two other houses, and a bunch of mangrove roots and water. Angus Grier lived in the closest house, and he was ninety if he was a day. And the kids who had rented the other place...they were stoned out of their minds most the time. There wasn't much reason to lock up his place. If a thief came by...well, hell, he was welcome to steal anything in the place.

Because once he drove away from it, Andy Latham knew that he was a different man.

# CHAPTER 3

Dane followed Kelsey back to the duplex.

She was probably going to accuse him of stalking her, but he still wanted to see that she got home safely. Besides, he could just knock on Cindy's door after he made sure Kelsey had gone on into Sheila's side.

He knew Kelsey was aware that he was following her, but she pretended not to see him as she parked, exited her cranberry Volvo and entered the house. Dane parked the Land Rover and took the steps up to Cindy's door. As he tapped on it, Cindy appeared at the door to the other half of the duplex, Sheila's half, now Kelsey's.

"Dane! Hey, we're over here."

"Hey, Cindy."

He walked across the tiled concrete front porch and greeted Cindy with a quick peck on the cheek. She never changed. Sweet and smart, Cindy always expected the best from everyone. But then, she'd never met with much personal adversity. Both her folks were still living just down the highway. She had two younger sisters and a ten-year-old brother. Her father, a transplanted Yankee, owned one of the largest charter fishing boat companies in the area.

Cindy had called to tell him that Kelsey was on her way out to talk to Andy Latham. Dane hadn't at all liked the idea of her being out there alone. Of course, he'd known that Kelsey wouldn't be particularly glad to see him out there—she would hardly think of him as a knight in shining armor—but he'd made tracks to get out there as soon as possible anyway.

"Come on in," Cindy said. "We were about to have quiche and beer." She wrinkled her nose. "Reheated quiche and beer. But it's still good. I can cook. Well, kind of, anyway."

"Sounds great, Cindy, but I already ate."

"Come in for a beer, at least. I mean, you're here, aren't you?" she demanded, blue eyes wide.

"Sure." He needed to talk to Kelsey, and it was damn certain *she* was never going to invite him in.

He followed Cindy into Sheila's side of the duplex. Kelsey was seated on a bar stool, a plate and a beer in front of her. Her shoes were off, one ankle curled around a leg of the stool. The sunglasses were gone, and he could see her eyes. Blue-green. Like a color that had been plucked right out of a shallow sea on a sunlit day.

He could see that she was surprised and definitely not pleased that Cindy had invited him in.

"Look who's here," Cindy said pleasantly.

"Surprise, surprise," Kelsey murmured.

"You're sure you don't want some quiche, Dane?" Cindy asked.

"No, thanks."

Cindy reached into the fridge and produced a bottle of beer. "But you'll have a beer with us, right?"

"Sure."

"Right. He hasn't had enough to drink today," Kelsey said.

For a moment Cindy looked as if she was going to try to ignore the obvious hostility between them, then she sighed, putting her hands on her hips. "Hey, kids, we're all grown-ups here."

"All right," Kelsey said. "Hi, Dane. Have a beer. You *are* all grown up. If you want to spend your life drinking the days away, I guess that's all right."

He stared at her and took a long swig from the bottle, ready to tell her that she hadn't seen him in years, she had no idea of what he did with his days, and she sure as hell had no right to judge him.

"That's right, Kelsey. If I want to be a drunk, it's my prerogative."

"Dane isn't a drunk, Kelsey," Cindy said.

"Sorry, then," Kelsey said. She made a point of yawning. "You know what, guys? I haven't had much sleep since I got back. Maybe you want to move your little party over to Cindy's half of the place."

"Maybe, but not yet," Dane said. He walked to the counter where she was sitting and set his beer bottle down. She tensed, and for a moment he thought she was going to jump up and try to escape.

But that would mean having to touch him because the way he was standing, at her side, hands on the counter, she would have to push past him to get by.

"So now you want to talk," she said.

"I'd have been happy to talk earlier—if you hadn't come on as such a bitch," he said.

She blinked, and he could hear her teeth clench. "You were drunk, and I was worried. And Nate had just told me that you and Sheila were...that you and Sheila had a big argument the last time he'd seen her, and that she'd told him afterward she was going out to your place. He said you weren't very nice to her."

She wasn't apologizing. She was still accusing him. And she sure as hell wasn't about to thank him for coming around when she might have been in trouble at Latham's. Of course, as far as any of them had ever known, Latham was just like a cockroach. Nasty as all hell, and germ-carrying, certainly, but not physically dangerous.

He inhaled a long breath before replying to Kelsey.

"Kelsey, I'm glad that your life is going so great that you feel you can judge everyone else. Although I'm curious as to how you got to be such a good judge of a man's level of alcohol consumption."

Her eyes narrowed. "I know you've been lying as low as pond scum, Dane, because Sheila told me."

"She did, did she? Kelsey, you need to listen to me. You haven't been around, and you don't know anything about anyone here anymore. What you've got is a bunch of hearsay and assumptions. Maybe you don't like what you think I've become, and maybe there's even some truth to it. But what you're doing here is dangerous. What do you think you are suddenly? Some kind of a crusader? Leave it alone. Quit running around accusing everyone of doing something to Sheila. You're going to get yourself into trouble."

Kelsey stared at him, eyes cool and hostile. "Dane, you didn't want to talk to me this afternoon, and now you're suddenly here telling me to keep my nose out of things. This is ridiculous. Apparently I'm the only one who's really concerned about Sheila. And since I *am* concerned, my nose is going to be everywhere until I know where she is. And I know you were seeing her."

"You're not listening to me. You're going off half-cocked and making a lot of assumptions. You know I was seeing Sheila because Nate told you so. Sheila hung around the Sea Shanty. So do I. So do Nate and Cindy—Cindy because she keeps up with old friends, Nate because he owns the place. And guess what? Lots of other people around here go there on a regular basis. It's the in place for the natives. Sheila saw dozens of people at the Sea Shanty. Big deal. But Andy Latham doesn't go there anymore, because Nate barred him. He got to be a little too obnoxious with some of the women customers. That's why Cindy called me when she knew you were going to go over and start throwing accusations at Latham."

Kelsey's eyes instantly shot toward Cindy with recrimination. Cindy flushed but shrugged, still feeling she had done the right thing.

Kelsey took a sip of her beer. "Latham is a horrible man. We all know it. He's a filthy, mean bastard—but that's all. He's scuzzy, not dangerous."

"How the hell do you know he isn't dangerous?" Dane demanded, wishing he weren't feeling his own temper soar. Kelsey knew he was right; she just wasn't about to admit it.

"He's been around for years," she said, waving a hand as if dismissing his words. "I used to go to that house when I was a kid. So did you, so did Cindy. He yelled, he was rude, and he created an environment no kid should have grown up in, but he never hurt anyone."

"Really? And here I thought you were Sheila's great friend. He sure as hell hurt *her.*"

He had her on that one, and she had the grace to flush. "When he was angry, he beat her a few times with a belt. He'd be arrested for child abuse now, but back then...parents used to spank their children."

"Strange. Mine never beat me with a belt. And neither did yours. Or Cindy's."

"Okay, he's a horrible man!"

"Listen to what you're saying. He *beat* her with a *belt.*"

"When our folks were in school, the deans used to walk around with big paddles."

He shook his head, growing angrier, fighting his rising temper and trying to tell himself that Kelsey wasn't his concern. If she wanted to be a stubborn idiot, there was nothing he could do.

But she was *his* concern.

He had to keep her from acting like a stubborn idiot. She would understand that—if only he could tell her the truth about Sheila.

But that was one thing he couldn't do. Kelsey would have his ass in jail so fast his head would spin. And then...

Then there would be nothing he could do.

"Don't go out there again," he said, forcing his jaw to un-clench and allow him to form words. His voice came out ragged and rough.

Her eyes narrowed further still, and she replied with cool, "who the hell are you to tell me what to do?" dignity.

"Look, Dane, no one around here is really paying any atten-tion to me. Don't you understand yet? Someone needs to be con-cerned. No one else is. Therefore, in my opinion, I have to be."

"It's not that we're not concerned," Cindy murmured.

They both ignored her. Dane spoke firmly. "Don't go out to Latham's again."

"Dammit, Dane!" she said, losing her composure at last, her eyes sizzling, her fingers tightening on her beer bottle. "Don't come on to me like the gestapo. You're not my father," she said.

He caught her eyes then, held them hard. "Let's hope not," he said.

She flushed slightly. Her gaze fell from his, and she studied the quiche she'd been pushing around her plate, the grip she had on her beer bottle becoming white-knuckled.

"Kelsey, I'm not trying to come on like anything or act like a father. It simply isn't a good idea to visit a man like that alone. Okay, maybe I am sounding like the gestapo. But he's not just mean and nasty, he's damned scary. Pay attention to me. Don't go near him again. *Please.*" He would try anything. It was im-perative that she understand Latham was dangerous.

She looked up at him, then looked down again quickly, silent for a moment.

"Kelsey, listen to him. He's right," Cindy suddenly pleaded.

Kelsey threw up her hands, almost knocking over her beer bot-tle, barely catching it. "Okay, look, both of you, I'm sorry. I was wrong. I shouldn't have gone out there, and I won't go visiting Latham alone again. Actually I wasn't planning on visiting him again anyway. It's not like it was a social call. But the trust funds mean that there's a connection between Latham and Sheila. I was just hoping that maybe she had said something to him. I want to believe with all my heart that Sheila is just being rude and careless, forgetting all about me. I'd love for someone to tell me she's on vacation in Switzerland with a wine baron. But I just don't believe it. And asking Andy Latham if he had seen her, if he knew where she was, seemed like an intelligent move to make. She may hate him, but whether she likes it or not, they're connected through her mother's will."

"He'd be the last person Sheila would go to," Cindy murmured.

"Yes, but because of the money, she might have told him if she was going to be away, or she might have made an appointment with him regarding the trust or something. Look, he's never been my favorite person, either. But I still don't think he's actually dangerous," Kelsey said, defending herself.

From somewhere a muted ringing sounded.

"Excuse me," she said, looking pointedly at Dane. He was still blocking her way. "Cell phone."

He backed away. Just a hair. She didn't want to touch him, but she was going to have to brush by him.

She did. She scraped by his taut form. She still carried the aroma of a subtle perfume.

Once past him, she dug into her purse, which she had tossed on the far end of the bar. She glanced at the caller ID and said a cheerful, "Hey!" into the phone. She listened to the voice at the other end, then spoke again. "No, she hasn't shown yet." She looked across the kitchen at Cindy and Dane, who were both staring at her. "I'm not alone," she said into her phone. "Cindy and Dane are here."

Cindy arched a brow to Dane, but her question was quickly answered.

"Larry says hello to you both," Kelsey said.

Larry Miller. The weekender who had almost been one of them. Dane had heard that Larry was around now and then, but he hadn't seen him. Larry's father had passed away, and his mother had moved somewhere up north. They had sold the condo they kept on the Keys, as well, so even Larry's little place was gone. Maybe property was what made a place home. He had Hurricane Bay, so perhaps it had been inevitable that he would come back.

Larry hadn't really been an islander, but he'd still run with their crowd. Good old Larry...

Poor Larry.

He had fallen in love with Sheila, married her, tried to give her the world. A decent guy. Studious, cautious, a talented artist.

"Tell him hello for me," Cindy said.

"Ditto."

Kelsey nodded. "Cindy and Dane say hello." She listened while Larry spoke, staring out the sliding glass door from the kitchen to the patio. "Yeah, I know, everyone is saying the same thing." She gazed at Cindy and Dane again. Her look said that phone calls should be private. But she didn't move away, and Dane wasn't about to be courteous and suggest he and Cindy go somewhere. Kelsey kept talking into her phone. "Maybe she'll show up, maybe she won't. Anyway, I'm still going to spend the week at the duplex. With Cindy. Yeah, she's right next door. Nate's in good shape—hey, he said he saw you a couple of weeks ago. You didn't mention that you'd been down here."

Whatever he said next, Kelsey didn't answer. "Listen, I'll call you as soon as I hear from Sheila or find out what she's up to, okay?"

She touched a button on her phone and returned it to her purse, then slid back up on the bar stool. "Larry is concerned," she said.

"Poor thing. He never fell out of love, did he?" Cindy said.

"Maybe not," Kelsey said. "He still cares about Sheila, but he's certainly gotten over her. He's been doing all right. He's great to look at, smart, has a good job. He was dating one of our models. Beautiful girl. But a man can move on and still think of his ex-wife as a special person. He doesn't get down here that often, but he still thinks of the old gang as his friends. Funny, though. He said he'd been down about a week ago and heard that Sheila was around, but he couldn't track her down. When I told him what I was doing with my vacation time, all he said was that he'd been down on business and hadn't had a chance to really do anything or see anyone."

"Maybe he didn't think it was worth mentioning. He must have come and gone really quickly. He didn't see me, either," Cindy said.

"He said he was down here with a client, just long enough for a drink and dinner," Kelsey said. "Apparently he saw Nate, though. But Nate didn't mention to me today that he'd seen Larry. That was strange, don't you think? Especially when he knows Larry and I work together." Kelsey had been musing aloud. She didn't seem to mind that she had spoken in front of Cindy, but when her eyes touched Dane's, she seemed to stiffen again.

Somehow he had become the enemy. Things hadn't been right between them for a long time. He hadn't expected hugs and kisses, but even so, he didn't want to be the enemy, not when it was so important that she listen to him. But she was in no mood for that now, so he might as well get going.

Dane set down his beer bottle. "Gotta go," he told Cindy, giving her a kiss on the cheek.

"You have to go? It's early," Cindy said.

"I have an appointment."

"A date?" Cindy asked hopefully.

"An appointment," he repeated.

"At night? Does it have anything to do with an exciting investigation?"

Dane laughed. "Cindy, so far I have surveillance cameras looking for disappearing bait and a few other jobs that are equally mundane." Well, that was both true and not true. He had taken a job with the principal of a local private school to tail a few of the rich teenagers who seemed to be getting their hands on a fair amount of drugs.

He was pretty sure he had the answer to that one. It had been at the top of his list of jobs to pursue...until this morning.

"Wow, Dane, you're just full of fire and energy," Kelsey said. She was speaking to him but studying her beer bottle as she peeled the label from it.

"See you, Kelsey," he said.

"Sure." She looked at him at last. "It's been great."

"Hey," Cindy said thoughtfully, as if she were totally oblivious to the last exchange, "you know, I've got a great idea, Dane. Why don't you have us over for a barbecue?"

"Cindy," Kelsey protested. "That's rude. We can't just invite ourselves over. And think about it. Dane likes his *mundane* lifestyle. I'm sure that's just what he wants to do. Get out of his lounge chair and cook for a group."

Dane had the feeling that he could turn into Emeril and Kelsey still wouldn't want to show up at his place to eat.

But Cindy was persisting. "Remember in the old days, when you and your dad had those great cookouts. Maybe Larry can come down for the weekend, and maybe Sheila will even have shown by then. Nate can get another bartender on and come, and who knows who else might be around."

"We'll see, Cindy," he said.

He was startled when Kelsey suddenly seemed to rouse herself and let go of her hostility. She slid off her bar stool, approaching him, but pausing a distance away. "Actually, Dane, you know, it would be nice if you had a barbecue and had us all over."

"You *want* to come visit ye olde town drunk?" he said, staring at her.

Cindy must have felt as if lightning were crackling around her, because she suddenly seemed anxious to get away from the two of them. "I'm going to wash the dishes," she said.

Kelsey stared at her. "We used paper," she reminded her.

Cindy gave Kelsey a little shove that almost sent her into Dane. "Look, you two, I don't know what's going on here, but good friends are hard to come by. Both of you, shape up. Kelsey, you're being a real bitch. Walk Dane to the door and tell him you don't think that he's a washed-up, inebriated has-been. Go on."

There was something going on in Kelsey's ever-calculating little mind, Dane knew, or else she would just have turned away with that air of superiority she could don like a cloak, walk herself into the bedroom, and shut the door.

"I'm being a bitch?" she said.

"Oh, yeah," Dane said. "Beyond a doubt. You're being a super bitch."

"And Dane is Mr. Nice Guy?" she said to Cindy.

"Actually I've been damned decent, considering the way you accosted me today."

"Go on, Kelsey. Walk Dane out."

"I'm sure Dane knows the way through the living room to the door, but what the heck. Come on, Dane."

He thought she was going to touch him, take his arm, but she apparently decided against it, crossing her arms over her chest as she walked to the door.

"You should have that barbecue," she said, opening the front door and leaning against the wall as she waited for him to exit.

He wasn't sure what the hell she was up to, but he was determined that she understand how dangerous any reckless course of action might be. She might have been unnerved earlier tonight, but she hadn't been nearly scared enough.

"Kelsey, *promise* me you're going to stay away from Andy Latham."

She shrugged. "I told you both, I was wrong, you were right. I only went to talk to him and find out if he knew anything about Sheila. I've talked to him. I have no reason to go back."

"All right." He hesitated. "Kelsey, seriously, get your nose out of this."

Her eyes seemed as opaque as clouds, hooded. "I'm the only one determined to find Sheila. I have to nose around."

"Look, I'm telling you, I *am* concerned. I swear to you..." He hesitated for a moment, thinking of the irony. "I swear there is no one more anxious than I am to find Sheila. I have a P.I. firm, Kelsey. Let me do this."

Her eyes narrowed. "So you *do* think there's a reason to worry about Sheila."

"Let me do the worrying—and the question asking."

She shrugged. "You're the P.I. Go for it."

He started out the door, aggravated and exasperated. He wanted to shake her. Make her understand. He also needed to get the hell out. He had to make that appointment.

"Kelsey..."

"I mean it. Go for it. I'll even hire you. Is that an inspiration for you? I assume your rates are high, but I can pay them. No slacking off, though. I want her found."

"Kelsey, I don't want your money. I told you—I want to find Sheila myself. You stay out of it."

She didn't agree that she would. Instead she persisted with her original question. "Are you going to have the barbecue?"

He froze where he was, half out the door. He turned back to her, suddenly realizing just why Kelsey was pushing so hard when he was certain she wanted to be nowhere near him.

"Kelsey, you want to come over and search my place? You don't need a special occasion for that. Come on over anytime."

There was the slightest flood of color to her cheeks, but she didn't flinch.

"If I wanted to search your house, you wouldn't care?"

"Not in the least."

"You should still have a barbecue."

"So you could have lots of help while you searched?" he said.

"Yes."

"Bye, Kelsey."

He strode away down the walk.

"What time do you start work in the mornings?" she called after him.

"Whenever the hell I feel like it!" He stopped, turning on his heel, staring at her. "You know...once I rise from my drunken stupor. And I lock my doors when I leave, so you'll have to call if you want a personal guide while you try to find incriminating evidence against me."

Kelsey had come out the doorway behind him and was standing on the porch.

He was about to walk away, aware that he would slam his way into his car. Instead he strode back to her so quickly that she didn't have time to back away.

"What the hell is it, Kelsey? What did I do to you that makes you mistrust *me*—yet you run out alone in the dark to see a man like Andy Latham?"

He hadn't touched her—he had managed not to do that. But he stood a breath away from her. He saw the flash of fire in her eyes and the tightness that gripped her from head to toe. He thought she was about to deny that there was any reason at all. But she didn't.

"You know what you did to me," she told him. Then she gritted her teeth, turning pale, and it was painfully apparent that she was horrified that the words had come out of her mouth.

"What I did to you?" he repeated. "I didn't do a damn thing to you, Kelsey. In fact, *I* should be angry for what you did to me. So that's what this is all about?"

"This is all about the fact that I came to see Sheila, but she's nowhere to be seen, and Nate said I should ask you because you had an argument with her and then she took off to your house. And she hasn't been seen since. And because you could have done anything with your life and you're spending it drinking yourself into some kind of oblivion in a lounge chair. It's because there's something going on, and you're the only one with the knowledge and the training to deal with it, but instead you're wasting your time in self-absorbed flagellation."

"You don't know anything about me, Kelsey. Nothing at all. Not anymore. Maybe I *should* have a barbecue. Let you tear up my place while I have friends around. Maybe I shouldn't trust you alone at my house."

With that, he made his way to his car. He managed to open the door without ripping it from its hinges and even closed it without slamming it.

In fact, he made it halfway down the block before punching the dashboard.

# CHAPTER 4

Jesse Crane was standing out by the dock when Dane returned.

Dane didn't particularly mind darkness himself, but he kept a floodlight trained on the front and rear entries to the house and the dock. The last thing he wanted was someone stumbling onto his place despite the huge Private Road notice on the turnoff to Hurricane Bay and taking an accidental dive into the water. He'd never had a fear of thieves; the value of Hurricane Bay was in the island itself. Most of what he had that might be considered of value had more of a sentimental worth, though he supposed some of the collections his folks had gathered were good ones.

Still, out on Hurricane Bay, he'd never even locked his doors—until today.

"You're late," Jesse called to him.

"Yeah, I know. Sorry."

"No big deal. I would have watched the TV, except the house is locked." Jesse was tall and gave the appearance of being lanky. He wasn't. He was honed to a *T*. His hair was nearly black, dead straight and worn short. His eyes were a light hazel, almost yellow, and he had a way of looking at a person as if he already knew everything they might be trying to hide. He'd been with the Metro-Dade force until his wife, also a cop, had been killed. At that point, he'd left the force and joined the tribal police.

He was Dane's second cousin, and he had mixed blood, as well. His just wasn't quite so complex of a cocktail, as he liked to tell Dane.

"When did you start locking the door?" Jesse asked him.

"Today. I'm setting up surveillance cameras, too."

"Your chosen line of work is getting to you?" Jesse said.

"Maybe. Come on in."

Dane opened the screen door, then unlocked the old Dade County pine door behind it. Both men stepped in.

The house was concrete block and stucco and Dade County pine, built against the storms that periodically ravaged the area. It had withstood a great deal, even being pounded by hurricanes, because the construction was so strong. The man who had owned the island before Dane's grandfather had been blown out even before they'd started naming storms. All he had wanted to do was unload the place; he'd called it Hurricane Bay, and the name had stuck. It was Dane's grandfather who'd built the house. Dade County pine was at a premium because it was almost impossible to acquire anymore. It repelled termites and stood strong against most of the dangers inherent in a subtropical climate. The living room was completely paneled with it. The house boasted two coral rock fireplaces, one in the master bedroom and the other in the living room. A large mantel had also been chiseled to match, and on it stood one of his father's great treasures, a stuffed 'gator called Big Tom in life, and—since the taxidermist had been excellent at his craft—for posterity. His father had caught the alligator, which had been terrorizing a residential canal in Homestead. The reptile hadn't gotten hold of any children, but he had managed to consume two poodles and a too-curious cat before being taken down.

A soft leather sofa, matching love seat and two armchairs

rounded out the grouping in front of the fireplace. The walls boasted some fine Audubon prints and interesting family photos.

"Want a beer?" Dane asked as they entered.

"Sure."

Jesse followed Dane through the dining room. The antique claw-foot dining table held Dane's computer and stacks of papers. They passed through the dining room to the kitchen, which fronted the house, along with the living and dining rooms. Way back when, his grandfather had figured people would want to be outside, so both the dining room and kitchen had large windows that could be opened up to the porch, where there were outside counters and rough wood tables. The back of the house faced both the dock and the little spit of man-made beach, so the floor plan made it easy to be outside most of the time.

Jesse leaned against the kitchen counter, looking out at the night and the water as Dane went into the refrigerator.

"It's been a while since I've been out here," Jesse said, accepting the can Dane handed him.

"Yeah?"

"Of course, you haven't been back all that long."

"Almost six months."

Jesse didn't comment. He knew what had brought Dane back. There was no need to talk about it.

"Okay, so what's going on?" Jesse asked. "Do I have a stray tribal member harassing the tourists? Is some local all pissed off because he lost big at bingo or something?"

Dane shook his head, thinking that his second cousin's dry expectations might have amused him at a different time.

"No, actually, I need to ask you about something."

"Shoot."

"A couple of months back, you found a strangling victim out in the Glades."

Jesse frowned and nodded. "Yeah, I found the body," he said. He studied his beer can. Then he looked at Dane again, his forehead still furrowed. "I've seen a hell of a lot, between Miami-Dade and just living out where fools can go astray. But...hell. That was bad."

"Mind telling me about it?"

"I think I talked to you at the time."

"You did, but I'd like to hear about it again."

"You have a reason."

"Yes, I do."

"Are you planning on sharing it with me."

"Soon. I just need a little time."

"You haven't found another body?"

"No."

Jesse studied him for a long moment but accepted the fact that Dane would tell him everything when he was ready.

"I think it was just about three months ago now. The first body was found three months before that, up in Broward County."

"And the Miami-Dade boys and Broward homicide think it was the same killer?"

Jesse inclined his head. "Looks like it. It's a tough case. Both bodies were found in such a bad state of decomposition, it's been a bitch for forensics."

"That's why it was so bad when you found the girl?"

"She'd been in the water almost two weeks, in a canal in the Everglades. I don't really need to tell you what that means, but suffice it to say that nature takes its course."

"So you think she was thrown into the canal by someone who knew the Everglades?"

"Not necessarily. There are a few pretty decent roads leading off of the Tamiami Trail. And the day I discovered her was...a Tuesday. Right after those torrential rains we had when it was supposed to be dry season. A Mack truck could have driven back there and the tire prints would have been washed out. Of course, a Mack truck would have sunk in the swamp, but you know what I mean. In that area, after heavy rains...you're not going to find anything resembling a print or a track. And since the body was in the water, tangled up in some tree roots, there wasn't even a way to tell exactly where it had gone in, since it might have traveled with the current."

"From what you told me at the time, and what I read in the paper," Dane said, "they knew she'd been strangled with a necktie, because it was still around her throat."

"Right. And it was a tie manufactured by the thousands, available in any department store in any state."

"Anything else?"

"She was naked, except for the tie. That's about it."

"Did you notice anything in particular when you found her?"

"Yeah, that she was dead. I didn't need to feel for a pulse. And where I found her...it's in an area that might be considered reservation land and might be counted as county. It's not one of those places anyone really wants to fight over. I roped off the scene where I found her and called in the Miami-Dade homicide guys. Specialists. She wasn't one of ours."

"You knew that from seeing the body?"

"I couldn't even have guaranteed you that she was a she from seeing the body," Jesse said.

"Then..."

"I'd have known if we'd been missing anyone," Jesse said. "We're one damned small tribe out there, you know. Less than five hundred. They pretty well wiped out the big numbers during the Indian wars and relocation. Bingo and the casino have been our best revenge, you know."

"They did identify her, right?"

"Cherie Madsen. Twenty-three, a dancer at a Miami strip club. She'd been a missing person at the time, and she was identified by her dental records."

"And did the police have any leads?"

"Sure, they had leads, but no real suspects. They traced every name they could find for the night she disappeared, but lots of

guys who go to strip clubs use cash and aren't necessarily regulars. They talked to all her old boyfriends, same as they talked
to everyone about the murder in Broward County. The first girl
was found in a canal off I-595. Same thing—she was in the water
at least a couple of weeks before she was discovered. Strangled,
tie around her neck. There had been rain that time, too. The body
had probably traveled. The girl was naked, and once again the
tie could have been bought anywhere. No way to get any prints.
The girl hadn't scratched her attacker, so there were no skin cells
beneath her nails, nothing. I have a friend in homicide at the
Broward sheriff's department, if you want to talk to him further
about the case. And you know the guy handling the case for
Miami-Dade. It's Hector Hernandez."

"Yes, I know him. I've known him for years. Big time fisherman, down here a lot. He's a good cop."

"Yeah, he's definitely a good cop. He can help you more than
I can, since you're apparently after something. I kept up with
the case some, since I found one of the victims," Jesse said quietly. "But not being Miami-Dade homicide anymore, I don't
have the same access to the experts. And it's not my case anymore, anyway. You know how small the Miccosukee force is.
Something like this, Miami-Dade comes in."

"Did you hear anything about a psychological profile?"

Jesse nodded again, taking a long swallow from his can. "The
cops in both counties got together and asked the FBI to give them
a hand with the profiling, and they brought in an expert who has
been pretty right on with each case he's profiled that has been
solved. White male, twenty-five to forty-five, has a day job,
maybe a wife and family, maybe not. Even though the second
girl was found out in the Everglades, the profiler is certain the
killer is a *white* male. Someone who knows the area and may
even know what happens to a body in the water. He probably
looks decent, maybe he's even good-looking, and he may have
a certain charisma. He's an organized killer. Nothing is left to

chance. He's smart enough to keep his prints off any traceable materials, use a condom and dump the bodies where nature will take care of the rest. There might be two different killers, one copycatting the other, but the homicide guys don't think so. They kept a few details about the first body secret, and those same details were also consistent with the second victim." Jesse shrugged, taking another long swallow from his beer can. "In private, of course, the homicide guys admit to having just about nothing to follow up on. Both girls were strippers. They've questioned every man they could get a lead on who was at either club the night the girl was last seen. They've questioned family and old boyfriends. They've looked for witnesses. They don't have prints, fibers, tire tracks or anything else. They haven't given up, but they've followed every lead they had, and the trail hasn't gotten them very far. It would be bull to suggest they're not hot on it because of what the girls did for a living. They're just working with nothing."

"I never suggested they weren't working every angle."

"You didn't, but some guy wrote it up in the paper that way."

"Was he questioned?"

"You bet. He was just some jerk who's down on the police. He writes up every scrap of corruption he can get his hands on. He tried to suggest years ago that the cops didn't really give a rat's ass when a psycho was killing hookers on Eighth Street. Then the cops cornered the killer and he had to eat his words. But there were witnesses on that case. At least they had the make and color of the car to go on. They don't seem to have a damned thing this time. Then there was the guy a while back who was killing working girls, cutting them up and stuffing them in suitcases. They thought they had it all solved when they were able to trace a guy to the last victim—except she hadn't been a prostitute, she'd been a lounge singer, and the guy they traced was her ex-boyfriend. Turned out he hadn't killed the prostitutes, he was just hoping to get away with murder by disposing of the body in the same manner. They caught him, but they still don't know who did in the other women."

"Think it could be the same man?"

"With a change in style? I don't know. I don't know enough about criminal psychology to answer that, but the guys I know seem to think they're looking for two different killers. Since they haven't found new bodies in suitcases in a while, they're afraid the guy they called the 'Bag-man' might have moved on. He was a slasher. This guy strangles. Apparently a different psychology brings about the difference in methods. Hey, you took a lot more classes in criminology than I ever did. You should know."

Dane shrugged. "It's not likely that a slasher would become a strangler," he said. "In this case, though...well, I just hoped you might have some insight. You saw the body in situ and all."

"I told you—I called in the specialists the minute I found her. I mean the *minute*. I knew damn well that I didn't have the man-power or equipment to investigate a crime scene like that, to pro-tect every little hair and fiber that might turn up." He was quiet for a moment, studying Dane. "So why your renewed interest in the case?" Jesse asked.

"Sheila's missing," Dane said. He was comfortable saying that much.

One of Jesse's dark brows arched against his forehead. "What do you mean, missing? Sheila is always off somewhere, and she always turns up again. Why are you worried and connecting her to this case? She doesn't fit the victim profile. Or has she started wearing pasties and dancing?"

"No. But...she was running pretty wild."

"She may still be running wild. Sheila's taken off for long pe-riods of time before, hasn't she? I don't think she came back to Key Largo much before you showed up down here again. And before that, if I understand it right, after her divorce from Larry, she took off for Europe for a while, came back and gambled in

Vegas, then hopped around some more before settling into renting that duplex with Cindy. Why would you suspect she might be a victim just because she didn't share her plans with anyone? Cindy told me that even after they rented the duplex, Sheila often went off for a few nights. Cindy would start getting worried, and then Sheila would suddenly call her from the Bahamas or somewhere to say she was all right."

"She hasn't called anyone this time."

"Still...well, you're talking about Sheila."

"Call it a hunch," Dane said.

Jesse stared at him. "It's more than a hunch, but, hey, you'll tell me when you're ready."

"I'm still dealing with it myself," Dane said.

"Have you been to the local cops?"

"No, but Kelsey is down. She was supposed to meet Sheila here. And she said something about having gone to the cops."

"I'm sure they mollified her and filled out a report. And that's about all you're going to get. Not that you haven't got decent guys working the Keys. It's just that Sheila is a grown woman, a woman known to leave her home for long periods of time without giving notice to those around her. She's over twenty-one and doesn't really owe explanations to anyone."

"She hasn't just gone off. I have to find—" He paused, wondering if he was being an ass, if he shouldn't just bring Jesse in on it now. But he wasn't ready. It was just this morning that he had seen the photograph. "I have to find her myself."

"If there's anything I can do, let me know."

"Thanks. How are you doing out there?"

"I'm doing well," Jesse said, swallowing the rest of his beer. "And I'm going to get going on this one beer. I don't think it would make for good public relations if a Miccosukee cop was stopped for driving under the influence. Come out and see me sometime. I'll show you where I found the girl, and I'll let you see the file I have on the incident."

"Great. Thanks. I'll take you up on that."

"Let me know when you're coming, so I can be available."

"You've managed to get your hands on a cell phone that can find a signal in the Glades?"

Jesse laughed. "No, not really. But the office can rouse me on the radio if I'm not around."

"I'll be out soon."

Dane walked Jesse out through the front of the house. A broad hallway stretched from the living room to the front foyer, a formal room decorated according to his mother's era, with a library to the right and a breakfast room to the left directly behind the kitchen. A curving stairway led to the two big bedrooms that took up the entire second floor of the residence.

They all used to slide down the banisters when they'd been kids. It had driven his mother crazy.

Jesse left by the front door, and Dane went along with him as he got into his car—his own, a beige Jeep, and not the patrol car he used when he was on duty. Jesse preferred his Jeep, though he was free to use the patrol car when he chose. There had been some torrential rains lately. Maybe he'd been afraid the road to Hurricane Bay would be badly rutted.

And sometimes he liked his own car when he was off the reservation because he got tired of tourists pointing at him as if he were Tonto on a pinto.

"You know, when you feel you're ready for my help, I'm there," Jesse told him.

"Yeah, I know. Thanks."

Jesse drove away.

Dane started back to the house, but hesitated, looking at the eaves over the porch that led to the roadside, the official entry, of the house. He mentally placed a security camera in the eaves. He'd get on it tomorrow.

He walked back in, heading for his computer. He sat down, keyed in some entries and followed them. For an hour, he gave his attention to every detail he could glean from the news articles he was able to call up online.

After a while, mind churning, he logged off, stretched and walked out back. He stared at the dock and walked around the angular corner that brought him from the dock and the deeper water to the spit of shallows and beach.

That was where she had been.

Rain, surf, sand, time. Nothing. The area looked as peaceful as ever.

He walked back into the house and looked around the living room, feeling a renewed surge of fury, sorrow and anger.

In his own room, he threw open the closet door, looked at the organized rows of clothing. The space where an article was missing. He'd been through it all in his head, over and over. He'd searched the house.

He went over it again.

The entire house, top to bottom. Out back, he trod lightly over the small dock, hopped aboard the Urchin and once again went slowly and minutely over every detail of his boat.

At last he went back to the house, locked both doors and made certain that his .38 special was loaded and beneath his pillow.

Still, sleep eluded him.

Someone had been in his house. And they had done a lot more than eat his porridge or sleep in his bed.

Only one thing had been taken.

He told himself he couldn't be sure. The house was filled with the accumulation of years.

Still, he knew in his gut that there was definitely one thing missing.

And that one thing could damn him.


Kelsey jerked up and nearly screamed at the sound of loud pounding at her door.

She hadn't wanted to admit it, but going out to Andy Latham's had spooked her. And Dane had been acting strangely, too. It was weird how life could change. She had adored him so much once; it had almost been hero worship. Then there had been the years when she kept a polite and civil distance at those few social occasions when they were at the same place at the same time. They'd gone from being best friends to stiff acquaintances. Then they hadn't seen each other at all for...two years, at least. Since the last time she had seen Sheila.

And now...

She could still hear Sheila's voice in her mind. She hadn't seen her in a long time, but she had known Sheila well. Known her when she was angry, caustic and careless of the feelings of others. Known her when she was depressed and down on herself. She knew the way Sheila sounded.

And this time, she had sounded...

*Scared.*

Kelsey had found herself upset when Dane left. And oddly frightened and unnerved when Cindy left—and she was only on the other side of the wall. Face it, she was actually feeling scared, though of what she didn't know, when she'd locked the door and gone to bed for the night. And she hadn't really slept. She'd dozed and awakened, dozed, and awakened again. She hadn't really been asleep when the knocking had sounded; it had just been so loud and sharp against the dark and quiet that it had startled her.

Bolting to a sitting position in the bed, she took a moment to tell herself that the noise was just someone knocking at the door—and thieves and psychos rarely knocked.

She crawled quickly out of bed. Since her night attire consisted of a long, heavy cotton, one-size-fits-most T-shirt with a frazzled duck saying something about needing coffee, she walked through the darkened house to the front door without a robe, not bothering with slippers, either.

Her mom still got mad at her for walking around without

shoes all the time. Even in the Keys. Walking around barefoot and getting your feet dirty made you look like white trash, or so Jennie said.

Amazed at the thoughts that came to mind in a darkened house in the middle of the night, Kelsey reached the door and looked out the peephole. The yellow porch light beamed down on two men: Nate Curry and Larry Miller.

She opened the door, no longer at all frightened, but quizzical and irritated. "What the hell are the two of you doing out here in the middle of the night?"

Nate, a true beach boy, tanned to pure gold, blue-eyed, blond-haired, seemed taken aback. "It's not the middle of the night. It's just after two."

"It's 2:00 a.m.," Larry said, his expression somewhat rueful. Even when he was standing in cutoffs in the sand, Larry Miller looked like an executive. His dark brown hair always gave the appearance of a neat, fresh cut. Kelsey didn't think she'd ever seen him anything but clean-shaven—five-o'clock shadow didn't dare darken his door. He was dressed casually in a polo shirt and knee-length Dockers, but both were pressed and clean. His boat shoes didn't have a scuff. The overnight bag he carried, which should have looked as laid-back as a duffle, bore a designer name. He had the profile to fit the image, as well. Features chiseled like a classic Greek statue.

"I don't close the bar on weeknights until 2:00 a.m.," Nate said. He stared from Larry to Kelsey. "Okay, so maybe to some people that's the middle of the night."

"I was just going to go to a hotel," Larry said, looking at Kelsey, still apologetic. "But I went by Nate's. He reminded me that this place has two bedrooms. And if Sheila shows, I can just bunk over with Cindy."

Kelsey stepped back, letting the men enter. "Larry, you're more than welcome here—as much as I am, surely. You'll have to take the spare room. I'm in Sheila's—I know it sounds silly, but it makes me feel closer to figuring out her moves somehow. But what are you doing down here at all?"

He shrugged. "Two things. You sounded upset on the phone, and I didn't want you to go getting all worried about Sheila. She's been known to take off before. Second...I don't know. You'd been to see Nate, Cindy was here, Dane had come over...I guess I was seized by a rush of nostalgia and decided I had to come down, too. My nostalgia was tempered with reason, of course—I didn't want you to be alone and upset."

Nate made his way past both of them. Unlike Larry, he unmistakably belonged here. His tan was straight from the beach, not acquired in any artificial bed. He had a complete ease of manner in cutoffs or swim trunks, a T-shirt or his bare chest. He could dress well when he needed to and looked like a million bucks. But an hour or so with a tie on, and Nate went crazy. He'd been born in the islands, and he loved them. He'd never had the least desire to leave. He'd gone far enough north to get a degree from Florida International University in hotel and restaurant management, just so he could further improve the Sea Shanty. A vacation to Nate meant taking a boat over to the Bahamas. He had no desire to head for the snow and couldn't care less if he ever saw a country that didn't offer a good reef for diving, sun, sand and warmth.

"You got coffee, Kelsey?" he asked, heading straight for the kitchen.

"Yes, I have coffee," she said, glancing at Larry with a shrug and following Nate. "But it's 2:00 a.m. You'll wind up staying awake all night."

"Nope. I never stay awake all night," Nate assured her. He was already digging through the cabinets.

She walked behind him, caught a prying hand and said, "If you want coffee, let me make decaf, and that way Larry and I can join you."

"She's in her mid-twenties, and already her spirit of adventure has departed," Nate said to Larry, over Kelsey's head.

"My dislike of lying awake all night unable to sleep has kicked in, that's all," Kelsey said. Giving Nate a little push out of the way, she found the decaf and began preparing the coffee.

"You got anything to eat in here?" Larry asked.

"You just came from Nate's place—why didn't you order food if you were hungry?" Kelsey asked. She didn't want to say that she was actually glad to see them, as annoying as they might be. They were giving her a pleasant sense of security.

"His late-night menu doesn't offer a lot," Larry said.

"Hey!" Nate protested. "Conch fritters, conch chowder, snapper sandwich, veggie burger, hamburger. What are you expecting at this hour of the night? A sissy fruit and yogurt salad, or some alfalfa sprouts?"

"Your eating habits will give you a heart attack one day," Larry said. "I can already hear your arteries choking."

"You're going to be one of those health freaks who does marathons and drops dead running down the block," Nate told him.

"You have cereal?" Larry asked Kelsey.

"Raisin bran. Help yourself." She was measuring coffee.

Larry had no problem helping himself to food. "Ah-ha! She has yogurt and fruit. I knew it."

"And beer," Nate said, taking one.

"You just left a bar."

"I never drink when I'm working my own bar."

"You just asked me for coffee."

"The coffee and the beer will cancel each other out."

Kelsey shook her head and let the coffee perk. She crawled up on a bar stool next to Larry. "What about work? We're both gone now."

"Tomorrow is Friday. I left a message with my secretary that I was working at home. I'll drive back in on Monday sometime," Larry said. "Don't worry, I'm a golden boy at work, you know that."

It was true.

"Um. Let's hope you're not so golden that they don't get the idea to cut my vacation short," Kelsey told him.

He laughed. "You're the golden girl. The idea lady. The creative genius. You're safe."

"Is that coffee done, Kelsey?" Nate asked.

"Looks like it. Why don't you pour me some, too?"

Larry jumped when the phone on the counter in front of the coffeepot rang.

"Who the hell would be calling at this hour?" Larry asked.

"Yeah, two o'clock in the morning," Kelsey murmured. "Answer it."

Larry did so. Even from where they were sitting, the others could hear Cindy's voice over the phone. She had recognized Larry's "Hello?" But she wanted to know what he was doing in Kelsey's place in the middle of the night.

"Time is relative," he told her. "Actually when I talked to Kelsey earlier, she sounded a little down, and I thought seeing you and Dane sounded really good, so I decided to play hooky from work and drive on down. For the weekend, at least."

Cindy said something Kelsey couldn't quite catch. Larry hung up the phone.

Kelsey and Nate both stared at Larry.

"She's on her way over," Larry said.

"Why not?" Kelsey said. "Time is relative." She got off her bar stool to walk to the front door and let Cindy in when she appeared in just a minute's time. It didn't take long to get from one side of a duplex to another.

"Hey!" Cindy said when Kelsey opened the door. She swept on in. Larry had come from the kitchen and greeted Cindy with a big hug.

"Wow!" he said as she hugged him back. "Little but powerful. I feel like I just got a hug from an anaconda."

"Sorry, too tight?" Cindy said.

Larry shook his head. "Hugs are never too tight. I just never realized before how powerful you are."

"It's a short thing. Being small, I work out a lot, so the big guys can't push me around. Kelsey, you should come to the gym with me tomorrow. I have a membership over at the new hotel. They've got all kinds of machines, a pool, a sauna.... If you work out, you'll feel better about everything."

"If Sheila shows up, I'll feel better about everything," Kelsey said.

Nate had joined them in the passage between the living room and kitchen. Along with Cindy and Larry, he stared at her. They were all looking at her as if they were adults and she was a child still convinced there was a Santa Claus.

"She's gone off for more than a week before," Cindy said.

"She left me for lots more than a week," Larry said. There was no pain in his voice. He was matter-of-fact about Sheila.

"She acts on whims," Nate said softly.

They still had that look in their eyes as they watched her. Kelsey shook her head. "Come on, now, we're her friends. We've got to be concerned."

Larry cleared his throat.

"Okay, so I was barely in touch with her for a couple of years. But you know what it's like. We all grew up together. We have a bond. At first Sheila just e-mailed me, and I e-mailed back. Then we talked. Then she said that she really needed to see me, because I knew her so well, and she could trust me with her deepest, darkest secrets. Then she told me she was feeling desperate, and please would I make arrangements to spend time with her. So, you see, don't you, why I'm so worried?"

Larry groaned softly. "Kelsey, don't you remember how pissed off Sheila was when you took my side during the divorce?"

"I didn't take your side. Larry, I don't take sides in the breakup of a marriage, which is always a very sad thing."

"Okay, you didn't take sides," Larry said. He stood staring at her for a moment, then groaned. "Well, great, I'm glad we're all best friends because it's still kind of embarrassing to admit all this. Don't you remember? She cheated. I was hurt. Really hurt. You were cool to her. I remember her standing in your office, and you telling Sheila that she had owed it to me to say the marriage wasn't working, that she shouldn't have hurt and humiliated me the way she did. She said you were her friend, so you should have understood whatever she had done. And you told her that she was a grown-up and could live the life she wanted, but she needed to start watching out for crushing other people."

Kelsey remembered the day well. Larry had just found out about what his wife had gotten up to. He'd blown an important presentation because of it, and she'd been worried about his job.

And it was true. Sheila *had* been angry with her, and she'd flounced out of the office. Next time they had made a date—at Sheila's insistence, because she had wanted to tell her side of the story—Sheila hadn't shown. The next time Sheila had tried to see her, Kelsey had still been angry herself. She'd come up with an excuse. And that had been it until just about six months ago, when Sheila started e-mailing her, and then the phone calls began.

"Sheila is our friend," Nate said quietly. "But she's kicked us all in the teeth."

They were all silent for a minute.

"So what are we supposed to do?" Kelsey said.

"You went to the police, right?" Nate said.

Kelsey nodded.

"Then we let them handle it. What else are you going to do?"

"Track her down," Kelsey said.

They all continued to stare at her. She let out a sigh of exasperation. "We follow her footsteps, talk to anyone she might have seen."

"Great," Nate said. "That would include the entire populace of the Keys. And let's not forget Miami."

"Dane has an investigations firm," Cindy said with impatience. "The smartest thing is to let him handle it."

"The problem with Dane is the same problem with you all," Kelsey said. She didn't know why she was reluctant to point out to Nate the fact that he had been the one to tell her he was pretty sure Dane and Sheila had been seeing each other as more than friends, and that then the two of them had argued at the bar, and that Sheila had implied she was heading out to Dane's place the last time he had seen her. "No one seems to be really worried," she said.

"Except you," Larry pointed out.

"All right, here's the deal," Cindy said. "Kelsey, tomorrow morning you come to the gym with me. I swear, it will make you feel better. Then we'll all go to see Dane. We'll have that barbecue at his place."

"He didn't exactly invite us for a barbecue tomorrow," Kelsey said.

Cindy waved a hand in the air as if being invited was entirely immaterial. "We'll bring all the stuff. We'll just show up at Hurricane Bay in the morning with all the fixings. He won't mind."

"Wait a minute," Nate said. "What time?"

"I don't know. Sometime in the morning," Cindy said.

"Morning is relative. It's morning now. Closing in on three," Nate said. "I wasn't planning on waking up too early."

"How about one?" Larry suggested. He yawned. "I'll sleep, Cindy and Kelsey can go get buff, buy the food, come back, then we all meet here and head over at one."

"There. We have a plan," Cindy said. "Good night. Kelsey. Will nine be too early for you?"

Kelsey had the feeling the last thing she was going to want to do in the morning was go to the gym.

"Sheila came with me sometimes," Cindy said. "You can ask around and find out if she said anything to anyone."

"Nine, then," Kelsey agreed.

"Night, guys," Cindy said. Walking past them, she let herself out.

"I should go, too," Nate said. He looked at Kelsey. "This seems strange," he told Larry.

"What's that?"

"Leaving you in a house, sleeping with my ex-wife."

"He's not sleeping with your ex-wife," Kelsey said.

"She won't sleep with me," Larry told Nate.

"No?"

"I've asked her," Larry said, winking at Kelsey. "She rebuffed me kindly, but with determination."

"She's like that."

"Hell, she married you."

"She married me because she was a friend who liked me. It was a mercy marriage, and that was all."

"She likes me, and she still won't sleep with me."

"Nate," Kelsey said firmly, "let's face it, you're just too pretty to be tied down by one woman. And, Larry, you're sleeping with one of the most beautiful women I've ever seen, and she seems to be nice, on top of it. Nate, go home. Larry, the extra bedroom is right there. Cindy is going to get me up in a matter of hours and make me do painful things to my body, so go away, both of you."

She pushed Nate toward the door. He protested playfully, "I can do painful things to your body, if that's what you want."

"Out!"

She shoved Nate out the door.

"Lock it," he told her from the outside.

"You bet," she said.

She knew that Nate was waiting to hear the sound of the bolt sliding into place. She obliged him. "It's locked."

"Good girl. Good night."

"Good night."

She turned around. Larry laughed, putting up his hands. "I'm on my way into the spare bedroom this minute."

To prove it, he turned and walked through the doorway and across the living room.

Kelsey returned to the kitchen for a moment and unplugged the coffee machine. She decided to set it up for the next morning. She'd gotten Cindy and Nate out, and Larry off to bed. She could go back to sleep.

Except that now she was restless.

The day had been busy. She was really exhausted. She wanted to lie down, close her eyes and black it all out.

But now, in the silence that came in the wake of the others' departures, she felt wired.

So tired, but wide-awake.

She gave the kitchen a thorough cleaning. When that was done, she looked around the living room. It was already clean. Sheila wasn't the type to keep bric-a-brac lying around. Nor did she pile up magazines or bills. Of course, she would have to have some kind of paperwork lying around. Utility bills, if nothing else. Kelsey made a mental note to go through every drawer in the place the next day and really start prying into Sheila's business. With that determination made, she returned to the bedroom at last. Sheila's room.

She lay down again, got up, washed her face, brushed her teeth, turned the television on to a cable movie. An old mummy movie. Black and white, with no computer or high-tech gimmicks, it was just a darned good movie. Good acting, lots of suspense.

She warned herself that she would fall asleep and dream about bandage-wrapped creatures rising from the grave to come after her.

But she didn't.

She dreamed about the past.

And hours later, when she awoke again to the streaking pink and gold colors of a new dawn, haggard and still exhausted, she wished that she *had* dreamed of ancient monsters.

They were far less unsettling than the memories of a not so distant time.

# CHAPTER 5

An endangered American crocodile had somehow made it into the waters just off Coconut Grove, so close to the marina that those who made a living scraping barnacles from the hulls of the many pleasure craft had been afraid to go into the water. But the wily reptile had been caught and brought back to a crocodile reserve. Two accidents had tied up US1, and a woman had been arrested for aggravated child abuse after bringing her injured baby to a local hospital. Another Hollywood star had been arrested on Miami Beach for DUI.

Waking early, Dane listened to the news on the television, then scoured the morning paper.

No bodies had been discovered in the last twenty-four hours. And it was daylight. Time to take the offensive. He owed it to himself—and to Sheila.

He left the house and started out with a visit to Gary Hansen at the local police station. Gary had come down from Minnesota. In the sun, his blond hair had turned to a platinum that was almost white. He always wore very dark sunglasses, mainly because his eyes were nearly as light a blue as his hair was a blond.

The sunlight hurt him. He was fair-skinned, as well, and despite the amount of sunblock he used, he was usually burned to a shade of brilliant pink most commonly found on tourists unaccustomed to the sun. But despite his body's seeming protest against the climate, Gary loved Key Largo. He was never leaving.

He was a decent guy of about forty, the kind who would slap a drunk driver in the can overnight without mercy, but who would deal mercifully with minor infractions of the law. He gave the appearance of moving slowly, of being a leisurely guy, but in the few cases that had brought them together since Dane had opened up shop in the area, he'd proven himself to be sharp as a tack.

"Hey, Dane, what's up? Caught any thieves on video?" Gary asked him.

"No, I just came in to ask you a few questions."

Gary groaned. "You're not going to ask me for files that aren't public domain, are you? There are laws to protect the criminals out there, you know."

Dane grinned at the joke despite his lack of humor at the moment. He took a seat on the edge of Gary's cluttered desk. "No, I think a friend of mine was in here yesterday. Seems we have another friend who hasn't been seen for a while."

Gary nodded, eyeing Dane closely as he leaned back in his swivel chair, lacing his fingers behind his head. He'd known exactly why Dane had come.

"Kelsey Cunningham. She reported that your friend Sheila hadn't been seen in a while."

"Have you done anything?"

"Filled out the papers. Asked a few questions."

"That's all?"

Gary hesitated, then shrugged. "Actually I would have come to see you today. Miss Cunningham said that Nate Curry out at the Sea Shanty told her Sheila was heading for your place the last time he'd seen her."

"She did. She came to my house. Left early the next morning. I haven't seen her since." That was God's truth. He hadn't seen her.

Not in person.

"Did she say anything to you about going away?" Gary asked him.

"No. Not to me."

"Well, there are some other locals she hangs with, who we might want to question...just for being questionable locals. Still, Miss Cunningham says that her friend's car is gone, as well. We'll treat the situation as a missing person, but from past history...this lady comes and goes as she pleases. Look, Dane, I know Sheila Warren, too. Not like you old-timers here know her, but I've met her, and I know about her. She isn't employed and lives off that trust fund left by her mother. She island hops, continent hops...seems to me she's a free spirit. Sorry, Dane, I know the woman is your friend. Maybe she's still a lot more, from what I've heard from a few people. But, hell, she's a grown woman. Apparently she...likes making new friends and traveling with them. Have you been hired by someone to look for her?"

"Yeah, myself."

"Great. We'll help each other. But...this isn't a big city like Miami or anything, but still, we had a big drug bust the other night, I've got to find a husband who broke his wife's jaw at the new hotel the other night...there's a string of burglaries, and...well, you know the routine. It's hard to get too concerned over a woman who regularly goes off with whomever she pleases whenever she feels like it."

"I understand your position. But I have a suggestion. Talk to Andy Latham, Sheila's stepfather."

"Yeah, I'd intended to do that." From his tone, Gary Hansen obviously considered it an unpleasant proposition. He eyed Dane for a minute. "I heard around town that Sheila was getting into drugs."

"To the best of my knowledge, she wasn't into anything heavy," Dane said. "She wasn't shooting up, if that's what you mean."

"How do you know?"

"Okay, she wasn't shooting into her arms, at any rate. I know because she was always bare-armed when I saw her."

"You did have a relationship with her for years, right?"

"Yeah. I wouldn't say high school sweethearts, because neither one of us was particularly sweet. After high school, I went away to college, and then into the service. Sheila went her own way."

"So it had all cooled down by now?" Gary said, still studying him. He didn't wait for Dane to answer. "Yeah, I guess it couldn't have been much of anything now. Heard about what happened up in St. Augustine. I'm sorry about that."

"Thanks. And as to Sheila, whether or not she was buying weed or pills on the street, I don't know. She might have been. It's an angle I wouldn't rule out."

"The problem with searching for Sheila is that there are miles and miles of angles that have to be checked out," Gary said.

"Keep me posted, will you?"

"Sure."

Dane stood and started for the door.

"Hey," Gary called.

"Yeah?"

"You keep me posted, too, huh?"

Dane nodded. He felt an uncomfortable rise of tension in his throat. It might be the best thing in the world if he did keep the cops posted with the truth.

The whole truth and nothing but the truth.

No, he'd thought it all out. There was nothing he knew that could help the cops do anything.

Except charge him with murder.

Working out with Cindy made Kelsey feel like a novice climber trying to scale Everest next to the pros.

She had never considered herself to be in particularly *bad* shape—she did slide on into the gym in Miami now and then, she loved to go bike riding on a decent day, and she spent at least several late afternoons a week in her condo pool.

But watching Cindy on an exercise bike was like watching a tornado set down. She seemed to pedal close to a mile a minute.

They shared no conversation at the cycles. Kelsey was lucky to be able to breathe while trying to appear to keep up with Cindy's speed.

From the cycles, they went on to free weights.

Cindy could apparently press more weight than most of the men. Two-hundred-something pounds. Kelsey didn't need to spot Cindy while she was lifting—something that probably wouldn't have done much good anyway, since she couldn't begin to lift the weight that Cindy could—because there was a roomful of muscle-bound guys more than ready to help out.

Kelsey played with the five-pound weights she used in her own exercise routine, said hello to all the lifters to whom Cindy introduced her, and decided that her own meager workout was done. Cindy, true to her word, asked if anyone had seen Sheila in the gym lately.

No one had.

Three guys—Jim Norris, Ralph Munroe and Ricky Esteban— apparently knew Sheila. And knew her fairly well.

None of them seemed in the least concerned about her whereabouts. Ralph was short and, with his muscles, seemed as wide as he was tall. Killer pecs. Jim was the opposite, so tall that the scope of his muscles seemed smaller, though certainly as well honed. The man didn't seem to have so much as a quarter inch of body fat. Ricky Esteban came in a body shape right between the other two; standing about six feet even, he had a very attractive build. He told Kelsey that he and Sheila had spent a night on the town about two weeks earlier, and he hadn't seen her since then.

He watched Kelsey with curious amber eyes, then told her, "You know...Sheila's the kind of girl who doesn't believe in double standards."

"Meaning...?" Kelsey asked him.

Ricky shrugged, dragging damp hair back off his forehead. "What's good for the gander is good for the goose. I guess I'm trying to say that she does whatever the hell she wants to do. It aggravates her that men seem to think nothing about going to a strip club, or that they can go to a bar at night in hopes of getting lucky with a total stranger, and that women generally get labeled—not nicely—for doing the same thing. She told me once that she was a voice for her sex."

Kelsey stared at him blankly as he went on. "What I'm trying to tell you is that you shouldn't be too worried. If Sheila met a guy and liked him, and he was heading to Alaska for the week, she wouldn't think twice about going with him."

"She would have called me," Kelsey insisted.

Ricky shrugged. Then his expression changed, and he asked her what she was doing with her vacation time in the Keys.

He was flattering—and damned good-looking.

She hesitated and wondered why she did. Dinner with him would probably be nice.

She gave him a vague answer, though, escaped out to the entry area and bought a bottle of water, then sat in one of the comfortable spa chairs to wait, breathe and hope the pain she'd incurred by trying to keep up with Cindy would go away.

She damned the fact that Dane Whitelaw had returned to Hurricane Bay. She wondered if, had she not seen him, she might have gone out with Ricky.

Ricky had admitted to dating Sheila.

Then again, she wasn't sure she had met a guy yet who hadn't dated Sheila. Everything she was learning was disturbing. And yet people kept telling her these things so she wouldn't worry.

Unfortunately, all these tidbits about Sheila's wild lifestyle only made her more concerned.

The bottle of water went quickly.

She wanted coffee.

The gym was very nice—Cindy had spoken the truth. There was the gym itself, along with a complete spa in the west wing of the new hotel. The spa sold all kinds of juices and herbal teas. Healthful offerings.

She just wanted coffee. Strong, caffeinated coffee.

As she debated heading out to the hotel area, she was startled to hear her name called.

"Kelsey? Kelsey Cunningham? It *is* you, isn't it?"

She twisted in her chair to see a man coming from the free weight room. He was a good six foot two and wearing a tank top, so it was apparent that he was muscular. He had hair so dark it was almost ebony, able to defy the effects of the sun that had tanned him to such a deep shade that he was nearly brown. His eyes were just as dark as his hair. Within two seconds she recognized him and smiled. "Jorge!"

He walked over to her, about to give her a hug, then backed off, apologizing. "Sorry, I'm sweating like a pig. If pigs really sweat. Quick kiss on the cheek. How are you? I haven't seen you in ages. Actually, I should have expected you—Sheila mentioned that you were coming down for vacation."

She rose and gave him a hug, despite the sweat. Jorge Marti hadn't been one of their intimate crowd, but he had been a friend. While they had all taken various jobs throughout their high school years, Jorge had really worked. His folks had come over during the Mariel boat lift from Cuba, and for many years had barely eked out an existence. Jorge hadn't spoken a word of English when he had arrived as a nine-year-old. Now his accent was barely discernible. They'd all liked him, and on those few occasions when he hadn't been studying or working, he'd spent his free time with them.

In high school, though, he'd had a period where he'd mixed with the wrong crowd. Only the intervention of Dane's father had kept him from going to jail and acquiring the kind of record that would have stayed with him all his life.

"Jorge, it's wonderful to see you. And yes, I came to meet Sheila, but it seems that she stood me up."

"Stood you up?"

"She isn't here. Have you seen her in the last week?"

"Sure...wait...no, I haven't. The last time I saw Sheila...was at the Sea Shanty. She'd been making the rounds, then ended up sitting with Dane. I think they had an argument or something. He left...and she left right after. Hey, have you talked to Dane?"

"Yes, I have."

"Well, you know Sheila."

Did she really know Sheila anymore?

"So how have you been?" he asker her.

"Great, thank you."

"Still doing commercials?"

"Commercials and print advertising."

"Great. And you're still working with Larry Miller?"

"Yes. In fact, Larry was the one who got me the job."

"Glad to hear it. You look wonderful."

"Thanks. So do you. How is your business doing?"

"I'm happy with it. I've got two captains working for me now, so I don't have to take out every charter myself. It was a good way to create a company, but man...it made for some long hard hours and very little social life."

She smiled. "Jorge, you were always the best worker, the go-getter. One day you'll probably have a fleet of ships to rival the navy, and captains for all of them." She thought about Dane and the way he appeared to be spending his life in a lounge chair with a beer. She didn't know what had happened in St. Augustine that had made him close up shop, then close up life. But here was Jorge, who had certainly been as beaten up as any man alive when he was a little kid, and he just kept moving forward. "And you've done it all from nothing," she added.

He looked at her peculiarly, almost as if he had been watching her mind working. "Remember where you are. Here we believe in smelling the flowers along the way, you know. We're in the Keys. Sun, sand and ocean breezes."

"Alcohol and drugs," she added.

"Well," he said, his tone light, "there is a fine line between making a place in the world and forgetting that we only live in it so long. So, are you planning to take the world by storm? Eventually own every advertising agency in the state?"

She gave him a rueful grin. "No. I'm sorry, did I sound as if getting ahead was the only important thing in the world?"

Jorge shook his head. "I was just remembering how you loved to paint, and how you always had a camera, no matter what we were doing. Still painting?"

"I still have a camera most of the time. As for painting..."

She never finished the sentence. Cindy came out, blond hair pulled back, her workout tank damp, her muscles gleaming with a sheen of perspiration. "Jorge!" she said with pleasure. "I didn't see you in there."

"I saw you, but you were lifting the equivalent of the Titanic, so I didn't interrupt," Jorge said.

Cindy gave him a kiss on the cheek, still smiling. "We're going to have a barbecue at Dane's in a couple of hours. Why don't you come?"

He looked surprised. "Dane invited everyone over for a barbecue?"

"Yes," Cindy said.

"No," Kelsey corrected.

"Yes," Cindy argued.

"We suggested he have one," Kelsey said. She looked at Cindy. "And we're surprising him with the time and date. You don't think we'll be welcome? Have you seen much of him since he's been back down here?"

"Sure, everyone from the old crowd runs into everyone else down here, what with Nate owning the Sea Shanty," Jorge said.

"Has he been...rude?" Kelsey queried.

"No, no, nothing like that. Quiet. Reclusive, maybe," Jorge said. "I've respected his privacy, that's all."

"Well, we're not going to let him be private anymore," Cindy said firmly. "Show up. We're going to make him have a good time."

"All right, maybe," Jorge said. He wrinkled his nose. "I'm off to the showers. Kelsey, great to have you home."

She wasn't really home, she thought. She was just passing through. "Thanks, Jorge."

He left them, heading into the men's locker room. Cindy sighed in his wake. "He is *so* good-looking."

"Yes, he is," Kelsey agreed. "He hasn't married? He isn't seeing anyone?"

"He works," Cindy said. "And I guess he sees lots of people. Oh, well, let's head out. We need showers, too," she said ruefully. "I must smell like a trucker who's been on the road for a week."

"You work out like a boxer aiming for the heavyweight championship," Kelsey told her.

Cindy laughed. "Like I said, I think it has something to do with being short. Let's go, shall we? Showers, then barbecue shopping. Too bad Dane didn't really plan this. He'd have gone out and brought us back lots of fresh fish. Maybe there will be something fresh at one of the markets. Or maybe we'll just go with red meat. Or chicken. Or both." She led the way out, hesitating as they exited the building. "I hope Jorge shows up," she said.

Dane had thought that he would have to drive all the way into the city of Miami and meet Hector Hernandez in the downtown area, but Hector had suggested that they meet at the seafood restaurant at the southern end of Florida City. Being with the Metro force meant that Hector handled anything to the Miami-Dade county lines, and that meant the Trail into the Everglades out to Collier County to the west, and Monroe County at the line just before the Keys. Where they met was still Hector's territory, although his assignments were more often in the city of Miami proper and the surrounding communities.

There were enough murders there alone to keep plenty of men busy, Hector had told him once. Not that he felt his beloved county was so bad. Put that many people together and bad things happened. That was the way of life, unfortunately. Miami-Dade had a tendency to have its bad news well publicized. But Hector didn't believe that a *place* could be bad. Now, as to people, well, they could be pure evil. And it was true that South Florida had endless miles of coastline, miles and miles of Everglades and the capacity to include almost any illicit operation known to man. It was incredibly easy to get rid of a body.

Yet the bodies usually surfaced. Eventually.

Hector was already there when Dane arrived, munching down on a big plate of calamari, drinking ice tea.

He grinned when he saw Dane, rose, shook his hand, still chewing.

"Good to see you. Since you asked me to lunch, I thought I'd order everything on the menu. Got surf and turf coming after this. Filet and lobster. Maine lobster. Love this place we call home, you know, but our overgrown crawfish don't come anywhere near close to the taste of the Maine guys. You're going to get one hell of a lunch bill. Detectives are underpaid, you know. I hope your new business in the Keys is going well."

He was a big man, resembling the old Frito Bandito.

"It's going all right," Dane said. "People are into the high-tech stuff these days. Store owners want camera setups, surveillance, tapes, all the kinds of stuff they've seen catch thieves on the television shows."

"Nothing too big, yet, huh?"

"You know life down there. A bit easier."

Hector made a face. "It would be easier up here if it weren't for all the fancy attorneys. We nabbed a guy who killed his wife and kids a couple of years ago, and they got him off. You know what his defense was? He hadn't meant to kill them. He'd been threatening her because he was convinced she was cheating on him. And the gun just went off. Three times. All three shots somehow accidental. You listen to what I'm saying, and you know it's crazy. But he got the right attorney, and the jury bought it. Can you believe it?"

Hector sat down again when Dane did. "Then there was the old guy who beat the old lady to death in the nursing home. He got off, too. The defense? His medication was wrong. And the old lady wanted to die. It was a mercy killing. Oh, yeah, he beat her mercifully. What really bothers me, though, is what a bad rap the city gets. And you know what? One of those survey companies just did a study on crime in the city. Seems that a lot of crazies like to come down here to do their dirty work. They're born and get crazy somewhere in the north, then come south to be homicidal. Not that we don't have our share of domestics," he said with a shake of his head. "Or greed. Stupid greed. I've got a case right now where some asshole shot an old man just to steal his car. That was a sorry one. The wife is inside, the husband goes out for the newspaper, sees the fellow trying to take his car and decides to stop him. The perp shoots the guy, gets blood on his clothes, goes inside the guy's house to steal a new outfit, and the wife is watching television all the time."

"Did you nab him?"

"Not yet, but we will. He left his bloody clothes on the victim's floor and went out without the wife ever knowing. The perp was no brain surgeon. He left fingerprints everywhere and has a rap sheet longer than the Bill of Rights. But you see what I mean? He shouldn't have been on the streets at all. He should have been locked up. There are too many loopholes in the law. And the prisons are so overcrowded that the parole boards are pushed into letting criminals go when they shouldn't. But you know how all that goes. And you didn't come here to ask me about any of the no-brainers."

Dane started to speak, but Hector lifted a hand. "Order first. Have the squid. They know their calamari here. Lightly dusted with breading, tender as a baby's bottom."

Dane ordered the yellowtail, instead, guaranteed fresh by their waitress. He opted for ice tea, as well, and when the waitress had gone, he plowed right in. "I'm interested in one of your open cases."

"The tie-strangling?" Hector said, wiping his mouth and reaching for his tea.

"Yeah. How did you know?"

"One in Dade, one in Broward. They're what we've got going right now with the biggest media attention and the least to go on. Both girls were strippers. If you were friends with one of them, your name has never come up in the investigation. What's your interest?"

"A friend of mine, a girl named Sheila Warren, hasn't been seen around in about a week," Dane said. He was going to stick with honesty while talking to Hector. The truth—just not the whole truth.

"Sheila..." Hector mused over the name for a moment. "Yeah, I know your friend Sheila. I've gone out on charters with your buddy Jorge Marti a few times when he had her aboard, cooking, running around, fishing...just being charming. Beautiful woman. Okay, before I keep going, is she a friend or more than a friend?"

"We were hot and heavy way back in the old days," Dane told him. "But we've both changed a lot. She'd gotten used to living a bit on the wild side, and she's been known to take off with new friends, so the local police aren't very concerned."

"But you are."

"Yeah."

Hector was quiet for a moment, mulling Dane's words as he chewed. Then he said, "I'm not sure where you're making the connection. Both girls strangled by the Necktie Strangler were strippers. And customers have gotten more than lap dances at both clubs by paying extra to have private 'shows.' Your friend wasn't a working girl, was she?"

"No. But she was definitely walking the wild side."

"So what makes you think the strangler might have gotten hold of her?"

"If I'm remembering correctly, both girls were missing persons before their bodies were discovered."

"True. Look, we haven't had much to go on. The bodies were badly decomposed. We haven't found so much as a fiber to give to forensics. We've questioned the families, the friends and the other employees at the clubs. We've tracked down customers through interviewing the proprietors about their regulars and through credit card receipts. Have we found all the customers? Hell, no. A lot of guys won't use a charge card at a strip club— their wives might want to know what they were doing there. We've had plain clothes guys sit around both clubs, watching for weirdos. And do you know what we've gotten?"

"What?"

"A hell of a lot of weirdos. But not a single lead has panned out."

Their waitress came to the table, delivering their food and refilling their glasses.

"I hope you're making the big bucks down there," Hector said, looking at his plate with relish. "Look at that baby! A two-pounder. I was so hungry, I almost ordered the five-pound guy. But then I thought about the old arteries."

Dane looked at Hector's plate. "I can see you're really concerned," he said dryly.

Hector shook his head. "It's all right. I start out the day with oatmeal." He waved a hand for the waitress. "I think I'm going to need a little more of that melted butter," he told her.

Dane took a bite of his fish. It was fresh, and broiled to perfection. "I hear there are details about the murders that are being held back from the media."

Hector had been smiling in delight at the succulent taste of his lobster. Now, he scowled. "Where'd you hear that? Oh, yeah, I forgot—you're related to Jesse Crane."

"Second cousins or something like that," Dane agreed.

"He tell you that?"

"No."

"Good, because it's not supposed to get out."

"So you're not going to tell me?"

"No," Hector said, but he pulled a pen from his breast pocket and started writing on the paper place mat beneath his plate. "But I will give you this. The names of both clubs—I'm pretty sure that both of these girls were targeted when they were working— and a few of the names of the girls we interviewed at each. Who knows? Maybe you'll get something we haven't been able to come up with. Sometimes these girls can spot a cop a mile away, and they're not always so willing to talk to the cops, even when their own lives might be in danger. And if you get anything, anything at all, you come to me with it, you hear?"

"If I get anything from a lead you've given me, you know damn well I'll come right to you."

Hector nodded.

Dane asked him about his family then. Hector told him about his teenaged boys with pride, while still managing to consume his entire meal and ask for dessert, and then coffee.

Dane had coffee, too. When it was served, he asked the waitress if they were in the smoking section, then pulled out a pack of cigarettes.

"Thought you gave that up," Hector said with a frown.

"Yeah, I did. I picked it up again just before I left St. Augustine."

Hector shook his head. "And you're giving me a hard time about the food I eat?"

"You've got a point," Dane said.

Hector downed his coffee, glanced at his watch and said, "I've got to get back to work. Thanks for the lunch. Good luck."

"You don't mind me in your territory, asking a few questions?"

"Hell no." Hector was standing, but he hesitated. "First body was found just about six months ago, second body was found just about three months ago. These guys...the profilers say they work in cycles. That could mean we're due for another body. They say that kind of killer doesn't stop. He keeps going. If anything... Never mind. You took classes in criminology."

"Yeah, but, if anything...what?"

"You know. The killings will just get worse. This guy probably started out squashing lizards as a kid. Maybe he went on to drown kittens, or take a BB gun and use it on puppies. It's likely he progressed to battery or rape, and then...well, now we have our bodies in the canals. That's the psyche of such a man. So believe me, I don't mind you asking questions at all. I don't feel the least possessive about finding a monster like this one. Just don't hold out on me, huh?"

Dane looked at Hector, an honestly good man, and was tempted to tell him all he really knew.

He couldn't.

Hector was too decent a guy. A by-the-book cop.

And Dane needed time. His palms felt itchy. He was determined now, but every once in a while, he felt a cold sweat break out as he wondered what the killer might do next.

"Hector, the minute I've got anything that might help you catch this guy—if and when I ever do—you know that I'll be in your office with the speed of light."

Hector nodded. "Thanks for the fish. And good luck. Who the hell knows? This guy could have moved on. They may be pulling strippers out of a bayou in Louisiana next. I wish I could say that we always get our man. Take care of yourself, Dane. Sorry about the situation in St. Augustine. I'm real sorry. Heard the fancy-pants lawyers got *him* off, too."

Dane folded the place mat Hector had written on. He thanked the waitress, paid the bill and decided he might as well start that night with the club in Miami.

He left the restaurant, mentally berating himself as he did so.

He *had* concentrated on psychology, human behavior and criminology during his years at VMI. While Joe had dived head-first into his love of flying, Dane had been studying with the men from the FBI offices at Quantico. His expertise in the service had been in enemy psychology, the study of religious and behavioral influences on the movements and actions of different peoples. He had worked in both diplomatic negotiations and in "observation tactics," out-of-uniform exercises among the populace in various zones of action in order to determine the mood and reactionary tendencies of the people.

But he'd been back a hell of a long time now. And though he'd opened his investigations agency in St. Augustine with energy and determination, even that seemed a long time ago. For all that he had learned in the classroom, he had discovered some basics—it was easy for people to become fanatical, and it wasn't always possible to discover just why people became brutally homicidal. Years of study, training and research came down to one dogma—there were simply some bad-ass people out there. Some wore their penchant for cruelty in a manner that was almost as easy to read as an open book. Some were well dressed, charming and could talk such a damned good line that in the very midst of destroying other lives, they could come off looking like victims themselves.

He realized that he'd come home to Key Largo knowing that he'd had to get the hell out of the St. Augustine area. And that he'd also come with the fatalistic belief that none of it had meant a fucking thing. He'd opened an agency again not because he'd been interested in the cases he might acquire but because he'd needed an income if he didn't want to go through his savings and his inheritance like toilet paper while literally leading the life of a lounge lizard, as Kelsey had accused him.

He could set a camera, a wire, any manner of surveillance, easily. He could keep an eye on hours of tape in the event of robbery or an employee pilfering from the till, of drug deals taking place in a parking lot. Easy. Like breathing. Waking up, showering, dressing.

No thought involved.

Maybe he *had* turned into a lounge lizard. Because his first thought, after the whack in the face of the photograph the other day, had been to lie low. To act normally, to watch, to wait.

Hell.

Maybe the old days were kicking back in. And maybe it was just an instinct for survival. He was suddenly as determined as all hell that he was going to crack what was going on.

Yeah, well, he had to be. He'd been bitter because he felt the system had failed him. So he'd walked away. It hadn't been the system. He had failed himself.

And then he had failed Sheila.

He owed it to her to find the truth.

Not to mention what the alternative could mean to him. Hell, this was Florida. He could get the death penalty.

He drove mechanically, traveling US1 southward as he had throughout his entire life. He gave the problem at hand the majority of his concentration until he pulled onto the private road to Hurricane Bay.

Then he groaned.

He had company.

Several cars were drawn up by the walkway. He recognized Cindy's minivan and Nate's full-size Wagoneer, with the name Sea Shanty and the mile marker of the establishment written in script along the side.

As he pulled up the gravel driveway in front of the house, Cindy came running around from the dockside of the property to meet him.

She was smiling as if it was Christmas.

"Dane, surprise! We've brought the barbecue to you."

# CHAPTER 6

Dane was definitely not delighted to be having a barbecue, Kelsey thought, seeing the tension in his features as he walked with Cindy around to the dock side of the house.

Cindy was smiling. She didn't seem to notice that Dane was less than pleased. "And look who made it down here," she was saying excitedly. "Larry Miller."

"Larry, hey, how are you?" Dane said. Larry had left the patio chair where he'd been sitting to walk over and shake Dane's hand. He was wearing a T-shirt, cutoffs and sandals, apparel similar to Nate's, but he still had a haircut that looked pure office. Nate was blond and shaggy, and looked like the native he was.

Some things didn't change.

Dane had been somewhere off the island, she thought. He was wearing chinos, dock shoes and a short-sleeved tailored shirt. Blue. A good color for him. It emphasized the dark quality of his eyes and the bronzed texture of his features. He was far from formally dressed, but in the heat and breezes and casual lifestyle here, ankle-length pants and a nonknit shirt were akin to being dressed up.

"I'm good, thanks, Larry. Nice to see you. What are you doing down here?"

Larry shrugged, grinning a little sheepishly. "Well, Kelsey was down here, and she was upset because Sheila didn't show. Then you were at the duplex, Cindy was there...and Nate. I admit it, I felt like a kid left out of a party. So I drove on down."

"Nice to see you here. It's been a while."

"Actually I've been down a few times here and there. But they've been business dinners, quick trips to a restaurant and back, and with a client. Every time I drove down, I'd think, man, I'm an hour away, and I love this place, and I never get here. So here I am."

"So we had to have a barbecue," Cindy said.

"Like old times," Nate put in. "Except, of course, that we meant to surprise you. Instead the tables were turned—we were the ones surprised when you weren't here. But I made these guys hang in for a while. I had faith that you'd show up eventually."

"But we meant to surprise you with no trouble to you at all, of course. You name it, we brought it," Cindy said with pleasure. "Hog dogs, hamburgers, steaks, chicken and fish. We brought the charcoal, corn on the cob—wrapped and ready for the grill, mind you—baking potatoes, salad, chips, beer and wine. Oh, and paper plates, napkins, paper cups, plastic utensils."

"Great," Dane said. The word was right, but Kelsey thought his inflection was off. He had the look of a man running down a street with a destination in mind, only to find a brick wall in his path.

At least he wasn't going to throw them off the property.

He'd had plans, she realized. But he was going to forgo those plans, rather than share them or make explanations.

Nate rose from the railing where he'd been sitting. "Hey, Dane, when did you start locking the house?"

Dane walked to the door, replying with a shrug. "I'm in the business of investigations," he said. "I supply people with security. I guess in telling people they need to lock up and take precautions I realized that I left my own place open all the time." He twisted his key in the lock and opened the door. He looked straight at Kelsey then. "Come in. The house is always open to you."

Nate walked in, carrying a cooler of groceries. Cindy followed, plucking a grocery bag from the floor of the porch. Larry did likewise, and Kelsey came last, aware that Dane was still staring at her, his hand on the door as he held it open. Her cheeks felt hot as she walked by him. Well, she had basically accused him of...something. At the very least, of keeping information regarding Sheila from them. And she had more or less told him that she was interested in coming here to search his house.

And here he was, opening the door.

She slid by.

"Didn't you want to get one of the bags?" he inquired politely.

She turned back, her flush seeping down to her throat. She picked up a bag, and he turned for the last two.

Cindy was already in the kitchen, emptying the bags. Nate was searching through the supplies for the charcoal. "I'll go right out and get the grill going, Dane, if that's all right?"

"Sounds like a good way to start, since it will take a while for the coals to heat up," Dane said. He walked over to the cooler Nate had brought in, helping himself to a beer.

"I hope they heat quickly. I'm starving," Cindy said.

"Everyone is starving," Larry said. "How about you, Dane?"

"Actually I just had lunch, so I'm fine. I'll get some bowls so we can break out the chips and dips for you guys while we wait to cook all that meat."

"I'll get the meat ready," Kelsey said, needing something to do. She delved through the bags until she found the hamburger meat, hot dogs, chicken, sirloins and seasonings. She found a place on the kitchen counter and started to form hamburger patties.

It felt strange, coming to Dane's place. Like the Sea Shanty, it seemed a bastion of all that had been good about her childhood. She had come here so often as a little kid. There was a lot of dockage, but not so much beach area in Key Largo as people tended to think. Hurricane Bay had both dockage and a spit of beach. Man-made, like a lot of the island itself, but it was beachfront, and over the years so much sand had been brought in that it was surprisingly clean and nice. The dock looked straight out on the Atlantic, ocean as far as the eye could see, while the beachfront area was protected by a curve in the property. Mangroves still surrounded the area. In fact, on the beach side of the house, lying on the sand, it was possible to feel as if you were marooned on a private subtropical isle in the middle of nowhere, with total privacy and a distance from the entire world. Many years ago, they had played pirates here. Dane's folks had never minded having kids around, whether they were actually with Dane or not.

Things had changed a little bit when his mother had died, but though his father had become something of a recluse, he had still welcomed the kids. Maybe he had done it in her memory, and maybe he had just liked kids himself. But there had always been something special here. Lemonade or ice tea and home-baked cookies when Dane's Mom was here, and canned soda and bags of Oreos once she was gone. The welcome always remained.

And the house was wonderful. A veritable museum.

"Watch the chicken," Cindy said.

"What?" Kelsey said, startled from her memories.

"The chicken. Wash it well, and don't let it get near anything else. Germs, bacteria...you know."

"I'll watch it like a hawk," Kelsey assured her dryly. Cindy gave her a grave nod. "Are these pieces ready? I'll take them on out."

They were alone in the kitchen. Kelsey could hear the guys talking out back around the barbecue.

"Cindy, actually, I know you'll do a much better job with the chicken than I will," Kelsey said. "You get to work here. I'll take this stuff out and let them get it going on the grill."

Kelsey didn't give Cindy a chance to protest. She picked up the plate of raw meat and headed out of the kitchen.

In the dining room, she paused. There, on the table, was

Dane's work station. His computer. Mail. Stacks of paper. Sheets of information he had apparently downloaded and printed out. She held still for a minute, listening to Cindy talk to herself about the dangers of salmonella. She moved forward a few feet and looked out the window to the deck, assuring herself that the men were still talking around the grill.

She balanced the plate of meat in her left hand and moved to the printer, where she saw that he had been downloading newspaper articles. She sifted through the sheets and saw that the columns all referred to the murders of two women. She placed the plate of meat on the table and picked up the top sheet. "Second Stripper Found in Canal." She scanned the article, but it wasn't really necessary. She remembered reading it when it had come out about three months ago. Cherie Madsen, twenty-three. A business major at a local university by day, a stripper by night. Her friends had said that she'd found it the best way to make the money for her tuition. She didn't intend to get old dancing and taking her clothes off, but she had always said that she was good at what she did and that it beat the hell out of selling clothing at a department store or working in a coffee bar. Cherie was her real name. She'd been reported missing about a week before her body had been discovered.

"Excuse me. We need the meat."

Kelsey was so startled that she dropped the paper. It wafted from the table to the floor, landing at Dane's feet.

She just looked at him wide-eyed. He betrayed nothing with his expression.

"Do me a favor. Don't get grease all over my papers."

"I—I wasn't. I just saw this headline. I remember when the murder was the top story in the news. Sad, huh? I didn't mean to get anything on your papers. The headline is kind of gripping, you know."

"It jumped right out and bit you, right? From the far end of the table."

She stood still, staring at him. He shrugged. "You told me you wanted to search the place. I don't know why I should be surprised. But I do have business that's confidential and that has nothing to do with Sheila. So...do you mind? And we *do* need the meat."

She shook her head. She moved forward to pick up the errant paper just as Dane reached down to get it himself. Their heads butted, and they both backed away. "Kelsey, take the meat out. I'll get my papers," he told her.

She nodded, picked up the plate and fled from the house. When she returned, having given the food to Larry to throw on the grill, she found Dane putting his piles of papers into the filing cabinets against the walls. She was about to go into the kitchen for more meat, but she hesitated, staring at his back. She knew he was aware that she was watching him.

"Why are you following the cases of the murdered strippers?" she asked him.

"None of your business, Kelsey."

"Do you think those stories have something to do with Sheila?"

He turned to her. "Do you think Sheila was stripping?"

"No."

"Then why do you think my interest has something to do with her?"

"Because you're supposed to be trying to find Sheila."

"I am."

"Then why—"

"You guys showed up over here for a barbecue," he reminded her.

"Kelsey?" Nate popped his head through the door. "You're supposed to be getting the rest of the meat."

"It's coming," she said.

Nate went back out. Kelsey stared at Dane. "I think you know something about Sheila that you're not telling me."

"Kelsey!" Nate said again, popping his head back in from the porch. "The meat. We need the meat."

"Okay," Kelsey said.

Again Nate's head retreated.

"Kelsey, I'll just get the meat," Dane said. He shoved his file drawer shut and walked past her to the kitchen. She followed him, picking up packages of buns and rolls.

"Make sure the chicken is cooked, really cooked," Cindy said, scrubbing her hands at the sink.

"Will do," Dane assured her.

Once they were outside, Kelsey started setting up the tables. The guys were talking about their favorite spots for fishing. Cindy came out carrying one of the coolers. Dane went to help her. Nate snorted, "She may be little, but she can bench press her own weight," he told Dane.

"That doesn't mean I don't like it when you all pitch in to help," Cindy told him.

"Dane can probably bench press his own weight, too," Larry told Nate.

"I think P.I.s are supposed to be in shape, aren't they?" Nate said.

"Either that or they're fat as houses and take up all the space behind their desks," Larry said.

"I think they come in all sizes," Dane said. He set the cooler down and stared out at the corner of the house. "Who else is coming?" he asked.

"Maybe it's Jorge Marti," Cindy said. "We asked him."

Kelsey set down a napkin and stared around the corner as well. She was suddenly aware of a horrible and overpowering odor.

"It sure as hell isn't Jorge," Dane said, starting down the porch steps and around the house. Kelsey found herself hurrying after him. She was right behind him when he came face-to-face with Andy Latham.

Latham was shirtless, in cutoff denims. He seemed to gleam with oil and sweat, and he was bearing a big bucket. The odor was coming from the bucket.

"You take your fish back! You take your rotten fish, and from now on, you keep the hell off my property, do you understand?"

Latham was shaking as he spoke. Whether it was with fear or fury, or a combination of both, Kelsey couldn't be certain.

"What are you talking about?" Dane demanded.

Latham turned the bucket over. Bloated, rotting fish spewed forth. They'd been dead a long time, and they'd been left in the sun. Some had exploded from the heat.

Dane stared from the fish on the ground to Latham, who took a step backward. "Oh, yeah, that's right, you're such a big man now. They taught you how to kill in the military, so what the hell, I just ought to be afraid and sit here and take everything you're dishing out on me," Latham said. He was still shaking, and still keeping a distance from Dane. "But you remember this, Mr. Tough Guy. A bullet goes through any man. You come on my property again and I'll put a bullet through your head." Latham backed up again.

"You ass!" Dane said. "I don't know what the hell you're talking about."

"The fish. The fucking fish! You came and dumped these right in front of the doorway."

"The hell I did!" Dane said.

"Who else?" Latham charged back. By then Larry had come to stand on one side of Dane and Nate on the other.

"I don't know who else. God knows, Latham, you'd never win a popularity contest around here," Dane told him.

Latham pointed a finger. At first Kelsey thought he was pointing at Dane, then realized he was pointing past Dane, at her.

"You! You little trouble-maker. You probably did this. Or you put the half-breed up to it. You...you'll get yours!" He was so angry, he was foaming at the mouth like a dog. Spitting as he spoke.

But just the same, he kept his distance.

Dane seemed to snap, taking a step forward. "You're as crazy as a loon, Latham. None of us dumped fish at your door. And if you threaten me or Kelsey again—"

Dane didn't finish speaking, because Latham broke in, shouting, "You heard him! You heard him. He's the one threatening *me*. You stay away from me. Stay away from me, and stay off my property, all of you!"

With that, he turned and ran.

"Whew!" Larry said.

"We're never going to be able to eat our barbecue with this stench in the yard," Cindy moaned. "What in God's name was all that about?"

"We'll eat in the house," Dane said. "Why don't you guys go get the food and bring it in? I'll get the fish picked up."

"Man, this is disgusting," Larry said.

"Get in the house. I'll get some bags and get it out of here before it permeates my whole place."

"I think he's gone crazy," Cindy said as they followed Dane. "Andy Latham never seemed really sane. Now I think he really has gone crazy."

As Dane went into the house, Kelsey started collecting the plates, plastic ware and cups she had been setting out on the porch tables.

"Cindy, hold that plate so that I can heap this food on it," Larry said. "Hey, who do you think really dumped these dead fish in his yard?"

Dane had already been in and out of the kitchen. He had two black plastic garbage bags in his hands and a roll of paper towels. "Who the hell knows?" he muttered. "Anyone could have done it." He walked away, followed by Nate. Cindy coughed and gagged. "I can't stand this. I've got to get into the house."

"We can't use the dining room," Larry said. "Dane's got it set up as an office."

"Head to the kitchen," Cindy said, leading the way.

A few minutes later Dane came in, followed by Nate and Jorge Marti.

"Jorge," Larry said, lifting his beer to greet the newcomer.

"Good to see you, Larry," Jorge said, walking over to shake Larry's hand.

"You made it," Cindy said with pleasure, walking over to kiss him on the cheek.

"Yeah, I got here just in time to be cleanup crew." He wrinkled his nose and lifted his hands. "I hear old man Latham paid a visit and brought food. Maybe he thought he was invited and that it was supposed to be a potluck occasion. Hey, gorgeous," he said, stopping by Kelsey. He kissed her cheek, as well. She kissed his back.

"That was one bad smell out there. How weird. Latham just came by and dumped a pile of rotting fish?"

"He thinks Dane dumped them on his property," Kelsey told him.

"Why would he think that?"

"Because I went out there last night to ask if he'd seen Sheila, and Dane followed me out at Cindy's insistence," Kelsey explained.

"Apparently he's crazy as a loon," Jorge said, shrugging. "I've heard the guy isn't making the catches he used to get anymore."

"Did you wash your hands?" Cindy demanded.

"With antibacterial soap," Dane said, walking into the kitchen. "We're safe, Cindy." He smiled at her, amused. "I swear it."

"He made us all scrub," Nate assured her, coming in behind Dane.

"Well, God knows what might be on those disgusting little fish corpses," Cindy said, making a face.

Nate went for a beer. "It was a real waste of good fresh fish," he said.

"The man is crazy, and that's all there is to it," Cindy said. "So, Jorge, how's the charter business going? The snowbirds are mostly gone now, with summer coming in full blast."

"Business is good," Jorge said, sitting on a bar stool and accepting a beer from Cindy and a plate of food from Larry. He lifted his drink to Larry. "Thanks to you Miami businessmen trying to shake the ties and white collars during the weekends. Lobster season is coming, too. I guess Latham hadn't heard from Sheila and none of you has, either?"

"No sign of Sheila," Larry agreed.

Jorge looked at Kelsey and smiled. "She'll show up."

"Sure," Kelsey said. She realized Dane was watching her. "She will show up, right, Dane?"

"Oh, yeah. I'm positive she will. Eventually," he said quietly.

Kelsey didn't like the way he said it. Not flippantly. And not with reassurance. He spoke with somber certainty. He knew something.

And it had to do with the murders of the two strippers, Kelsey thought. Putting it all together scared her to death, but she knew he wasn't going to share whatever it was that he knew with her. Whatever he was onto...

She had a computer, too.

Dane thanked God for the placement of his property and house. The stench had been enough to choke a dung beetle, but with the breezes going through, it didn't last long. In fact, with the fish double-tied in trash bags and set back for disposal, the afternoon and evening became so nice that they were able to head outside after they had eaten. He set up the volleyball net, and they played a few games. They switched teammates and sides, but somehow, Kelsey always wound up on the other side of the net from him.

The exertion of playing sent them all into the water, but again, though there was a lot of dunking and fooling around, Kelsey kept her distance. Later, they all rinsed the saltwater off with the hose he had rigged up as a shower by the porch, then dried off and ate dessert—packaged brownies—outside. The brownies were so-so. The coffee Kelsey ground and brewed was great. He hadn't figured out yet if she was simply keeping her distance from him because she was never going to forgive him for the night that followed Joe's funeral, or if she was actually afraid of him. He damned himself for not filing away his downloads before leaving the house that morning, but then, he hadn't expected company.

Now she knew he was interested in the murders. All the better, once the reason for his interest was known.

Dane finished his coffee and lit a cigarette. Cindy and Jorge were sitting on the porch swing, talking about gym equipment. Larry had begun passionately explaining the value of top-notch advertising to Nate.

Kelsey had headed out on the dock and was sitting there with her cup of coffee, watching the sun begin to set.

He rose, determined to join her. He knew that she heard him coming over the wooden decking, but she didn't look up. At first he thought that she was staring at his boats, both of which she had seen before, the snappy little Donzi for zipping around on quick trips, and his larger boat, the thirty-eight-foot Chris-Craft. The Chris-Craft was probably the one material object that meant a lot to him. He and his father had chosen the boat, refurbished it together, and spent countless hours on her out at sea. She could sleep six but still offered an enormous captain's cabin along with private guest quarters, a huge galley and salon, and large deck spaces. She was an old girl now, built in the early eighties, but he had tended her lovingly over the years.

But Kelsey wasn't staring at his boats. She was simply looking down at the wood of the deck. She wasn't seeing anything at all.

Dane sat next to her on the dock, where she dangled her legs over the edge. The wary look in her eyes as he joined her was disturbing.

"Hey, it *is* my dock."

She nodded. "You're right. It *is* your dock." She hesitated for a moment, staring at the water. "Your dock. I was actually just wishing that there was still something here, in the Keys, that was mine. It's strange, not having a place here. You know, the house doesn't even exist anymore."

"I know. So...how are your folks?" he asked.

"Good, thanks. Doing really well. You knew that they moved to Orlando?"

He nodded. "Yeah, I knew."

"I guess you weren't very far from them when you were up in St. Augustine."

"Probably not. Just a few hours."

"You never saw them?"

He shook his head. "I was always afraid that I would just be...well, a reminder of Joe."

"They'd probably really like to see you."

"I don't know. It was hard on them."

"It was hard on everyone."

"Joe was their son. And your brother."

"Your best friend."

She was actually looking at him again, and the mistrust seemed to have faded from her eyes for a moment. He found himself looking ahead at the dazzle of the sun on the water, rather than at her.

"Actually I thought that it was harder on you than anyone else." He paused for just a moment. "Do you remember feeling that—"

"I don't want to remember," she said. There was an edge to her voice. He knew what she didn't want to remember.

"Don't go getting your hackles up," he said. "I'm talking about the break you had with your parents. Joe worried about it."

"Oh," she said, her cheeks growing bright. "You mean...the way I thought they preferred their son?"

"Yeah," he said softly. He was treading on personal ground. She would either get furious and walk away, or else they would have a chance to bridge the gap that lay between them.

She kicked her feet in the water like a kid, watching the waves she made. "I felt, after Joe died, that I didn't quite come up to what he had been in their eyes. And that my folks really had loved him more, and that I wasn't anywhere near as important." There was a curious, wistful expression on her face. Kelsey was beautiful. Her hair had dried in the breeze and was wafting around the perfectly molded contours of her face. Her eyes reflected the water. She was still in shorts and a bathing suit top. Her throat was long and smooth, and her breasts rose high and tight against the bikini bra. He had taken a seat close enough that their skin nearly touched. Something was stirring within him.

So much time yawned between them. She'd been his best friend's kid sister, so the instinct to protect and defend had always been there. The instinct to touch her, to have her, had only pushed to the surface once. Now both waged war within him. She brought out something protective in him. He realized, as he had on that long-ago night, that she also brought out a hell of a lot more.

Odd that something so brief could be remembered so long. So clearly.

He tamped a lid on the urge to reach out and touch her.

He lifted a hand. "Your dad was gung-ho military. Joe followed in his footsteps. Naturally he was interested in every move Joe made."

She laughed. "You're being kind. To my father, the sun rose and set on Joe. And I still remember feeling totally inadequate because I didn't seem to be able to do anything to make my brother's loss any easier for my parents. For so many reasons, I was in such sorry shape then, and I did such sorry things—"

She broke off. He could feel the warmth emanating from her.

He was sure that he had been one of those "sorry things."

He decided to ignore that for the moment.

"They always loved you equally, you know. Like I said, Joe just had a lot in common with your dad."

She smiled, and the curve of her lips was both rueful and nostalgic. "Hey, it's okay, time has gone by, and I don't need any assurance. Actually the past is one of the reasons things are so good between us now. Dad called me a couple of years ago and asked me to come up and spend some time with them. I did. We sat together one night, and he apologized to me, told me that he probably had set more store in Joe, and that it had been shameful of him not to realize that he had shown so much favoritism. We both cried, drank too much, talked about Joe all night, and fixed everything that might have been wrong. I see my folks often now. It's only a four, four and half hour drive up to their new place. They're not on the water. They have a couple of acres in an area zoned for horses. Dad and Mom have started riding together, and they're thinking about buying a couple of horses of their own."

"I'm glad to hear they're doing so well."

"Thanks."

The silence stretched out between them. Not a comfortable silence. She drew her knees in, rested her chin on them and looked at him. "So what happened in St. Augustine?" she asked him.

He felt himself stiffen. "Someone died."

A frown tensed her brow. "And it was your fault?"

"Yes. No. Look, it's not something I like to talk about."

"Hey, you came out and sat down next to me."

"Yeah, I did. So how is your life? No marriages after Nate over there?"

He heard the sound of her teeth grating. "No. No marriages. How about you? Is it true? Have you and Sheila been getting close again?"

He shook his head, aggravated, trying not to lose patience. He stared at Kelsey, and she stiffened where she sat, not turning from him, but definitely tense. "What is it that you still haven't figured out? Sheila was looking for something, and it wasn't me. Yes, we hung out together at the bar. Yes, she came out here. But I wasn't in the best shape to try to solve her psychological problems, and she certainly wasn't any kind of a balm for me."

"But you were the last person to see her."

"No, I'm certain that someone else saw her."

"Who?"

"Dammit, Kelsey, that's what I don't know."

"You think she's dead," Kelsey said, watching him.

"Kelsey, I'll find Sheila."

"Hey, out there!"

They were interrupted by the call from the yard. Looking back, they saw Cindy, Larry, Nate and Jorge standing and waving.

Dane got to his feet and instinctively reached down to give Kelsey a hand. To his surprise, she accepted the lift and didn't wrench away immediately.

"We're going to take off," Nate called. "I've got to go by the bar."

"I need a real shower," Larry said.

"I may have a hot date," Cindy contributed.

"I *am* someone's hot date," Jorge said.

Dane walked back along the dock and reached the yard. Cindy took a step toward him before he could reach the group, rising on tiptoe to kiss his cheek. "Thanks for letting us invite ourselves over."

"Thanks for everything you brought."

"Just call us dial-a-party," Nate said. "Hey, come by the bar later, if you can. I've got a new band starting tonight. They do everything. Pop-rock, jazz, reggae, calypso...you'll like them."

"I'll try to make it."

"I'm off," Jorge said, lifting a hand with his keys in it. "Thanks, all of you. It's good to get together."

"Yeah. We'll have to do it again," Larry said. "We're heading back to the duplex," he said to Kelsey. "Are you coming?"

"I've got my own car. I'll be along."

"You sure?" Larry said.

"I'm sure that's my car," Kelsey said, smiling.

"No, I meant—"

"Kelsey will be right along," Dane assured him. "I have plans tonight."

He thought that maybe her cheeks reddened, but she replied

smoothly to Larry, "I'm just going to make sure we picked up any messes we made in Dane's place." She turned and started for his house. The others took off for their cars, waving their last goodbyes.

Dane looked at the dying sunset. Strip clubs didn't get going until later anyway. He followed Kelsey into the house.

She was in the kitchen, rinsing out the last chip bowl.

He leaned in the doorway, watching her. "Are you sure you don't want to go through the rest of my papers?"

She turned and looked at him innocently. His gaze slipped to her breasts. He forced it back to her eyes.

"I have my own computer, you know."

"What?"

"I don't need to go through your papers. I can download old newspaper articles just the same as you can."

He clenched his teeth with aggravation. "Kelsey, leave it, please."

"I just want to know what you're going to do to find Sheila."

"I will do everything in my power. Kelsey, please, trust me on this. Let me do the investigating."

"There's a little coffee left. Do you want more, or should I just pour it down the drain?"

"No, I'll drink it."

He walked over to the coffeepot.

"I'll get it for you," she said.

He paused. Kelsey was suddenly being far too nice.

"You know...I think I left my lighter outside. Why don't you join me for coffee? I'll meet you in the living room."

He walked out of the kitchen and through the house. Outside, he leaned against the support wall and looked in through the dining-room window. He watched as Kelsey came out of the kitchen, set the cups down on the coffee table and looked around the room. She was headed back toward the dining room when something caught her eye. He frowned, seeing Kelsey get down on the floor on her hands and knees.

He walked back in. She jumped up as he did so, her cheeks bright red. "What the hell are you doing?" he demanded.

She stared at him in silence for a moment. "Just friends," she said. "There was nothing hot and heavy going on? There was nothing serious?"

"What are you talking about now?" he asked, aggravated.

She dangled something in front of him. An earring. Sheila's earring.

He crossed his arms over his chest, staring at her. "So?"

"This is Sheila's earring."

"You know that?"

"Of course I know that."

"How?"

"I gave her these earrings. The stones are emeralds. They were my gift to her when she was the maid of honor at my wedding."

"So Sheila lost her earring. What does that mean? She's been in this house many times."

"Right. But her earring was here, on your living-room floor. If you look at the way the loop closes, these aren't the kind of earrings that just fall out."

"Kelsey, what the hell are you saying?"

"You two were...you were having an affair again."

He walked over to where she stood, staring into her eyes as he plucked the earring from her fingers. "All right. One more time, Sheila was here. I never said to anyone that she wasn't. Were we having an affair? No. We honestly were not having an affair. Nothing so grand. Did we have sex one night? Yes. One night. We both knew that even what we'd had as kids was long over. Did I do something horrible and evil to Sheila? No. Pay attention here. *No.* There it is, the truth. And I really don't give a damn whether you believe me or not. Take it or leave it."

Kelsey's teal eyes lit hard on his for a long moment. Then she brushed past him. He didn't move and didn't turn.

He heard the sound of the door closing as she left his house.

# CHAPTER 7

Kelsey was surprised to arrive at the duplex and find that neither Larry nor Cindy had gotten back before her. They had probably gone with Nate to the Sea Shanty. Or else the hot date Cindy had mentioned was with Jorge. She had no desire to follow them and have a more social night, and was relieved at first to be back alone. She wanted to shower, huddle into bed and sleep. It was unlikely that she would sleep easily, but at least she could shower, get into bed and mull over her thoughts of the night.

Strange, though, the minute she turned off her car's engine, she felt her solitude. The night wasn't still; there was a soft breeze blowing. But the trees and shrubbery seemed to hang heavily around the driveway and create a host of shadows. The short distance from the driveway to the house became very long. Darkness almost seemed to whirl in pockets of ebony, constantly changing the shapes that were nothing but illusion but appeared to be sinister creatures lurking in the night.

They had forgotten to turn on a porch light. It was only the street lamps, standing high and at a distance, that gave any glow to the night and turned the lengths of branches into bony fingers, stretching out over the yard.

Kelsey realized she was just sitting in her car, staring at the house.

She told herself she was ridiculous, opened the car door and started for the duplex. None of the shadows jumped after her, though breezes rustled the branches, seeming to create a whisper on the night air. To her annoyance, she fumbled with the key while getting it into the lock. Once she had gotten the door open, she burst in, then turned and closed the door as if there were a tiger on her tail. She locked it quickly, then stood in the entry feeling like a fool. Shadows. She didn't tend to be afraid of them, or of darkness, or of the night.

Yet as she walked through the living room to the kitchen and dining area, tossing her purse on a chair, she felt uneasiness creep over her.

The strange sense that she wasn't alone.

She found herself retracing her footsteps to the front door, as anxious to get out again as she had been to get in. But before she reached the door, she managed to tell herself she was being absurd. The duplex had been locked. There was nothing out of order that she could see. There was no reason to think she was anything but alone.

Still, with the uncanny sense of something being off persisting, she decided that her first course of action had to be an inspection of the apartment. Living room. Definitely no one there, unless it was an ant-size person. She opened the door to the second bedroom where Larry was sleeping, going to the bath and looking behind the shower curtain, then checking out the closet.

She was feeling silly again when she thought she heard a sound...like a thumping, coming from the back. Standing in a closet that held nothing but a few of Larry's shirts, she felt a chill sweep through her. Great. She was inspecting the house like a sane person, but if there did happen to be an intruder, she had nothing with which to defend herself other than a tailored shirt and a hanger.

Great.

She looked around the bedroom. Nothing. She stepped back into the living room and decided her best bet for protection was one of the heavy pewter candlesticks on the coffee table. She grabbed one and walked toward the back.

Great. The porch light wasn't on but the lights inside were. If there was someone lurking in the shadows in the back, they would be hidden in darkness. She might as well be on widescreen television.

Kelsey hit the switch on the wall, pitching the main room into darkness. She inched into the dining area and quickly hit the lights there, as well.

Now the world seemed a pool of darkness.

She stood still, listening. Night sounds came to her, almost imperceptibly. The breeze against the house, the rustle of branches. The longer she stared out through the plate glass, the more her eyes adjusted to the darkness. Seconds stretched into minutes. Minutes seemed an eternity. She realized she wasn't breathing and exhaled a long stream of air, then inhaled. She neither saw nor heard anything out of the ordinary. After a while she once again felt like a fool. She left her silent vigil at the back window and walked into her bedroom.

Sheila's bedroom.

The drapes were open in there, as well. She could see out to the back. A long palm frond dipped low over the pool, as if it were a bony hand with pointing fingers, indicating some horror within the water. She chastised herself for her ridiculous imagination and total cowardice. She still had a death grip on the candlestick.

The moonlight showed little more than shapes in the room. She was almost frozen with the fear that one of them would move. Again she stood still and waited. She almost screamed aloud when she heard another thumping sound from the back, not by the pool, but by the fence to her right.

Nine-one-one, nine-one-one, nine-one-one, just call the police! her mind raged. But call the police and tell them what? That she had heard a thumping noise from her backyard?

So much for being alone, for being grateful for solitude. Where the hell was Larry?

Cindy?

Anyone?

Dane had been looking up information on murdered strippers. He had gone to bed with Sheila. He had caught her snooping through his work. Maybe she was getting too close to the truth. Maybe he had followed her home, and now he was out there, thinking she should share Sheila's fate.

She formed the thoughts in her mind, but she didn't believe them. Dane couldn't have followed her so quickly. He certainly couldn't have been here before her.

Besides, she didn't want to believe evil of Dane. How insane.

She kept staring out into the darkness, watching, fighting the sense of panic. The shadow-shapes in the room seemed to loom larger. The bed, she knew. The chair. The wing shape was merely the jacket she had tossed over the back of it.

Nothing was changed, she was certain.

And yet...

She had the oddest sensation that someone other than herself had been in here.

*Sheila...*

She almost said the name aloud. Was she fine, perhaps in hiding for some reason, slipping in and out of her own home without telling a soul, simply because she was afraid?

But with no valid reason, no logic, no sense, she was just as certain that Sheila hadn't returned as she was that someone had been in the room.

Staring out the back, straining to see, to hear, she almost missed the sound that came from the front of the house.

But she didn't.

Subtle, soft, barely perceptible. But a sound. A clicking. A soft clicking. Like a door opening. With stealth and menace.

The front door. She had locked it.

Hadn't she?

Had she imagined the sound? Worked herself into such a silly panic that she was imagining noises everywhere?

But no...once again, some form of sixth sense or instinct was kicking in.

She was not alone in the house.

The thumping had come from the back. The clicking had come from the front. If she had really heard either.

She realized that she was standing like a deer in the road, blinded by the lights of an oncoming car, standing still and simply awaiting the deadly impact.

In a single instant, she decided that she would rather take her chances outside than be trapped inside the house with a...

Killer.

In a whir of motion, she reached for the latch on the sliding door leading out to the porch, pool and yard. The door didn't give. She pulled at it, then realized there was another latch closer to the floor. She bent down to unlock it.

And then she knew.

There really was someone in the house.

She could hear the swift quiet footsteps against the carpet. She could feel the displacement of the air, as someone was rushing toward her, out of the shadows, out of the darkness.

She gripped her candlestick tightly in her left hand and pulled at the sliding glass door once again with her left. She pulled hard, with an adrenaline-charged strength that sent the glass sliding with a vengeance across the runner.

But before Kelsey could catch her balance and go flying out, the phantom that had been only sound became real as a figure burst through the bedroom door and came barreling toward her.

With no choice, she turned rather than flee, ready to attack in self-defense.

In a split second, she lifted the candlestick.

And screamed.

There were no prints on the Polaroid.

Dane knew it. He hadn't brought the photo into any lab; he just knew that he was dealing with someone who had carefully plotted every aspect of his crime.

He had once heard an FBI profiler give a lecture on the perfect crime. He'd claimed there was no such thing.

But sometimes, by accident, a killer could commit a perfect crime. When a woman was murdered, the husband, ex-husband, boyfriend or lover, immediately fell under suspicion. Except in the case of serial crime. Most of the time, serial killers committed their crimes against strangers. And when there was no one with whom to compare physical and trace evidence, the evidence, no matter how carefully collected, was of little use. Husbands, lovers and boyfriends were easy to track down; strangers were not so easy to find.

There were always clues.

But what had gone on here had been, at the least, orchestrated with extreme detail and careful planning. Accidents could create a perfect crime. This killer had planned on accidents of nature. There were so many tiny fragments with which forensic experts could now work. Prints and blood were huge by comparison; in a lab, a case could be made with a tuft of carpet, a broken strand of hair, a remnant of ash.

*Could.*

Nature could preserve. Insects could give time lines and tell a million tales.

But nature could also take away. And the whipping fury of a storm could wipe away any trace evidence.

So much for his own powers of observation, his training, his years in the military.

The killer had known when he was away. Had known when he would return. The killer had performed his savage act when Dane had been gone. He had delivered the photo when Dane had been gone.

But not before any evidence had been destroyed. He had planned his act to coincide with the storm. A violent storm, with whipping winds, a massive surge. Normally it would have made sense to go through the motions. To follow procedure. But Dane knew that he had been targeted, watched and used. He was intended to take the rap, to go to prison and possibly to meet his fate through lethal injection. The crime had almost been a challenge.

None of it made sense when brought beneath the scrutiny of everything he had ever learned. The Necktie Strangler was considered, by all the law enforcement agencies that were involved, to be a serial *signature* killer. Often a serial killer's MO might change. He might target strippers who practiced prostitution on the side, then change to picking up women who were merely promiscuous. But the man's *signature* had been in his acts against the bodies of his victims, the fact that he had left them stripped, with the weapon of their strangulation still around their necks. He didn't leave the bodies in the open; he hid them in the water, knowing that time and the elements would take their toll on the corpses. Though this implied organization and planning, it didn't fit with a body being left on his property—and a Polaroid picture of the body being taken, then shoved beneath his door.

There were, of course, killers who wanted to be caught. Killers who knew they couldn't stop but still had enough conscience left to want to be.

Tonight, as he stared at the picture, stomach still churning at the sight, nerves raw, emotions burned and cold, he felt again the sorrow. And the tumult. If he brought this piece of evidence in, he would go to jail. He had owned the old Polaroid camera that had taken the shot.

He had owned the tie that was knotted around her neck.

Any evidence pointing to the real killer had been washed away in the fury of the elements.

*Sheila had been with him. There might still be DNA evidence on the body that could prove it.*

And yet...

Hiding the picture was withholding evidence. He loathed what he was doing. If his actions brought about another woman's death...

He closed his eyes. If he was arrested, another woman might still be murdered. Because they would be holding the wrong man.

Kelsey was already convinced he was involved. She would be passionately determined on justice for Sheila.

He rose, ready to leave the house, a man with things to do, people to see, and a desperation to do them all before time closed in on him.

He returned the photo to the place beneath the floorboard in his bedroom and headed out. But before he was out the door, his phone rang. He let the machine pick up. He was surprised to hear Jesse Crane's voice.

"Dane, call me. They've found another body in a canal."

"Kelsey!" Larry yelled.

He said her name with barely enough time to prevent her from bringing the heavy pewter candlestick down on his head.

"Larry!"

The room was suddenly flooded with light. She and Larry were caught in a bizarre embrace. Nate and Cindy were standing in the doorway.

"I could have killed you!" Kelsey said furiously. "What were you doing, sneaking around in here?"

"Me? We came home and heard someone creeping around the

house, and there were no lights and no sign of you," Larry protested.

Shaking, Kelsey dropped the candlestick. Larry jumped away, watching it fall.

"We really thought someone had broken in," Cindy said. "Kelsey, you didn't have any lights on. I whispered your name, but I guess you didn't hear me."

"Why didn't you just call my name loudly?" Kelsey asked.

"We couldn't call your name loudly if there was a thief or a...or a thief," Nate said lamely.

Kelsey exhaled a long breath. "I thought I heard someone sneaking around. And I heard a thumping sound out back."

"There's a mango tree out there. The fruit was probably falling," Cindy said impatiently.

"Let's take a walk out back and look around anyway," Larry said.

He walked past Kelsey. They all followed. The whole thing had been silly, she thought, with her sneaking around in the darkness and thinking someone was about to attack her, and the three of them certain that *she* was the intruder. And still, when they walked out back, they were all unnerved.

Larry laughed suddenly. "Nothing out here but a pool."

"Grass and trees," Cindy said, sounding almost giddy with relief.

Kelsey turned around, wanting to feel more relieved than she did. "Well, I have to admit, I'm glad you're all back."

"It's getting late," Nate murmured. He looked at Kelsey. "Maybe I'll bunk out on the sofa."

She was about to tell him that wasn't necessary, since Larry was staying in the guest room, but then Cindy chimed in again. "You don't need to sleep on the sofa here when there's an extra bedroom in my half of the place. If any of us gets the heebie-jeebies in the middle of the night, we can just bang on the walls."

"Doesn't sound like such a bad idea," Larry said.

"Okay, then, I'm off to bed," Cindy said. She gave Kelsey a hug and started back into the house. They all turned and followed her.

"Wait," Larry said, checking the glass doors to the back and assuring himself that the rear of the house was completely secured. He gave a satisfied nod to Kelsey. "I'll lock the front once the crew is out."

"Great. See everyone in the morning," Kelsey said.

She closed the door to her room once they were all out but found herself standing still, listening intently until she had heard Larry lock and bolt the front.

The light was on in her room. Larry was out front, the house was full. She still felt that sensation of uneasiness.

She turned and leaned against the door, surveying the room, and she knew what was still bothering her. There wasn't anything that was an exact giveaway, but she still felt as if someone had been there. Someone who hadn't come to rob them, who hadn't taken anything. Someone who had come to do something worse. To invade...

To invade what?

She didn't know. But the pillow didn't seem to be on the bed at quite the angle that she had left it. The spread seemed to be a bit off. The items on the dresser seemed to have been moved just a fraction of an inch.

Kelsey checked the door again, searched the closet and the bath. She was definitely alone now.

She hesitated, then looked under the pillow.

Sheila's diary remained right where Sheila had left it.

Yet it, too, seemed to have been moved. Just a fraction of an inch...

Maybe she was simply losing her mind, so convinced that something terrible had befallen Sheila that she was making up evil ghosts in her mind.

Telling herself that she was crazy didn't seem to help any. Kelsey took a long shower, a couple of Tylenol and went to bed.

And stared into the murky darkness of the room, eyes wide-open, listening...

Listening...

Andy Latham, who was as crazy as a loon, was convinced they had thrown dead fish in his yard. And then there was Dane, who was behaving so suspiciously. He'd slept with Sheila, then she had disappeared. He'd been the last one to see her, and now he was reading about the Necktie Strangler. But Dane couldn't be guilty....

Why not?

Because she didn't want him to be.

A branch tapped on her window. She almost screamed aloud, then realized it was just a branch and she was being ridiculous. She had been so frightened tonight over nothing; they had all been stalking one another, when there had been no one here, no one outside....

Logic didn't matter.

In the night, in the dark, she was suddenly very afraid.

"Jesse," Dane said, grabbing the phone.

"Dane, good, you're there."

"Is it...could it be...?"

"No, definitely not Sheila. Some fishermen pulled up a body today. Just bones. They've been taken to the morgue, but the medical examiner said the victim has definitely been dead nine months to a year. They'll try to ID her as soon as possible, of course."

"But it was the Necktie Strangler?"

"They aren't even sure of the cause of death. But the preliminary investigation suggests it's a young woman. And if they do connect her to the other murders, it means our guy started off long before any of us suspected. I don't have much real information to give you yet, but I wanted to let you know. The bones were found just west of Shark Valley. And I wanted you to know that it wasn't Sheila, so you wouldn't worry when you saw it in the papers."

"Thanks, Jesse."

"Ready to tell me what's going on yet?"

"Soon. I want to do a little more investigating first."

"I'm here if you need me."

"Thanks."

Dane hung up, then left the house as he had intended. It was late, but there were some places in South Florida where the night was just beginning.

Morning was hell.

Sunlight made its way through the drapes, and, though muted, it seemed to pierce Kelsey's eyes with a vengeance. She had barely slept.

Rising, she drew the drapes anyway, recoiling and blinking in pain as the light increased. Still, it was the best way to wake up.

She jumped in and out of the shower, dressed, then made coffee. With her first cup, she felt more awake. And then foolish. Larry was still asleep in the spare room, and the shadows of the previous night became benign trees, gently waving in the breeze. Fear faded. Determination returned.

She thought about turning on her computer and tracking down the stories Dane had been reading, but decided instead that if she was looking for Sheila, first she needed to delve more deeply into her friend's life. She returned to her room, second cup of coffee in hand, and reached beneath the pillow for Sheila's diary.

It still surprised Kelsey that Sheila had kept any kind of a diary. She had always seemed far too busy living life to take the time to put anything down on paper.

The diary began shortly after Sheila had moved back to the Keys. The first page was a simple entry.

*Home again, home again, home again. Things change, and yet they don't change at all.*

Two days later, there was another entry.

*The tourists are flocking. Busy little bees. Almost had to drag a lady out of a chair at the bar at Nate's. I told him he needed reserved stools for the locals. Naturally, being Nate, he took me seriously and tried to explain that he couldn't do that. And he had the nerve to say I wasn't really a local anymore. Ah, men, how quickly they forget. But that's okay.*

*Most of them are far too forgettable themselves.*

The next few entries were basically just as mundane, yet typically Sheila.

*How strange Dane has become. Somber. Not like him. Cool, though, that he's come back now, too. Told him I might wind up needing his services. He gave me a really strange look. God knows what he's heard about my past. I told him I wasn't thinking about stud service, that I might want to use him as a private eye. He said I should hire someone better. Poor guy. Wonder what happened. He won't talk about it. Thought he was just lying around drunk in a lounge chair, but he wasn't drunk, since he was drinking soda water, or so Nate said. He was just lying around. Strange to see Dane so beat, yet when he looks at you, when you see his eyes...well, there's life in there yet. Just have to reach him. Ah, well, I'm living in a piece of Paradise. Lots of pretty boys on the water. Better yet, lots of pretty rich boys on the water. Still, sometimes the old boys are the best boys. Time will tell. Meanwhile...*

*Saw Izzy.*

*Now there's quite a high.*

*Good old Izzy. His stuff just gets better and better.*

*And old Izzy isn't bad himself. He likes to bargain. Which is okay by me. Izzy has Latin rhythm down pat. Running his stuff keeps him in good shape. Another laugh. Officially he's in the fishing trade. Some fish. He takes tourists out and makes them so happy they couldn't care less if they get any fish. Cindy says she sees him at the gym now and then, but he must be working hard at his craft—running! What do I care? I'm hardly the FBI or DEA. Not likely. No, I'm the down and dirty kind, but hell, what would you expect? Still, the way he flirts and bargains is pretty cool. Makes me feel...okay, not exactly Madonna-Like-A-Virgin-ish, but damn cool close.*

*Combine Izzy and the stuff...*

*Not a bad deal. And I really do have one hell of a good time. If I were a guy, no one would think a thing about it. The shrink said I'm looking for something I can't have. He's full of shit. I was married. I had the good-looking guy with money, and I was bored to death. Maybe he was just the wrong guy. But if so, I threw away being what the other guy was looking for years ago. Just reread this, and I'm not making sense, even to myself. But maybe I don't want to make sense. Maybe I don't want to see the truth, even if it's just for my eyes only.*

A knock on the bedroom door startled Kelsey so badly she might as well have been a guilty teenager. She jumped up and shoved the diary beneath the pillow.

"Hey, Kels? You awake in there, kid?"

"Yeah, yeah, Larry, I'm awake."

She walked across the room, glancing at her watch. It was already one in the afternoon. She opened her door. Larry, somehow still looking like a *GQ* advertisement in shorts and a crew neck shirt, was smiling at her. "What do you think this is, vacation?" he teased. "Want to get some lunch?"

"Lunch?"

"Yeah, you know, the meal that's typically eaten sometime around noon."

"Lunch? No," Kelsey said, making a sudden decision. "I've got a few errands to run. But I'd love to have dinner. Let's meet at the new fish place just past Nate's at seven. How's that?"

She didn't really care how it was. She brushed past him, already on her way out for her purse and keys.

"Wait a minute, Kelsey. First of all, we'll probably hurt Nate's feelings if we eat somewhere else. And second, where on earth are you going? Cindy is going to wake up and want to know where you are. We were all spooked last night. She'll be worried, then she'll be pissed at me for letting you go."

She paused at the door. "You're right, we don't want to hurt anyone's feelings. We'll meet at Nate's place at seven sharp." Then she left before he could ask any more questions or give her any further argument.

Jesse Crane leaned against his desk and handed Dane the top dispatch from the stack. As Dane read, Jesse talked. "Looks like our killer has been busy a lot longer than any of us suspected. Forensics found remnants of threads around the neck. Down here, in the Everglades and the heat, a body can decompose quickly, but the ME's office still estimates the girl had been dead close to a year. There's no damage to the bones, though there's also no proof that she didn't drown. There were remnants of fabric found in the muck near the bones, and forensics may be able to discover what they came from. No actual clothing, no purses or shoes or other personal effects of the victims have been found, so it's quite possible that the remnants came from a tie. They managed to identify her quickly. Her name was Alsie Greer, aka Janice Thorson, aka Lydia Farning. She had a nice long rap sheet for drugs and prostitution, and worked in a really low-down joint up in Palm Beach County. Alsie cared for her teeth, though. She'd been reported missing eleven months ago, and the computer matched up the dental records right away. That was a lucky break. You know how long it can take just to identify a victim, much less—"

"Find a killer," Dane ended.

Jesse shrugged. "The statistics say there are probably a couple hundred serial killers at work in the country at any given time. And most of them are never caught."

"This one has to be caught. You know that or there will be more victims. And it looks as if he's picking up his pace."

Jesse shook his head. "Dane, we really don't have a clue as

to what his pace is. South Florida holds endless miles of waterways. You know that as well as I do. Last year they finally found four teenagers who'd been missing for almost twenty years. They'd driven into a canal and disappeared without a trace. And the businessman from Philadelphia who disappeared after a night on the town? He was found in a Fort Lauderdale canal after more than a decade. The list of people found in the water after they've been missing for years is staggering."

Jesse nodded. It wasn't that South Florida law enforcement didn't have excellent dive teams, because they did. Some of the best in the world. It was that the waterways were endless and often mucky, murky and dense with vegetation. Thanks to the divers, many people survived after driving into canals, and most of the time the missing were found. But then there were times when finding someone in the endless waterways was like finding the proverbial needle in a haystack.

"Come on," Jesse said, taking the paper from Dane and setting it on the desk. "I'll take you out to the site where the remains were found."

They took Dane's Jeep, though. The road they followed wasn't nearly as bad as many of the seldom used paths into the Everglades. It was treacherous country for the unwary, though. Summertime heat was on, and though the area had gone through a drought, it had turned to storm season. Technically the Everglades was not a swamp. The whole area was really an incredibly slow-moving river, heavily subject to the whims of nature. After the recent storm, the gator holes and canals were deep. One twist of the steering wheel could land a car in the water and muck, and then the car and its inhabitants could disappear from view, maybe forever.

Today, as they drove, the sky was a beautiful blue, with light tufting clouds. There was a breeze, bending the saw grass low, like shimmering sheaves of green wheat. They passed canals where unwary egrets, herons and other water birds played perilously close to the watchful gaze of alligators, their bodies cooled from the brutal heat beneath the water's surface, their eerie, reptilian eyes sharp and ever on the alert just above the water's edge.

"There's another storm moving across the Atlantic," Jesse said.

"Yeah, I saw the paper," Dane said.

"They think it's going to turn up and head for the Carolinas," Jesse commented.

"They tend to do that."

"I think this guy likes to dispose of his victims just before a storm," Jesse said. "I think he even plans his murders by the weather."

Dane felt a strange chill despite the near hundred degree heat of the day.

Jesse was right. The killer would strike again soon.

"Whether that storm turns north or not, we're probably in for some weather...in three, four days' time," Dane murmured.

"Better stop ahead. We'll move down to the waterfront on foot."

The term "waterfront" didn't actually apply. Once they stepped out of the car, they were in several inches of muddy water. The muck oozed around their feet and created sucking sounds with each step they took.

A few minutes' walk took them to the actual canal, swollen against its banks. A Metro-Dade uniformed officer stood an unhappy guard beside the yellow crime tape that surrounded the area where the body had been found. The man miserably swatted at a mosquito and greeted Jesse with a hello, then nodded at his introduction to Dane.

There wasn't much to see at the actual site. Dane knew that forensics experts and crime scene investigators had spent the morning looking for any minute scrap of evidence—a hair, a fiber, anything at all that might one day link the victim to a suspect, should a suspect ever be apprehended. The tiniest carpet fiber from a vehicle could link a killer to his victim. Forensics had made convictions possible in many cases where it had seemed there was no hope. A perpetrator always left some tiny piece of physical evidence behind, just as he took some piece of evidence with him, a victim's blood, a fiber from their clothing, a strand of hair.

But after nearly a year in a swamp...

"See what I mean, though? The road isn't your average tourist track," Jesse said. "But it's more than possible to get your average vehicle near enough to dispose of a body. Of course, it's also possible that the body traveled."

Dane nodded, looking around. The heat was intense. The buzzing of the flies and mosquitoes was like a monotonous song. This was one instance when the detectives were going to have to rely on the age-old methods of hunches and a lot of footwork.

"I went up to the Broward club last night," Dane told Jesse.

"Yeah?"

"The girls are leery about talking," Dane said. He shrugged. "They're convinced they're safe because one of them has already been killed, and the killer seems smart enough not to strike in the same place twice. They don't trust the police, and I spent a lot of time trying to convince the girls I wasn't a cop."

"Did you learn anything?"

"Not yet, but I believe I will. I want to get into the Miami club, as well. Jesse, I didn't have time to read everything on that report. When this girl disappeared, someone evidently filled out a missing persons report, right? So I'm assuming her friends and co-workers were questioned."

"I've pulled up what information is in the records. It's the same story. She was at work one night. She wasn't there the next. She lived alone. Neighbors don't remember anything. She might have come home, she might not have. She left the club sometime between four and five in the morning, and that's the last time anyone can remember seeing her. In this case, she didn't drive, so there wasn't a question of looking for her car. There was no record of her calling a cab from work, and though her cell phone disappeared with her, the company records were requested, and there were no calls to a cab company. The last place she contacted was a language school—she had asked about taking French lessons. She never went to the school, though, so that was a dead end. She'd had a boyfriend, but he checked out. There were witnesses to prove he'd been at a party in West Palm the night—or early morning—she disappeared. He passed out in the living room at the party, and there were four people to attest to the fact that he didn't wake up until after the girl's shift started the next night. The police in three counties are following every lead, not that there are many. Warnings are going out on the news daily. And other than that...well, the population down here is in the millions, once you take in the three counties. Every possible lead dries up. You know that can happen. A killer is usually caught when he slips up. This guy hasn't slipped up yet. And the police can't interrogate every man who steps into a strip club in South Florida."

"I think I can narrow it down," Dane said.

Jesse studied him gravely.

"The Necktie Strangler has to be someone I know," Dane said.

"Someone you know?" A deep, concerned furrow creased Jesse's forehead

"Or someone who knows me," Dane said.

He wasn't ready to elaborate further. Jesse, being Jesse, would accept that.

Dane decided to end the conversation there.

"I've got to get back. There's a lot I have to do. And I don't think I have a lot of time."

# CHAPTER 8

The sign read simply Izzy's Charters.

Izzy Garcia's fishing boat, the *Lady Havana,* was docked next to a dozen others. Kelsey was glad for the other people around. From what she understood, Izzy was ostensibly living the perfect Keys life, working when he chose, then taking off for the pure pleasure of it when he chose, as well. But if the rumor was true—which she was certain it was—Izzy *didn't* actually take off for the pure pleasure of it. He ran drugs.

She wasn't sure why some government agency hadn't cornered him by now. Except that he was probably good at what he did. He knew every tiny island and inlet, Gulf-side and Atlantic-side, of the Keys, knew when to hold and when to fold, and how to rid himself of a cargo quickly.

He had apparently taken out a morning charter. What seemed to be a family of tourists hovered on the dock, two kids watching with fascination as Izzy gutted and filleted their catch. His knife was sharp, his expertise with it swift and fascinating. Kelsey had spent many an hour with a fresh catch herself, and she was nowhere near as good as Izzy. Few people probably were.

She hadn't seen him in years, but she recognized him right away. He was tall and bronzed, more wiry than massive, but Kelsey had to admit that he was very good-looking in what she might term a "smarmy" way. His hair would have been long if it weren't so curly, oily and dark. His face was lean, with a sharp chin and narrow cheekbones. His eyes were deep-set and very dark. He moved with a strange, natural grace, and knowing Sheila, Kelsey knew what Sheila saw in the man. His tan was so dark that he was beyond bronze and more the color of nutshell brown. His skin was shiny in the sun and heat. Like many a boat man, he was in nothing but cutoffs. His feet were bare.

As if he sensed her standing on the dock, he looked up. Since she'd had no trouble recognizing him, it shouldn't have been strange that he recognized her immediately.

"Kelsey Cunningham," he breathed, pausing for a moment as he stared her up and down. Again Kelsey understood Sheila's attraction. There was nothing hidden in the way he looked at her. His assessment was slow and complete. He didn't just undress a woman with his eyes, he went all the way.

"Is that the last of them?" the mother of the two children asked. Her nose was white with sunscreen. Her cheeks, missing the protection, were lobster-red.

"The last," Izzy said, still staring at Kelsey, a curious smile twisting his full lips. He wrapped the fish in brown paper kept at the dockside station for just that purpose. "Don't overcook the fish. Just a little olive oil in the pan, a touch of butter..." He brought his fingers to his lips and made a kissing sound, still looking at Kelsey. "Voilà! Your fillets will be like butter themselves!"

"Thank you," the husband said. He had the kind of belly that protruded over the waistband of his shorts. The slice of stomach that was revealed was as red as his wife's cheeks.

The group started to move off. Izzy finally looked away from Kelsey. "A tip is customary," he said flatly.

"Oh, yeah, sure," the man said, digging in his damp pockets.

"Tip him good, Daddy!" the little girl said. "He helped me catch my fish."

"Oh, yeah, sure, we had a great time," the man said, giving Izzy a wad of bills.

Izzy grinned. "Of course. Little girls, just like little boys, should learn to catch fish. To go for it all in life, right...Susie?"

"My name is Shelly," the little girl said, frowning.

"Ah, yes, Shelly." Izzy tousled her hair, grinning. "Of course. And now you know how to catch fish with the best of them."

"My fish was bigger," the little boy said.

"You both did well," Izzy said complimentarily.

The kids seemed happy, as did the parents. They waved as they walked away from the dock, studying Kelsey curiously and nodding as they passed her.

"Think she's his girlfriend?" the little girl asked the little boy in a whisper as they passed.

"I'll bet he has a dozen girlfriends!" the boy said confidently. "At least a dozen."

Izzy laughed, watching them go. "So...Kelsey Cunningham. What an honor—and a surprise. So, have you come to be one of my girlfriends? City life getting to you? Did you come down to slum it with a real man?"

She walked to the table where the flies buzzed around the fish remains. "I came down to see Sheila," she said.

His smile didn't alter a hair. He shrugged. "Sheila. Now there's an unusual woman. A real woman. Maybe more of a real woman than I am a real man."

"So you've seen her?"

"Of course I've seen her. She knows where to come when she needs me."

"Lately? Have you seen her lately?"

He set his hands on his hips and cocked his head, thinking. "I saw her...eight days ago? I think. Before the storm."

"Not since?"

"No, I don't think so. You know Sheila. She comes, she goes."

"Were you seeing her...regularly?"

Izzy let out a long laugh. "Was I *fucking* Sheila? Is that what you want to know?"

Kelsey suddenly felt both a surge of anger and a sense of her own stupidity. What the hell did she think—that Izzy was going to confess he'd taken Sheila off and dumped her in the ocean?

She started to turn away. She was startled when his hand fell on her shoulder and he quickly apologized. "Kelsey, don't go so fast. I'm sorry. You were never mean to me, you were never interested in me, either, but I'm just surprised to see you, that's all. But if I can help you, I'd be happy to. So are you concerned about what Sheila has been doing—or what Sheila has been getting? Did you come to me for...something?"

Despite herself, she felt her cheeks flood with color. He thought she had come to an old acquaintance to make a drug purchase.

"I was supposed to meet Sheila here on Thursday. She hasn't shown up yet."

He made a face that clearly showed her that she was talking about no time at all, the way Sheila would see it.

"Sheila sees me one day...then disappears for a week or more. She has other things to do." His long lashes swept over his eyes for a moment. "So many people to meet. Me, I fulfill some of her needs. But she has...many needs, and I can't satisfy them all." As if sensing her discomfort, he changed the subject. "Would you like to come aboard? I've got cold drinks in the refrigerator."

He picked up on her hesitation immediately.

"I don't bite—unless I'm asked to."

It might be the stupidest thing in the world to walk onto his boat. But the dock was filled with people. A lot of the charter fishing captains took out a morning group and an afternoon group. They were all between right now. At least a dozen people would see her when she stepped aboard. And she wanted to see for herself where Sheila had been spending time.

"Sure. I'd like to see the boat. And I'd love a cold soda."

He arched a brow in surprise that she had agreed so readily. Then he smiled broadly. "Miss Cunningham, do come into my parlor. I promise to be on my best behavior."

Kelsey followed him from the dock, taking his hand as he helped her jump down to the deck of the *Lady Havana*.

"You haven't joined the DEA or anything have you, Kelsey?" he queried. "Because I know damn well you don't trust me."

He was still holding her hand. She didn't allow herself to pull it away, though she wanted to, and finally he released her.

"I'm just worried about Sheila."

"I'll tell you what I can."

They didn't stay on deck. He led the way to the few short steps that descended into the cabin.

Dane's concentration had been on focusing the lens of his camera on Izzy Garcia. Bringing his face into full view as best as possible from this distance. He clicked a picture, then another, then a third. A decent full frontal shot as Izzy stepped off his boat. A good profile shot as he turned to the woman passenger, assisting her from the boat. Then, on the dock, cleaning his fish.

He was patient in his quest, waiting for a good, clear shot. He stared at the dock area, where the object of his attention was working. He refocused, noting the mother, father and two children. Then, through his lens, he saw Kelsey.

Hair pulled back into a cool ponytail, she was in a tank top, shorts and deck shoes.

From the midst of a tangle of sea grape trees, Dane watched in amazement as Kelsey disappeared from view, entering the cabin of Izzy's boat.

He hadn't expected to find her here. And he sure as hell hadn't intended to confront Izzy himself. If he were even halfway rational, he wouldn't confront Izzy now.

But he couldn't see Kelsey. And that suddenly meant that he wasn't rational at all.

He pocketed the small camera in the cargo shorts he was wearing and headed toward the dock.

Kelsey was an idiot.

At this moment Dane didn't just dislike Izzy Garcia, he hated the man.

Though he could travel the distance from the off road hummock to the sandy path, the dock and then the boat in a matter of moments, he thought even that was too long a time for Kelsey to be alone with Izzy Garcia.

His heart rate and sense of unease escalated when he saw Izzy on deck again, releasing his mooring lines.

"Shit!" Dane swore, suddenly at a sprinter's pace as his feet hit the dock.

The *Lady Havana* was already pulling away from her berth.

"We'll just take a little spin out on the water," he'd said, again offering his smile of amusement at her obvious mistrust. "Twenty people just saw you get onboard," he'd reminded her. "And I have another charter in less than an hour. But that way no one will be able to interrupt us. I can talk to you."

Then he'd left her in the cabin and gone up top. She was still nervous, but he was right—she had gotten on his boat in broad daylight, in front of plenty of witnesses. And Izzy had never done anything to her or to anyone she knew.

Unless, of course, Sheila...

She could swim, she reasoned with herself. If she didn't like what was going on, she could just jump overboard and swim to safety.

Besides, she wanted a few moments alone in the cabin. Time to snoop. Not a lot of time, but she was willing to use anything she could get.

Of course, not only was she looking for a needle in a haystack, she didn't even know what needle she was looking for. But she'd found Sheila's earring at Dane's, and though he'd had a reason for it, she'd learned something.

Actually, more than she'd wanted to know. But it was important to know everything.

And here, in Izzy's boat...

Charts by the radio. And Izzy's cell phone. She glanced up the steps to see him busy on deck and hit the phone book key on Izzy's phone to get his stored numbers. She was carrying a small knit bag, so it was easy to find a pen and paper. She started writing, keeping her eyes on the steps. He was going to have to steer out of the marina area. That would take at least a few minutes.

She found the number to the duplex and the number to Sheila's cell phone. And others that startled her. Cindy's number, Nate's...Dane's. Dane's number at the house and at the office he had rented on US1. More numbers. Even the number to *her* house. She was so surprised that she froze for a minute, then started writing again. She didn't recognize half the area codes.

She heard his footsteps overhead. He was still maneuvering the boat out of the channel.

In a frenzy, she wrote down every number she could. She wondered if she would be able to decipher her own chicken scrawl later. She heard the motor idling down and quickly set down the phone and looked around the cabin. A simple place, loaded with fishing gear. A refrigerator, a small cooktop, a door reading Head. A small archway to an aft bunk. Cushioned seats lined both sides. She lifted the seats, knowing there was storage beneath. More fishing gear. A couple of metal boxes holding...what? A woman's bikini, neatly folded. Sandals on top. Sheila's? A purse...

Kelsey glanced back toward the steps. Listened. The motor was still running. She opened the purse. Lipstick, pen, small plastic bag holding a greenish-brown tobacco-like substance. She sniffed it. Grass. A compact initialed with the letters *SEW*. Sheila Elizabeth Warren.

The motor went still.

Kelsey dropped the purse back in the seat, closed the cushion lid. Sat. She was breathing as if she had just run a marathon. She willed her heart to stop pounding.

Izzy came down the steps. "Soda or beer?"

"Just a soda, please."

She was amazed to hear her own voice. It was low, calm, polite. It should have been a squeak.

"Cola or lemon-lime? Store brand, I'm afraid. Fishing charters don't pay enough for me to supply the tourists with anything better. Besides, out in the heat, on the ocean, what do they care? If they catch fish, they're happy. Half of them don't even eat fish. They just like to catch them, watch them struggle and say they caught the biggest one. What do you think that says about people?"

"I think it says most people realize that the big fish are born to hunt the little fish. That they rip apart their own kind at the first sign of weakness," Kelsey said.

"Not like people, eh?"

"Is it your opinion that people rip other people apart when they sense weakness?" Kelsey asked him.

"Me? I've seen it happen, if that's what you're asking. I saw the revolution in Cuba, the good and the bad. Little children helping old people, old people sacrificing themselves for the children. I saw a man jump into the sea and drown so that the overloaded raft he was on would make it across the sea. And I saw another man knock his wife from a raft so he could survive himself. All this I saw as a child. Yes, I would say it formed opinions in my mind."

"So whatever you do to anyone is all right, so long as it helps you survive?"

Izzy laughed, bringing Kelsey a soda and sitting at her side. Close. Brown legs against hers. "No. I think what I do is all right when I fulfill other people's needs. I told you, I fulfilled many of Sheila's needs. But look at you, Kelsey. Such a pretty girl.

And a sweet girl, mostly. But you're so stiff. This is right, and this is wrong. I bet you've never even jaywalked. And now you work for an uppity advertising agency. You go to long lunches with clients at the best restaurants, silly places where they take ten words to describe a piece of lettuce. I bet you live in a gated complex, up high, looking down at the world."

"Are you going to tell me about Sheila?"

"You know Sheila."

"Not like you know Sheila."

"Right. And I like Sheila. There's no pretense about her. She knows how to have fun. And while she's having fun, she takes what she wants. If a man appeals to her, she goes after him and enjoys him. If he has money and gives her beautiful jewelry, all the better. If he's jealous, she laughs. She'll order filet mignon or a hamburger, drink champagne or a beer, have sex on the sand, in the mud...wherever."

"How deep into drugs was she?" Kelsey demanded.

Izzy smiled, white teeth flashing against his bronze skin. "Did she shoot heroine? No. Did she enjoy some good pot or hash? *Sí*. And ecstasy? Oh, yes, Sheila is a woman of the senses. You see, I didn't have the diamonds to give her, but I had something else. A world of fantasy—and, of course, myself. What I offer is good. Safe drugs."

"Safe drugs?" she inquired.

"See, there you are, Miss Moralist, Miss Purist, perfect little nose in the air. You've got to learn to have fun. Let your hair down." He set a hand on her knee.

She moved it, staring at him.

He was amused. "You married Nate. He runs a bar. You think drunks are safer than people who've smoked a few joints?"

"Izzy, it doesn't matter what anyone's moral opinion is, it's legal to drink and it's illegal to do drugs."

"I still think you need a joint. You should chill out a little."

"Izzy, I don't want to chill out. I want to find Sheila."

He frowned suddenly. "I told you. Sheila comes, and Sheila goes. Except that..."

"Except that *what,* Izzy. Please, help me."

He shrugged. "Sheila did tell me that she had been a fool. She said that when a man was part of the past, he should be kept in the past." He hesitated, then looked at her squarely. "You know, Sheila saw a lot as a child, too. Maybe that's why we understand each other so well."

"What are you talking about?"

"She never talked to you about her mother?"

"Her mother? Her mother died."

"She did. But she was a busy lady before that. She and old Andy Latham, they were two of a kind. She had the money, but she was willing to do a lot of things for old Andy. And that included looking away."

"Looking away from what?"

Izzy suddenly stood, shaking his head. "Talk to Sheila. I've said too much. It's not my business to share."

"Izzy, please, that's why I'm here. What exactly are you saying? That Sheila's mother ran around after she married Latham?"

"She ran around *with* Latham is what I'm telling you. He needed more than...more than just one woman. Maybe two women. Maybe just watching. And Sheila...she saw a lot."

"Izzy, please, stop talking in riddles."

He walked back to her suddenly, arms braced on the wall to either side of her, his face just inches from hers. "Sheila has done too much, but you...you haven't done enough. Kelsey Cunningham. I always liked the sound of your name. Good Kelsey, beautiful Kelsey, prim and proper Kelsey. Take a chance, Kelsey. Life is to be lived. I can show you why Sheila couldn't stay away from me."

"Don't you have a charter this afternoon?" she asked him.

"Screw them."

He moved closer, but Kelsey wasn't afraid, just impatient. She wanted to get back to talking about Sheila and what Izzy knew about her. She wanted to know what Sheila had meant when she told him that the men in her past should remain there.

"Izzy—"

"*Sí?*" His dark-lashed eyes were half closed; his face was barely an inch from hers.

She was about to respond when an explosive slam suddenly sounded in the cabin and Izzy was jerked away from her as if by the hand of God. A too-familiar voice rang out in fury.

"Get the hell away from her, you drug-dealing asshole!"

Izzy had gone flying and crashed against the door to the Head. In the middle of the cabin, dripping sea water, stood Dane Whitelaw. Dark hair was plastered against his head. His feet and chest were bare, but his cargo shorts dripped like a leaky hull.

"Dane, what the hell are you doing here?" she asked angrily.

Izzy had recovered from his impact with the door. He shook off the blow, stood and pulled a switchblade from the pocket of his cutoffs.

"Izzy! Drop it. Dane, what the hell is the matter with you?"

Both men ignored her. Dane's face was set, harsh. Izzy looked ready to kill. He came forward in a rush.

She had never seen what Dane was capable of before, and he scared her. Izzy was a well-built man, muscled and lithe. But Dane sidestepped him in a second, smashing the arm with the blade and capturing him in a headlock.

"Stop it!" Kelsey screamed, leaping to her feet, grabbing Dane's right arm.

"Get the knife, Kelsey."

She picked up the switchblade, shaking, and realizing she didn't even know how to close the weapon.

Izzy swore in Spanish, a spew of venom, frightening. But Dane's headlock kept him from moving.

"Topside, Izzy," Dane said. "And get this rust bucket back into her berth."

Izzy kept swearing, but Dane was dragging him toward the steps. Dane determinedly forced Izzy up, then out to the open deck. Kelsey followed behind, shouting at Dane. "What the hell are you doing here? He was just talking to me about Sheila!"

"What the hell are *you* doing here? Trying to meet the same fate?" Dane countered. He shoved Izzy toward the helm. The two of them stood like a pair of game cocks, tension knotting them so tightly that they seemed like a display of bulging neck veins and wet muscle, like a pair of fighters about to be photographed for an anatomy class.

"You have no right to be here, Whitelaw," Izzy said. "Kelsey chose to come aboard. I can have you arrested for breaking and entering, and assault and battery."

"Izzy, I can have you arrested for so many felonies, your head would spin."

"You can't have me arrested for what you think, Whitelaw, and you have no proof of anything."

"You might be surprised at what kind of proof I have, Garcia."

Kelsey didn't have the slightest idea what was going on, but Dane's words gave Izzy pause. He turned around, cursing Dane in Spanish. She and Dane were both well enough acquainted with the language to know what he was saying, but the words had no effect on Dane, who didn't move, just stood stolidly watching as Izzy raised anchor and gunned the motor. The sound of it suddenly filled the air, and he walked to the helm, guiding the *Lady Havana* back toward the marina.

As the boat moved, the breeze picked up. Other boats filled the horizon, sailboats, fishing boats, dive boats. The sky remained blue, lightly touched by clouds. Oddly beautiful.

As the *Lady Havana* slowed into the "No Wake" zone, they all remained stiffly silent. When they reached the berth, Dane leaped from the boat, ready to tie her to the moorings. As the two men secured the boat as naturally as men who had been working together all their lives, it seemed impossible to believe that they had just been at each other's throats. The moment the boat was tied, Dane reached down to help Kelsey onto the dock. She ignored his hand, hopping out. She had been around boats just as long as the two of them had.

Izzy's afternoon group, five men of varying ages, all pale, two with the paunchy bellies of the weekday-business-warrior-week-end-couch-potato, were waiting on the dock, confused because there had been no boat waiting for them.

Dane spoke softly. "Don't even think about taking Kelsey out again, Izzy."

"Why? You afraid of what I'll say to her?"

"I'm afraid of what you'll do to her. You want to discuss this more now, or do you want to carry on your business and take your tourists out?"

Izzy turned his back on Dane. His easy smile back in place, he approached one of the waiting party with his hand extended. "Señor Huntsville. Good. You're on time."

As Izzy kept talking to his group. Dane started walking down the dock, toward the path out to the parking lot.

Kelsey ran after him, tapping him angrily on the back and forcing him to turn around.

"Look, I don't need a bodyguard. I could have taken care of myself with Izzy."

"You think so?"

"We were talking."

"Kelsey, you can't even close a switchblade."

"So? Izzy wasn't going to rape and kill me."

He looked at her with disgust and turned, ready to walk away again.

"Dane!"

"What?" He turned back with aggravation.

"What the hell just went on back there? How did you get on the boat? Why were you so convinced I was in danger, and what is it that you think Izzy has done?"

"Izzy is scum. I can just about prove that he's the supplier behind the drugs being sold at the local high school. He's dangerous, Kelsey, whether you want to believe it or not. As to how I got there, I hitched a ride on a dive boat, dove in and swam across. I destroyed a shirt and lost a good pair of boat shoes in the process, too. And what the hell kind of thanks do I get from you? None. You're too busy telling me that you didn't need a bodyguard."

"I've known Izzy most of my life."

"So? Did you know he has a rap sheet for assault? Or that he was also accused of date rape? The girl refused to prosecute, probably because she was paid off. I just didn't want to see you in her position. You don't want to believe me? Talk to Hans at the sheriff's office."

Kelsey could feel her cheeks going red as he spoke. Maybe she *had* been crazy. *Really* crazy. She had found a purse that definitely belonged to Sheila, but then again, he hadn't denied that he saw Sheila frequently.

Sheila's earring had been at Dane's. Her purse had been on Izzy's boat.

Then there were all the numbers she'd found on Izzy's cell phone.

It was true that for a few minutes she had been afraid. But now she found herself inclined to believe that Izzy wouldn't have hurt her, nor would he have forced her into anything. He had pushed, but pushing was his way.

"Lots of people saw me get on that boat. Only an idiot would have harmed me."

"Or a guy so aggressive and confident he believes himself immune to the law. But hey, Kelsey, what the hell? I'm the last person you want help from, right?"

"It's not that, Dane, but you really don't have to follow me around."

"I wasn't following you around, Kelsey. I simply happened to be there at the same time you were. But what the hell, you're right. You're free and over twenty-one. I can't stop you. Just keep on seeing every psychotic scumbag in town. I'll do my best to quit trying to keep you from putting yourself in harm's way."

"Excuse me, but how the hell am I supposed to know *you're* not a psychotic scumbag?"

He turned and started walking again. She found herself following him, regretting her words already.

"Okay, I don't *think* you're a psychotic scumbag." He was still moving. He either didn't notice or didn't appreciate the light touch she had tried to give her words. "Dane, I'll buy you a new pair of shoes," she told him.

He kept walking.

"And I'll replace your shirt."

He was still walking. She could have kicked herself for following him, but she couldn't stop herself. "He told me things I didn't know, Dane. And he might have told me more."

He stopped at last and turned back to face her. "You've known Sheila forever. What could he have told you that you didn't already know?"

"That...well, I always knew Andy Latham was a creep, but according to Izzy, Sheila's mother was just as bad."

Dane studied her for a long moment. "That's a surprise to you? And you think it will help you find Sheila now?"

"Everything I learn is a help, Dane. And—" She broke off. Dane wasn't telling her everything, so she wasn't going to tell him everything.

"And what?"

She shook her head. "I just feel that if I could have talked to him long enough, he might have said something that would have helped. I think Sheila was spending a lot of time with him, off and on."

He looked down at the ground for a minute, then met her eyes again. "Kelsey, if you were going to spend time with everyone Sheila had been seeing, you'd need way more than a week's vacation." He waved a hand in the air. "Sheila was...it was almost as if she was on a quest to prove that she could have whoever she wanted whenever she wanted him."

"But why? If we knew, it might lead us to her. Or to whatever...happened to her. We have to find out why."

"I *will* find out why. I told you that."

She was silent for a minute. "But I could find out things you don't know."

"Not a chance."

"Oh?"

"Why do you say that?" His eyes narrowed.

She shrugged. "Because people who might not be willing to talk to you might be willing to talk to me."

She walked past him.

"Where are you going?"

She hesitated. "Back to the duplex. Are you going to follow me?"

"You're really going back there? You're not going to go into the computer and see if you can find another violent career criminal to visit?"

"I'm really going back to the duplex."

He nodded, then headed for his Jeep.

"Are you coming over?" she asked him.

He shook his head. "I have things to do."

She hesitated, watching him climb into the Jeep. He turned on the motor and took a pair of sunglasses from the dashboard, but he didn't move the car. He just watched her through the dark lenses.

"We're meeting for dinner at Nate's at seven," she told him. "Care to join us?"

She could read no emotion on his features, and she couldn't see his eyes.

"Yeah, I'll be there," he said.

She turned and got into her car. A block down the street, she realized that, despite what he'd said, he was following her. He wasn't even pretending not to. When she parked at the duplex, though, he remained in his car. She walked over to him. "Are you coming in?"

"No, I just thought I'd see you safely in."

"I thought you didn't care if I put myself into dangerous situations anymore."

"I lied." He adjusted his glasses. "Go inside, Kelsey."

She turned impatiently and walked to the door, fitting her key into the lock. She stepped inside, calling Larry's name. He didn't respond, but she hadn't expected him to, since his car wasn't in the driveway. She hesitated before closing the door, remembering her uneasiness the night before. She ran through the duplex, checking out closets and bathrooms, then back to the front. Dane was still there, still staring impassively out from behind his sunglasses. She waved to him and closed the door, listening to him drive away.

She hesitated. Her half of the duplex was empty, and she knew it. So why did she still have the feeling that someone had been there who shouldn't have been? That someone had searched the rooms? That the space had somehow been violated.

She glanced at her watch. It wasn't quite three. She had plenty of time to run over the list of numbers she had taken from Izzy's cell phone. She walked to the kitchen, set her purse down and dug out the paper. She marked off the numbers she knew, amazed that he seemed to have so many that should have meant nothing to him at this stage of all their lives. He had Larry's home phone keyed in, as well as her own, and that of the company where they both worked. Nate's home, Nate's business. Cindy. Dane. There was one listed only as "JM." She was willing to bet that number was Jorge Marti's. Just to double-check, she went to the phone and punched in the numbers. The phone rang, and then an answering machine picked up. "Hi, this is Jorge. Please leave a message. I'll get back to you as soon as possible."

She hesitated, then said quickly, "Hi, Jorge, it's Kelsey Cunningham. A group of us are meeting at seven at Nate's for sup-per. We'd love it if you could join us."

She hung up, then picked up the phone again, ready to try an-other number. After a moment she hung up without dialing, not wanting to call from the duplex.

Everyone had caller ID these days.

She drummed her fingers on the counter, wondering why she hadn't told Dane about Sheila's purse being on Izzy's boat, or that she had taken the numbers from his phone.

She really didn't know what the hell to do with the numbers. She knew it was somehow important that Izzy not only had all their numbers, but that he kept them on his cell phone. But as to finding out anything about the other numbers...she really didn't know how to go about it.

Dane would. He was a private investigator.

Maybe she would tell him. Soon. She was still disturbed by the fact that Sheila's earring had been at his house. That he had admitted to sleeping with her just before she disappeared.

What did it all mean?

Dane arrived at the Sea Shanty late. Before joining the group, he observed them from the doorway. Cindy was looking small but perfect in a backless sheath that showed off the definition of her shoulders, pecs and back. Larry was as perfectly pressed and tailored as ever in tan slacks and a black short-sleeved knit. Nate was wearing a surf shirt and knee-length Dockers, and he was enthusiastically discussing something with Larry. Kelsey was leaning back in her chair, her hair shimmering in the Tiki lights, curling over her bare shoulders. Her dress was a flowered strapless concoction that clung to every curve of her body. She was listening to the man in the chair at her left, Jorge Marti.

Jorge looked good. Dark, handsome, he was the only one in a jacket. His navy shirt was open at the throat underneath the beige blazer. Like Kelsey, he had the knack of looking both well-dressed and casual. Whatever he was saying to her was making her laugh.

Before joining the group, Dane discreetly took a few photos. Then he slid the small waterproof camera into the pocket of his black windbreaker and strode over to join them at their table.

Kelsey heard him coming and looked up. He couldn't tell if she was pleased by his arrival or not. Cindy, as always, jumped up with the effusive pleasure she showed to all her friends. "Dane, we were afraid you weren't coming."

"Sorry I'm late," he said, sitting and picking up a menu, though he knew it by heart. "Jorge, how are you doing?"

"Great, thanks. You?"

"Moving right along," he said. "I hope I didn't keep you all from ordering?"

"We're in the Keys," Larry said. "We're not supposed to be in any hurry. We planned on giving you half an hour, at least. Then we figured we'd spend another fifteen minutes being disappointed that you hadn't joined us."

"I knew you'd show," Nate said. "By the way, those hidden cameras worked great. Fired a kid today. Caught him right on tape with his hand in the till. Thanks, man. You saved me a bundle."

"What can I say? Security works," Dane said.

"I guess it's good," Larry volunteered. He smiled at Kelsey across the table. "I don't know. At work, I feel like Big Brother is watching. The frigging cameras move. They follow you around."

Dane gave him a rueful smile. "Good cameras. They're probably expensive. They must think highly of the work you do."

Larry sniffed. "Either that, or they think we're going to make off with all their art supplies. Ah, well, such is corporate life."

"Since Dane is here, let's order," Cindy said. She looked at the suddenly silent group. "Okay, it's the Keys, but I live here all the time, and I'm starving."

Laughter followed her words. Nate summoned the waiter, and they ordered. "I hope you're not disappointed," he said. "This place isn't exactly gourmet."

"We'll go gourmet another night," Kelsey assured him. "Tonight we'll go with friendship and down-home good food."

"Thanks, sweetie." He lifted his glass toward her. She lifted hers in return. "To the best ex-wife I've ever had."

"Thanks. Of course, I'm the *only* ex-wife you've ever had."

"Scary to think I could have gotten married over and over again." Nate shuddered. "I think you've made me a single man for the rest of my life."

"Great, there's a real testimonial," Kelsey groaned.

"No, no, I didn't mean it that way," Nate protested. "None of us really seem cut out for marriage. Take Cindy, for instance. She may end up an old maid."

"Thanks for the compliment," Cindy murmured.

"We're all in the same boat. I'm a reformed man, Dane doesn't show the least inclination toward marriage, God knows what goes on in Kelsey's mind, Jorge, you're still on the loose. And Larry...Larry and Sheila were a total disaster."

"We weren't a total disaster. I still love her," Larry said.

"Sheila wasn't meant for marriage," Jorge said, without meeting Larry's eyes.

Larry shrugged. "You guys don't all have to stare at your drinks. Let's face it, my ex-wife has hopped into bed with every guy here." He lifted a hand before any of them could protest. "Not while we were married—not with you guys, anyway—and if I'm wrong, I don't want to know. But it's true, I still love her."

Dane noticed that Kelsey was staring at her ex-husband. He wondered if she knew about her ex's relationship with Sheila, or that he had been just as big a lech as any other man alive.

"Okay, here's to you for being such a decent guy," Cindy said. "But you know what? Guys will sleep with anyone."

"Oh, yeah. I'm just a walking pile of testosterone," Larry said.

Cindy had to laugh. Even Dane felt the twitch of a smile at the other man's mournful tone. "Kelsey says you're dating a model."

"She *is* pretty gorgeous," Larry admitted.

Cindy continued. "That's the problem. There just aren't that many decent guys out there anymore. And all the ones I know are my old friends."

"That doesn't mean we aren't willing to oblige you in any way you might desire," Larry told her, grinning.

"See what I mean? You're dating a gorgeous model, but you're ready to oblige me."

"Hey, I was kidding. Besides, who knows what the future holds? It's awfully easy to find yourself available. I learned that the hard way."

Cindy smiled. "Poor Larry. I'll keep the offer in mind—for the future, of course. I just hate to lose a really good friend by dating him."

"Hey, Kels didn't just date me. She married me and divorced me, and we're still friends," Nate said. "But then, I took the divorce awfully well."

Kelsey stared at him, shaking her head. "Nate..."

"Hey, it's your loss. Isn't that what they say?"

"My loss. You're a good guy, Nate," Kelsey assured him.

"Hey, at least she divorced you before sleeping with half the town," Larry said.

"You know, Larry, you have Kelsey in the office with you all the time," Cindy pointed out.

Kelsey groaned. "I never date co-workers."

"And she means it, dammit," Larry said.

Kelsey shrugged. "I hate to lose friends, too, and I also hate the idea of being uncomfortable at work if it didn't work out."

"Good policy," Jorge said. "You should never date clients, either." He spoke casually, but when he met Dane's eyes, he blushed, despite his dark complexion, and looked uncomfortable. Dane wondered just how much his friends knew about what had happened in St. Augustine. Enough, apparently.

"This whole conversation is depressing me," Cindy said.

"In that case, we'll talk about something else," Larry told her.

"Oh!" Cindy said. "Did you hear that they dug up another skeleton in the Everglades?"

A dead silence followed her words. Dane studied the faces around him, wondering whether they were afraid to ask if the remains might belong to Sheila.

Kelsey sounded as if she was strangling as she asked, "Bones? Just...bones?"

"Uh-huh," Cindy said. "They've been out there almost a year. That's what they reported on the evening news, anyway. Apparently the police suspect that the woman might have been a victim of the Necktie Strangler. They've already managed to ID her. Another stripper, thank God. Lord, that sounds awful, doesn't it? It's not that I have anything against strippers. Everybody has to make a living. Except that it seems the victims were all prostitutes on the side. And that's why I'm grateful. This guy is targeting a certain kind of woman. If there was a killer on the loose who chose his victims randomly...well, I know I'm not desperate enough to start hooking, so I don't have to be afraid of my own shadow."

"You should always be careful," Dane told her.

"I wish we knew where Sheila was," Nate said.

"Sheila doesn't work in a strip club," Jorge said.

"But the way she behaves..." Larry murmured.

"Right. Taking off without letting anyone know," Cindy said firmly, refusing to acknowledge any similarities with the dead women. "Sheila is fine, and she'll show up soon. I know it."

There was silence again.

"Wow, what a fun time we're having," Nate groaned. "Anybody here have anything cheerful to talk about?" Nate said. "So far we've gone through failed marriage, the lack of romance in our lives, our worry about Sheila, and, just to make us all a little more anxious, we've thrown in a serial killer."

Jorge turned to Kelsey, who was still looking worried. "Sheila is going to be all right."

*No, she's not,* Dane wanted to shout.

Which would be an insane move.

"We can talk about politics," Cindy suggested.

Nate groaned more loudly this time. "Hell, let's throw in abortion, gun control and religion. We won't have to worry about being old friends by the end of the night."

"Hey, Kelsey," Jorge said. "Are you planning on doing any painting while you're down here."

"Maybe. I haven't done any in a long time," she said.

Jorge began talking about some of the areas she might want to sketch. Then Cindy asked Dane about his work, while Nate and Larry turned to a discussion about a new rock group from the Keys that was starting to gain national prominence. The food came and went; coffee and dessert were served. Dane glanced at his watch.

He looked across the table to find that Kelsey was studying him. He leaned as close to her as he could. "You're not visiting anyone tonight, are you?"

She arched a brow. "I'm here with friends."

"Stay with them," he told her. Then he rose. "I've got to get going. This was great, seeing everyone. And just to assure you all of the success of my career, let me get the check, Nate."

Nate grinned. "Hell, no. I'm getting it here. You can get it on...say Monday. We'll try that nouvelle cuisine place right down the road. It will be much cheaper for me that way."

"Nate!" Kelsey protested.

Dane was unperturbed. "That's fine with me. Monday night. Seven again?"

"Seven," Cindy agreed. "Ugh. Monday is a workday."

"That from Miss Workaholic," Jorge teased.

"True—usually. But with us all together now...I'd love to just play for a few days. Head out to the beach. Go boating, diving, exploring. Like when we were kids."

"Actually I wasn't part of most of your excursions back in those days," Jorge said. "I feel a bit like an intruder here. Sure you want me along?"

"Oh, definitely," Kelsey said, looking at Jorge.

"Of course we want you to join us," Cindy said.

"You've got to be there," Dane said, nodding his agreement with the others. "Nate, thanks for dinner. The Sea Shanty rules, as always. Good night, all."

He waved and headed out, taking the path for the parking lot.

He hesitated, hearing a rustle in the bushes. He looked back.

He could see a touch of color through the foliage. Someone's shirt?

He walked again.

Listened.

Yup. He was being followed.

# CHAPTER 9

Earlier Kelsey had planned to leave the Sea Shanty and head straight back to the duplex for a tub of hot water, a cup of tea, a Tylenol P.M. and a night's sound sleep.

Instead she forced herself to sit tight for a moment when Dane left, then feigned a yawn and begged off. She left quickly and followed Dane's footsteps. When he stopped to light a cigarette, she froze. As soon as he was in his Jeep and heading out of the lot, she ran for her own car, gunned the engine and sent pebbles flying as she hurried to catch him. He had entered the flow of traffic, heading north.

Her hands were shaking on the wheel. Dane knew something he wasn't telling. She was sure of it.

Of course, she wasn't giving him all the information *she* had, either. Meanwhile, she was determined to follow him tonight.

Dane's relationship with Sheila still disturbed her.

Why? She shouldn't have been surprised that he had slept with Sheila. It hadn't been anything new. They had been a duo all through high school, after all. And she hadn't needed to find the earring or hear from Dane himself that he had been with

Sheila. When she had first reached Key Largo and Sheila hadn't been there, she had heard right away from Cindy that Sheila had been seeing Dane.

Before that, on the phone, Sheila had told her that she was seeing him, though there had been a strange wistful tone to her voice that hadn't seemed to fit the words.

Kelsey realized how badly she wanted to believe in Dane. She didn't know why. Maybe it was impossible to be with him without feeling an attraction. After all, he had been Joe's best friend. There for most of her life. Older, handsome, assured, determined on his future, confident in his ability to get where he wanted to go.

Or maybe it was just because of *that* night.

As she drove, trying to focus on following the Jeep, she found that a certain honesty was bubbling to the surface.

She shouldn't have come to Key Largo. She had been married to Nate—a disaster from start to finish—but she didn't feel a thing when she was near him except for an old affection. She'd spent one night with Dane and all she had to do was see his face to feel a rush of sexual longing so strong it was humiliating. She could tell herself whatever she wanted, she could lie or hide it from others, but it was hard to keep the truth from herself. She didn't want to mistrust Dane, she didn't want to think that he had come home to waste his life, and she hadn't wanted to believe he had been back with Sheila.

But he had been.

She was able to keep a safe distance behind him while the highway was divided into four lines. But then they hit US1 on the way back to the mainland and Florida City. The road narrowed to two lanes and there were several cars between them at that point, so she could no longer see his Jeep.

But there was nowhere for him to go except north. She stuck to the tail of the car ahead of her as she drove. She didn't know why, but she hadn't expected Dane to leave Key Largo. She hadn't expected such a long drive, but, checking her gas tank, she knew she was fine. As long as she didn't lose him once they reached Florida City.

Coming up to Florida City, she strained to catch sight of his Jeep. She found him and followed, taking the ramp onto the turnpike.

At the toll booth, she had to scramble for change to get through. He had shot on ahead of her. She hit the gas hard, trying to keep up. Eventually he took the turnoff for South Miami. Amazingly she didn't lose him when he exited, back onto US1. He didn't drive far from the exit. She saw the Jeep pull into the parking lot of a strip club.

She drove by once, then returned and entered the parking lot. She surveyed the area. The club was called Legs. It sat in the middle of the parking lot; a strip mall stretched behind the freestanding building. Ironically the mall included a day care center, a health food store, a coffee shop, an insurance agency and a gym.

The parking spaces nearest the club were filled. The lot was large, stretching back to where a border of trees separated the property from the gas station next door. Floodlights illuminated the area, so though the area by the trees seemed a bit dark and foreboding, the rest of the parking lot seemed to be fine.

Kelsey found a space in the far back row, next to the trees. She parked the car but remained in it, staring at the club. She wasn't sure what to do. She'd never been inside a place like that before and had no idea if single women ever just wandered into such a place. She'd been invited once to go on a girls' night out to a male strip club, but something had come up at the office, and she'd been too tired to join the others.

She sat in the car for another couple of minutes, then got angry with herself. She was an adult. Surely she could walk into such an establishment without feeling like a guilty child.

Of course, she wanted to walk in without Dane seeing her, and without attracting attention.

Only one thing to do.

She exited the car and strode across the parking lot. Odd, she already felt as if she were walking peculiarly.

The door opened as she approached it. She was afraid she would find herself immediately accosted by a bunch of drunks.

There were no drunks, just the doorman. Or bouncer. He wasn't more than six feet even, but his shoulders appeared to be about three feet wide. He was wearing a casual suit and had a pleasant smile. "Welcome to Legs," he told her.

"Thanks," she murmured. She started to walk by, blinking to adjust to the dark and smoky club where, strangely enough, a country tune was playing.

"Excuse me," the man called to her.

"Yes?"

"I'm sorry, there's a cover. Pay right over there."

"Oh, of course."

So much for not attracting attention. She saw the booth where a woman was sitting. She wasn't exactly topless, but strategic lace-rimmed holes in her shirt meant she might as well be.

Kelsey tried not to stare as she paid the admission, then slipped into the club. She was grateful that she could slink around the back of the room, far from the stage, and take a seat in a dark corner.

She wasn't sure what she had expected. A pack of dirty old men with scraggly cheeks and beer bellies, all leaning around the stage, tongues hanging out.

Maybe she'd been watching too much television.

The club was actually rather nice. She had expected something seedy, with dirty floors, dank walls and rough, litter-strewn tables. But though the place was dark and smoky, the tables surrounding the stage were clean, polished wood, sporting candles and even fresh flowers. She liked the darkness; it allowed her to feel invisible.

She looked around. The customers were not what she'd expected.

For the most part, they were clean-shaven. Or, if they had facial hair, it seemed to be trimmed and in good order. Some were dressed casually in denims and polo shirts, and some were in suits.

Some were with women. *Normal*-looking women.

Okay, Kelsey, she asked herself, just what is normal?

It wasn't time to get into a philosophical debate with herself. She had come to find out what Dane was doing.

At the moment, country music was playing because the performance was...country. The girl on stage was a tall, beautiful blonde. As Kelsey took her chair, the girl was removing her hat and swirling her hair. She wore a white-tasseled skirt and matching jacket and moved with a sensuality that defied the wholesome lyrics of the song.

The cocktail waitress who came to her table was wearing a short black skirt and low-cut silver bustier. She was pleasant and professional, and didn't seem either surprised or annoyed when Kelsey asked for soda water with lime.

There were catcalls rising around the room. The girl on stage shed the short skirt to reveal a G-string, a pretty piece of nothing so studded with rhinestones that they might as well have been glued to her skin.

"Hi there."

Kelsey looked up. A nicely dressed, older man with steel gray hair was standing by her table.

"Hi."

"Are you alone?" he asked. "Want company?"

"No...I'm waiting for my fiancé. But thank you."

She breathed a sigh of relief when he moved away. The waitress returned with her drink, and this time she seemed to eye Kelsey curiously.

"Thanks," Kelsey told her.

The woman smiled. "You look nervous. Don't worry. They don't let guys come on too hard to the women here—customers or dancers—unless it's obvious that's what they want. Did you come here looking for some action?" she asked.

"No, I...I'm waiting for my fiancé."

"Sure."

The woman wasn't going to press it, but Kelsey knew she wasn't buying that for a minute. "Actually, I've never been in a place like this. I just wanted to see what it was like."

The waitress smiled again. "You mean you followed your old man here to find out if he was just out with the guys or ordering a private lap dance?"

Kelsey was surprised to hear herself laugh. "No, honestly, I just came to see what the club was all about."

The woman suddenly frowned. "You're not from the press, are you? This really is a decent establishment, and after Cherie was found, the cops and the news people were all over us. If you're here to start writing more moralistic trash—"

"I'm not! I swear, I'm not a reporter," Kelsey said.

"All right, then," the woman said, nodding. "If you need any help—if any of these guys come on too strong—you let me know."

"Thanks. Thanks very much."

The woman shook her head. "You look like a babe in the woods," she said as she walked away.

Kelsey was a little irritated by the remark. The cocktail waitress didn't look as if she could be over twenty-two by any stretch of the imagination. She knew she was definitely older, and surely more mature, than her newfound champion.

A babe in the woods...

Her eyes scanned the tables, and at last she saw Dane. He was in the front row. He had a drink in front of him, something clear with lime. Just like hers. Dane was drinking soda water, too. His attention was on the cowgirl, who had shed the white-fringed top.

The woman on stage was beautiful. Perfectly built. Kelsey wondered why she had always thought that only desperate women would take to dancing like this for an income. This woman could clearly do whatever she wanted, and yet she was here.

The woman moved along the stage, dancing, achieving positions that surely were matched only by the world's best contortionists. Her eyes were on Dane, and he seemed to be returning the stare.

"Hey there, cutie."

This time the man who approached Kelsey slid right into the chair across from her. He was younger, and one of the scruffier-looking patrons in the place. She met his eyes across the table. "I'm not alone."

"Sure looks that way."

From her purse, her cell phone started ringing. She dived for her bag, wondering who was calling her at this hour, yet glad of the chance to pick up the phone and end this conversation before it began. She stared at the man as she hit the talk button. "Do you mind?"

He didn't move.

"Kelsey? Kelsey, is that you?" It was Larry on the other end.

"Yes, sweetheart, it's me," she said.

"Sweetheart?" Larry echoed dubiously.

"What's up?" she asked cheerfully.

"I was worried. You didn't come back. I was afraid you'd decided to take off and throttle old man Latham or something like that."

"No, I'm fine."

"What the hell is that music in the background?"

"I'm having a drink."

"Kelsey, you don't sound like yourself. And you called *me* sweetheart. If you're in any kind of trouble, I'll come and get you, wherever you are."

"That's wonderful. But I'm fine." She lowered her voice, made it soft and husky. "We'll discuss all that...later."

"Kelsey, now I'm really worried."

"Oh, don't be worried." She stared at the man at her table. "No one's bothering me here. I know you're built like Conan the Barbarian, honey, but you really don't need to rush to my rescue. Honestly, I can handle myself."

To her surprise, either she sounded good or she must have looked as if she meant it. The man threw up his hands, rose irritably and walked away.

"Kelsey, since when have I been built like Conan the Barbarian? You aren't making the least bit of sense. Where the hell are you?"

"Just at a club, having a soda. Larry, I know I'm sounding ridiculous, but, please, it's okay. I'll explain later. Don't worry about me. I swear I'm fine, and I promise I'll call you if I have any problem whatsoever. Bye now. Get some sleep."

She clicked off before he could keep talking.

She did so just in time to keep Larry from really worrying, since it seemed that the entire place was now kicking into a chorus of "Home on the Range" to go along with the antics of the cowgirl on stage. The girl had lost all semblance of a top, and her bottom half was the next closest thing to completely bare.

The men in the place had all made an almost comical shift, leaning closer to the stage, even those men who were with their wives or girlfriends.

The cowgirl lay down and started gyrating sensuously on her back again. Then she got up and, with the sinuous movements of a prowling cat, she made her way to the tables closest to the stage. She was there to accept money from the appreciative audience, and there was only one place for them to put the bills they were eagerly pulling from their wallets.

As Kelsey watched, Dane leaned forward, tucking one in. He smiled at the cowgirl, who seemed to watch him a second longer than the other men who added to her collection.

Kelsey realized that she was grinding her teeth and staring down at her soda as if she had been watching something not just sexual, but intimate. It made her furious with Dane, despite the logic flooding through her and telling her that she had no reason to be offended—he was an adult male without a commitment to any woman, so he certainly had the right to attend a strip club and slide bills into a dancer's G-string if he chose.

She wanted to slosh a drink over his head.

"You seem to be doing all right, honey."

She was startled to find the waitress standing at her side, giving her a broad grin.

"I'm fine, thanks." She noticed that Dane's waitress had gone back to his table. He was talking with the girl, and he had taken something from the pocket of his jacket and was showing it to her.

"Want another soda water?"

"Pardon?"

"Another soda water?"

"Sure, thank you."

"That's Katia," the waitress said. "She's the best. I wish I could move like that."

"So do I," Kelsey murmured, and realized she meant it. Katia the cowgirl had evidently had years of dance lessons before beginning her career with the pole.

"She's a nice woman."

Kelsey looked up at the waitress. For some reason the woman seemed bent on proving to Kelsey that the people who worked there weren't as shady as most people supposed.

"I'm sure she is."

The waitress was staring at the stage. "She and Cherie were really good friends."

Kelsey instantly remembered the news articles she had scanned at Dane's. "Cherie...she was the girl who worked here who...was murdered."

The waitress, still looking at the stage, nodded. "She was a really sweet kid. Some guy had broken her heart, but she was determined to make it through school and get ahead in life. She always quoted that old adage about success being the best revenge. I knew...I knew she was giving some guys more than lap dances, and...I guess she went off with the wrong one."

"Aren't you afraid now when you leave here?" Kelsey asked her.

"Hey, Sophie! We need another round over here," a heavyset man in a business suit called. He was at a table with a number of well-dressed Japanese men.

"Coming," the waitress called. She told Kelsey quickly, "Since I'm Sophie—Sophie Smithfield—I guess I'd better get moving. I'll be back."

The waitress moved on. The cowgirl had left the stage, and "Sheherazade" was being announced next. The music changed to something Arabic and exotic. The new dancer was definitely exotic herself; she was almond skinned, with dark slanting eyes and a head of rich dark hair that cascaded down her back.

Kelsey watched Dane again. He was leaning back in his chair, arms crossed over his chest as he watched the stage. The waitress approached him again, slipping him a note.

A few minutes later, he rose and walked toward the back of the club, disappearing through a door at the left. Kelsey gave thanks for the darkness, which had kept him from seeing her.

Frustrated, she stared after him. She felt the rise of illogical anger once again.

"Another soda," Sophie said, arriving at her side and placing the drink in front of her.

"Thanks. I'll take the check, too, I guess."

"Sure thing. Oh, you asked if I was afraid to work here now. Not really. There's a super nice homicide guy on the case. He seems to really care that Cherie was killed. And he told us that this guy is no idiot. He'll move on and choose his next victim somewhere else—if they can't catch him first, of course."

"That's good to hear. But you've still got to be really careful, you know."

"Of course."

Sophie gave her the check, and Kelsey produced a large bill and told Sophie to keep the change.

"That's really nice of you."

"Thanks. *You* were really nice. I might have felt like a real idiot, sitting here by myself, but talking to you helped."

"Come back sometime."

"I might. I swear I'm not a reporter or a cop, but I might ask you more about Cherie sometime, if you don't mind."

"Why?"

"I have a friend who is missing."

"A dancer?"

"No, but...well, it's complicated. I'll explain sometime."

"Sure, and thanks again."

Sophie started to walk away. Kelsey rose and stopped her quickly. "Sophie, that door back there...where does it lead?"

"Back there? That's where the guys go to get private lap dances."

Sophie smiled and moved on. Patrons were calling her again.

Kelsey made her way out of the club, then hesitated just outside the door. One of the floodlights that had illuminated the parking lot had evidently burned out. The lot suddenly seemed very dark, and she was parked across the way, under the trees.

As she stood there, the door opened behind her. She almost jumped. It was just a couple, leaving for the night. They gave Kelsey a friendly smile and moved past her.

She sprang into action herself, moving quickly across the parking lot.

Shadows seemed to lurk everywhere.

The couple's car was close to the door. Kelsey's was not. They got into their car. She kept walking.

A shadow loomed, looking high and tall. She thought it was a man, then realized it was just one of the trees separating the parking lot from the gas station beyond.

She exhaled a sigh of relief and purposely slowed her footsteps, since she could hear the thumping of her heart. She didn't know why she was suddenly so scared. There was no real reason, except that it was night.

*And a girl had left here one night, never to return. Her decomposed body had been found floating in a canal.*

She heard laughter and spun around.

Just another couple leaving.

She kept walking, her pace quickening once again. Then, like Lot's wife, she found herself turning back.

The entry to the club was in deep shadow, the bouncer nowhere in sight. There was definitely the shadow of a man this time.

And he was watching her. As he moved from the doorway to the parking lot, she was certain he was looking directly at her. Without the floodlight, she couldn't see his face, couldn't tell anything about him. Except that he was tall, his build formidable.

Even at a distance, she heard his footsteps in the otherwise silent parking lot. Sharp, fast, coming her way.

Her keys were out. She clicked the button to unlock her car and moved briskly toward it. The footsteps kept coming. She quickened her pace. Behind her, the footsteps quickened, as well.

Kelsey began to run.

She reached her car door and threw it open, sliding into the driver's seat. She reached for the door handle to slam the car shut.

But a hand fell on the frame of the door, stopping her.

"Not so fast!"

Kelsey opened her mouth to let out an earsplitting scream.

Nate Curry looked down the length of the bar, saw that everyone seemed to have a full glass and gave a little nod of satisfaction. He'd brought on a new kid, a college junior from the

University of Miami, so he wouldn't have to feel so wed to the place himself. Since he'd been joining his friends tonight, he hadn't planned on working at all, but hell, being here, he had to kick in. Especially since he was down one employee, after uncovering the thefts. But the new kid, Bill Edgeham, seemed to have everything under control. The Saturday night band was playing as usual, conch fritters and chowder were being served right and left, the tables were filled, and the bar was busy. A good Saturday night—even if the gang had all departed long before he had thought they would. Kelsey and Cindy usually loved to dance. And it was fun to party with the old crowd. Fun...and, of course, intriguing as all hell.

He still felt uneasy. He wished Kelsey hadn't left so quickly. And he wished that she'd gone straight home, which he knew she hadn't. Larry had called earlier to say she hadn't returned to the duplex, wondering if Nate knew where she was. He was worried about her; she was so determined to delve where she shouldn't in her attempt to find Sheila.

At the end of the bar, he picked up the phone and called the duplex.

Larry picked up. "Have you heard from Kelsey yet?" Nate asked, trying not to sound too anxious.

"Yeah, I talked to her."

"Well, where the hell is she?"

"At some club. I don't know what she's doing. She sounded strange, kept calling me sweetheart, and said something about me being built like Conan the Barbarian."

Nate frowned. "You?"

"Hey, I resent that. I'm in good shape."

"Yeah, but hardly Mr. Universe."

"Don't go sounding jealous on me. She didn't mean anything by it. She said she was at a club. She was probably just talking like that to keep the sharks away, though what the hell she was doing in a club to begin with if she was avoiding sharks, I don't know."

"But she was all right?"

"She said she was fine, and that she'd call me if she had any problem."

Nate couldn't help feeling a little rise of resentment, even though he'd barely been married to Kelsey for a month, and that many years ago now. She'd cried rivers when she'd broken it off with him, sorry that she had used him as solace the way she had, begging him to forgive her. She'd sworn that she would always love him—as a friend.

He wound the phone cord around his fingers. Kelsey and Sheila. As different as night and day. Kelsey, who felt she'd sinned the minute she was with him, because she had to admit both to herself and to him that she didn't love him.

Sheila, who was generous to a fault. Heedless of anything she did with a guy, whether she loved him or not.

And here he was, feeling a rush of heat to his face and a burn of anger in his soul because Kelsey had said that she would call Larry if she needed anything. Well, what the hell. He and Kelsey had hardly been married. Kelsey and Larry worked together.

*But I'm closer to you, Kelsey. Closer in your heart. And I know you. Even if you've forgotten the time when we were close. I remember. I'm the one you should depend on.*

"Nate, you there?" Larry asked.

"Yeah, sorry. Well, I was just worried. But since you've talked to her and know that she's okay, then I'll quit worrying."

"I never said she was okay. She's got me worried. She's obsessed with finding Sheila." Larry's sigh came through loud and clear. "She just hasn't gotten it yet, that Sheila will show up when she's ready."

Nate felt a prickling at his nape. "Yeah, sure."

"If Kelsey doesn't get back soon, I'll call you."

"You're going to stay up?"

"Sure. I've got work here with me. I can always stay up."

"All right. See ya. And tell Kelsey to give me a call in the morning. Unless you don't hear from her. Then call me, because I'll be worried."

"Of course."

Nate hung up and turned just in time to see Andy Latham, his eyes wild, standing on the other side of the bar.

"Latham, I told you, you can't come here anymore. The women complain."

Latham shot out a fist, catching Nate hard in the jaw before he could duck.


"Damn!"

Dane swore as he clamped his hand over Kelsey's mouth. He looked around the parking lot. No one was anywhere near them, and the music blaring from the club would drown out pretty much anything, anyway.

Cars were going by on US1, but not one of them had even slowed.

"What the hell are you trying to do, get me arrested?" he asked Kelsey angrily.

She caught his fingers, drawing his hand from her mouth. Her blue-green eyes met his with a narrowed anger. "What the hell are *you* trying to do, give me a heart attack?"

"I followed you out to your car. Hell, you saw me. You turned around and looked right at me."

"I saw *someone.* I didn't know it was you. Why the hell were you following me like that?" she demanded.

"That's not the question of the hour," he told her, voice harsher than he had intended. It was disturbing, though, to realize how easily he had been able to accost her.

And the way that she had screamed...without anyone noticing at all.

"Why were *you* following *me?*" he demanded, his words sharp.

She stared at him where he leaned against the open car door.

"What makes you think I was following you?" she asked.

"How about the fact that you jumped up the minute I left dinner, and then you followed me."

"Maybe not. Maybe I just decided to check this place out on the same night you did." She didn't intend to admit a thing.

"Kelsey, you suck as a liar."

"Say that I actually *did* follow you. Maybe my reasons were entirely innocent."

Dane felt himself growing impatient. "Entirely innocent? Right. You followed a man to a strip club. What were your innocent reasons? You decided to get your jollies by watching me get a lap dance?"

Kelsey looked away from him, hating the flush that filled her cheeks. "Don't be ridiculous."

"Then what do you think you were doing?"

"Trying to figure out what *you* were doing."

"Stuffing money into G-strings. That was obvious, I'm certain. But then I know I don't have to tell you anything, because you were watching me from the minute you walked into the club."

She looked startled. "You didn't see me. I was in the—"

"Kelsey, I knew you were following me all the way north, and I saw you the minute you tried to walk in without paying."

"I didn't know you had to pay!"

"Kelsey, I don't know what the hell to do with you. I've told you often enough that you have to trust me. All you do is get yourself into trouble. So far, you've had a confrontation with Latham, and you've gotten me into a fight with Izzy Garcia. One would think you would have gone home tonight. Will you please listen to me now? I want to find Sheila just as much as you do. More. Dammit, Kelsey, let me handle it."

She looked straight ahead again. "I can see how you were handling it."

"Did it bother you?" he inquired, amazed that he could feel amused.

"Your sex life is your own concern."

"I don't know, Kelsey. You're looking like a disapproving schoolmarm at the moment."

"I don't give a damn if you fu—" She cut herself off, fell silent, then said, "I'm just not real sure that your current...techniques will do anything to help in your investigation."

"Kelsey, this *is* a strip club."

"A strip club where a murder victim worked," Kelsey said.

Dane exhaled a long breath, shaking his head. "Isn't that the point? I'm here, therefore you don't have to be."

"I do have to be," she said stubbornly. "You're following the tracks of a murderer known as the Necktie Strangler." She looked at him then with a certain naked anguish in her eyes. "You think that Sheila is dead, don't you?"

He was silent for a long time. Then he told her, "Move over."

"Move over? You don't need to ride with me. Your Jeep is here."

"Yeah, and we'll just leave it here for now. I don't particularly like the idea of you riding back down to Key Largo alone."

"Dane, I drive alone all the time. I'm a career woman, living alone in Miami, a fairly street smart kid."

"It's almost an hour's drive back. Move over."

"You know, I don't have to go back to Key Largo tonight. My condo is fifteen minutes away, just down US1, on Brickell. I'll be fine."

He straightened and quickly walked around to the passenger side, then opened the door and sat before she could think to lock him out.

"Go. I'm just dying to see your condo."

"You're not going to stay at my condo. Certainly not tonight," she told him.

There she was, he thought. The imperious Kelsey.

"I touched a stripper? Does that make me diseased?"

"You didn't need to touch a stripper to be an unwanted houseguest, Dane," she said flatly.

"You want to talk, Kelsey? Get to the bottom of some things? Then drive."

She stared stubbornly at the windshield, jaw clenched. He was sure she was mulling over the possibility of dragging him out of her car.

Evidently she thought better of it.

She twisted her key in the ignition. The car roared to life.

"I hope they tow your Jeep," she said.

"Oh, I doubt it. The club stays open until 5:00 a.m., and by then the coffee shop is open, so there's no reason why there shouldn't be a car parked in the lot."

"Sounds like you know the place well," she said, eyes on the road as she pulled out on to the highway.

"Well enough."

"I see."

"Just drive, Kelsey."

# CHAPTER 10

It felt strange, having Dane come into her condominium with her, Kelsey thought. He always seemed to be observing everything, dark eyes watching as she flashed her pass to the guard on duty at the gate, looking over the parking beneath the building, noting the security cameras in the lobby as they walked to the elevators.

He didn't speak, and neither did she, as they rode to the fifteenth floor. He gave his attention to the hallway again as they left the elevator and walked to her unit.

"How many apartments on each floor?" he asked.

"Four. There are actually four towers," she told him, opening her front door. "Four apartments on each of sixteen floors per tower. In the center of the building, there's a rec room, and out back, a pool."

He followed her into the condo. She turned on the lights, wondering why it felt so odd to have Dane here.

Because, she decided, this was *her* life now. Her life in which she had moved forward. It wasn't part of the past.

The past was what should bother her. But it had been comfortable, being back at Hurricane Bay, though maybe it had been comfortable in a bad way. She had experienced a proprietary feeling at Hurricane Bay that she never should have felt. The place was his. Just because she had been welcome all the time as a child, that didn't give her any right to feel as if she were home when she was there.

She stood in the hallway, waiting as he surveyed the entry, living room and kitchen. He walked to the large plate-glass window and looked out on the bay.

"Nice view."

"Yes."

"Small rooms."

She shrugged. "It's an expensive area. This is what I could afford. I took it because I do like the view."

He stared out the window for a moment, then turned to her. "Aren't you going to offer me something?"

"You want a drink?"

He laughed. "You sound as if you've joined the Temperance League. No, I don't mean a drink. Coffee or tea would be nice."

She walked into the kitchen and opened the refrigerator. "Regular, flavored or decaf?"

"Regular."

He remained by the window, just staring out, as she measured coffee and poured water. While the coffee brewed, she came around the counter, leaned against the wall and watched him.

"Well?"

"Well what?"

"We're here so you can tell me why you're trying to track Sheila down at a strip club," she reminded him.

He turned and looked at her, studying her in silence for a minute. "Kelsey, I keep telling you to stay out of this. And I mean it. You're dangerous to yourself and everyone else. But I have the feeling there's something you're not telling me. That you have an insight into the whole thing that I'm missing. From just about the minute you showed up, you were on *my* tail over Sheila's disappearance. *Mine.*"

"That's not fair. You're the one who followed me over to Latham's, and you were the one who went ballistic when I went to Izzy's boat to question him about Sheila."

"That was *after* you stormed after me. I was first. Why?"

She shrugged. "Come on, Dane. You know the reason. I got in, there was no Sheila. Cindy hadn't seen her since she'd been at Nate's place. Cindy suggested that I talk to you. She said you and Sheila had been talking at Nate's. She was convinced you two were doing a lot more than talking. And she was right." He didn't argue with her; just kept standing by the plate-glass window, watching her. "Cindy told me that you'd been different since you got back. Bitter in a way she'd never seen you before. And prone to, well, like the song says, wasting away in Margaritaville."

"There's more to it than that," he told her. "Unless you've really been carrying a grudge all these years. Andy Latham is downright slimy and scary, but you immediately decided to come after me, forgetting all about him until later that day. And Izzy is a pure sleaze, but you only decided that you just had to go talk to him today."

She was startled by his words, which were spoken dispassionately, as if he wasn't judging her, wasn't feeling offended.

"Don't be ridiculous," she said. "You were the last one seen with Sheila, that's all."

"That can't be all," he said, shaking his head, dark eyes on her intently, giving her the impression that she was a book being read. "When you were making plans to meet Sheila, she must have said something to you, implied something. And anything she said could be important now."

"She never said she was going to strip clubs, if that's what you mean."

Her comment didn't perturb him in the least. "So what did she say?"

"You mean...after she e-mailed me the first time?"

"Of course." His eyes narrowed suspiciously. "Did she write something else?"

"No," she lied.

He didn't know about the diary. But the diary hadn't really given her anything yet.

"Dammit, Kelsey, give me something to go on here."

"Why were you in that strip club?"

He stared at her for a long time. "Because I *am* trying to track down the Necktie Strangler. I didn't go in the back for a lap dance, Kelsey. I was showing the girls pictures of people."

"People? Who?"

"Andy Latham, Izzy Garcia..."

"And?"

"The cowgirl was good friends with the murdered girl. She's going to study the photos I gave her and see if she can remember anyone."

"She couldn't tell you now?"

"She wasn't sure. She wanted to take time to look at all the faces. And I couldn't stay."

"Why?"

"You were leaving."

"I was only going to drive home."

"Yeah, sure."

"Where did you think I was going?"

"God knows. After your visit to Izzy, nothing would surprise me. Kelsey, will you please tell me about Sheila? What she said on the phone or in her e-mail. Anything that might help."

Kelsey hesitated, then shrugged. "I heard from her for the first time in ages when she e-mailed me after renting the other half of the duplex where Cindy was living. She said that being back as a permanent resident was strange. You were different and distant. One time she'd write that you needed help, the next time she'd write that *she* needed help. She was chatty about Nate and

Cindy, and she wrote about Jorge and Izzy, as well. She admitted to drinking quite a bit, and I think—well, now I know—she was doing drugs, as well." Kelsey paused for a minute. "She wrote that she was having some strange problems, but that she didn't want to go into them. That her past was catching up with her. She said she really needed to see me. And that was why I decided to come down and spend a week with her."

"And that's it? That's why you were all over *me* first thing?"

Kelsey stared at him for a long moment. His dark eyes never wavered in their intense perusal of her.

"No."

"Then what?"

"She said that she needed to talk to you. Really talk to you. Because she was nervous."

"If she was nervous about something, and the something was me, why would it be me she wanted to talk to?" he demanded.

Kelsey threw up her hands. "I don't know. But everything led to you. Her e-mails led to you, Cindy and Nate both told me about Sheila being with you at the bar, then going off after you. And that's the last time anyone saw her. And you admit to having a relationship with her."

"It wasn't a *relationship*," he murmured, looking away from her for a moment and staring out at the lights of the city again.

"Okay, so you slept with her."

"Once. And she couldn't have written to you about that, because that was the last time I saw her. And I told you how it happened."

She threw up her hands. "It's just that Sheila always implied something about you. And your name came up first with everyone. That's it. Really," she said.

Dane never seemed to give anything away in his voice, or with his eyes, his face. Yet she thought he looked relieved.

"So you aren't still bearing a grudge?"

She lowered her eyes. "We were one night, ages ago, in another lifetime."

"Yeah, well, we're feeling the same thing now."

"Oh? What?"

"That we both failed Sheila. But I'm begging you, Kelsey—please be careful. Don't follow me to strip clubs. Don't go to Latham's. Or to Izzy Garcia's. Give me a chance. Believe in me."

She watched him for a long moment. "Dammit it, Dane, I want to. But I want to know...things."

"Such as?"

"To start with, I want to know what happened in St. Augustine."

For a moment Kelsey thought he was going to remain silent, rejecting the question as totally irrelevant, but then he shrugged. "You really want to know? Right now?"

"You want me to trust you. To believe you really want to find Sheila. So let's start with what happened in St. Augustine." She was silent for a moment, then added, "Please. I'd really like to know."

"I'm not sure what you've heard," he said.

"Nothing, really. I suppose I was so determined to find Sheila that I didn't ask many questions. I know that something went wrong." She hesitated. "And that one of your clients was killed."

"Yes, a woman was killed. And she was more than a client," he said.

Kelsey thought he was going to end it there, he paused for so long.

"You'd been in St. Augustine for a while, right?" she asked, prodding despite the fact that he might turn around and inform her curtly that it really wasn't any of her business. He was silent again for a minute, then seemed to decide it didn't make any difference. He was still wary of her, and probably with good reason. It was true—she had gone after him, when she had first seen him at Nate's, as if he were the most detestable being alive, something she hadn't quite understood herself.

Or maybe she did. Better to go in attacking than be dismissed as an annoyance from the past. No, that wasn't quite it. Better to go in attacking than wonder how you could still want someone after so many years, still care so deeply when there had been so much so wrong.

"Right," he said, eyes on her as if he could see the soul beneath the flesh. "You really want the whole story?"

"I do."

"All right. I had been working up there for a couple of years. Nice life. I liked it. The ocean was still at my fingertips, but it wasn't Key Largo. And...I just didn't want to go back to Key Largo."

Kelsey understood what he meant.

"I'd heard you were up there," she murmured. She suddenly felt warm and uncomfortable, remembering the morning when he'd left. Three days after her brother's funeral. She hadn't seen him off at the small airport. She'd fled his house as if all the demons of hell had been after her. She could remember hearing his voice, calling her name. And she could remember seeing him standing at the top of his driveway, a towel around his hips, watching as she gunned her car and drove away.

He'd flown back to his base, and a week later, he'd been back overseas. His father had been dead by then, and Joe was gone, as well. He'd never called or written. The way he was watching her now, she knew they were both remembering that time.

"I knew the minute I went back after my leave that I wasn't going to become career military like my father. And St. Augustine seemed pleasantly tame after I'd gotten out of the service. Not that I hadn't opted for the kind of work I was doing in the Middle East and Eastern Europe. Joe loved to fly, and he was good, really good. I loved to filter into a different society and find out about the way people thought, and why, how they were likely to react to a situation. I liked the prospect that I could save lives by finding out about terrorist activities or ethnic purges before they could take place. My knowledge of a number of languages was useful, and with my strange coloring—both so dark and so light—it wasn't easy for anyone to figure out my ethnic background. I was young, and despite some of the horrors I had seen, I still believed in my own immortality. After Joe died, though, things just changed. I wasn't so sure that I was anything more than a grain of sand on an endless beach. I wasn't as sharp as I had been, and twice, I almost got myself killed. I had some money, so I found an agency in Key Largo to see to the maintenance of Hurricane Bay so I could wander around a while. Finally I knew I still wanted to live in Florida. Not too far south. Not too close to home. St. Augustine had history and a certain charm. The city was small, but not too small. It was on the water, but far from Hurricane Bay. Joe was gone, my father was gone, God knew what steps Sheila was taking to get where she wanted to go...and you had run."

"I hadn't really run. Not at that point. I went away to college," she said.

Dane shook his head. "No. You had already run. You were running the morning I last saw you. So there was no point in going home. Oh, Larry was coming and going, Cindy was around, and Nate was entrenched at the Sea Shanty, but I knew there was something of the past that we could never recapture, and I didn't want to look back. I toyed with the idea of hiring on at a police department in the north of the state, but after my years in the military, I wasn't ready to start taking orders again. So I got my license and opened an investigation firm. Which was tedious at times."

"From what I understand, very tedious," Kelsey said. "Hours and hours of just sitting around, watching people."

"Sometimes, yes. But I was my own boss, so I could take on the cases that interested me. Still, a lot of the work I took on was small stuff. I wasn't going to save the world with what I did, but I had to find a niche in the civilian world, which isn't always easy when your training has equipped you to infiltrate and—" He hesitated, looking at her again. "And kill people. Anyway, I was good at what I did, so I started gaining a certain respect in the area. I took a lot of cases in Jacksonville. Bigger cases, more interesting cases. A few with some really high profile companies.

Sabotage, fraud. I had a small but decent place on the water, a dock for the Donzi...a good enough lifestyle in the off-hours, and plenty of work to make me feel useful, and worthy of the fairly exorbitant fees I charge. Then I met Kathy Nottingham."

"The woman who died," Kelsey murmured.

"The first time she came into the office, she was very nervous. She walked in, a beautiful young woman in dark glasses. She didn't have a deep mystery about her, though—she just wanted a standard service, information about her husband. I told her that I wasn't working domestic cases anymore. But then, when she finally took off the glasses, I saw the shiner she'd been given. She said she was clumsy, tripped, some excuse. The usual. She wanted to have her husband followed. She knew that he was seeing other women and she didn't care, she just wanted out, but he didn't intend to let her go. She had to find a way to force his hand. I tried to tell her again that I wasn't taking that kind of case, but there was something about her...I told her I knew she was lying, that she didn't need a P.I., she needed the police. But she was afraid that if she called the police, her husband would kill her. She said she had heard that I was discreet. She thought that if she had enough against her husband, she could get a divorce and custody of her children. I agreed to help her, if she'd get help herself. Anyway, to make a long story short, I couldn't budge her that day. She said that as long as he thought she'd be his good little wife at home, he'd shove her around a little but keep up with the life he was living. She had to operate in secret until she had enough to really get away.

"I started feeling really sorry for her. She'd been a poor kid who'd gotten married right out of high school to an older guy with an income. She'd gotten pregnant right away. And right away, he'd gotten angry when the dishes weren't set out on the table properly, when a piece of dirty clothing was left for a minute in the bathroom, when she wasn't perfect. At first he only yelled. Then he started pushing her around. Dragging her over to point out where a vase was off center or a glass had been left. She was so frightened that day that I finally swore I wouldn't give her away to anyone, and that I would help her. So I started to follow her husband. I got pictures and video of him in compromising situations. And when I'd see Kathy again, she'd be wearing more bruises.

"Finally I got really angry. I was afraid I was just going to go up to the guy and belt him in the jaw—which wouldn't have helped her. I told her I couldn't help her anymore if she didn't get out, and I convinced her that no one should live with such abuse. She took her two little girls and left him, and headed straight into a shelter. Her husband realized how badly it could go against him when the first thing we did was get a restraining order against him. He sent his lawyer to give her anything she wanted. She was kinder and fairer than he deserved. She said it wasn't for him but for their children—she didn't want the girls to lose their father. Every kid had a right to love their parents—both of them. She was still afraid, but she went through with the divorce. I was with her in court, and afterward, I told him that if he ever touched her again, I'd kill him. He seemed to believe the threat. He acted as if he was ashamed, and just grateful that she was still going to let him see the kids. She got the house, custody, and he got a weekend with his daughters once a month. He wasn't allowed to go inside the house. He was to pick up the girls outside and return them outside. On the street, in full view of neighbors and passersby. Time went by, months, and she seemed to blossom like a rose. She got a job as a hostess at a restaurant. She was happy."

"And you two started seeing each other," Kelsey said.

"Right. She loved the water, boats...a day in the sun. Just existing, without being afraid. I enjoyed her company. She was so alive, intrigued by every little thing she hadn't experienced before."

"And then...?"

"Then one day he went to pick up the kids. And he ran her

right into the garage door. She was pronounced dead on the way to the hospital."

"My God, I'm so sorry," Kelsey said. Silence stretched between them. "He was arrested, right? He went to trial?"

"Oh yeah. He went to trial. The police had him before I could get my hands on him. I was so livid, I could have gone up for murder myself." He stopped and looked at Kelsey, a certain mistrust in his dark eyes again, along with a flat honesty. "He got out on bail, and I ran into him at a club and wound up in jail for a night. I might have killed him if I hadn't been stopped. When he went to trial, he got off with manslaughter. He convinced a jury that it had been a terrible accident, that he had thought he had his car in Reverse...anyway, he'll be out in a few years."

"Dane, that's horrible, and I'm so sorry, but how was it your fault?"

He sat, still staring out at the water. "I should have seen that the danger was still there, that he was homicidal, and that he wasn't really going to let her get away. There I was, a guy with his own P.I. agency, ex-military, and in the end, I couldn't do a damn thing to protect her. And the bastard got away with it."

Kelsey shook her head. "It's not your fault. No one can guard another human being every minute of the day. She decided he had the right to see his children. Because of that, he managed to kill her. What could you have done?"

"I could have—should have—seen just how deadly he could be. Most of the time, men who beat their wives are cowards who fold as soon as someone strikes back. He played the part. He was remorseful. He was ashamed. He said he knew he needed help. He was polite and followed the rules set up by the court. Kathy even believed that in time he might marry again and be decent to another woman. But all the while, he was just being devious and cunning, waiting for his opportunity. And when it came, he seized it, but because he'd been clever and played his part well, he got away with a vicious, premeditated murder."

"No one can really read another human being," Kelsey said.

"Yeah? Well, I should have been able to. So you were right. Bottom line, I fucked up big time in St. Augustine and came back to waste away in self-remorse. I just really didn't give a damn. I would have been happy to drink the hours away. It wasn't a sense of decency that made me open up an agency down here— sheer tedium did it. I couldn't drink enough to make the day any shorter. Then, after a while, I guess I became alcoholed out. And I didn't want to piss away everything my father had done. Cindy is a good kid, Nate's place is pleasant... I started thinking living down here again wasn't so bad. Then Sheila came around again. Seeing the way she was living should have scared the hell out of me. I found myself being disgusted and angry instead. I lectured her. But not enough. I slept with her. I shouldn't have. She'd asked me for a 'mercy fuck.' It was so wrong in so many ways. At the time I was still wallowing, but living and breathing. And now, according to all accounts, I was the last person around here to have seen her...to have seen her."

Kelsey wondered at his strange hesitation. It was as if he had been about to say *I was the last person around here to have seen her alive.*

"Except that I wasn't," he said flatly. Then he stared at her, impatient and angry. "The point is, I've screwed things up with Sheila, too, so you don't have to hound me every step of the way and put yourself in jeopardy. I intend to find out what happened to her, and I don't need your money or your pressure to do it. In the meantime, though, I want you to stay the hell out of it. Do you understand?"

His sudden about-face took her off guard. "You seem convinced she ran into the Necktie Strangler," Kelsey said, her voice rigid. "A guy who kills strippers and prostitutes. I'm neither."

"Sheila didn't actually fit the description, either."

"She was running around, living the wild life," Kelsey said.

"And you're running in her footsteps."

"So let me run with you."

"No. Not on your life. You should go back to work. Hell, if Sheila *is* in a canal somewhere, she might not be found for years. Jesus Christ, they're always dragging out someone who's been under water for years...decades, even. Kelsey, have you gone daft? The cops might not be able to solve this thing. Sometimes serial killers are caught, and sometimes they're not. Do me a big goddamned favor and don't make me feel responsible for your death, too."

So much for any closeness that might have sprung up between them. Kelsey rose abruptly. "Let's go. I'll drive you back to your car."

"No."

"Who's daft now? This is my place, and I don't want you here. I'll drive you back to your car, or you can take a taxi."

He looked up at her, dark eyes hostile, face set. "What are you going to do, Kelsey? Throw me out?"

"That's exactly what I'm doing."

"I'm not going. You'll have to call the cops."

The challenge in his eyes was so great that she was tempted to do it, just to drag him down a peg. But she wasn't going to, and she knew it.

She walked away from him, going to the hall closet. She dragged out a pillow and sheets and went back to throw them at him where he remained stubbornly seated.

She didn't say a word to him, just turned again and retreated to her bedroom. She slammed the door and locked it. Childish. And pathetic. He wasn't coming after her.

She was both wired and tired as hell. Determined that she was going to salvage a few hours' sleep, she decided that she was going to pretend he wasn't on her couch. Mechanically she went through the steps to prepare for bed, brushing her teeth with such determination she was lucky she didn't rub her gums raw, then standing beneath what must have been the hottest shower endurable by man. She dressed in her most comfortable, threadbare cotton nightshirt, turned off the lights and crawled beneath the covers.

Her eyes remained open and fixed on the darkness.

The events since Sheila had failed to appear at the duplex ran like a broken tape through her mind. *Dane had opened up to her tonight. A lot. Not enough. He had not been pleased to find them at his house yesterday. He thought Sheila had been a victim of the Necktie Strangler. Why? Why think that, just because she had disappeared? Yes, Sheila had been running wild. Yes, she had been seeing Izzy Garcia. A lot. But Dane was the one she'd been with last. Izzy had had Sheila's purse on his boat, but she hadn't told Dane. Why not? Dane was still holding something back from her.*

*He'd gone to the strip club. She'd followed him. Home had held nothing for him, no reason to come back to Key Largo. She had run...run from the very beginning. Sheila had gone to him. Necktie Strangler. He had failed someone he had loved. Wasn't going to fail again. Didn't need her or her money. He wanted her out of it. Sheila had been seeing so many people. They all admitted it. Larry had said that every man at the table had slept with his ex-wife. No denials.*

*Nate had never told her about being with Sheila. Maybe he had been too embarrassed, too polite, or maybe just too macho at heart to say he hadn't had what every other man there had had.*

*She'd been with Dane last. There had been something there. Sheila had gone to him...because after all these years, the good, the bad, the friendship, there had always been that* thing *about Dane that made him seem strong and compelling and sexual. A thing that compelled and drew...*

*Kelsey had run. He had run. They had all run. Just like a first-grade reader. Run...run...run. Because Joe had died. Because she shouldn't have needed to be held so badly. She shouldn't have found something so strong that it had swept the pain away. She shouldn't have been with a man who had once been Sheila's.*

*Sheila was gone.... Necktie Strangler, strip clubs, bars, drugs, she could have been into anything. He had been the last one to see her....*

Kelsey kept staring into the darkness.

When she finally rose, it wasn't with a real plan. But she got out of bed and opened the door. Tea, a drink, something to make her sleep.

She walked back out to the living room.

It was dark, only the dim lights of the city drifting softly in. The sheets were on the couch. He was stretched out, one below him, one on top of him. His chest was bare. His clothing lay on the coffee table.

Sleeping? She couldn't see his eyes without approaching him.

She veered from her path to the kitchen. She stood over him. His fingers were laced behind his head, and he was watching her.

"What?" he asked curtly.

"I just...wanted to see if you were sleeping."

"You've seen."

She nodded.

She was startled, but she didn't jump back when he suddenly swung into a sitting position with a silent speed like lightning. He reached up and caught her wrist.

"What do you want, Kelsey?"

She could feel the pulse beating in the vein in her throat. Breath coming too fast. Blood on fire, racing through her veins.

She hadn't come out for tea.

She felt the heat in his fingers where they wrapped around her wrist. She didn't need light to visualize his hands. Large. Callused. Bronzed. Fingers long, nails clipped short. Blunt, no-nonsense hands. Time had never changed the way they felt against flesh.

She had never been able to read people, but she felt something hot and hostile flowing from his touch. She ignored the hostile. And felt the hot. Ignored whatever might be in the midnight darkness of his gaze, both brooding and sharp upon her, despite the shadows in which she stood.

"What, Kelsey?"

"Well, hell," she drawled out. "I couldn't sleep. I thought I'd see about a mercy fuck myself."

"That isn't you, Kelsey. The words don't even fit your mouth."

Burning with humiliation, she tried to wrench her hand free. She didn't succeed, but found herself drawn down on his sheet-covered lap, feeling the warm heat of his breath against her cheek, aware that he was naked beneath the sheet.

"I didn't say I wouldn't oblige," he told her.

# CHAPTER II

To say that Kelsey—stone-cold sober and asking for sex—was far more than he'd ever imagined would have been a serious understatement. To say that the simple fact of Kelsey being on his lap was pure and instant arousal would be an even greater one. Everything in him went rigid, and he knew he sounded like a Doberman when he added, "On one condition."

One condition. Christ, he was giving her conditions.

"Condition?" she said. A whisper. Soft as the air, smooth as silk, one word sending the blood coursing roughly through him. Kelsey's magnificent backside on his thigh, her breath teasing his lips, warmth enough to jump-start a generator. Man, was he a liar.

"You're not going to run out at dawn."

"Where would I run? It's my apartment."

"You'd find a place. But you won't. I like to wake up next to a woman."

She blinked. "Did you wake up next to Sheila?"

"No. And did I hurt her in any way? No. But you know that, or you wouldn't be here. And I don't want to hear her name again. Not now." He threaded his fingers into her hair, drawing her face down to his before either of them could ruin it with any more words. Her lips parted instantly under his, her mouth sweet and deep with the seduction of liquid honey. He had a million intentions. A seduction so damned good she would never forget it. But when she shifted in his arms, her fingers running into his hair, cradling his head, the sheet fell away.

The soft cotton of her nightshirt rode up.

She wasn't wearing anything beneath.

He shoved his hands beneath the fabric while his mouth remained locked onto hers, tongue creating ravishment, deep, wet, molten. His fingers ran over her torso, settled beneath the firm fullness of her breasts, ran over the circumference, caressing, exploring. Her nipples were as taut and hard as marbles, and a breath seemed to escape from her mouth into his as he touched her. She shimmied convulsively against him, and he brought his hands down the length of her back to her buttocks, marveling at the feel of her flesh and the round tension of muscle beneath. He shifted her until she was straddling him right where he sat, lifting her just enough to bring her back down on the instant erection she had so effortlessly created. Their kiss broke and she gasped, head tossed back as her body gloved his sex, wet and giving as he brought her slowly down until he was fully inside her. She shuddered against him, head falling against his shoulder for a moment as he let her adapt to the invasion. Then his hands were on her hips and he was moving her, she was moving herself, and they were desperately bucking together like a pair of kids stealing time in the old man's Chevy. There wasn't a lot of time to think, to really rue the fact that he'd been far less than a slow and sensual lover. The eroticism of her flesh against his and the near rabid pulse of their movement were like a spiral to a carnal heaven. The sound of their breathing, the staccato beating of their hearts, seemed like a driving thunder. Her fingers dug into his shoulders, nails pressing his flesh. He managed to wrench the nightshirt over her head and toss it into a corner of the room without missing a beat. Her breasts fell against his face. His tongue moved over them as she rose and fell. His lips latched around one pebbled nipple and aureola, suckling, evoking a soft gasping cry on the wind they'd created. He felt himself bottling up desperately. Prayed for an iota of control. Moved her harder, faster. Listened to the sweet beat of their bodies, damp and writhing, sliding against each other. He couldn't take it. His arms wound around her. He ground her down against him, teeth gritting as he prayed. He heard the expulsion of her breath, felt the tension drain out of her, her body suddenly seeming to collapse against his. He thanked God. In a split second, he let himself go. His body constricted and erupted in climax, held and released, and he pulled her even more tightly against him, wet and pliant as he pulsed and withered within.

Her head rested against him. They were both sheened with sweat, wet and hot and cooling. She didn't move at all but remained on top of him, hair damp and streaming over his chest, tickling his nose.

"You're not running," he said softly after a moment, smoothing her hair but otherwise remaining still, glad to have her remain so intimately against him.

"I don't think I can move," she murmured against his chest.

They lay content for several seconds. Dane was dimly aware of a muted sound.

And then, contrary to her words, she suddenly leaped to her feet and went running across the room to the dining area, dragging his sheet with her.

"What the hell...?"

"Cell phone," she said.

"Cell phone? Great," he muttered.

She had already reached the table where she had left her purse and was digging through it with one hand while draping the sheet around herself with the other.

"I have to answer it," she told him. "I forgot. Larry will be worried."

"Larry will be worried?" He didn't know why he was so irritated. He had no great claim to Kelsey's time or attention, and he had been less than the world's greatest lover in the last few minutes, though it had seemed like great sex nonetheless, so Larry's call was definitely unwelcome.

"Hello?" she said into the phone. "Yes, I'm fine."

He rose himself, grasping for the bottom sheet, and walked over to where she stood. "Is there a reason Larry gets to know where you are at night? Something going on there?"

She covered the little phone.

"Don't be ridiculous." Even in shadow, the look she gave him was scathing. "He was in love with Sheila forever, until this new girl finally came around."

She moved her hand. He could hear the crackle of words from the other end.

"No, no, it's all right. I'm in my condo in the city. We were at a club in Miami. We...Dane and I. It was really late, so we're going to drive back in the morning."

There was a pause as Larry spoke on the other end.

"I know it's really morning now. Larry, I'm sorry. I should have remembered to call you back. We're going to catch a few hours' sleep and be back." She listened again. "No! Is he all right?"

"What's going on?" Dane asked.

The phone crackled.

"Yes, it's Dane. He's awake, of course." She hesitated for a split second. "He was sleeping on the couch. He heard the phone, too."

Larry said something else.

"What's going on?" Dane repeated.

Kelsey told him. "Andy Latham went into the Sea Shanty and belted Nate in the jaw."

"What? Why?"

She waved a hand at him to indicate that she couldn't hear what Larry was saying. "Something about more fish," she said.

"More fish?" He reached for the phone. She surrendered it.

"Larry, what about the fish?"

"Dane?" Larry said from the other end. "Jeez, you two had me worried. I didn't really think too much about Sheila being gone, but when Kels said that she was at a club earlier, then never came back...I was sitting here like a worried parent. Then Nate calls, nursing his jaw, because old man Latham walked into the Sea Shanty, straight up to him, and belted him in the jaw. I wasn't there, but it caused quite an uproar. Latham is sobering up in jail, but he claimed it was because 'one of us snot-nosed kids' kept throwing dead fish on his property. Bizarre, huh?"

"Definitely."

"He's crazy as a coot," Larry said. "But they've got him cooling his heels right now, though they'll have to let him go in the morning."

"Tell him we're heading back right now," Kelsey urged at his side.

Dane looked at her in the shadows, then glanced to the plate-glass window, where darkness was beginning to ease into the softer, pastel tinted shades of day.

He wondered when he would next get the chance to see Kelsey standing next to him in a sheet.

"You know, there's really no reason."

"I'd feel better if we were back."

"I'd feel better if we just moved this into the bedroom."

The blood seemed to drain from her face, but she said, "I'm not running anywhere, Dane. I'd just feel better if we drove back now."

He still wondered when he would see her in a sheet again. And he wished he'd given her a hell of a lot more to remember.

"What?" Larry said from the cell.

"Nothing." Dane stared at Kelsey. "I was just saying she

should get some sleep, but Kelsey wants to get back, so we'll be there in a couple of hours."

"Hey, tell her as long as we all know she's all right..."

Kelsey was already heading for her bedroom. The sheet wasn't really wrapped around her all that well.

"I'm going to take a shower," she said.

She had her front covered just fine, but she undoubtedly didn't know that the long sleek line of her back was bare, and one buttock was exposed.

"Yeah, we'll see you soon," Dane said.

He didn't hear Larry's reply. He pushed the end button on the cell, tossed it back in Kelsey's purse and followed her.

He'd already proven he could be quick.

The water was already running; she stood beneath the spray. He joined her. The water sluiced down over the two of them as she gave him a reproachful look. "We've really got to get back."

"We will."

"Then..."

"Right after I lick you all over."

"We said we'd be right there."

"I'll lick quickly." He pulled her against him. Soaking wet, smooth as velvet. Kelsey was tall, but still several inches shorter than he was. Each part of her seemed to fit in a perfect place against him. He pressed his lips to her throat. Found the pulse. His hands slipped over the wetness of her breasts, down around her hips, between her legs.

"Dane..."

"Quickly...but thoroughly."

He picked her up, lifted her from the shower stall. He didn't bother with the water. It dripped from them as he carried her into her bedroom. They were still soaked when he brought her down on the designer sheets of her bed.

"We're wrecking the bed," she murmured.

"It will dry by the time you get back."

Wet, tasting faintly of soap, she was delicious. He'd promised "all over," so he went for it. Throat, belly, lips, long and lingeringly, inner thighs, dead between them, long and lingeringly again. So much for quickly. Kelsey forgot time. The pastels of morning were beating back the grays. She was bathed in soft golden yellows. He made a mental note of just how she looked, tanned against the softness of pale sheets, belly flat, legs wickedly long, breasts full, body writhing...words incoherent as they escaped her lips. He felt himself drown in her taste, musky on his tongue. When he sank completely into her at last, he'd aroused himself to a frenzy and time no longer mattered. She moved as only Kelsey could move. The world came down to the driving desire for release. Damp bed, Kelsey, wet flesh, sliding, rocking, friction, Kelsey, words, whispers, cries. Explosion...

But once again, he had barely eased his weight off her before she was shooting up.

"I'm going into the shower. Alone. For two seconds," she said. Pleading.

"Sure." He lay there as she left.

A moment later, she was out. He strolled into the shower himself.

Within ten minutes, they were on the road.

Two hours out, two hours in.

Aboard his main boat, *Free as the Sea,* Jorge Marti could see the night lights of the marina. He was almost back. The night was cool, touched by the ocean breeze, which had been heightened by the storms out on the Atlantic. Hurricane season. There was always a weather system sliding off the African coast. And if that wasn't enough, killer winds would form in the Gulf, slip off the Yucatán Peninsula, the islands or South America, and whip into something lethal right before they struck.

Then the winds would churn, making a beeline for the Florida coast, or maybe turning in a matter of seconds and heading straight toward the Carolinas.

Fishermen and charter captains always paid attention to the weather forecasts. They listened carefully and learned to make sane judgments. Of course, there were times—more often in the Keys than on the mainland—when evacuations were mandatory.

Tonight...

Tonight the forces of nature, far out over endless miles of water, simply made the ocean a thing of pure beauty. A gentle, deceptive softness kissed the air.

It was beautiful coming in. The very first edges of dawn were beginning to break. He had planned on beating the light. Maybe he would. His mantra kept running through his head.

Run slow...run slow...

The soft sound of his motor, just above an idle, still seemed as loud as a chorus of growls. Yet looking ahead, he could see that there was a stir of life on the dock. Fishermen began their day with the coming of light. But the activity seemed natural. People arriving...not so many, only the real fishermen. The lights were shining an iridescent yellow. Joe Palumbo, who kept his boats two berths down, was loading groceries onto the deck. Izzy Garcia's *Lady Havana,* farther down the way, was showing lights. Old man O'Connell, who was so wizened and brown no one could really estimate his age, was at work on the aft of his boat. Nothing unusual.

Two hours out...

Two hours in.

Dawn was still just a promise.

Jorge guided the boat carefully past all the buoys, keeping his wake down to nothing more than a ripple. He ran with his lights and speed conforming to all laws and regulations.

He came in close enough to see old man O'Connell's face. He looked up, waved. Jorge forced a smile, waved back.

He cut his motor.

He brought in the *Free as the Sea,* running from the helm to the rigging, securing her first with one tie, then leaping to the dock to bring her closer in before hopping back down to secure her completely.

He was standing on the dock, securing the last tie, when he felt a tap on his shoulder.

His blood ran cold, and he felt a sheen of sweat break out on his skin.

He turned. Izzy Garcia was standing there, staring at him.

"Izzy. Hey."

*"Estúpido,"* Izzy said softly, reverting to Spanish. "I will be blamed for what you are doing."

Jorge stiffened, staring at Izzy. The light was becoming more pronounced.

"I don't know what you're talking about."

"Yes you do."

"Izzy, you'll never be accused of my...crimes."

Izzy threw up his hands. "If I go aboard your boat now, I will find nothing there?"

"With what you do, you should get off my ass," Jorge said quietly.

"I say again, if I go aboard your boat, I will find nothing there?"

Jorge was in good shape. He worked hard, when he wasn't working, he went to the gym. Nor was he a coward.

But Izzy was honed like a razor blade.

Jorge was still tempted to smash him in the face, though it would accomplish nothing. He would wind up lying on the dock, bleeding like a freshly killed fish. An ambulance and the police would come for him.

Or the coroner's wagon.

And there was more to lose than his life.

"I have sometimes kept silent when I shouldn't have," Jorge reminded Izzy. "You owe me the same."

"You've kept silent?" Izzy sounded amused. "I have seen

things I shouldn't have seen. I have seen parcels go into the water...from your boat."

"I've seen what you discard into the water as well...from *your* boat."

"So we have both seen things go into the water. And how do we prove that now? But I play a game I know how to play. And you...well, you are all emotion and passion, and you will get caught. So you do what you must. But I tell you this. You get me in trouble with the law on anything, *amigo,* and I will kill you," Izzy told him. "Do you understand? I will not blink. I will kill you, and they will never find your body."

Over Izzy's shoulder, Jorge could see that the activity on the dock was growing. It was time for him to deliver his package. And Izzy was still threatening him, though naturally it appeared that they were doing nothing but having a friendly conversation.

"I will never get you in trouble."

"You remember that. Every second."

"I just said, I will never get you in trouble."

Izzy nodded. "All right. Just so long as you know. You do so, you are a dead man." He folded his hands together. Very powerful hands. He tightened them, as if showing Jorge just what he could do with them.

Jorge wished he had a gun. Bang, bang, you're dead. Then it wouldn't matter how tough and powerful Izzy thought he was.

Bang, bang...

Jorge allowed himself the luxury of watching Izzy fall limply to the dock in his mind's eye.

No guns. That would just destroy them both.

"I hear you, Izzy," Jorge said.

Izzy smiled again. A scary smile, and yet Jorge could see why women thought it had a certain dangerous appeal.

Loathing him, Jorge watched as his countryman walked away down the dock.

Pink light emerged in the sky, but the air remained touched by a distant storm.

The day was serene.

Jorge turned quickly back to his boat to complete his night run without further incident.

The ride was both too long and too short.

Intimacy could be very strange.

In the condo, it had been as if time had rushed away. Kelsey *knew* Dane, as she had known him years ago. Dressed, sitting next to him as he drove her car, she studied his face and realized anew how much time had passed. She didn't know him at all anymore. And yet, maybe it was time to speak out loud about her reasons for being so quick to think him capable of harming Sheila.

"Dane?"

"Yeah?" He was deep in thought.

"I think I came right after you because of what had happened...years ago."

He glanced her way. "You *think?*"

She instantly grew defensive. "Hey, excuse me, by your own admission you were the last one to see Sheila."

He shook his head. "You want to go way back? There was nothing wrong with what we did. Joe was your brother and my best friend. We were always close as kids, even when I was tight with Sheila, which I wasn't at the time. You came to me for comfort. We wound up in bed. I was fine with it, you weren't. Sheila and I weren't together, and you still felt as if you'd intruded on something private that was hers. Well, I *wasn't* hers. Hadn't been for some time. She was already moving in the direction she intended to go. She wanted a hell of a lot more than love from a man, though I don't think she even knew herself just what that was. The sad thing is, Sheila wouldn't have blinked before sleeping with someone you loved."

"It wasn't just Sheila," Kelsey told him. She shook her head. "My brother was dead. And there I was...enjoying life."

"Kelsey, as long as we are alive, we have to live. And that's all you were doing. Joe would have understood."

"It's all easy now, isn't it?" she murmured.

He shook his head firmly. "Nothing is easy now."

She was silent for a minute. "All right, you can tell me now that I was a fool when I ran away before, but look at what you just did. You came back to Hurricane Bay to waste your life. You said it yourself. You were only pretending to go through the motions of making a living."

He stared at her. "Maybe. Or maybe, whether I knew it or not, I came back to pick up the pieces of my life."

"You looked like a drunk that day."

"I have been a drunk."

"So...?"

"Kelsey, that night, with you, after Joe died, I found out that I want to survive. There's something about life...we want to live it. And while we have it, that's what we do—we live. I intend to make it past...all this."

She didn't have a chance to reply. They had pulled into the parking lot where he'd left his Jeep.

The coffee shop was already doing business, though it was slow and laid-back, on a Sunday morning.

"Sit tight," Dane told her, after he had left the driver's seat and she had taken it. "Please. Okay?"

She nodded.

He left her in the car, walked into the coffee shop, and returned within minutes with two cups of coffee and the morning paper.

"Kelsey, I'm begging you, please go straight back to the duplex. I'll be right behind you."

"Dane, it's daylight. And I'm not a stripper or a hooker. I live a dull and boring life, with all my fantasies going into ad campaigns."

"Maybe so. But we've already established the fact that you're bent on visiting men who may be psychotic killers. Please, promise me you'll go straight back to the duplex."

She nodded, waited until he was in his Jeep, then started out along the road for home.

As he had promised, he followed right behind her.

Stupid-ass thing to do.

Stone-cold sober, by the light of day, Andy Latham knew that what he had done had been one really big stupid-ass thing to do.

He sat in his jail cell. Day had come. They brought him coffee and breakfast. Breakfast wasn't too bad—for jail. The coffee was good.

He rubbed his chin and felt the stubble on it. He must look like hell. Clothes slept in, hair unkempt. It was the alcohol. Usually, he was smart enough not to drink too much. But last night...

It was the fish. The dead fish in his yard. Again and again. And he couldn't help but believe it was those uppity rich kids throwing the bloated corpses in his yard. The smell...

He had smelled fish all his life. His sense of smell was both inured and heightened. Fresh fish smelled good. Dead and decomposing fish smelled like such awful rot that it could make a strong man vomit. It was as if someone knew how he hated the smell once the creatures started going bad.

He'd had too much to drink, and he'd lost his temper. It had felt good when he'd bashed Nate in the face. Now he knew that it had just been stupid. All the things he'd done in his life, and he'd avoided a cell—until now.

But here he was, all because he'd popped a rich kid in the nose.

A cold sweat suddenly broke out over his flesh.

He had to get out of here. Had to get out and had to get out fast.

He heard a jangle of keys. Someone coming toward his cell. Sheriff Gary Hansen. Pink-faced as always. The fool should move back to the north. Some people belonged here, some people didn't. Hansen didn't belong, yet he seemed to think he owned the island.

The door to his cell opened. Andy stood up, wavering just a little. Not because he was still drunk, because he'd been sitting too long. And because he was wary of Hanson.

"What's going on?" he demanded.

"Your attorney is here. Looks like you get to go home," Hansen said. "If it were up to me, they'd lock you up for a hell of a lot longer. Unfortunately there's still such a thing as due process."

"They ought to fire your ass for saying that," Latham told him, his mouth twitching uncomfortably as he spoke. His eye was twitching, too. Hell, maybe he could sue the sheriff's department.

"You're going before the judge, you'll post bail and walk away," Hansen said, staring at him with disgust. "But don't get too cocky there, *Mr.* Latham. You'll still be charged with assault and battery. And you may yet do some real jail time."

Andy Latham paused right by Hansen. "And you, you porker. You might still trip one day and dry up in the sun, just like a slug. Or fall off your boat and drown. The fish would be delighted."

"Get out, Latham, before I think of a way to hold you longer."

Latham left. His attorney, a fastidious man in a suit, despite the heat, was waiting. He looked good. Andy found himself suddenly burning with an inner fury. He could look good, too. He could be a handsome man, appealing. He had his charms. He had proven it many times.

It was all right to smell like fresh fish.

Just not decayed fish. He needed a bath. A beer to chase away the trembling from the night before. He needed to grab a nap, change his clothes...

And get away.

He thanked God for the due process of law.

When Kelsey pulled into the driveway of the duplex, she was startled to see the front door to her side open and Larry, Nate and Cindy come running out to greet her, like a welcoming committee for a long lost child.

She barely got the door open and a foot on the ground before Nate was pulling her out, hugging her. Then Larry, then Cindy, all chastising her at the same time.

"You scared us to death!" That came from Nate.

"You just took off after dinner without saying a word." Larry was reproachful.

"Thank God you're back," Cindy said.

Dane's Jeep pulled in behind her car. Both Larry and Nate looked at him as if he had done something totally morally reprehensible.

"We were worried," Nate said indignantly.

It was then that Kelsey got a good look at his face. The left side was swollen and red, his eye area bluish and swollen.

Kelsey gently touched the other side of his face. "Are you all right?"

"Oh, yeah, sure, I'm all right. I'm more embarrassed than anything. Humiliated that I let a slug like Latham get past my guard."

"What could you have done?" Kelsey said. "He walked up to you and slugged you, right?"

"He's in jail, isn't he?" Dane asked quietly.

"I'm fine, and yes, Latham is in jail. But you know they won't hold him long. He'll be out on bail. And slugging someone isn't like a capital offense or anything."

"But you're going to press charges," Dane persisted.

"Part of me feels badly," Nate said. "He's such a loser, I'll just be adding to the degradation that is his life. But then again, he's a scary piece of scum, so, yeah, I'll press charges. Though I guess the state is already doing that. I don't know that much about the law."

"I believe you'll have to press charges," Dane said.

"It's hot as hell out here. Let's go in," Cindy said.

Dane shook his head. "I'm going over to the jail. I want to see if Gary Hansen will let me talk to Latham," he said. "You're

all going to hang out together today, right?" He stared mean-
ingfully at Kelsey.

Nate and Larry each slipped an arm around her. "We won't
let her out of our sight," Nate said possessively.

Kelsey frowned, looking at Dane. She had thought that he
would stick around. That she would have time to talk to him.

She wanted to kick herself. They'd had so much time together
and she hadn't said anything. And now she suddenly wanted to
spill everything. She wanted to tell him what she'd seen on Izzy
Garcia's boat. She wanted to give him the phone numbers she'd
stolen and let him try to figure out why Izzy had them.

She wanted to tell him that Sheila had kept a diary, and that
she was ready to quit running around, questioning people, until
she had read the entire thing.

"We'll take good care of our Kels," Larry said.

She was between them, finding their joint embrace kind of
sweet, but when Dane started toward the Jeep, she pulled away.

"Wait just one second," she said, running after him.

Seated in the Jeep, he looked up at her with weary exasperation. "Kelsey—"

"Shut up and listen. I...yesterday, on Izzy's boat...I prowled
around a little before you, er...arrived. I found Sheila's purse in
the storage compartment beneath the seat, port side. And I took
these...." She dug quickly in her own bag, producing the list of
phone numbers. "These numbers were programmed into his cell."

He stared at her incredulously. "You're giving these to
me...*now?*" he said.

She stared back at him. "Better late than never—isn't that
what they say?"

She heard his teeth grate. "Yeah, I guess it is. You've got my
cell number, Kelsey. Anything, anything at all...get hold of me
right away."

"All right."

"*Anything,* Kelsey."

"I'm not an idiot, Dane."

His expression told her that she had done little to prove it, but he didn't say anything else, just gunned the motor of the Jeep and pulled out onto the road.

"You know what we should do?"

Cindy was behind her, her voice as cheerful as ever.

"What should we do?"

"Just take off. Get in a boat, take off for a few hours. We can dive, snorkel, fish. Get away. Just us. The old guard."

"Cindy, there are things..."

"We're all worried sick about Sheila, Kelsey."

She nodded. Of course. "I'm really tired, too."

"So are we because last night we were up late worrying about you."

"I told Larry I was okay, that I was with Dane."

"You know us...we stayed up anyway. C'mon, let's take off. It *is* Sunday, you know."

"You want to go to church?"

"The next best thing. Let's head out to the reef and the Christ statue. Say a little prayer under water. Kelsey, we have to quit driving ourselves crazy."

Larry had come up to them. "There's an idea. Come on, Kels. Let's do something."

"Whose boat?"

"Nate has his down at the same marina where Izzy and Jorge keep their charter boats. He has plenty of gear on board for all of us. We'll just do a day trip."

Kelsey thought quickly. She wanted to read the diary, but she could take it with her. If she stayed at the duplex, she would just read and pace, read and pace.

Maybe they were right.

"All right. If that's what you all want to do. I need a few minutes to grab a few things."

"Me, too," Cindy said.

"What? What's up?" Nate asked.

"You're taking us out for a spin," Larry told him.

"A spin?" Nate said.

"On your boat," Cindy told him.

He threw up his hands. "What the hell."

Kelsey walked past him into the house. She went to her bedroom, digging into the suitcase she hadn't really unpacked for a bathing suit, shorts, T-shirt and cover-up. She had started for the bed to grab the diary from beneath her pillow when a strange sensation told her that she wasn't alone. She held still, looking around the room. Again she realized that things were just slightly out of order.

She turned to the door of her bedroom. Nate was standing there, good eye soulful.

"Sorry, Kels. I didn't mean to disturb your privacy. It was a long night. You know, after Latham slugged me and the cops came and I spent hours with ice on my face, worrying about the fact that you hadn't come home and that you were calling from some club...and that...well, that you were with Dane."

"You shouldn't have been worried if you knew I was with Dane."

He shrugged. "Okay, maybe I was jealous."

"Jealous? Nate, after all this time? I thought we were friends, good friends."

"We are, Kelsey. It's just that I still get one of those macho, possessive things going on now and then. Oh, nothing serious. I'm over it. Really. Hell, I like Dane. And I guess we all saw something there all those years ago when you...well, when you didn't know it."

She just stared at him, brows raised.

He lowered his head. "Anyway, I started looking around. I wasn't digging into your things, honestly. But Sheila had mentioned something to me once about keeping a diary. I thought I'd look around for it."

"Did you find it?" Kelsey asked cautiously.

He shook his head. "But I didn't want you to think you were crazy, and I didn't want to lie to a friend. I was looking around in here last night. Or this morning. Whenever the hell it was."

She nodded, still watching him speculatively. He appeared so sheepish that she decided not to yell or lecture.

Larry suddenly appeared behind Nate. "Are you two ready?"

"Just a second," Kelsey said. "Would the two of you get out of here? For just a minute?"

"Oh, sorry." Larry turned and walked away. Nate followed and closed the door softly in his wake.

She walked quickly to the bed and found the diary, then stuffed it into the canvas bag she was bringing for their day at sea.

*"He's gone. Out? Free?"*

Dane was incredulous as he stared at Gary Hansen.

Hansen, seated at his desk, stared back at Dane, shaking his head. "What the hell did you think I could do? A drunk punched a guy in the face. The drunk had an attorney. I don't make the laws, I uphold them. And besides, Dane, Andy Latham may not be a popular man around here, but hell, what can you do? He got drunk and punched Nate. You can't execute the guy for that."

Dane exhaled a long breath.

Hansen's eyes narrowed. "What's with you?"

"What's with me? Gary, his stepdaughter is missing and we've had dead women popping up in the water."

"Dane, there's still nothing to say that Sheila Warren won't come back anytime. She could come sashaying in any day now, be incredulous that we had the gall to want to know where she was and with who."

"And there's nothing to say that she will," Dane said flatly.

Gary leaned forward. "Dane, you find a reason for me to keep Andy Latham in here and I'll be happy to oblige. Like I said, I don't make the laws, I uphold them. And I can promise you, I'm not the only lawman in the country sick to my stomach at the ability of fancy lawyers to let criminals walk. But as it goes right now, Andy Latham is walking free. Legally."

"How about you keep an eye on him, then?"

"We're trying to do just that. But you know what? We have to cover a hell of a lot of people and a hell of a lot of area. You keep an eye on him, too, if you're so damned convinced he's dangerous."

"He's proven he's dangerous."

"By punching a guy in a bar?" Gary shook his head in weary disgust. "Dane, do you know how many men we'd have to keep under permanent lock and key if that were a crime punishable by years of incarceration?"

"Sorry, Gary. Sorry."

"Get me something. I'd love to see him put away."

Dane left the sheriff's office and drove out to Latham's place. The guy wasn't there. His truck wasn't parked in the driveway.

He tried a few of the local hangouts but could find no sight of his quarry.

Dane stopped at a local donut shop for more coffee, gazing over the list of numbers Kelsey had given him. Why the hell had she taken so long to tell him about Sheila's purse being on Izzy's boat—and about the numbers? He felt a chill along his spine, knowing that Izzy had been keeping tabs on all his old acquaintances.

Coffee in hand, he headed out for the docks and Izzy Garcia.

His cell phone rang. He picked it up quickly.

"Dane, it's Kelsey. What happened with Latham?"

"Nothing. They'd already let him out."

"They let him out?"

"Yeah, yeah, he's out. Where are you? What are you doing? Your voice is fading in and out."

"Oh, we decided to spend the day out on the water. Cindy thinks it will be good for all of us."

"Out on the water?" He wasn't sure why that disturbed him.

"Yeah. Don't worry. We've taken Nate's boat. It's just Larry, Nate, Cindy—and oh! We ran into Jorge at the docks, and his captains are taking out all his charters, so he decided to tag along, too. We're going to do the tourist thing, go to the Christ statue, see the tropical fish. You know, all that stuff. We'll come back in around—"

The phone went dead in his hands. He clenched his teeth, telling himself that she had just gotten out of satellite range somehow. He dialed her back. A taped voice told him that Kelsey Cunningham wasn't available and to please leave a message. With an oath, he tossed his phone down.

He was already heading to the marina.

But when he arrived, Izzy's boat was gone. Naturally. Charter time.

He stared at the dock impotently, thought of all the things he could do to make wise use of his time, then turned and walked to his car.

Screw it.

Something was bothering him. Something he couldn't fathom.

When he got back to Hurricane Bay, he didn't even go in the house. He headed straight for his boat.

# CHAPTER 12

Kelsey lay on the deck. The sun was brilliant, a fantastic orb in an unbelievably blue sky. Larry had mentioned that the National Weather Service was still talking about a storm, but according to the forecast, the tropical depression now being called Hannah was heading toward the Carolinas. Kelsey still thought the sky was beautiful in the way it often was just days before the wind really ripped and the rain came in a deluge.

Lack of sleep had meant they were all fairly exhausted when they started out, but Cindy had been right. Being out on the sea was great. They had chosen to visit a few of the popular reefs around John Pennecamp Coral Reef State Park. The underwater park was protected, so there was an abundance of fish for them to look at. They started off north of French Reef, diving down to the wreck of the *Benwood*. The *Benwood* had been hit by a torpedo during World War II, then, while trying to get home, hit hard by another ship. Now she hosted a wealth of undersea wildlife. Beneath the surface, Nate pointed out a big grouper and mouthed a name. Old Henry. She hadn't seen him before. Sometime during the last few years he must have realized with his little fish brain that Pennecamp was a good place to live.

They stopped at Key Largo Dry Rocks, as Cindy had suggested, and went down to the Christ of the Deep Statue, a copy of the Christ of the Abyss Statue in the Mediterranean Sea just off Genoa. It had been a gift from an Italian industrialist. It was a beautiful statue, about twenty feet beneath the surface, arms upraised, face sculpted with peace and serenity.

After waiting for the tourists from the hired dive boats to leave, they all paused around it. Cindy folded her hands in prayer and they all followed suit. A while later they rose, and Nate suggested that they leave the park behind and do some fishing in legal waters. They hadn't made any plans for a restaurant for dinner that night, so a good catch of fresh snapper, dolphin fish or grouper would be good.

After just having met Old Henry, Kelsey was more in the mood for dolphin than grouper. Lying on the deck, feeling the air and the sun, she gave half her attention to the discussion going on between Larry, Nate and Jorge.

Jorge said that since they didn't seem to be catching anything from the boat, they should think about doing a little spearfishing.

Kelsey glanced at Cindy, who was lying on a towel near her. She appeared to be sleeping.

Kelsey had almost dozed a few times herself, but she had brought Sheila's diary topside with her to read as she lay in the sun. So far, she wasn't getting anywhere. Sheila had written about the men she met, but there were too many of them to keep track of. Plus she often used initials that meant nothing to Kelsey. So far, especially since she had sheathed the diary in a plastic book saver, no one had asked her what she was reading. She often had a book or a sketch pad with her, and she loved reading, just as Cindy loathed it, so apparently no one thought it worth bothering to ask about.

Just as she had very nearly dozed off again, she came to a section that alerted her.

*Saw the asshole my mother married again yesterday. Had to see him to go to the bank. He was all dressed up. Told me he was enjoying a new nightlife and meeting lots of women, real women. They found him appealing.*

*I don't care what he says. He can take a bath and pour on a liter of cologne, but he'll still smell like rotten fish. He always did. I told him so, too. Maybe that's why I left the Keys before. I can't stand the smell of rotten fish. Always reminds me of him. Reminds me of being a kid. Reminds me of the things he made me do.*

*I don't want to remember.*

Despite the heat of the sun, Kelsey felt cold. She closed the diary, biting her lip as she stared up at the sky. She should have known. She had been naive all her life. Sheila hadn't really spelled it out, and neither had Izzy, but suddenly she knew the truth.

Andy Latham had molested Sheila when she had been a child. And if the things Izzy had said were true, he had done it with—if not her mother's consent—at least her mother's knowledge.

*Poor Sheila! What a rotten life. And now...*

Out of the blue, tears stung her eyes. Maybe just because she was so tired.

And maybe because she knew, just knew, that Sheila was dead. They could pray at the Christ Statue all day, and all they could hope to achieve for Sheila was peace.

She closed her eyes. For a moment she almost felt sick to her stomach. Then she was outraged. When Sheila had become an adult, she should have brought charges against her stepfather.

She pushed herself up on her arms, suddenly needing to get into the water again. Rinse off, cool down—except that she had chills. Rinse off and warm up, then. The water was warm today, especially here in the shallows.

She started, realizing that Nate was sitting next to her. Cindy was gone and Nate was there.

"Hey."

"Hey. You okay?" he asked her.

She nodded.

"Really, really worried, though, huh?"

"Yeah."

"So am I."

She watched him. He hugged his knees to his chest. "Sheila was really going off in a bad way. I tried to talk to her, but..." He hesitated, then stared at Kelsey. "I really did care about her. You know..." Again he hesitated. "Well, you heard Larry last night. I had my fling with Sheila, too."

"Yeah, I heard Larry."

"I always loved you best, though."

"Nate, you know how much I care about you. I always will. But you don't have to apologize to me for sleeping with Sheila. We've been divorced for a very long time. And it was wrong to begin with, our getting married."

He looked away for a moment, then back at her. "Why do you think we barely lasted a month? Was there...something the matter with me?"

"No!" Kelsey protested quickly. "Nate...it was me. I hurt you, and I had no right to. I didn't really want to be married. I was just so hurt when Joe died, and I felt that...that I needed to belong to someone who was...mine, I guess. There wasn't a thing wrong with you then or now. You're handsome, charming and dependable."

He looked at the sky again, then lowered his head and his voice, as if someone might hear him. "Was I..."

"Were you what?"

"Okay in bed?" He sounded anxious.

"You were just fine," she assured him.

He still looked uncertain. Then he made a funny face, wincing. "I don't think that's what Sheila would say. She made some comment that I think was out of a movie. That you needed a microscope and a tweezer to find anything if you wanted to have sex."

Kelsey quickly lowered her head, determined to hide her smile. Leave it to Sheila.

"She was just being mean, Nate. You must know that. I mean...well, you made it through school, you were on the football team...you've been in locker rooms, and surely you've been with other women. You know what she said wasn't true."

"Didn't do much for my ego, though."

"I can imagine. But you know Sheila. She has a habit of striking below the belt. But..." She hesitated. "Nate, you know she was writing to me, calling me...and I've had a chance to read a few of the things she wrote in her diary. All these years, Sheila has been a bitch. She could be mean as a kid, but we all tolerated her. You know why?"

"We're a pack of fools? There weren't that many kids to hang around with?"

She shook her head. "I think Latham abused Sheila from the time she was a little kid. I'm pretty sure that's why she had no respect for sex whatsoever. And I think that, even when she cared about people, she hurt them. She was probably afraid to care too much about anyone. And if you use people, then they usually don't get a chance to use you in return."

"You think it was that bad?"

"Nate, I don't really know anything. Sheila kept things hidden from all of us. But I think that growing up must have been horrible for her."

"And then her mother died."

"Yeah. And she loved her mother, but I think maybe she wasn't much better than Latham."

"You mean her mother allowed whatever went on?"

"Maybe. Like I said, I don't really know anything. But I don't think you should let anything Sheila said upset you, or even give your ego the slightest scratch. Sometimes she just liked to strike out at people. I think she hurt you just because...it's better to hurt someone than to be hurt by them."

He squinted, looking up at the sun again.

"I could see it if we'd been headed for a monogamous situation or something like that. She just wound up being with me." He hesitated, then shrugged. "I think...I think she wanted Dane. But Dane had come back not wanting anybody. Of course, though they came back at nearly the same time, I think Sheila had been through half the lower Keys before he even came on the scene. And she knew about him...knew that his life hadn't been going real well. Do you think everybody has one great love in life, and even when it doesn't work, it's always there?"

"I don't know. But the world is full of people. And a lot of them are very nice." She paused, frowning at him. "Nate...are you saying that Sheila was the great love in your life and she crushed you?"

He started to laugh. "Hell no. You were the great love in my life. And *you* crushed me."

Kelsey felt the color flood her face. "Oh God, Nate, I am so sorry."

"Hey, that was years ago. Don't go apologizing. You just gave me back my manhood. I'm grateful to hear from you that I didn't suck as a lover. And I hope you're not lying to make me feel better."

"You didn't suck as a lover. I did."

He brushed her cheek with his knuckles. "All you had to do was be and you were great. But..."

"But?"

"You weren't really there. You were never really there. I thought...I thought there was someone else. Then you became a workaholic after we split up. You were never dating when I talked to you. Are you..."

"Am I what?"

"Nothing."

"Am I *what?*"

"Gay?"

She felt her cheeks darken again. "No."

"Hey, there's nothing wrong with it if you are."

"I agree. But I'm not. And I do date. Just not often. You're right. I have been something of a workaholic."

He leaned closer to her suddenly. "You know, girls, more than men, experiment."

"What are you talking about?"

"When Larry made that comment that Sheila had slept with everyone at the table, he meant everyone—and he wasn't off by much. That is, if you're being honest."

"I still don't get you."

"I think Cindy and Sheila had a thing."

"You think?"

"I do think so."

"I don't think you should say things unless you know they're absolutely true," Kelsey said. "And maybe not even then. If they did...experiment, as you say, it isn't our business."

"Sure. Sorry."

"Dammit, Nate, don't be sorry. I just think you should watch what you say."

"Yeah, maybe. And I do believe Cindy is looking for the right guy, though the years are going by."

"We're not living in the Civil War era. We don't become old maids at the age of seventeen or eighteen anymore," she told him dryly.

"Right." He shook his head. "Man, I'm sorry about Sheila. And I'm sorry as hell I let that asshole stepfather of hers get a fist on me! Wish I could have belted him back."

"I'm glad you didn't The fact that you restrained yourself probably makes it a clearer case of assault."

Nate laughed. "Hell, it had nothing to do with restraint. He caught me by surprise and I fell flat. And by then...the cops seemed to be right behind him. I will prosecute, though. For Sheila. Because she was a friend...even if she did set out to humiliate me. At least...well, now I understand."

He rose suddenly. "They're still talking about spearfishing. Are you coming?"

"Maybe I'll come in later." She grimaced. "I never really liked spearfishing."

"Oh, yeah. Big difference. Catch a fish on a hook and let it flop around and asphyxiate, or shoot it cleanly with a spear."

"We can, you know, just order in a pizza," Kelsey said.

"Where's your spirit of adventure, woman?" Nate asked. "We need to eat fish!"

"We can order anchovies on the pizza."

He gave her a look of disgust. "We're going to have fresh fish. And if you don't catch any, you're going to get to clean them."

"Maybe I'll join you guys. Give me a few minutes. And if all else fails, I will call for that pizza."

He let out a sigh, still staring at her. "Good book?"

"Um." She nodded and smiled at him, feeling a bit of a guilty twinge. Then she gave her attention back to the diary, aware that he walked off with a snort of impatience.

*Men. Men, men, men. Can't live with 'em, can't get them when they're nice and then shoot them when they become obnoxious.*

*The best ones out there—the cutest, the funniest, the most courteous—are all gay. They're even the best built, half the time. They make the best friends, that's for sure.*

*Maybe I should go that way myself. Try it, anyway. I can make anyone think I love them. It's fun.*

*But I need more. Want more. Just what do I want? I should probably be in therapy. Good old Larry. He always told me I needed help. He's too involved. He thinks he can fix me, and we'll fall in love all over again, even get married again. Poor boy. I know I'm self-destructive. I'm trying to get even with someone. Or prove something. I really should get therapy. There's something in me. Every time I get near someone, I have to prove I can seduce him. And I get something from everyone, like a little trophy. I think even the fact that women are supposed to be so much more selective and discreet makes me want to prove everyone wrong. I hope Kelsey comes. I want to spill all this to her. I need to tell her how I'm suddenly afraid, even though I'm not sure why.*

*Once upon a time I might have been in love. But even then, the evil seed was blooming in me. I know some people would say it wasn't my fault. But if it wasn't my fault, why do I always feel so guilty?*

*Dane is at Nate's all the time. Oops, there I go again.*

*Hafta have, hafta have. Hafta prove I can take what I want. I think it's the chase. I need so much. But maybe not in this instance.*

*Okay, I will look into a therapist.*

Kelsey set the diary down, feeling a strange chill sweep through her. *Had* Sheila made a play for Cindy just to experiment with her own prowess?

She stood, feeling acutely uncomfortable. She didn't really want to know all the private thoughts, emotions and deeds, of her friends.

But she felt she had to finish the diary if she was ever to have a chance of finding Sheila.

Or of finding out what had happened to her.

Because, like Dane, she was beginning to sense that Sheila was dead.

She realized that, despite the chill that had swept through her, she was baking. At least she'd had the sense to apply sunblock. She looked around. The others were all in the water and the dive flag was up on the boat.

She walked aft. She saw Cindy's head bob to the surface, then Larry's. They were laughing about something.

Their voices carried over the water. "What the hell were you aiming at, Cindy? We can't eat a cute little yellow tang for dinner."

"You didn't see the snapper?"

"We're not down here to massacre fish, children," Larry called back.

"I'll get a bigger fish," Cindy assured him.

Her head disappeared beneath the water.

Kelsey looked around. Since they had anchored, several boats had joined them at the sandy-bottomed fishing spot. The sun was glinting so brightly, she couldn't make out much about them. The charter captains often came here. On the outskirts of Pennecamp, where fishing was allowed, there could be a good catch. Fish naively left the safety of Pennecamp and wandered into the area where they were fair game.

Kelsey went over to the equipment and found her mask and snorkel. She leaned over the port side of the boat to spit in her mask and rinse it, then jumped into the water.

Dane had tried many of the usual haunts before trying the fishing spot. He didn't know why, but his sense of anxiety had been growing ever since he had learned that Andy Latham was back on the streets.

Latham had a tendency to fish the Gulf side, but when the fishing was poor there he went over to the Atlantic.

The shallow bank near Pennecamp was a favored spot. Some of the best reefs were close by, and not far away was a small, barren island, almost a sand spit, with a few tenacious grasses and trees. It was a popular picnic spot for boaters. Beneath the water's surface there were long spits of sand, as well, making it a safe place to anchor without harming the coral, while still being close enough to several small outcroppings of reef where the fish tarried before—hopefully—falling prey to rod and reel. There was also the wreck of a fishing boat that had gone down before they had been born. It provided a place for barnacles to form and sea life to find a home. It made the spot a special place, good for fishing, diving and, especially, for snorkeling, since the water ranged from twenty to forty feet deep.

As he motored in slowly, Dane surveyed the boats already anchored there.

"Bingo," he said softly.

He could see the *Lady Havana, Free as the Sea,* Nate's *Madonna,* and two of the other charter boats that went out from the same marina. Jorge Marti wouldn't be captaining the *Free as the Sea,* since he was with Kelsey and the others.

Izzy Garcia might well be aboard the *Lady Havana,* though.

He set his anchor and picked up his binoculars. He could see the groups aboard the *Lady Havana,* the *Free as the Sea* and the other two charters, the *Key Kiwi* and the *Sea She.* He studied the *Lady Havana* closely, but he didn't see Izzy among the men with their rods.

He turned to study the *Madonna.* There was no one topside, and the dive flag was up.

He set the binoculars down. The view before him was almost picture-perfect, entirely serene. The day was spectacular, without even the customary puffs of white clouds above him. The sky was a crystal blue, the sea shimmering in shades of blue and green. The waves were light, without a hint of chop, and the boats at anchor rocked gently where they lay.

And yet...

He should have been on the phone with the women he had met at the strip clubs, pushing and prodding to find out if they recognized any of the people in his pictures. He should have been tracking down Andy Latham, calling every number from the list Kelsey had taken from Izzy's cell phone, or bribing or conniving a friend at the phone company to give him names and addresses for those numbers he didn't know.

Instead he was here.

There was no reason to suspect that Kelsey should be in any kind of danger. She wasn't a stripper, and she didn't lead Sheila's lifestyle.

But she never shut up. She was determined to find Sheila. She was always asking questions, and her questions were an awful lot like accusations.

The temptation to get in the water and find her was overwhelming. He felt like an Alfred Hitchcock trailer. "Have you ever had a premonition...?"

Dane put up his own dive flag, went for his snorkel equipment and dived in. Surfacing, he headed straight for the area where the *Madonna* lay at anchor.

Kelsey took a deep breath and dived. She could see Cindy ahead of her. Cindy could be a pure predator. She had apparently shaken Larry, having decided he would scare her fish away and ruin her catch. Now she was headed toward the scattered coral.

Something brushed Kelsey. She instinctively moved, then realized it was only a piece of seaweed. There was a lot of it today. Whatever was happening with the storm out in the Atlantic might be driving it in.

She surfaced and took another gulp of air.

Her lung capacity was good. Probably because she had grown up an islander and spent almost as much time in the water as she had on land the whole time she was growing up. They were all good, of course, though Larry wasn't quite up to par with the rest of them. But then, he had been a weekender. And no one was quite as good as Dane, but then...well, he was Dane.

Joe had been as good, though.

Kelsey swam toward the coral and found a tiny flatfish digging into the sand. She teased it with a finger and watched as it dug deeper. She surfaced and found herself pulling away from a big patch of seaweed again. For a moment she floated, staring up at the sky. She found herself thinking that she was going to make a point of calling her parents that night. She remembered her feeling, after the initial anguish of Joe's death, of failure that she wasn't all that Joe had been, the perfect son.

It all seemed so petty now.

She was grateful to them; she loved them so much. They were so normal and they did love her. They had given her a good home, a good education and so many of the silly things she had wanted over the years.

She had not led Sheila's life.

She turned in the water, took a deep breath and made another dive.

She was very close to what could be classified as a reel reef. And, she realized, she was by the old wreck. How far had she come from the boat? As experienced as she was, she never went diving alone, and even when snorkeling, she was careful to stay close to the others. The best swimmers in the world could drown because they were too confident in their own abilities.

She would surface, get her bearings and head back.

Now, she saw, she was right over the wreck. The scattered coral near it was intriguing. As she headed up, she was surprised to catch a glimpse of green curling around one of the larger pieces near the rusting hull of the boat, and she found herself taking a breath and slipping beneath the surface again. She dived down low to the ground, wondering if a moray eel was making a home here. She swam deep. Tangs, parrot fish and medium-size grouper swam past her, the grouper eyeing her warily. She kept her distance, circling, watching.

She was startled at a whooshing sound in the water, close by.

She spun around and saw nothing, but the fish that had been near her were all darting to and fro in sudden confusion and fear.

She turned around in a full circle but still saw nothing.

The old boat sat decaying in the sand and rock, silent and still.

The fish around her slowed again, their movements easy through the water.

As she turned back to the little spit of coral rock, she was pleased to spot an eel. It poked its head out from a hole in the formation of living rock, then ducked its head back in.

Treading water, she waited at a safe distance, anxious to see the moray again. She'd missed being in the water like this. She loved the serenity in the water, the beauty of the creatures that lived there.

The moray tentatively peered out.

She was careful not to move.

How long had she been down? At one time she could make almost five minutes. She probably wasn't that good anymore.

The eel seemed to accept her.

Then...

It jerked back so suddenly it was almost like a disappearance into thin air—or water, as the case might be.

She heard the whooshing sound again...

And saw...

A streak of silver.

A spear...

Some idiot was spearfishing right here, with her in the water. Surely, despite the coral and the seaweed, she could be seen.

She couldn't see anyone attached to the spear that had just shot by her, dangerously close.

She looked around...and again...the whoosh.

Damn tourists!

Was someone in the hulk of the old boat, thinking they could do better if they were hidden in the rotting wood and rusting metal of the wreck?

She got ready to kick her way to the surface, out of the fishing grounds. Before she could do so, she nearly screamed as a hand landed on her shoulder.

She turned in alarm. Dane. He grasped her hand, pulling her upward.

They broke the surface together.

"Dane, what the hell are you doing here? You scared me half to death!"

"*I* nearly scared *you* to death? Jesus, someone down there is using you for target practice! Get back to the boat, Kelsey."

"Back to the boat? Where are you going?"

"Back to find out who is down there."

He pulled free, about to dive. She grabbed his hair, jerking him back up. His dripping head and blazing eyes reappeared.

"Dane, you idiot, there are tourists down there who don't know what they're doing! You've got to come with me. We'll call the Coast Guard."

"Kelsey, dammit, get back to the boat. I don't think that's some dumb tourist taking potshots. Let me go."

"You're not going after someone with a speargun. You're unarmed!"

"Kelsey..." He was impatient.

"Dane!" She was adamant.

"Kelsey, go back to the boat. Now."

"But—"

He dived. She didn't stop him, but she couldn't turn and leave him, either. She surveyed the ocean floor beneath her.

She could see the coral, but the fish had all disappeared.

The old wreck sat like a silent sentinel, as it had for years. No activity was evident in or around it.

She couldn't see Dane.

Seconds ticked by with agonizing slowness, but she still couldn't see Dane.

Or any sign of life.

Minutes.

Minutes went by.

He was good. He could hold his breath for a long time.

She still couldn't see him. How far had he gone? Where had he gone?

She gasped, inhaling water along with air as she felt a hand on her back. She turned, coughing, treading water as she wheezed and struggled for breath. Dane. He had come from the other direction.

"I told you to get the hell out of the water!"

"Don't yell at me!"

"Kelsey, you idiot, I think someone was trying to kill you."

"Here? With at least half a dozen boats around? Dane, it was some idiot tourist who should be arrested. You were in as much danger as I was."

"We may still be in danger, Kelsey, and while I'm wearing a dive knife sheathed at my ankle, you haven't any protection but a blue bikini. So swim, Kelsey. Let's both get back to the damn boat."

She turned and started for the boat, but she couldn't help thinking he was crazy. No one would want to kill her.

And yet...

*Why would someone search for concealment in order to spearfish?*

*Unless they were fishing for a human prey.*

# CHAPTER 13

When they reached the boat, Larry was just climbing up the ladder. He was jubilant.

"Will you look at this? I got a dolphin fish—a big one. Cindy, Nate and Jorge got *nada*. Call me a weekender, will ya? Look at this baby. Hey, Dane, where the hell did you come from?"

"Where the hell did you catch that?" Dane demanded. Larry's smile faded, and he pointed north, away from the wreck. "Over there somewhere," he said, scowling. "What the hell's the matter with you?"

When they reached the ladder, Dane urged Kelsey to go first, then followed her up.

Kelsey, sorry that Dane had been so curt when Larry was so excited, explained quickly. "Larry, someone was over by the wreck with a speargun, and they missed me by a matter of inches."

"Damn!" He stared at Dane, who was dripping onto the deck. "Stupid tourists. Did you tell them to stop?"

"We couldn't find them," Dane said. "But I'm calling the Coast Guard and reporting the incident. Where are the others?"

"Coming in."

Dane, his hands on his hips, was staring toward the other boats still anchored nearby.

"It's gone," he said.

"What's gone?" Larry asked, perplexed. The spear he had held so proudly, bearing his captured fish, was now lowered by his side.

"Izzy's boat. The *Lady Havana.*"

"It was out there?" Larry said.

Dane nodded, studying the fishermen still at anchor. "Jorge's boat is gone, too."

"Jorge is with us."

"I know. But his boat was here when I anchored."

"So?"

"So we need to know exactly who was out here."

"Those charters usually just do rod and reel fishing," Larry said.

"I know."

Jorge came climbing up the ladder, his spear empty. "Hey, Dane," he said in greeting.

"Where were you?" Dane asked him.

Jorge frowned and looked down at his torso, glistening from the sea. He looked back at Dane. "In the water."

"Where were you spearfishing?" Dane clarified.

"Toward the boats in the crescent there. Why?"

"Someone nearly speared Kelsey," Larry explained.

"What?"

Cindy was on the ladder then, with Nate right behind her. "Maybe we should explain this to everyone all at once," Kelsey murmured.

"I'm calling the Coast Guard," Dane said, and headed below deck to use Nate's radio.

Kelsey wound up explaining. They were all indignant, and certain that anyone so careless with a speargun had to be a tourist.

"I mean, come on, Kels," Larry said. "Why would anyone be aiming at you?"

She shook her head. "I don't know."

Dane had come back topside.

"You really called the Coast Guard?" Nate said slowly, as if they might wind up getting someone in trouble for a piece of stupidity.

"What happened was serious," Dane said.

Cindy was frowning. "Dane...how did you get here?"

He sighed and pointed. "My boat."

"Oh. You were just coming out to join us?" Nate said.

"Something like that."

"Cool," Nate murmured. "Hey...they're all leaving."

"Did any of the rest of you notice what other boats were out here?" Dane asked.

They looked at each other. "I didn't even notice that Jorge's *Free as the Sea* was out here," Larry admitted ruefully.

"And I hadn't seen Izzy's boat," Kelsey said. She hadn't paid the least attention to the other boats. She had been involved in the diary, and then she had gone in the water.

Dane looked at them all one by one. Kelsey could feel a certain tension rising. "You were all within sight of each other, right?"

A silence followed his words.

"Kelsey was right—we should have decided to order pizza," Nate said, staring hard at Dane.

They heard the loud blast of a horn from a Coast Guard cutter, and a moment later the vessel was lining up with theirs and an officer hopped aboard the *Madonna.* He was young, and very serious and attentive as Dane told him that he had gone looking for Kelsey, only to see a spear go streaking through the water, nearly missing her.

"Well, who shot it?"

"I don't know," Dane said impatiently, ruffling the feathers of the young officer. "She was nearly killed. There were at least two spears, maybe more. And whoever shot them was hidden somewhere. In the wreck, I imagine."

Then the officer stared at them all curiously, since they had obviously been spearfishing.

"Every one of us knows how dangerous a speargun can be," Nate said firmly.

"And we weren't anywhere near the wreck," Cindy said.

The officer took information from each of them, then asked what other boats they'd seen in the area. Dane rattled off the names of at least five of other boats anchored.

"We'll do what we can," the young officer said, then shook his head. "If you'd only seen someone..."

"Yeah, I know that," Dane said impatiently, "but when you're being shot at, you try not to swim right back into danger."

"And you're sure," the officer said, narrowing his eyes at the group once again, "that none of you was...careless in any way?"

"We're positive," Jorge said with disdain.

"Right," Larry murmured. He nodded toward Kelsey and Dane, and said, "Humans there." He picked up his catch. "Fish here. We know the difference."

Once again the officer stiffened. "You don't need to be sarcastic. We're on the water to save lives."

"Of course. And you do an excellent job," Cindy soothed.

"We deal with drug peddlers, modern-day pirates who would just as soon shoot you as look at you, refugees and—"

"Assholes," Nate supplied.

The officer lifted a brow and at last cracked a small smile. "Yeah. So if I offended you with my questions, at least you'll understand why."

"No one is offended. We appreciate your work," Dane said carefully. "But you will check out everyone on those other boats, won't you?"

"Yes, we will. I know most of these boats. And you think there were a few more with names you didn't catch?"

Dane nodded. "Yeah." He sounded angry with himself.

"You didn't mention that boat over there." He pointed.

"She's mine," Dane said.

"Oh? So you came out in two different boats?"

"I knew my friends were out here," Dane said.

"And you just happened to dive in the water and found your friend in danger from an unseen spear fisherman?"

"Yes," Dane said. Kelsey realized then that everyone was staring at Dane.

"Good timing," the officer said.

"Yes, it was."

The officer kept staring at him.

"I don't even own a speargun. I was never into spearfishing," Dane said impatiently.

"All right. We'll do our best." He handed Dane a card. "I've got your name and numbers. And you can contact me if you think of anything else," he said.

Dane accepted the card. "Thanks."

The officer returned to his boat, leaving them with a cross between a wave and a salute.

They were left alone, silent for a few minutes, staring at one another.

"I guess it's a pizza kind of night after all," Cindy said, trying to break the spell of silence with a light tone.

"I think we should head back in," Nate said stiffly, his eyes on Dane. "I'll bring you back to your boat."

"What about my fish?" Larry asked sorrowfully.

"We'll clean him and freeze him at the duplex," Cindy said.

"But it's fresh now."

"It won't feed us all," Cindy said.

"Well I can't exactly throw him back. He's as dead as dead can be."

"All right, we can have dolphin tidbits with our pizza."

Nate pulled in the anchor as they spoke and started the motor. As it roared to life, Dane leaned close to Kelsey.

"Come with me."

"I can't."

"Why not?"

"My things are all on board this boat. It'll take me ten minutes to get them all together."

"Leave them, then."

"I have things I can't leave."

"Nothing is more important than your life, is it?"

She stared at him incredulously. "You know, I can see where you think I was an idiot for running over to Andy Latham's. And it might have been even stupider to go on board Izzy Garcia's boat alone with him. But this is a group of our oldest friends."

"Yeah, great. We've barely seen each other in years."

"I've barely seen *you* in years."

"Kelsey, someone was shooting at you."

"None of these guys."

"Wouldn't it be nice if your belief in the goodness of man was a guarantee?" he murmured, then returned to the original topic. "What the hell can you have on board that's so damned important?"

She looked at him and hesitated for a moment, then said, "Sheila's diary."

For once she took Dane completely by surprise. But he was able to mask his emotions almost instantly.

"Who knows?" he asked in a whisper so low she barely heard it above the hum of the motor and whipping of the wind.

"No one."

Apparently Nate didn't plan on tying up with Dane's boat. He cut the motor about twenty yards away. Normally it would have been no big deal. The day was still beautiful, the sun hot. There was no reason why Dane shouldn't swim back. The problem was the reason why they'd stopped where they had.

Nate was wearing a resentful and stony expression.

"Dane, we're going to make it a pizza party tonight," Cindy said cheerfully, speaking loudly, since Nate was revving the motor in a ridiculously impatient manner.

Dane smiled at Cindy. "Pizza party," he muttered beneath his breath.

"Oh, yeah, it's going to be just great. A really happy, friendly occasion," Kelsey said. She stared at Dane. The moments of fear she had felt beneath the water were quickly fading. This episode in her life definitely had a logical explanation. One they used often, to explain any aggravation.

Tourists.

They could be annoying as hell, but the Keys could hardly exist without them.

Dane walked aft to dive off the end of the boat. "Dane, you're coming over, right?" Cindy called hopefully.

Bless Cindy, Kelsey thought. Ever the peacekeeper. Just what *had* her relationship with Sheila been? Kelsey couldn't help but wonder.

She felt queasy. She wasn't going to go through life wondering about Sheila and everyone she knew.

Yes she was. Until they found Sheila.

"I wouldn't miss it for the world," Dane assured Cindy.

He leaped over the hull and into the water. Kelsey could see him swim with clean, swift strokes to his own boat.

Nate didn't wait for him to board.

He gunned the motor, and they headed back for the marina.

As he headed in, Dane tried to keep a vein of rationality running through his head.

Kelsey was right. Their entire group of friends could hardly be conspirators in the Necktie Strangler cases. And Kelsey wouldn't be alone with anyone for the next few hours, not since they were all heading for the duplex to order pizza.

He'd never felt like quite such a madman in his life, not knowing what to do first. He needed to talk to the strippers again and find out if the girls could pick out anyone from the pictures he had brought to them. He needed to accost Izzy Garcia before he could get rid of Sheila's purse, and he also needed to be with Kelsey. The whole thing was getting crazier by the minute.

Kelsey wasn't a stripper or a prostitute, so she shouldn't be in any danger. Except that she had been asking questions.

So why would anyone want to kill Kelsey, even if she had gone around asking questions of everyone?

Perhaps because she'd gotten too close to the truth.

He made his decision as he headed back toward the Key. Veer to the left, he brought his boat straight in to Hurricane Bay and made it as fast as he could to the duplex.

Or, veer to the right and head for the marina.

As they brought the *Madonna* into her berth, Kelsey was surprised to see that the young Coast Guard officer had decided not to waste any time. The majority of the charter boats were back in, and it appeared that a number of officers were walking the docks, talking with each captain and his passengers.

She paused, seeing that a tall, well-built black officer was on Izzy's deck.

"Want to hang around?" Larry asked her.

She shook her head. "No, I'd rather let those guys do their work and get back to the duplex." She looked at him. "What can I do? Run around and stare at everyone they're questioning?"

Cindy was behind her. "You know, that might not be such a bad idea. Give them the eye, see if anyone breaks down and confesses."

"No one is going to break down and confess. Let's get out of here. I want to take a shower, chill out and order pizza."

They kept walking toward the parking lot. Kelsey hadn't been lying. She needed a shower. The sun seemed to be baking the sea salt permanently into her flesh. Though it was dropping now, the heat was still so intense that it shimmered over the pavement. She wanted a long shower, soft, clean clothing and the company of no one but friends.

"Think Dane will show up?" Jorge asked.

"We can hope not," Nate said, casting a sideways glare at Kelsey. "*She'll* just let him in if he does."

"Oh, come on, Nate!" Larry said. "Kelsey could have been killed. Naturally he's afraid. Especially after he fucked up in St. Augustine."

"How do we know *he* wasn't down there with a speargun?" Nate said.

"He didn't come out of the water with a speargun," Jorge reminded them. He had stopped walking. "I wonder if I shouldn't stay behind for a bit. Check on my captain, see what's happening on my own boat. I'll be there later, though, so don't count me out."

"Of course not," Kelsey told him. "We all need showers, downtime. Let's do the pizza thing about seven or eight, how's that?"

"Good by me," Jorge said. He lifted a hand to them and started back for the dock and the berth where the *Free as the Sea* was docked.

"Nate, chill," Cindy commanded.

"How many years have I known that guy?" Nate said. "And he suggests that *we* might have been careless with spearguns. Hell, was he suggesting one of us might really have been down there on purpose, trying to hit Kelsey?"

"Nate, he reacted to a situation, that's all. He's got a thing for Kelsey, always has had, and we all know it," Larry said with a deep sigh of impatience. "I'm not going to throw out a friendship over this. Do you really want to? Hell, the guy has helped you. He set up the cameras that caught your thief, and he spends half his life at the Sea Shanty."

Nate shrugged, dug around in the pocket of the short-sleeved tailored shirt he'd thrown on, found a pack of cigarettes and lit one. His fingers were shaking.

"I thought you quit," Cindy said with reproach.

"Yeah, I did."

Cindy shook her head and started walking toward the parking lot again.

"Hey, guys, come on, this is my vacation time," Larry said.

Nate nodded. "Okay, okay. Let's go get ready for our cozy little pizza party." He hesitated suddenly, looking back toward the dock.

"What is it?" Kelsey asked him.

"I was just thinking...do you think old Andy Latham might have gotten in his boat and gone out there? Even Dane said that he didn't notice the names of all the boats out there. Do you think Latham could be smart enough to go after you like that? Would he even be capable of such planning and subterfuge? I mean, whoever was down there was either one lucky asshole or one very clever would-be killer."

Kelsey looked at Nate. "I don't know. I really don't know," she said. "But if Latham's boat had been there, don't you think one of us would have noticed it?"

"Hell, I didn't even notice that Jorge's boat was there, and Jorge was with us," Nate said.

"I didn't notice what other boats were out there because I wasn't paying any attention. But if Latham's boat had been out there, Dane would have seen it."

Cindy turned back "Are you guys coming? If Latham was out there, who the hell says he was even on his *own* boat? Please, can we go? I feel like a salt lick for an entire herd of cattle. What-ever happened out there doesn't matter right now, because we're all together. Let's hit it."

Kelsey and Nate started walking, but Kelsey found herself stopping and looking back again.

Izzy Garcia was standing barefoot on his dock, hands on his hips. Staring after her.

She couldn't see his eyes or read his features. But even at a distance, it was easy to read his body language.

The man was furious.

Sunday afternoons tended to be crazy, which Dane knew. He returned to his house, docked his boat, opted for a two-second shower and clean clothes, then drove down to the marina.

Sunday evenings could be quiet. Dead quiet.

In the time it took him to get back, the activity at the marina had died away. But it was Izzy Garcia he wanted to see first, and the *Lady Havana* was at her berth.

He left his car and hurried down the walkway until he reached Izzy's charter boat.

He glanced at his watch and then at the sky. It was nearly nightfall. On a Sunday night that meant a lot of people were heading north to Miami-Dade and beyond to prepare for Monday morning and the workweek. The tourists and daytime fishermen had taken their catches and headed on home or to their hotels. Cocktail time was drifting into the dinner hour at the local restaurants. But the hectic pace at the marina had slowed to the lazy crawl that came at the end of such a day.

Dane headed straight for the *Lady Havana*. There was no sign of Izzy or anyone else on the boat. He jumped lightly from the dock to the deck. The *Lady Havana* rocked ever so slightly at her mooring.

Before he could reach the cabin, Izzy emerged. His features were so tense it looked as if he barely had enough skin to stretch across the bone structure of his face.

"Took you longer than I thought," he told Dane, and headed back down into the cabin. He opened the refrigerator as Dane followed. *"Tú quieres una cerveza?"*

"No, I don't want a beer. I want answers."

Izzy took out a beer for himself, popped the top and swallowed for a long time before lowering the can with a sigh and staring at Dane again, as if he were watching a rabid dog.

"Maybe the pressure is making you *loco, amigo,*" he said. "Now you think that I take out a charter, leave the clients on board, grab a speargun and go after a woman everyone has always liked?"

"So the Coast Guard came."

"Oh, yeah, the Coast Guard came." He waved an arm vaguely

to indicate the cabin. "To the others, they ask a few questions. Me? Me they grill for twenty minutes."

"You *are* a dope-peddler. Occupational hazzard," Dane said. "You know, cops and such wanting to talk to you."

Izzy gave him an icy smile. "You think I'm selling at the high school?"

"Yeah, I do."

Izzy shook his head. "I sell recreation to adults. Maybe some people with whom I've worked have gotten careless and greedy. I will make it stop."

"What do you think, Izzy? That you can make me stop wanting to nail your ass?"

"You're not here about the drugs today. You're here about Kelsey. No, it's more than that. You're here about Sheila."

"Someone tried to nail Kelsey in the water today. And Sheila..."

"You think Sheila is dead."

Dane didn't respond.

Izzy walked through the cabin, lifting the seat cover on the port side of the boat and pulling out Sheila's purse. "You have come for this, I believe. Kelsey found it. I knew that, of course. But I don't know where Sheila is. Maybe she is dead. Sheila played in many scary places. Maybe she knew things she shouldn't have known. And maybe she did things she shouldn't have done. But I didn't kill her. Here, you take this. Go ahead and waste your time hounding me. I didn't kill Sheila. I could swear to that, but it wouldn't mean shit to you if I did so. I didn't go in the water with a spear gun, and I didn't kill Sheila. Now get the fuck off my boat."

Dane didn't move.

"You keep an interesting set of numbers in your phone, Izzy," he said.

Izzy swallowed the rest of the beer. "Yes, I watch everyone. I know where everyone is and what they are doing. It's good to know things about people. Maybe I'll become a private investigator, too, one day. And maybe I'll be better than you. I make it my business to know what goes on with the people who think they know me too well."

"Izzy, I would never claim to know you too well. I just know *about* you."

"That thing. In St. Augustine. What happened wasn't your fault."

Dane felt his jaw twist, but he didn't allow his emotion to show.

"Trying to suck up to me?"

"Why? I don't need to suck up to you. You can't prove anything against me."

"I must be awfully close."

"I don't think so. You see, that is why I make it my business to know about the people around me."

"If you make it your business to know about people, why can't you tell me more about Sheila?"

Izzy arched a brow, then gave Dane a sardonic grimace. "No one really knew about Sheila. She couldn't anticipate her own movements. But you—you should be careful. Here you are on my boat. The big military man who learned all about killing." He mimed aiming a gun with his fingers. "Don't you know? Even tough guys can be killed by the crazy people out here. And even some who are not crazy, just businessmen. You could wind up dead, you know."

"Now, now, Izzy. First you suck up to me, then you threaten me."

"Hey, I'm just talking. Pointing out some of the facts of life."

"Tell me, Izzy, would you happen to be the Necktie Strangler?"

Izzy could be a good actor, Dane knew, but the look he gave him then registered genuine surprise. Then he tightened his features into a snarl of real disgust. For a moment Dane thought he was going to spit on the floor of his own cabin.

But he didn't. "The Necktie Strangler? Do you think I'm some psycho? Look around you. I do well with women, my friend. Very well. Perhaps not with women like Kelsey, who think they know me too well, same as you. But you should see some of the corporate wives who come aboard this boat with their paunchy husbands. They long for a man who doesn't have a fat white tire for a middle. The Necktie Strangler...he is some sick reject, desperate, seeking revenge, perhaps. Or maybe he was just born bad. Evil. He is probably what they call a bad seed. And I am not. I've chosen my way in life. I like to take a few chances. I disagree with some laws, but I am not evil inside."

"You're quite the upstanding citizen, Izzy."

"Yes, I am. And you should know this—*if* I wanted someone dead, it would not be like that. Perhaps you should look at some of your friends. Why don't you find out what Jorge Marti does out on the ocean in the middle of the night?"

"Why don't you just tell me?"

"I don't actually know for certain," Izzy said. "That's the truth. But I know that he is out there. And I know that whatever he does, he does in darkness. There, I've told you what I know and what I've seen," Izzy told him. "Now get off my boat. I've given you what was Sheila's. Yes, she left it here when I saw her last, but that was before *you* saw her last. If what you really want is the truth about Sheila, you're wasting your time with me. I didn't kill her. It did not even occur to me that she might be dead or a victim of the Necktie Strangler—which apparently you do, or why accuse me of being such a man? I didn't hurt Sheila. Ever. I gave her a great deal of pleasure, actually. So, lay off. Get off my ass and leave me alone."

Dane folded his arms over his chest. "If you know anything, Izzy, it would be good for you to tell me."

"I've told you all I know. Now will you leave? Or were you planning on beating me to a pulp. Maybe break my arm?"

"Your face, actually," Dane said. "But I can't afford to spend a night in jail." He started out of the cabin and up topside, to the deck. Izzy followed him.

On deck, he stopped. "What about those rape charges that were filed against you, Izzy?"

"Filed and dropped," Izzy said.

"Maybe the lady was afraid she might wake up dead one morning."

He smiled. "And maybe the little *puta* realized she wasn't going to get anything. She filed charges because she wanted a one-woman man. And that's not me. She got pissed off because she wasn't so special. That's it. You're going now? You'll leave me alone?"

"I'm going, Izzy. But I'll be damned if I'll leave you alone."

"Remember, everyone says Sheila was with you the last time anyone saw her." He smiled. "Alive, that is."

Dane was tempted to risk a night in jail for one good wallop. Just one punch, enough to flatten Izzy's nose. Instead Dane took a long stride that brought him from the deck of the *Lady Havana* to the dock. Then he turned back. "Be seeing you, Izzy."

Izzy just glared.

Dane strode along the dock. With or without Izzy's approval, he intended to talk to Jorge Marti. But the *Free as the Sea* was not in her berth.

Well, maybe that wouldn't matter. Jorge would be coming for pizza at the duplex. He knew that he himself would be hardly wanted there, not after today. Nate was the most put out.

Too damn bad.

Nate and the others had been in the water with spearguns.

He stood on the dock for a moment, watching the ripple of water in the place where Jorge's boat should have been berthed.

Then he turned and headed back for the parking lot.

Izzy was still topside on the *Lady Havana,* watching him every step of the way as he departed.

He hated Izzy because of what Izzy did.

He'd learned a hell of a lot about the man when he'd been hired by the private school to find out who was supplying the kids. Discreetly placed cameras had caught a number of the pushers in the act.

Thus far, though, even when threatened with prison, no one had been willing to identify Izzy as their supplier.

The guy was the epitome of bad news. Sleaze. Slime. A pusher.

But was he a cold-blooded, organized psychopath who killed with his bare hands?

Dane stopped, lit a cigarette and looked back over the flame of his match.

The man was still watching. And he knew that Dane was watching him.

Izzy lifted a hand, formed his fingers into the shape of a pointed gun, pretended to aim and fire, and then smiled.

Dane ignored him and started walking again. He could still feel the heat of Izzy's gaze as the man watched him while he reached his Jeep, stepped into it, gunned the engine and left the parking lot behind.

"What?" Kelsey cried, startled.

She had jumped at the sound of the knock against her bedroom door.

She hadn't really been scared, just startled, because she had become so engrossed in what she was doing.

She was seated on the floor in front of Sheila's dresser, still wrapped in a towel after her shower. She wasn't sure what had made her suddenly decide to lift the lining beneath Sheila's elegant undergarments before getting dressed, but her curiosity had been rewarded. A folder had yielded all kinds of interesting papers, even if they weren't particularly relevant to her disappearance. An award Sheila had earned for being top speller at the local competition when she was in third grade. A picture of her and Dane together at his high school prom. A half-written letter to Larry, trying to explain why she couldn't stay married to him. A page, apparently written when she had been very young, on which she practiced her penmanship with the line *I hate my stepfather* written over and over again.

"Kels, can I come in?"

Larry. She jumped up, wrapping her towel more securely around her and cracking the door open.

"Hey," she murmured. "Sorry, have I been a long time? Are the others here?"

"No, no, it's all right. Cindy is still next door, and Nate went by the bar just to check on things. He called and said he'll be along. The pizza place doesn't deliver, so I'm going to go pick up our order. I wrote you a note—it's there on the table—but then I thought I'd just see if you were out of the shower before I left."

"I'm out. I'll get dressed right away, just in case anyone shows up while you're out."

"Can you think of anything else? I ordered one pizza with just cheese, one pepperoni, one vegetarian, and an order of anchovies on the side."

"Anchovies on the side sounds great. Anyone who likes little hairs on their pizza is welcome to them."

"Do we need beer, soda, wine?"

"I went shopping when I got here. We're fine."

"Maybe I'll pick up an extra six-pack."

"Whatever you think."

"All right, then, see you soon."

She closed her bedroom door when Larry left and returned to the dresser. She dropped the towel and she suddenly found herself looking toward the rear window. The drapes were open. There was faint light out in the patio and pool area, but bright light in the bedroom.

She cursed herself, grabbing the towel, suddenly afraid that she was being watched. She grabbed her underwear and bra and raced into the bathroom, then discovered that she was shaking as she slipped into them. Of course. What she had done was idiotic. Every woman knew not to dress with her shades open.

And great. Now she was wearing a bra and underwear, but her

jeans were still in the dresser. She was really getting stupider with every passing moment. She should have simply closed the drapes.

And now...here she was.

She was suddenly afraid to stay in the bathroom. Afraid that she might find herself trapped there if the someone watching her made it into the house.

No one could get into the house.

Larry would have locked the door.

What if he hadn't?

She could lock the bathroom door and hole up until Larry returned, Cindy came over, or one of the others showed up.

She reached for the knob, all the while assuring herself that she was being ridiculous. But then she thought she heard another knob turning. Someone coming into her bedroom...

She waited in absolute stillness...and listened.

Seconds...minutes...

She exhaled, unaware that she had been holding her breath. It sounded to her like a jet engine. She was afraid that she might have missed some subtle noise beneath it. She held her breath again. Nothing. Nothing...

She was becoming ridiculously paranoid.

Kelsey opened the bathroom door.

And screamed.

# CHAPTER 14

Dane tried in vain to find Andy Latham. His truck wasn't at his house, and his fishing boat wasn't tied to the pier.

He tried the usual hangouts, the bars Latham frequented, and found no sign of him.

As he pulled out of the parking lot of one hole-in-the-wall, his cell phone rang.

A soft female voice spoke tentatively on the other end. "Dane?"

"Yes?"

"It's Katia. From Legs."

He stopped the car, pulling back into a parking space to listen attentively. "Katia, hey. Thanks for getting back to me. Did the pictures jar anything in your memory?"

"Yes."

"Which one?" he asked, hearing the tight sound of his own voice.

She let out a long sigh. "The scary thing is, I see so many people. They all look familiar. Every face in the shots you gave me seemed familiar. You could probably give me a picture of some old geezer who was European royalty a hundred years ago and he would look familiar."

Dane lowered his head, listening, rubbing his temples.

"So...you might have seen these guys...and you might not have seen them."

"Well, yes."

"Thanks, Katia. I appreciate you trying."

He was ready to hit the end button on his phone when she spoke softly again. "I said they all looked somewhat familiar. But one of them...I know one of them has been coming for months."

Dane's heart quickened again. "Who?" he asked.

His hands tightened around the wheel as she answered him.

"Kelsey?"

Cindy burst into the bedroom just as Kelsey cut off her own scream.

"What is it?" Cindy demanded.

A face in the window. Or had it been? There was now a large lizard where she was certain she had seen, at the least, the shadow of a head. A very large lizard.

"Anole," she said, exhaling.

"What?" Cindy asked.

"There's an anole, a big lizard, on the window."

"You screamed because of an anole?" Cindy said incredulously. "You've seen them all your life, Kelsey. Kelsey?"

She could feel that she was still white and shaky. She didn't know if paranoia was setting in, or if she really had seen a face in the shadows.

She stared at Cindy suddenly. "Is Larry still gone? How did you get in?"

"Larry should be back any minute. I let myself in with my key when you didn't answer my knock. Kelsey, maybe you should go on home. Maybe this whole thing with Sheila isn't good for you. You're taking it all so much to heart, and..."

"And what?" Kelsey stared at her.

Cindy shook her head. "I don't know. Have you done something to someone? It's possible someone was taking potshots at you in the water. And now you're seeing faces in the window. Kelsey, I'm going to be more worried about you than Sheila if this keeps up."

Kelsey stared at Cindy. "Maybe there *was* someone in the backyard."

Cindy answered slowly and carefully. "Right. Maybe."

"Well, I intend to look back there. For footprints or something."

"You think we have a Peeping Tom?"

"Maybe. Maybe it's something worse."

"We can check it out," Cindy said. "Of course, we can wait for the guys, too. On second thought, I may be buffer than either Nate or Larry."

"No, you're right, we should wait. There's safety in numbers."

"And there may be safety in clothing, too," Cindy said dryly, pointing out Kelsey's state of semiundress. "Were you planning on an underwear pizza party? The guys would appreciate it, I'm sure."

Kelsey reached for a pair of jeans and a knit shirt, sliding them on quickly. She strode quickly across the room then, drawing the drapes. The anole darted away when it sensed her approach.

She closed her eyes, wishing she weren't still feeling so shaky. There couldn't have been anyone out there. Her slightest movement had caused the anole to scamper away in panic. It never would have stayed on the window if someone else had been out there.

"Hello? Kelsey? Cindy?"

"It's Jorge," Cindy said, pleased. "He can go out with us." She raised her voice. "Hey, Jorge, we're here, in the bedroom."

"How did Jorge get into the house?" Kelsey said.

"I must have left the door open," Cindy said. Kelsey stared at her. "Well, I heard you scream, I opened the door as quickly as possible...and I must have left it open." Kelsey was still staring at her. "You were screaming," Cindy said. "I thought you were in trouble."

"Well, thanks, it's good to know you're ready to run to my rescue."

"You can count on me in any lizard situation," Cindy said dryly. "Hey...?"

Kelsey looked across the room. Jorge had come to the door. In dark jeans, a navy cotton shirt, with fresh washed, combed back hair and the slight scent of a pleasant aftershave, Jorge was both attractive and reassuring, built to take on the creatures of the night.

"You two all right?"

"Kelsey thinks she might have seen a Peeping Tom," Cindy explained.

"Or a big lizard," Kelsey admitted ruefully.

"You have to watch out for the lizards around here," Jorge said gravely. "They seem to be watching all the time. Just like Big Brother."

"Maybe we'll find out that the lizards are aliens, and they've been waiting all these years to take over the earth," Cindy murmured.

"Want me to check the yard?" Jorge asked.

"Let's all check the yard." Kelsey said. She started to open the sliding glass doors that led out to the back.

"Wait, I'll head out that way," Jorge said. "You go out the front, and that way, if there's a Peeping Tom, we'll know it because you'll see him trying to get away."

Jorge went out the back. Cindy and Kelsey went out to the front porch and ran right into Nate and Larry.

"Hey, guys, I found Nate out here, which is good, because even I—weekly-businessman-perfect-athlete that I am—cannot handle the pizza boxes and drinks all in one," Larry said. Then he frowned, staring at them. "You didn't come out to help with the pizza, did you?"

"We're checking out the yard," Cindy said.

"For lethal lizards," Kelsey explained.

"Lethal lizards? You think there's a gator back there or something?" Larry asked.

"No, just a big anole," Kelsey responded. She took the pizza boxes from Larry and nearly ran with them into the kitchen. Cindy was behind her with the sodas and beer. Then they hurried to rejoin the men, following them through the tall wooden gate of the privacy fence on the side of the house and around the back. They got to the window in question, but there was nothing there, and nothing seemed disturbed at all.

"Any footprints?" Cindy asked.

"Lizard prints?" Larry said.

"People prints," Cindy said with exasperation.

"I sure don't see any," Nate said.

Jorge was standing about five feet from the window, looking at them in dismay. "Well, actually, now there are lots of them."

"Just what are we looking for?" Larry asked. "A lizard or a person?"

"Signs that someone was here," Cindy murmured.

"I thought someone might have been back here in the yard," Kelsey said. "I—I thought I saw someone. Maybe it was just a shadow or something," she added lamely.

"She definitely did see a lizard," Cindy said. "I saw it, too."

"Let's check under all the trees," Larry said. They all split up to look around the yard.

"The pool looks nice tonight," Jorge said.

"We can always dive right in," Larry said.

"We've left all our suits behind," Nate reminded him.

"There's skinny dipping," Larry suggested.

"Or just underwear," Cindy said. "Kelsey will be all set. She's wearing her good stuff tonight."

Kelsey smiled vaguely at Cindy. If someone had been in the yard, he had left by the gate. Or else he had been in really good physical condition and scaled the wooden privacy fence around the rear of the duplex.

"There's another car out front," Cindy said.

"Let's go back in," Kelsey said suddenly. "It must be Dane."

"So he did come," Nate murmured.

"Maybe we shouldn't mention all this," Cindy said. "Dane really seems to be on edge lately."

"Good idea. Don't say anything," Kelsey said. Jorge was staring at her, frowning. "He'd rip apart the entire backyard because I saw a lizard," she explained.

"And accuse us all of being Peeping Toms," Nate said.

"Shh," Cindy said.

Dane was out of the Jeep. He saw the open gate and joined them.

"What are you all doing?" he asked.

"We just decided to come outside and see the night," Cindy said. "It's a beautiful night."

"Yeah. But wouldn't it be more beautiful from the patio?" Dane asked.

"Um, well, we were just trying to find an anole. There was a really big one on Kelsey's window a while ago."

"Hey, the pizza is getting cold," Kelsey said. Dane didn't seem inclined to press the point. He was watching Jorge, and she was curious at the way he was staring at the other man.

"We can eat out on the patio," Cindy suggested.

"That sounds great," Kelsey said. She automatically started for the sliding doors to the bedroom, while the others began to go around the front. "We can get in right here," she called.

"Yes, but then we'd have to tromp through your bedroom," Jorge said.

"It doesn't matter."

"We'll go around the front." Dane snapped out the words. The others froze, staring at him.

He looked at the group. "Oh, what the hell. Jorge, I have to talk to you."

Jorge's face, though darkly tanned, turned ashen. "Oh?"

"Let's go for a ride," Dane said quietly.

"All right," Jorge said.

"Wait a minute. You haven't even had any pizza," Cindy protested.

"It's all right," Jorge said.

Kelsey and the others stared in amazement as Dane turned and started for his Jeep, Jorge following behind him.

"Well, hell, leave it to Dane to spoil the damn party," Nate said.

"You don't think that...that Dane thinks...Jorge might have had something to do with Sheila's disappearance, do you?" Cindy asked.

"Of course not!" Larry protested. His words sounded hollow.

They stood in the yard in silence for long seconds.

"Well..." Nate said.

Kelsey threw up her hands. "Let's go get the pizza."

They walked through the house and into the kitchen. They were quiet, politely passing paper plates and plastic cups.

"It is beautiful outside," Kelsey said. "Why don't we sit around the pool?"

"Sounds good."

A few minutes later, the four of them were gathered around the pool.

"Hey, that depression is stalled over the Bahamas," Larry said.

"Hannah, right?" Cindy said.

"Yeah, they're calling it Hannah. Right now, it's still supposed to be heading for the Carolinas. I hope it doesn't turn. Since Andrew, every time it looks like the wind might blow hard they want to evacuate the Keys."

"That's natural. It's dangerous down here when a really big storm hits."

"Well, yes, but evacuating...man, I hate it. We don't get tourists for weeks afterward."

"I don't mind the lack of tourists," Cindy said. "I just hate it because all the fast-food restaurants close, and we have no electricity, which means no air-conditioning.

"The duplex is high. I think it would take a major storm for us to have to leave here."

"Nothing is high here," Larry argued.

"But we're not right on the beach. And when they evacuate...the traffic, oh, Lord!"

"If the storm is over the Bahamas, it will probably go north," Kelsey said. The pizza was good, she was hungry, but this was strange. She still hadn't shaken the feeling that someone had been in the yard. And when Dane had told Jorge that they needed to talk, Jorge had looked like a man who had been caught at something bad.

And yet the four of them were sitting here talking about the weather.

"A penny for your thoughts," Larry said to Kelsey.

"They're probably not worth it," she replied lightly.

"She's thinking, wow, let's all strip naked and jump in the pool," Nate suggested.

She smiled at him slowly, shaking her head.

"Okay, I tried. She's wondering why our friend the gestapo came in and hauled off Jorge," Nate said. "Am I right?"

"Of course."

"But none of us could possibly believe..." Cindy murmured.

"We should call him," Larry said. "Tell him we're a group and demand to be let in on this."

Kelsey stared at him.

"Well?"

"I think you're right," she said. "Let me grab my phone from inside." She crumpled her pizza plate, stood and went inside for her cell phone. She dialed Dane's cell number.

It rang and rang and rang. At last his voice came on.

"Dane, dammit it, you can't just run in, drag Jorge out and not give us anything resembling an explanation," she said. Then she frowned and clicked off.

"What did he say?" Nate demanded.

Kelsey let out a sigh. "Nothing."

"What?" Cindy protested.

"Nothing. I just got aggressive with his answering machine."

"He's not answering the phone?" Cindy said.

"No." Frustrated, Kelsey sat back down on a lounge chair.

They were all silent again for a minute.

"Well..." Larry said.

"Yes?" Cindy spoke, but they all looked at him.

"There's the whole skinny-dipping thing," he suggested.

Cindy moaned. Silence fell again.

"Damn." Nate yawned. "Well, this just sucks. We're all exhausted. No one has had any sleep in forever, and now—"

He broke off suddenly, his body tense.

"What now?" Kelsey said.

"I think I heard something."

They all jumped up and raced back around the side of the house.

"Dammit! I could swear..." Larry said. "Did you see a flash of...color, fabric, a person...?"

"Going out the gate?" Nate said. "Hell, why are we waiting? Let's find out."

He was already running.

Larry was at his heels.

Kelsey stared at Cindy. In tacit agreement, they burst into a run themselves.


Dane didn't speak at all until they were on the highway. He knew exactly where he was going, and apparently Jorge knew, as well.

"We're going to the marina?" he said. He seemed calm now that they were away from the others.

"It's as good as any place to talk."

"This is about my activities at night in the boat?" Jorge said.

"And more."

"I did not think..." Jorge began, but he didn't finish.

"You didn't think what? That you'd get caught?"

"I didn't think that you...I didn't think that you'd involve yourself."

"Not involve myself? When who knows how many women have been murdered and Sheila is missing?" Dane was so astounded by Jorge's attitude that he nearly missed the turnoff. The Jeep jerked its way into the parking lot and ground to a halt.

Jorge was staring at him incredulously. "I haven't murdered anyone. What are you talking about?"

"The strippers. The victims of the Necktie Strangler."

Jorge shook his head, frowning. "I am guilty, but not of murder."

Dane sat silently for a minute. "Someone witnessed you dumping something into the ocean, Jorge. And I'd like to know what it was."

Jorge said nothing at first, then insisted, "I have never killed anyone."

Dane stared ahead through the windshield. "A stripper at the club where Cherie Mardsen worked saw you there. Many times. She's pretty certain you were there the night Cherie disappeared. Sure enough to testify to it in court."

Jorge laughed, then buried his face in his hands. "You talked to a stripper. Which stripper?"

"Her name doesn't matter right now."

"Yes, it does," Jorge said. He looked around, then turned to Dane. "So you think I may be a killer, but you're talking to me alone."

"Right."

"Why?"

"Because you're an old friend."

"You're not afraid of me?"

"No. However, I am armed."

"Of course. You would be," Jorge said. "Maybe you don't really have anything on me."

"Maybe I don't, though I do have witnesses to your activities. But I intend to let you explain them first—if you can. Want to talk?"

Jorge let out a long sigh. "Sure." Then he hesitated and looked away before turning back to Dane. "Okay, like I said, I am guilty of illegal activity. But not murder."

"Go on."

"You said you talked to a stripper. But not a girl named Marisa Martinez."

Dane frowned and shook his head, studying Jorge. "No, I didn't speak with a girl named Marisa. Why?"

"I had business with her."

"What business?"

Jorge hesitated again. "I can show you. But...I have to trust you. If I can't trust you, then you'll have to drive me to the police."

Dane shook his head. "Jorge, if you're doing something illegal—"

"Illegal, but not...bad," Jorge said.

"All right, Jorge. If you can convince me that what you're doing isn't bad...then we'll leave it alone. But if you're pushing drugs..."

"That's Izzy's business. I think I can convince you that you need to look beyond what you have seen," Jorge said.

"I'll give you a chance."

"And I'm taking that chance," Jorge said.

"Well?"

"Drive. I'll tell you where to go."

Dane stared at him warily for a moment.

"You're armed, and I'm not," Jorge said. "You can search me if you want. Please, drive."

Dane stared at Jorge, then revved the engine. A minute later they were back out on the highway.

Running didn't get them anywhere. When they reached the sidewalk, Nate and Larry were already there, staring down the little byway that led to US1.

"What? What did you see?" Kelsey asked breathlessly.

"I think someone did run through here," Larry said.

"Not just someone," Nate added.

"Who, then? What the hell is going on?" Cindy demanded.

"I...I don't know," Larry said. "I can't guarantee it, but it might have been..."

"What?" Kelsey exploded.

"A truck. A beatup old tank of a truck," Larry said.

"Old man Latham's truck," Nate explained.

"You think Andy Latham might have been here? In the yard, staring in Kelsey's window, then hiding until he could get away?" Cindy asked.

"Maybe," Larry said. "I wouldn't put it past him."

"It's Nate he's pissed at, though," Larry said.

"I think he hates all of us," Cindy murmured. She stared at Kelsey. "Maybe you did see more than a lizard. I think we should call the police."

"Definitely. That asshole slugged me last night, and who knows what he's doing now? Stalking all of us," Nate said. "Yeah. I'm going in. I'm calling Gary Hansen's office."

"We can't prove anything. We didn't really see anything," Kelsey said.

"We should report the incident, anyway," Nate insisted.

Kelsey nodded. He was right.

They all traipsed back inside, where Nate went to the phone and called the sheriff's office.

Dane was wary as they drove down a side street, but it was true—he was armed, and Jorge wasn't. He was also pretty certain that in a fight, he wouldn't have any trouble taking Jorge down. But the street was a quiet one. And if Jorge was running drugs, it was hardly likely he would have admitted it while they were sitting in the parking lot at the marina.

But it was important to pursue this. Now.

"Just down the street," Jorge said.

Dane pulled into a yard. It was neatly kept. Someone had planted perennials in the little boxed garden area surrounding the house.

The car in the yard was an old Chevy. Like the yard, it showed signs of careful upkeep. The house itself was small but whitewashed.

It didn't look like a crack house.

Jorge got out of the car. Dane followed him as he started up the path to the house and knocked at the door.

A woman's voice answered, sounding wary. The door didn't open.

Jorge spoke to her quickly in Spanish, identifying himself. Dane's understanding of the language was good, but Jorge was speaking so quickly that he couldn't catch everything. But Jorge wasn't warning her that he was out there with someone dangerous, that much Dane could comprehend. He was assuring her that everything was all right.

The door opened slowly.

They stepped into a small living room. The furniture was sparse but polished. A handmade quilt covered an old battered couch. The tile beneath the throw rug was scrubbed and shiny.

The woman who had let them enter was young, in her mid-twenties. She was exotically beautiful, with huge brown eyes, deep bronze skin, long, dark hair, and a willowy, hourglass figure. She looked at Jorge, then at Dane.

"Marisa, *este hombre es un amigo mio,*" Jorge said. "Dane Whitelaw."

"*Hola,*" Marisa said gravely, shaking his hand.

"Dane, Marisa works at the club."

"Nice to meet you."

"She is applying for her citizenship," Jorge went on to explain.

"Good for you," Dane said.

She apparently understood some English, because she smiled and said, "Thank you."

"Call Jose," Jorge said softly.

Her eyes widened with alarm.

"It will be all right," Jorge said. "Please, call Jose."

Marisa looked at Jorge. She was clearly afraid, but she trusted Jorge.

"Jose!" She walked toward a small hallway that must have led to the bedrooms. "Please, Jose, come out."

A moment later a boy of about six came running out of the bedroom, straight to the woman. She settled her arms protectively around his shoulders as he stood before her, staring up at Jorge and Dane with the same large dark eyes as Marisa. He smiled at Jorge but looked suspiciously at Dane.

Jorge turned to Dane.

"Marisa is my reason for being at the strip club. Jose is my cargo. Marisa came here several years ago from Cuba. On a raft. Marisa and her husband were parted when they left, and Jose was with his father. Their raft began to leak, and they had to go back. She has been trying for years through legal channels to get her son here. Last year his father died. He was left alone with a very old grandmother who wanted him to come here to his mother. She tried other means. Then she came to me."

"So...you earn your living smuggling refugees out of Cuba?" Dane said.

Jorge stiffened and stared at him with the coldest gaze Dane had ever known.

"Not me. There are others who take every cent desperate people have ever made. Not me. I do this because I love my countrymen, because I came here myself, because I love my new country. I do it for all that I have been given."

Dane was silent. The little boy was looking up at him. Dane ruffled his hair. "So what were you dumping in the ocean?" he asked Jorge.

"I lost a passenger once. A very old man. He wanted to touch the shores of a free country before he died. He didn't make it.

I...had to cast the body to the sea. I couldn't explain how I had come by it if I had not."

Dane smiled at Marisa. "Thanks," he said softly. He grinned at the boy, mussed his hair once again.

Then he turned and started from the house.

Jorge followed him. "You can't turn me in. You can't tell anyone about Jose."

Dane stopped. "Dammit, Jorge, I'm not going to turn in the kid."

"I have not lied to you about anything. I am scared every time I make a run. Scared to death. But it's something I must do, something I owe to myself, to God. I would never hurt a woman, I swear that to you."

"Okay, Jorge, I believe you."

"So now...?"

"So now let's go back and have pizza."

Jorge studied his face. Then nodded. "Pizza. It will be cold, but it won't matter. You don't know what a world is like without fast food and pizza."

"Actually, I've seen many worlds without fast food and pizza," Dane told him dryly. "But in this world if our pizza's cold, we can order another one. So let's go."

They returned to the car. Back on the highway, Dane asked Jorge, "You're absolutely sure you were nowhere near that wreck today?"

Jorge looked over at him. "Dane, if I had seen anything, I'd be the first to say so."

"Okay, so were you, Larry, Nate and Cindy near each other all the time?"

"Sure."

"You saw them?"

"Of course. Well, not always...but there were only moments when we weren't together." Jorge spun on him suddenly, angry. "Izzy was so quick to tell you about my activities. Have you talked to him?"

"Obviously."

Jorge stared ahead. "Maybe you should talk to him some more."

"Is there something you know that I don't?" Dane asked.

Jorge shook his head in frustration. "I wish there was. Hey! Look—a sheriff's car. There are Gary Hansen and one of his deputies in front of the duplex."

Dane drove quickly onto the embankment near the front of the duplex. The motor was barely off before he was out of the car and racing toward the front door, his heart thundering with panic.

"Dane, hey!" Gary Hansen called out.

Dane looked like a thundercloud, all dark-haired menace as he walked toward the porch. Kelsey looked up as he came toward them.

"What the hell happened?" Dane demanded.

"The folks here think they might have had a visitor," Hansen said.

"A visitor?" Dane's eyes were fixed on Kelsey.

"I thought there might have been someone in the yard. Then, when we were eating our pizza out on the patio, Nate thought he saw something, so we all ran out front, where he and Larry thought they saw a truck that might have been Andy Latham's."

Dane stared at Gary. He didn't say a word; he didn't have to. Gary quickly answered his unspoken question.

"Dane, dammit, I told you, I uphold the laws, I don't make them. And so far all he's done is punch Nate and maybe trespass."

"He has to be picked up," Dane said.

"I've got an APB out on him," Gary assured him. "We can bring him in on suspicion of trespassing, something like that. But if you want me to hold him, dammit, you've got to come up with something for me to hold him *on*."

"Bring him in," Dane said, running his fingers through his dark hair. "Bring him in, and I'll come up with cause to hold him."

"You'd better. Because I haven't got squat."

Gary started down the walk toward his car. Dane stared at Kelsey, and she stared back.

"Pack up a few things."

"What? Why?"

"You're coming to my house."

Kelsey frowned. "Dane, Larry is here, and Cindy is right next door."

"Please," he managed to say quietly, gritting his teeth. "Come to my house."

Kelsey stared at him. Scary. She had slept with him last night, and now she didn't know if she trusted him or not.

No...

She did trust him. As much as she trusted anyone.

And still...

"Kelsey, please."

She didn't want to be afraid the way she had been earlier. Seeing a face in a window, wondering if it was real or just a product of her overexcited imagination.

"Come in for a few minutes." She looked past him, frowning, and saw that Jorge was right behind him. She stared at the two of them. "Is everything all right with you two?"

"Just fine," Dane said curtly.

"Are you going to explain?" she asked them.

"No," they said in unison.

"Great. And I'm supposed to go sleep at your house," she said to Dane.

Jorge set a hand on her arm. "It's all right."

"I have your blessing?" she inquired, a half smile curving her lips.

Jorge grinned and nodded.

"Great. Well, then, you two go on in and explain yourselves to the others, have some pizza. Beer and sodas are in the refrigerator." She stared at Dane, whose dark eyes never gave away a damn thing. She exhaled. She was uneasy. No, flat-out scared. But, right or wrong, she wanted to be with him.

"I guess I'll go pack a few things."

# CHAPTER 15

As Kelsey walked back through the apartment, she heard Nate, Larry and Cindy discussing Andy Latham and wondering why he was so convinced that one of them was throwing dead fish on his property. They were clustered together in the living room, and had moved on from pizza and beer to coffee and Oreos.

"Is Gary Hansen going to do anything?" Larry asked her, stretching to get a kink out of his neck.

"Yes, he's going to try to pick him up, and he can probably hold him for about twenty-four hours, but he can't really keep him unless we can come up with something on him. By the way, Jorge and Dane are back."

The announcement was unnecessary, because by that time the group could clearly see Jorge and Dane walking in behind her.

"Did you eat all the pizza?" Jorge asked.

"No, the leftovers are in the refrigerator," Cindy said. "Want me to heat it up for you?"

"I can manage," Dane said.

"Did you two duke it out or something?" Nate asked.

Kelsey went to the bedroom and closed the door behind her.

They could figure it out between themselves, she decided. What-ever was going on, Dane and Jorge had decided not to tell her.

She sat down again in front of the drawer where she had been digging through Sheila's things. She separated out the papers she had already gone over and started leafing through some of the others. She came to a picture that looked as if it had been drawn by a small child. It had been, of course. Sheila's name was scrawled at the bottom right.

The drawing was done with the simple strokes of a grade school art class. Arms and legs were little more than sticks.

What was disturbing was that the picture, despite its simplis-tic form, was very real. It depicted a man and a child, his arm around the little girl. Not around her shoulders or her waist. Lower. His smile was little more than a slash of color, and yet it captured a strange sense of evil. The girl was clearly afraid of the man. Studying the crude crayon drawing, Kelsey bit her lip. She wondered if anything she was seeing could prove that Andy Latham had been a child molester.

She doubted that either Sheila's diary or her old drawing would be enough in a court of law, not without Sheila here to do something about it. Gary Hansen knew just as well as they did that Andy Latham should be locked up, but like he had said, he didn't make the laws, he just upheld them.

She stashed the picture, the rest of the papers and Sheila's diary in an overnight bag and grabbed a few more things. She walked back out to the living room with the bag packed.

"What's that?" Larry asked in surprise, an Oreo halfway to his lips.

Dane was seated in the armchair next to the sofa. He had a large coffee cup in his hands. He looked at Kelsey over the rim of it and replied to Larry. "Kelsey is going to stay with me at Hurricane Bay tonight."

"Oh," Larry said.

They all stared at Kelsey.

"That didn't take very long," Larry murmured.

"Well, I guess we've all known all along that there was...something between them," Cindy said.

"Still, three days," Larry said, looking at Kelsey with a shake of his head.

"Three days," Nate echoed.

"Three days—and how many years?" Jorge said.

"I guess I just never realized before that Kelsey and Dane knew each other so quite well," Larry said.

Larry looked at Kelsey, still confused. "Did Sheila know?"

"Did Sheila know what? That I'm going to stay at Hurricane Bay tonight because I'm spooked by what happened here?" Kelsey asked, unable to repress a certain irritation that she seemed to have three extra parents judging her actions.

"About you and Dane," Larry said with a sigh.

"There wasn't—isn't—any 'me and Dane,'" Kelsey said. "I'm just sleeping at Hurricane Bay tonight."

"It's because he thinks one of us tried to kill you with a speargun," Nate said suddenly, angrily. "And I guess you think so, too."

"No!" Kelsey protested. "Nate, that's not it at all. I'm just a little uneasy about Andy Latham or someone sneaking into the yard and watching me."

"I'm here, too, you know," Larry said.

"And I live in the other half of the house," Cindy added.

"You could have come to my house," Nate said, eyeing her levelly.

"I'm glad I'm not in the middle of this one," Jorge murmured.

Nate kept staring at Kelsey as he said, "She's always been in love with him." He offered her a rueful smile.

Kelsey groaned, dropping the bag and staring at the lot of them. "I'm here, right here, you don't need to talk around me. Dane made me the first offer, so I'm just going over to Hurricane Bay for the night. I'll figure it all out from there tomorrow. Is that all right?"

Larry looked at Nate. "He was in the armed forces. And he's a private investigator."

"Carries a big gun," Nate agreed.

"Larry, if you're feeling protective, I may just stay on this side tonight, in Kelsey's bed," Cindy said.

"Sheila's bed," Kelsey corrected.

None of them said anything, their silence seeming to indicate that they shared her fear that something bad had happened to Sheila. No one even tried to suggest that Sheila might show up that night.

"There's a plan. Cindy, who can bench-press twice her own weight, is going to let me feel protective," Larry said.

Jorge crumpled his pizza plate in his hand. "Well, I know where I'm sleeping—in my own bed. I'll wish you all good night."

He nodded around the group, then looked at Dane, who was just walking in from the kitchen. Kelsey was both baffled and curious. Dane nodded back at Jorge, as if the two of them had come to some new understanding that went beyond anything she could begin to comprehend.

It was nice, of course, since they had been friends for a very long time. But it was also annoying as all hell. She felt very much on the outside.

"I guess I'm going, too," Nate said, rising.

"And we'll be on our way. I'm about to drop," Kelsey said.

Nate was standing behind her. "Oh, yeah. I'll bet you're going right to sleep," he said softly.

She stared at him, frowning. "Do you remember that we didn't sleep at all last night? We came rushing back here because Latham decked you."

"Thanks for the concern," he said. He started out the door, then turned back. "Hey, Larry, if Latham really is getting freaky, you two do need to watch it, being here. Make sure you lock up tight."

"We'll do a thorough inspection of all windows and doors before going to sleep," Cindy assured him.

"Of course," Larry said, "we could all go to Hurricane Bay and be safe."

"Except that we're not all invited," Jorge said. "Good night." He headed out for his car.

"Good night, and, Cindy, Larry, really do lock up," Kelsey said.

"I'm on it," Cindy assured her.

Nate didn't say goodbye; he just watched Kelsey as she climbed into the Jeep beside Dane. As they left, Cindy and Larry waved from the door. Nate at last lifted a hand.

When the others had left, Cindy looked at the two men. "It's not actually a surprise."

"You mean Kelsey going off with Dane?" Larry said.

"Of course. Nate, you're the one who used to tell me all the time that you thought something went on between them years ago."

"Yeah," Nate said.

"So why didn't they stay together?" Larry asked.

"Who knows? Maybe Kelsey felt she had betrayed Sheila or something like that."

Larry made a snorting sound. "How could anyone betray Sheila?" he asked.

"Poor Larry." Cindy put her hand on his arm. "I know she hurt you, but...but I think sometimes that she just must have been...is...so messed up inside that she couldn't help it." She watched him, hesitating for a minute. She was about to make a confession. "I...could tell you..."

"What?" Larry asked her.

"Never mind. Let's take a walk through my place, check it out, lock it up and come back here."

"You think someone might have broken into your place?" Nate asked.

"I don't know, but I'll feel better if we look around. I'm like Kelsey, just feeling a little spooked."

"Whatever makes you happy," Larry said.

"Can't hurt," Nate told Cindy. "Maybe I'll hang around on

the couch tonight. We'll all be here then. Would that make you feel better?"

Larry groaned. "Just because I'm usually in a suit doesn't mean I haven't got balls, you know."

Cindy laughed. "Larry, we're not questioning your manly credentials."

"Right," Nate said. "Actually I might stay just because I'm spooked myself, and I'm not sure I want to drive home alone. I had Dane set up cameras and stuff for security at work, but hell...we haven't locked our doors around here for years. Larry, you can protect me, too."

"Cool," Larry said. "Let's start with Cindy's place, then."

They locked the door to Sheila's place, and Cindy unlocked the door to the other side of the house.

"Want us to hang out in the living room?" Larry asked.

"No, I want you to follow me every step of the way."

They did. They went through every room, checked out every closet, then made sure every door was locked. Just as an extra precaution, they shoved a mop handle against the sliding door in the back bedroom that corresponded with the one where Kelsey had been sleeping. Larry found a broken broom to use for the same purpose off the dining and living area.

"Happy?" Larry asked.

"I am," Cindy said.

"Okay, now we go through the other side," Nate said.

They walked through the house together, then secured the doors, taking extra care with the back where Kelsey had slept and where Cindy would sleep that night.

"Am I crazy?" Nate murmured, looking out the window before closing the drapes. "Are we all crazy? Kelsey might have seen a head—or she might have seen a lizard. I might have seen a flash of someone—or it might have been my imagination. We might have seen Latham's car—and we might not have seen it."

"We're all overtired," Cindy said. "We've hardly had any sleep at all."

"All right, well...there's my bunk," Nate said, indicating the couch. "I guess you two are beat."

"Exhausted," Cindy agreed. "But...not quite ready to sleep. I shouldn't have had that coffee. I'm wired."

"I know how to cure that," Nate said.

"How?" Cindy asked.

"Let's have another beer."

"Great. Then we can sit around and talk about old times," Larry said dryly.

"If we have two beers, who knows what I may wind up telling you," Cindy said.

"Something scandalous?" Larry asked.

"Low down and dirty," Cindy said.

"I'm on my way for the beers," Nate told her.

"I wish you would tell me what went on with Jorge," Kelsey said. "You came in the first time as if you wanted to throttle him. You came back in later as if you were his best buddy."

"I wouldn't say that," Dane told her, pulling onto the road to Hurricane Bay. "Jorge just explained a few things, that's all. No one is off the hook yet."

"Off the hook? Dane, I know that I've been the one pressing to find out what happened to Sheila, but I think you're becoming paranoid."

"Kelsey, have you forgotten that someone shot at you with a speargun today?"

She turned in the seat, staring at him. "There were lots of boats out there today. You didn't even catch the names of all of them. And let's face it, most of the problems down here are caused by tourists who don't know what they're doing. And if someone around here is guilty of any of this, it has to be Andy Latham."

"I'm sure he *is* guilty of something. But that doesn't explain a lot of the things that have been going on. I didn't really look at all the boats out there today—I was too anxious to hook up with all of you—but I think I would have noticed Latham's boat. It's a floating cesspool." Dane shook his head. "Besides, I can't see Andy Latham having the intelligence to track you down, take a speargun and manage to hide himself so well."

"If he is the Necktie Strangler, he's certainly demonstrated his intelligence," Kelsey said. "He's managed to dispose of his victims so that they don't surface until it's almost impossible for the police to get evidence from the bodies."

Dane brought the car to a halt and turned off the engine. "All right, I'll grant you that."

"And if anyone was running around the yard tonight, it must have been Latham. Nate was almost certain it was Latham's truck he saw."

Dane looked at her. "Okay, Latham is the prime suspect. Now we just need some proof. Or at least something that connects him to the victims."

"If we find Sheila and she's been..." Kelsey's voice faltered.

"Yes, *if* we find Sheila," he said simply. "Here, give me your bag."

He took the small canvas bag she had brought and exited the car. Kelsey followed him to the back door and noted that he now locked both the bolts.

"You're worried about something out here?" she said.

"I'm just worried in general," he told her.

As soon as they were inside, he was careful to lock the door again.

She had paused just in the entry. "Make yourself at home," he told her, walking past her.

"Strange, isn't it? I do feel at home here."

"Because it hasn't changed a hell of a lot, probably."

"Yes, but *we've* all changed, haven't we?"

"Maybe. And maybe not. Want something to drink? Are you hungry? Hell, I guess you're exhausted. I am."

"Yeah, I'm beat. And I know where the kitchen is," Kelsey said. She hesitated. "Where do you want me?"

"In my room," he said ruefully. "I get the impression you're still not really sure you trust me."

She took the bag from him. "Miss a chance to inspect your bedroom? Not on your life." She started for the stairway in the front, then paused. "You're going to let me go up there without supervision?"

"I have a few calls to make," he told her.

"All right. Who are you calling?"

"I promise I'll tell you if anything pans out, how's that?"

"I don't think I can beat an answer out of you, so I guess it will have to do." She hesitated, watching him.

"Yes?"

"If you take too long, you know I'll be asleep."

A slow, rueful grin cut across his face. "I'll keep that in mind."

Kelsey went up the stairs.

The threesome at the duplex were actually on their third beers when Nate urged Cindy to make good on her earlier remark.

"C'mon," he pressed. "I've confessed my horrendous dating experiences. The time I got that really hot model into bed and passed out from too much booze. Then the obvious, of course—that I couldn't keep my wife a full month. And Larry has told us all how he caught his pecker in his zipper on his first date with that art assistant. Come on, Cindy—you got us going on guy talk. You're going to have to join in. And this should be different—I mean, you're not likely to tell us you couldn't get it up."

"No..." Cindy said slowly.

"Jeez, come on," Larry prodded. "Nate and I only spilled the far-from-macho beans to get you talking."

"All right." Cindy stared at them. "I had a thing with...another woman."

"Whoa!" Nate said.

"I wound up really humiliated."

"What happened?" Larry demanded.

"Who with? It wasn't Kelsey, was it? Or wasn't she telling the truth when she said she's not gay?"

Cindy shook her head. "Not Kelsey. And, Nate, dammit, quit worrying that you weren't a good lover and that's why your marriage didn't last. I think it's obvious now what made Kelsey tick all the time."

"A better man," Nate said.

Cindy shook her head determinedly. "A different man. That's all, Nate. A different man."

"Hey, hey, hey. Enough of the rah-rah for Nate. Come on, Cindy. Do we know this broad you slept with?"

"Oh yeah."

"Who?" Nate demanded.

"I know," Larry said, eyeing Cindy over his can of beer. "Sheila."

"Sheila?" Nate exploded. "How did she fit you into her schedule between men?"

Cindy smiled. "Oh...we were doing this same thing one night. Sitting here, drinking wine. We just started talking, kind of like this, about men. I was telling her about all my bad dates, lousy relationships. I had just been out with this guy who sold T-shirts wholesale. The entire time we were doing business, he was as nice as could be. We go out for dinner, and right off he wants to head for his hotel room."

"Let's get back on topic here. What happened with you and Sheila?"

"She gave me the speech about her own life—saying I might as well get what I could out of a guy, because they were all like that at heart."

"I wasn't. I loved her," Larry said.

"She said you loved her too much," Cindy told Larry.

"Maybe."

"Come on, Cindy, get to the good part," Nate urged.

"I'm not even sure where it started," she said. "I guess we decided that, on the whole, the male of the species was a total louse. Except for gay guys. They're great but unavailable. She said that was why women often preferred other women. They were nicer, sensitive...decent. The next thing I knew, she was rubbing my shoulders. She said I needed a hot bath. We wound up in the bath together with a ton of bubbles and more wine, and when we got out, she started drying me off. And she...well, she just touched the right places, and I was really drunk, and then...the things she could do..."

"Yeah, we know," Nate said huskily.

"Well, anyway, we slept together. I woke up with a terrible hangover, feeling ridiculous and uneasy. Sheila started laughing and telling me not to worry about it, she wasn't getting into anything permanent with me—I had actually been an experiment. She just wanted to prove to herself that she could seduce anyone, male or female. I was pretty pissed off—and big time embarrassed. I don't think we spoke to each other for days after that. But she was always so blasé about everything. In a week it was as if it had never happened."

"That was probably a record," Nate said. "I doubt if she ever remembered any guy she slept with for more than a week."

"Except for Dane," Larry said.

"Her thing with Dane was weird," Cindy said, shaking her head. "She wanted him, but she would push him away when he tried to get too close."

"She knew she couldn't be what Dane was looking for," Nate said. "Partly because she was Sheila...and maybe she even knew he'd had a thing for Kelsey all those years. And this time around, she knew he had been in love with that woman in St. Augustine." He was quiet for a minute, then said, "Okay, Sheila drank with you and sympathized about bad dates. I'm doing the same thing. And I'd sure love to get into a tub with you and a bunch of bubbles. What do you think?"

Cindy just laughed.

Cindy curled into Sheila's bed at long last. She was beyond exhaustion, and though she had had a great time staying up and talking with Nate and Larry, she knew she was going to regret it in the morning. She loved what she did, really enjoyed the stores, the people she met and, especially, buying the things they would sell, but it was still work. Nate could cruise into work when he felt like it, and Larry was on vacation, though he'd said he planned to do some work on the computer. She was the only one who was going to have to get up in a few hours' time.

Still, it was fun. She liked having the old crowd back. Not that she hadn't had Nate around forever, or that she hadn't seen Dane a fair amount since he'd been back. But she'd missed Kelsey. And Jorge. Spending time with Jorge was great.

She snuggled beneath the blankets, glad the air-conditioning worked so well. She lived in Key Largo because she had no desire to live anywhere else. One day she would probably be as wrinkled as a prune from her hours in the sun—despite the sunblock she had learned at a young age to apply on a continual basis—but she had no desire to live anywhere else in the world. The sun was wonderful, the water was wonderful. Snorkeling, diving, all of it. The reefs, the people, the food, the drinks...and now, the return of old friends.

Heat was great by day. At night, though, it was great to cuddle beneath the blankets in the chill blast of the air-conditioning.

The best of both worlds.

She turned and plumped her pillow, knowing she really needed to sleep.

She had almost drifted off when she was suddenly wide-awake again.

At first she didn't know what had disturbed her. She just lay there in the darkness, her eyes wide-open, her body tense from head to toe.

Then...

A rustling. Outside.

She turned and stared at the window, but of course she had made certain the drapes were closed before she went to bed, so she couldn't see a thing. She wondered if she was really hearing something, or if she was suffering from belated nerves.

She told herself that she was safe. Larry was in the other bedroom; Nate was on the sofa.

At last the tension in her muscles began to ease. She closed her eyes.

Then her lids flew open again.

There was someone out there. Someone trying to jimmy the lock on the sliding glass door.

"Hello? *Hola?*"

"Jorge, it's Dane."

"Dane?" Jorge sounded puzzled.

"Sorry, were you sleeping?"

"Yeah, but no big deal. What's up?"

"I'd like to talk to your friend again."

"Why?" Jorge asked suspiciously. "You said you wouldn't—"

"Jorge, I don't want to send the boy back to Cuba. I just need to talk to your friend. I showed Katia some pictures. That's how I knew that you'd been at the club. But she wasn't sure about the others. She thinks everyone I showed her might have been there at one time or another. Which is logical, I guess. She sees so many men. But maybe Marisa could help. I want to be sure she's seen all the pictures, too."

"She's probably sleeping now."

"I know. But I'd like to see her first thing in the morning."

"All right."

"Were you planning on working?"

"I have captains who can work my boats," Jorge reminded him, a low touch of pride in his voice. And then he added quietly, "Except when I must go to sea myself."

"Meet me at the gas station up on the highway by my place. Nine o'clock too early?"

"No. Not for you."

Jorge hung up.

Dane looked at the clock. There wasn't much else he could do until morning. Not on the phone.

He stood quickly, and headed for the stairs.

Cindy let out a scream that could have roused the dead. She jumped up and tore out of the room. In the broad hallway outside the bedroom, she collided with Nate.

"What is it?" he demanded. His blond hair was tousled, almost standing on end. He was clad only in a pair of blue silk boxers.

"The back!"

Larry, nothing but a sheet tied around his waist, came rushing out of his room.

"What the hell...?"

"There's someone at the sliding glass door," Cindy said, trying to be calm.

"You're certain?" Nate said. "You're not just having leftover jitters?"

"I heard someone!"

Larry started into the bedroom, heading for the drapes.

"I'm going out the front. Hope we can catch him this time," Nate said. Heedless of his shiny blue boxers, he headed right for the front door, unlocked it and went out.

Cindy watched Nate go, then ran after Larry. She reached the room just as he wrenched the drapes away from the window.

There was no one on the patio.

"I'm going around to find Nate," Cindy said.

"I'm right behind you."

Larry followed after her. She had just reached the door when she heard him curse.

"Shit!"

She turned back. Larry had tripped on his sheet. He was on the floor, in the buff. Despite herself, she felt the urge to laugh. She didn't want to stare at him. He looked like a kid on a bear rug, ready for one of those embarrassing photos parents liked to show their kids.

"I'm going to catch up with Nate. Come on," she said.

Cindy ran out the front door. She tore around to the side gate, which gaped open.

"Nate?" she realized that she had whispered his name.

He didn't reply.

"Nate?" she persisted, raising her voice slightly.

Still no reply. He had to be out there.

She hurried along the side of the house, walking quickly, then running, anxious to reach the patio, where Nate had to be.

Suddenly she staggered, a shooting pain going through her head. She blinked, wondering what she had done, and tried to take a step.

She careened to the ground instead.

Kelsey really should have gone to sleep.

But she was waiting for Dane, and she knew it. When he didn't come right away, she knew she would fall asleep if she didn't do something, so she turned on the television, sitting up in bed and using the remote. Nice bed, she thought. Big. Comfortable. Four pillows at the headboard. The room wasn't overly neat—Dane had fishing magazines strewn about and some kind of trade journal describing new security products. Across from the bed was a bookshelf with an interesting assortment of titles: copies of the classics, military manuals, books on the local flora and fauna, a lot on the Everglades, and the paperback thrillers he liked to read for pleasure.

The room was done in a combination of hardwood and rattan. It was a masculine room that still welcomed a feminine presence. She felt ridiculously comfortable and at home.

Dane even had a good mattress. Clean, cool sheets. Comfy pillows.

Don't get too comfortable, girl, she warned herself. She led a different life. A fast-paced life in the advertising world. She'd only been home a matter of days, and already it seemed as if the years since her last visit meant nothing, were hardly even real. She had ended up exactly where she wanted to be. But it was a bad move. She didn't know Dane anymore. She doubted that he wanted any more than a few days with her. He'd been hurt in St. Augustine, so here he was. She'd actually gone to him and asked him to sleep with her. She was sure that was no hardship for him. But he'd slept with Sheila, as well. Before she had disappeared. She needed to think about this situation, keep her emotions in reserve.

And yet all that seemed to matter was that she was here with him now. Granted, he was downstairs. And she had warned him that she might fall asleep. Hmm. But she had also insisted that he find Sheila. And whatever he was doing, she was certain, had to do with that goal.

With that in mind, she jumped out of bed and dug into the bag she had brought along. She drew out the picture Sheila had drawn in grade school. Sheila was no artist, yet the picture was more disturbing than if it had been a perfect likeness.

She kept going through the papers, then picked up Sheila's diary, wishing that it gave more away. A diary was supposed to allow for total freedom of thought, but Sheila had only rambled. Kelsey flipped pages, wishing she could find something. Sheila did refer to people. Nate was a "silly dear." And Larry loved her so much, she wished she had been able to settle down with him. He still called her, just to make sure she didn't need anything. Izzy remained at the top of her list for fun. She enjoyed Jorge's company, but he lacked that true edge of dangerous excitement—

and the ability to see her as a real equal—that Izzy had. If only Izzy didn't mind that she loved to go to bars and pick up strangers.

The only time she ever mentioned fear was in reference to Dane. In needing to talk to Dane.

But Dane had been right. If she was afraid of him, why would he be the one she turned to when she needed to talk?

She cast the diary down in exasperation. "Sheila, why the hell didn't you just come right out and say something? It was *your* diary," she said aloud.

She picked up the papers again. Riffling through them, she was startled to find another drawing she had missed earlier.

The drawing was more like doodling. But once again it depicted a man and a girl. Or a woman. The man had the woman by the throat.

"What did you find?"

Dane's voice startled her and she nearly threw the drawing into the air. He was standing in the bedroom doorway, watching her.

"A sketch Sheila did," she told him.

He walked over to the bed, taking the sketch, staring at it. Dane so seldom gave anything away. But his look as he stared at the picture was disturbed and sorrowful.

"You think she was drawing Andy Latham?" he asked.

Kelsey shrugged. "Who can tell? She wasn't much of an artist."

He looked at the journal on the bed, still encased in the book cover.

"Sheila's diary?"

"Yes," she admitted.

"And...?"

"Nothing. She talks about everyone, but...nothing."

"I should read it."

Kelsey shrugged. "Sure. Maybe you can find something I can't."

"Not tonight. I don't think I could make sense of anything tonight."

She met his eyes. "I guess you're really tired."

"Well, there's tired and then there's tired."

"Oh?"

"I'm too tired to read." He set the journal on the nightstand and collected the papers Kelsey had scattered on the bed, piling them on top of the journal. He sat on the side of the bed, looking at her. "You've got great shoulders, Kelsey."

"Thanks."

"Can I assume the fact that they're naked shoulders means that the rest of you is also naked underneath that sheet?"

"You can assume anything you want. But you are a private investigator. I'm sure you can think of some way to find out."

"Yes, I'm sure I can."

He didn't touch her then, but rose, turning off the light. He picked up the remote control and flicked off the television.

The room wasn't completely dark. They were on the second floor, and Hurricane Bay was a private island. The drapes were pulled back. Pools of soft moonlight spilled into the room.

He undressed in haste, shoes kicked off at the foot of the bed, pants and briefs discarded there. He pulled his knit shirt over his head and it, too, fell on the pile.

He pulled the sheets from Kelsey.

"Looks like my assumption was right."

"Wow, you're really good at what you do."

"Thanks, ma'am."

"I meant investigating."

"I didn't."

Kelsey laughed as he crawled in beside her.

"Humble," she murmured, as she felt the length of his body slide next to hers, hard, hot and vibrant.

"Do you want humble...or good?"

"Well you'd better be damn good now," she told him.

She saw him grin in the moonlight. "All right."

Kelsey curled her arms around him. She'd been exhausted, but suddenly she was wide-awake.

His lips found hers. He could kiss in a way that created a carnal and intimate illusion of everything he was about to do with his body. Her legs were parted by the length of his. Their mouths were locked in an open, wet fusion when he thrust deeply into her, bringing her to the brink in a matter of seconds. She wanted to hold on, to savor the moment of deepening penetration, but then he moved...and moved.

She thought she was going to die. But just when she reached that point, he withdrew. His lips started moving then. Over her shoulders, which he complimented in whispers once again. Teasing against her collarbone. Doing incredible things to her breasts.

She couldn't bear it. She pressed against him, turning the tide. There was so much of Dane she wanted to explore. Taste, treasure. She nuzzled against the hair on his chest, ran her lips and tongue in delicate kisses over his throat, down to his hips.

Great legs...

Six-pack belly. He kept himself in shape.

She teased him everywhere...then slid her mouth down the length of his sex. She heard his single expulsion of breath as he savored her every move.

He flipped her down in a sudden movement with a sound almost like a growl. Then he returned the caresses. Belly, thighs...

Between.

She tugged at his hair. He came to her.

She thanked God they were on an island, she shrieked so loudly.

And then they lay there, locked together. She was aware of the dim moonlight. And of Dane. The feel of him, sheened with sweat, beside her. So alive.

"Well?" he murmured, lips against her ear.

She smiled, turning into him, running her fingers through his hair. "You'll do."

"Thanks." He rose above her suddenly. "I'm not always so good, you know."

"Oh?"

"It's you," he said. "You're incredibly inspiring."

"I try," she said, then added. "With you."

She couldn't see his features as he lay by her side again. She curled against him, exhausted. In moments she was asleep.

She awoke to find that he was up, dressed and ready to go out. She was startled to see that there was a gun on the bed next to her.

"It's a .38 special," he told her. "You know how to use it?"

"I...yes. I haven't touched a gun in years, but...I used to go to the shooting range with Joe fairly frequently."

"Good. I'll be about an hour. I'll lock up behind me, but keep that with you—even in the shower."

He kissed her forehead.

"Where are you going?"

"To see a stripper."

"Really."

"Yes, really. But I'll be right back."

She didn't press him, because he wasn't there to press. She heard his footsteps as he hurried down the stairs.

She lay in bed, wanting to get up, eyeing the gun. It had been a while. But she did know how to use it.

She closed her eyes, and was startled when the phone rang.

She picked it up, wondering if she should have. "Hello?"

"Kelsey?"

"Yes." It was Nate. His tone was strange.

"What is it? What's the matter?"

"Are you up? I'm coming out."

"Nate, dammit, what the hell is the matter?"

"Two things, Kels. Cindy is in the hospital."

"Why? My God, Nate, what happened?"

He went on as if he hadn't heard her.

"Cindy is in the hospital...and they've found another body." He hesitated for a fraction of a second.

"And they think this one is Sheila."

# CHAPTER 16

Cold seeped into Kelsey. A chill deeper than anything she had ever felt before.

It wasn't like the day when the military had arrived to say that Joe had been killed in action. That had been agony, anguish deeper than any physical trauma could ever inflict.

But even when Joe had died, she hadn't felt this chill. Joe had died doing what he considered his duty as an American.

Sheila had been murdered. And the anguish now lay in knowing that Sheila must have been terrified, that she must have suffered not just pain, but fear.

And the chill came from the fact that her murderer was still out there.

"Kelsey?"

"Who called?"

"A policeman called this morning and asked us to come down and identity her remains. They couldn't get hold of Andy Latham, so they tried to find Larry. Where's Dane?"

"Gone. I'm not sure where."

"All right. I'm on my way out to get you. Dane's got an in with both Gary Hansen and the Metro-Dade cops. I'm sure they'll get hold of him. Get dressed. I can be there in five minutes."

"Yes, all right." She was so distraught about Sheila that she'd almost forgotten the first news he had given her. "Wait! What happened to Cindy? You said she's in the hospital. Is she going to be all right?"

"God, yes, sorry. She thought she heard someone at the sliding glass door to the bedroom last night. I went out the back, she and Larry went out the front, and she was running, and we think she ran into the hurricane awning. Anyway, she knocked herself out. The E.R. doctor said she needed to stay in the hospital, just for observation." He hesitated. "We're supposed to pick her up this afternoon. I haven't told her that they think...that they think they've found Sheila. We thought we'd let her get out of the hospital first. Be ready, okay?"

"I will."

Kelsey hung up the phone and jumped out of bed. If she thought about dressing, she wouldn't think about Sheila.

Wrong.

All she could think about was Sheila.

Her dread had proven to be far too real.

Tears stung her eyes as she hopped in and out of the shower, then threw on clothing. She didn't think to brush her hair. She didn't even glance at the gun Dane had left on the other side of the bed, just ran downstairs, wondering if Nate had arrived and she hadn't heard him. She looked out the peephole in the front, but no one was there.

She looked out back.

Nate had arrived.

He was standing on the little spit of beach to the far left of the dock.

She hit the lock and exited the house, hurrying over to him. She hesitated. He was standing there, hands in his pockets, shoulders slumped, just staring at the sand.

"Nate?"

He turned to her, the sun casting a strange glow over his features.

"There you are," he said softly.

He walked to her, placing his hands on her shoulders. His eyes were curiously dry. "Kelsey," he said.

He drew her to him.

His grip was hard.

And painful.

They had found her.

Dane had barely reached the gas station before Gary Hansen gave him the call. She had been found on the Gulf side by a couple of kids out fishing around the numerous little islets that were little more than a few mangroves grouped together.

Due to the condition of the body—and the tie around her neck—she had been brought to the Miami-Dade County morgue for autopsy. Since she'd been fished out of the water where she'd been caught among the roots of the trees, there wasn't much the crime scene investigators could do, but they were out there working. Hector Hernandez had told Dane that he was welcome to meet him at the morgue; they were going to need a positive identification, and they weren't sure Larry was going to be up to it.

Dane met Jorge long enough to tell him what had happened, then drove north as quickly as he could. He had given Jorge a picture of Andy Latham and asked him to go show it to Marisa and ask her if she recognized the man.

Hector was well acquainted with the morgue. At the desk, he was directed to what they called cell five. It was where she had been taken, awaiting autopsy.

When Dane entered, Hector had his notebook out as he spoke with Dr. Alfred Gray. Hector waved a hand to indicate to the medical examiner that it was all right to keep speaking with Dane in the room. Sheila had been in the water approximately seven to twelve days, but since she had last been seen a week ago Friday, he thought it likely that she had been killed soon after.

"You were the last one to see her, right?" Hector asked Dane.

"The last one to admit it," Dane replied.

He had seen the dead before. Those who had died peacefully, and those who had died after the ravages of a long illness. He had seen people who had been shot, bombed and stabbed, the casualties of war.

He had never seen anything like Sheila.

What the water and its inhabitants had done to her once beautiful face and figure went beyond terrible. The crabs had chewed on her. Fish had nibbled fingers and flesh. And then, of course, there had been the death itself. Strangulation was not a pretty way to go.

And the tie. His tie. The pattern still visible, despite the ravages of water, fish and muck.

"It is Sheila Warren, though, right?" Hector asked him.

Dane nodded.

Hector was studying him gravely. He wanted to turn away. He felt Hector's eyes, but kept studying Sheila's face.

"We tried to contact her stepfather, but his boat isn't docked and his car is nowhere to be found."

Dane stared at Hector. "I've been looking for him myself, ever since Gary Hansen had to release him after he made bail. His boat and car were both gone yesterday, as well."

The medical examiner covered Sheila's face.

"Is there a place where Dane and I can talk for a minute?" Hector asked Dr. Gray.

"My office. Down the hall."

Dane followed Hector out of cell five and down the hall. Gray's door was closed but not locked.

The office was strange, though perhaps the eclectic decor within was to be expected. A skeleton hung from a metal stand. Dane knew it was human, not a copy. The skull on the desk, however, was an excellently crafted medical tool made of plastic. There was a stack of eight by ten photos on the desk. Morgue photos.

Hector sat in the doctor's chair, indicating that Dane should take the chair in front of him. Dane sat, folded his hands in his lap and looked at Hector.

"You came to me about the Necktie Strangler when Sheila was just among the missing. I need to know why you thought we were going to find Sheila like this," he told Dane.

"That's not a great mystery," Dane said, despite the fact that it seemed every one of his muscles was tightening like piano wire. "She was missing—missing women have been showing up in the canals lately."

"And you've been looking for Andy Latham, who has disappeared, at least for the moment. Want to tell me why?"

"Because he's a scumbag, and Sheila hated him," Dane said. Staring at Hector, he still saw Sheila's face. Sheila's beautiful face...

Never to be beautiful again.

Sheila, who had said, "Dane, help me."

He felt sick. He didn't usually get queasy at the sight of death.

*He didn't usually see a woman he had known all his life, slept with, grown up with, dead, and not just dead...dead the way Sheila was...lying on a slab at the morgue. Sheila was beyond suffering now. And beyond help.*

There was a tap at the door, and it opened. Dr. Gray didn't enter, he just spoke briefly.

"Hector," Dr. Gray said, "if you're done...we're going to get started on her right away. You'll have my report the minute we're finished."

"Thank you," Hector said gravely.

The door closed. Hector looked at Dane again. Dane realized his palms were sweating.

"Come on, Dane," Hector said. "Talk to me."

\*\*\*

"Hey! Let's go!"

It was Larry. He was on the dock.

Nate released Kelsey, staring down into her eyes. He shook his head in misery. "I didn't mean to...I just started thinking...oh, God, Kels, I had a death grip on you there...I'm sorry, I just...I just..."

She nodded. "Let's go."

She walked over to Larry, who looked like hell. His eyes were swollen, the rims nearly crimson.

"It—it may not be her," Kelsey said.

Neither of them answered her as they walked to the car. She knew that, in their hearts, all three of them knew that the woman in the morgue was going to be Sheila Warren.

Nate had trouble opening his car door.

"Are you all right to drive?" she asked him.

He stared at her. "I'm fine. Honestly. Come up, we've got to get up to Miami."

Larry got into the back seat. Kelsey took the front. They drove in silence.

"Kelsey Cunningham, an old friend, showed up here a few days ago because she was supposed to meet Sheila."

"I know who she is," Hector acknowledged.

"Kelsey was extremely concerned right away. She didn't believe Sheila would have gone off without telling her, not when they had arranged to get together. She came to me—and then she went out to Andy Latham's. Another friend called to tell me that she was out there, so I went after her and got her. Not because I knew anything, but because, like I said, Latham is a sleazebag. Always has been. We—Sheila's friends—believe she was probably molested by him as a child. Then Latham showed up at my house when we were having a barbecue. He dumped off a pile of rotting fish. Accused us—or me—of having dropped them on his property."

"Did you?"

"Come on, Hector, what do you think? Of course I didn't."

"Go on."

"Last night Kelsey thought someone was out in the yard at the duplex. She's staying at Sheila's place. They called Gary Hansen, so the cops came out."

"Are you sure it was Latham?"

"Sheila's ex-husband, Larry, and Nate Curry were both there, and they thought they saw Latham's truck drive away."

"They thought."

Dane lifted his hands. "Hector, I wasn't there at the time. I'm telling you what they told me. But they called Gary Hansen."

"And?"

"By the time Gary came out, they'd all tramped all over the yard."

"Did anyone dust for prints?"

"No. But..."

"But what?"

"I think he wears gloves. Some kind of gloves, most of the time. Diving gloves, fishing gloves. You know yourself, the Necktie Strangler is no fool."

"Is there anything else?"

"Yes."

"What?"

"Yesterday they all went fishing. When I heard that Latham had been released, I set out to find them. And I did. They were spearfishing. I found Kelsey, and while we were down there, a couple of spears came shooting by—far too close."

"Who was shooting? Did you find Latham down there?"

"No. I didn't find anyone."

"And did you do anything?"

"Hell, yes, we called the Coast Guard."

Hector eased back in his chair. "You're a private investigator, and you didn't find out who was shooting at her?"

"I went down...but Kelsey wouldn't go back to the damn boat without me. I didn't get to search long, because I was too afraid someone was going to find his mark."

"But you think Latham might have been out there?"

Dane shrugged.

Hector leaned forward. "All right. If Latham is the Necktie Strangler and he was determined to kill his own stepdaughter, he'd have known, once the deed was done, that she was dead. Why would he be staking out the duplex?"

Dane exhaled a sharp breath. "To kill Kelsey," he said. And he straightened. "She's out at my place now. Alone. And no one knows where the hell Latham is."

Hector shook his head. "She's not alone," he said.

"But—"

The door to the office opened, and a man, apparently a plain-clothes officer, stepped in.

"The ex-husband and his friends have made it?" Hector asked.

The man nodded. "The M.E. took the morgue photo out to the ex and his friends just a minute ago," he told Hector. "They gave us another positive ID. They're out there now."

*The ex-husband and his friends...*

"Fine, I'll go speak with them right now," Hector said. "Come with me," he told Dane.

They left the office and headed out to the reception area. "I dislike sounding clichéd, Dane, but you're not planning any va-cations or anything, are you?" Hector asked.

"Am I planning on leaving town? Definitely not. But I sure as hell hope you're looking for Andy Latham, not wasting time suspecting me."

"We are. And I assume you'll be doing the same. In town, of course."

"Yes."

"I'm going to need a lot more against Andy Latham to hold him, much less to get the D.A.'s office to put together a sound case. So far...well, I hope you can give me more than the fact that you don't like him and his stepdaughter hated him. And that he dumped dead fish on your property, and people *think* they saw him sneaking around."

"He may have been hanging around the strip club where one of the other girls who was killed worked. Where she was working the night before she disappeared."

Hector stopped in the hallway, staring at him again. "And you have found this out...how?"

"One of the girls thinks she may have seen him."

Hector was still staring at him. "I spent days at that strip club."

"You had nothing to give the girls. I brought in pictures. And you know as well as I do that girls practicing prostitution on the side aren't going to talk to the police."

As they were standing there in the hallway, Dane's cell phone began to ring. He ignored it for a moment, staring at Hector.

"Answer it."

He did. It was Jorge, and he was excited.

"Marisa says she has definitely seen Andy Latham at the club."

Hector was still watching him, and Dane was pretty sure he had been able to hear Jorge's words.

"Thanks, Jorge."

"What now?" Jorge asked.

He winced. "Marisa may be asked to testify."

"She will have to go to court?" Jorge sounded alarmed.

"She's legal, right?"

"Yes."

"Then there's no problem, Jorge."

"I pray that you are right."

Jorge hung up. His last words sounded as if he felt he had somehow been betrayed. Unfortunately there was no way for Dane to call him back and reassure him.

"You heard?" Dane asked Hector.

Hector nodded.

"Gary Hansen put out an APB on Latham last night."

Hector arched a brow. "That's good. But now the APB will have to be amended. He'll be wanted on suspicion of murder."

They walked out to the reception room. Larry, Nate and Kelsey were there. Kelsey's red, tearstained eyes widened at the sight of him. Larry was ashen. His eyes were red-rimmed as well.

"It's Sheila," Larry said. "Oh, God. It's really Sheila. I had hoped...knowing Sheila...I just kept believing that she'd walk back in, irritated that we were so worried. That she would say she had just gone off to Paris or Rome...or, hell, Tampa. But it's Sheila...."

He was going to break down again. Kelsey put an arm around him.

Larry covered his face with his hands.

Hector stood by him, his features both sympathetic and resolute. He was a homicide detective, a man who had been the bearer of such news before.

"Thank you very much for coming down. You were called in as the closest to kin we could find. I'm sorry, very sorry. And I assure you, we are doing everything we can to catch the killer."

Larry nodded, getting a grip on himself.

"We're free to go?" Nate asked.

"Of course. I'll know where to find you when I need to ask more questions."

"We all have cell phones," Nate said.

Hector stared at Dane. "We'll catch him."

"You need to find Latham."

"Oh, we will." Hector was still staring at him. He turned and walked back toward the autopsy rooms.

"Let's get back," Nate told him.

"I need a drink," Larry murmured.

"We'll get Cindy...break it to her and go to the Sea Shanty. We'll be together."

The three of them rose.

"Kelsey," Dane said, "drive with me."

She looked at the other two, worried.

"Drive with me," Dane repeated.

"Go with him," Nate told her. "Larry and I are all right. We'll pick up Cindy and meet you at the Sea Shanty."

"All right," Kelsey murmured.

As they stepped out to the parking lot, the sky was overcast. "Looks like we're in for some weather," Nate said.

But none of them cared about the weather anymore, even when it started to spit and sprinkle as they parted, walking to their cars.

"We'll be right there," Kelsey called as the two men walked off. "They look like a pair of lost puppies," she said to Dane.

"And you...you're all right?"

She gazed at him ruefully. "No. But I'm not going to fall apart. I'm too busy being angry at myself right now."

"Trust me," he said. "Everyone has regrets."

*Help me, Dane.*

As they drove, silent tears trickled down Kelsey's cheeks. She wiped them away angrily. "There are people who will say she was asking for it. They'll never know what a horrible childhood she had, that she was always running. She was always trying to escape, always trying to get somewhere."

"Yes," Dane said softly.

She stared at him suddenly. "My God! You don't know."

He almost veered off the road. "Know what?"

"About Cindy."

"What about Cindy?"

"They're picking her up from the hospital. They thought they heard someone in the yard again last night, and all started running around. From what Nate told me, she ran right into one of the storm shutters and knocked herself out."

"They thought they heard someone and started running around outside again?" he said with distress.

"I guess Nate went out one way, and Larry and Cindy went out the other, trying to catch whoever it was."

"They should have kept still and called Gary Hansen," Dane said, dismayed. "They might have caught him."

"So you think someone really was out there—even though the police had been by already?"

"I don't just think it was someone, I think it was Andy Latham," he told her.

"But if it's Andy...Sheila is dead."

"Hector just made the same point."

"So...?"

"Dammit, Kelsey, don't you see? You're in danger."

"Why me?"

"Who the hell knows?" he asked her. "Because you went after him. Because you were her friend. Because he's psychotic. Perhaps because he thinks she might have said something to you. I don't know." He paused and looked at her. "I don't know, but you're staying with me and close to me. All right?"

She didn't look his way. She was staring out the window. She had to be afraid.

She had seen Sheila's morgue photo.

"Kelsey?"

"Yes, of course, I'll stay with you."

"We have a bit of a detour to make. It will only take a few minutes."

She glanced at him at last.

He reached in his pocket and handed her his cell phone. "Call Jorge. Tell him we're on our way to the gas station to meet him. I need to see Marisa."

She frowned but did as he asked.

They arrived at the Sea Shanty later than the others because of the "detour" they had taken. They had met Jorge, who was upset about Sheila but understood Dane's need to see Marisa.

They had driven to the neat little house on the outskirts of town, and she had met the young Latina stripper, who was strangely shy, incredibly sweet, and stalwart despite her fear of the authorities when Dane explained that it was imperative for her to contact Hector Hernandez and explain to him that she had seen Andy Latham at the club.

Jorge listened quietly the whole time. When Dane had finished, the girl rose and told Jorge that she wanted to go right away. She had a friend at the house, so she could leave. She wasn't due at work until later.

Kelsey still didn't entirely understand what had been happening.

"Why is she afraid to go to the police?"

"Her son was just smuggled in from Cuba."

"But...he's her son. Won't the immigration laws protect him? Does he have a father back in Cuba, or family that will fight for him?"

Dane shook his head. "No."

"Then I'm sure he'll be all right."

Dane looked at her, and she knew that he didn't want to betray a confidence, even to her. And then she understood.

Jorge Marti had smuggled the boy in.

"Oh," she said softly. She didn't intend to make Dane say more. But she felt a strange warmth inside. She was proud of Jorge. The world could be awful. What had happened to Sheila was beyond awful.

But there were wonderful people in the world, as well.

"They'll have reached the Sea Shanty before us," Dane said. "Let's just say we stopped for gas."

"Sure."

The others were indeed there. Cindy hopped up and hugged Kelsey tightly, then did the same to Dane. They didn't speak about Sheila right away, and Kelsey quickly asked her how she was.

Cindy was dismissive of her own injury and as distraught as

the others about Sheila. Kelsey saw, when they took their seats at the table, that she had finished her first beer and was pouring her second.

Kelsey, at the end of the table, frowned with concern as she watched her. "You just had a major crack on the head. Should you be drinking like that?"

"I don't know any other way to drink," Cindy said, trying to speak lightly.

"Cindy..."

"I didn't take any of the pain medication they sent home with me. I'd rather douse myself with beer."

"But if you have a concussion..."

"I'm fine," Cindy insisted. "I was fine last night, but they wanted me to stay for observation. They observed me. I'm fine. I don't even have a knot on my head anymore."

"You're sure you hit the hurricane shutter?" Kelsey asked.

"What else? I was running around barefoot like an idiot." She paused and actually smiled. "Kelsey, it was just a comedy of errors. Nate went out the back. In beautiful blue boxers, I'll have you know. Larry was following me—in the buff, except for a sheet. It all happened so fast. We wanted to catch the bastard. Larry tripped on his sheet, on the way out. He was cute as could be," she said, trying to make Larry smile. She glanced at him affectionately where he was seated at the rough wood table beside her. "Naked as a jay, tummy down on the sheet. Great butt, Larry. Just thought you should know. Anyway, stupid me, I kept going, I was running, and...pow, I went down."

"You didn't see the hurricane shutter?" Kelsey asked.

"If I'd seen it, I wouldn't have slammed into it."

Dane, next to Kelsey, leaned forward. "I think she's trying to find out if you're certain that you were hit by the hurricane shutter."

"Well, what else could it have been?" Cindy asked.

Dane looked at Nate and Larry.

Nate shrugged. "I found her under the shutter."

Larry seemed to emerge from his fog enough to join the conversation. "Nate had just reached her when I managed to wrap the sheet around me again and get out there, but yes, the hurricane shutter was right there."

"And had anyone tried to jimmy the lock?" Dane asked.

Nate and Larry looked at each other.

"I don't know," Nate admitted.

"You didn't call Gary Hansen's office?" Dane said.

"Shit, we called an ambulance. We were worried about Cindy. We went into the hospital with her."

"And later...?"

"Later we were half dead, and we fell asleep...and then we got the call about Sheila," Nate said.

"But...you still haven't called the cops to check the yard?"

"Jesus Christ, Dane!" Larry exploded. "We just found out that Sheila is dead."

"Murdered," Nate said, staring at his beer.

Dane leaned forward. "And I intend to see that her murderer is caught," he said angrily.

"All of you, stop it," Kelsey protested.

"Dane, call the cops now—they'll go out and look around. Maybe Gary can even post a man at the duplex."

"Yeah, he will. The police are on the lookout for Latham," Dane said. "Excuse me while I make that call."

"Wait. Wait just a minute. We need to make a toast. To Sheila. To tell her we loved her," Cindy said. "No matter what her sins may have been."

"Right. We're the ones who cared," Larry said. "I mean, that matters, doesn't it? We all loved her. In the end, what matters is that you had people who cared."

Nate poured from the pitcher on the table into two more glasses for Dane and Kelsey. Then they all solemnly raised their glasses.

"To Sheila," Kelsey said.

"May she rest in peace," Nate added.

"Let's pray that she's found it at last," Cindy murmured.

"Amen," Dane said.

Then he rose and left the table. Cindy watched him go.

"At least..."

"What?" Nate said.

"At least Dane has...something to do. He can help catch Sheila's killer...Latham, if it really is Andy Latham. While we...well, we're just sitting here, and we can't do anything but think about her. I'm glad about Dane, though. When he first came back to the Keys..." She looked at Kelsey and shrugged. "It looked like he was going to become a lounge rat."

Dane was standing about twenty feet away. As she watched him, Kelsey thought that it was a fitting day.

Rain had followed them.

It had stopped now. But the sky, usually so bright and blue, was gray.

Dead gray.

As if he read her mind, Nate said, "The day is right for mourning, isn't it?" He lifted his glass, as if to heaven.

"See, Sheila? Even the elements know you're gone. The day is weeping." He set down his glass and studied his beer. "We'll get that sick bastard," he murmured. "Count on it, Sheila. We're going to get him."

Dane came back and sat down. He sipped his beer, set it down and looked around.

"What's the matter?" Cindy asked him.

He smiled ruefully and shook his head. "I don't know." Then he said, "Excuse me." He stood again, and walked through the restaurant, then went out toward the parking lot.

"What are you doing?" Kelsey asked him when he returned a few minutes later.

"Nothing, I guess. Being really paranoid. I thought I saw someone."

"I'm sure you did," Nate said, indicating the tables near them, where tourists sat, having stopped in for the lazy, rainy afternoon. "Customers. It's a public establishment, Dane."

"Yeah, I know. I just had a strange feeling."

"Did you see anything?" Cindy asked, perplexed.

"No. Just a feeling."

"We're all having them," Larry murmured. He shrugged. "After all, we know there's a murderer somewhere out there."

# CHAPTER 17

By seven that night, they had eaten and commiserated, and they were silent with one another. Dane had kept in touch with Gary Hansen, but there had been no sign of Andy Latham. They also learned from Hector Hernandez that the police were sorry to intrude, but they would all be needed for questioning, as Sheila was now a murder victim and not just a missing person.

Kelsey watched Dane's face as he spoke with Hector on the phone. His features were almost as dark as the day. She was certain that he, as the last one to see Sheila, was going to bear the greatest scrutiny, even if the police were looking for Andy Latham and might be able to tie him to all the murders.

Cindy and Larry drank heavily, but Nate was as slow in imbibing his beer as Dane and Kelsey. He had made himself the designated driver.

They stayed at the Sea Shanty until tacitly agreeing that it was time to go.

Nate, Larry and Cindy were determined to spend the night in the duplex, and they were actually hoping that the backyard prowler was going to show up, since Gary Hansen had a man from the sheriff's department stationed at the house.

They left after a round of hugs and with the knowledge that they all needed some sleep.

Dane was silent as he and Kelsey headed out to Hurricane Bay. The weather still seemed fitting. The sky had gone from dull pewter to the deep gray of a battleship. As he parked the Jeep, the wind was whipping around them, but at the moment it wasn't raining. He got out and headed for the house, then turned. Kelsey thought he was heading for the docks, but he wasn't.

She frowned as she watched him walk to the same spit of the beach where Nate had stood earlier that day.

She walked up behind him. He knew that she was there.

"I failed her," he said after a moment.

Kelsey felt the same way herself. "We didn't fail her," she said. "We were all her friends—despite her sins. Then again, it's not as if we're all without our quirks and problems. She was friends with all of us, too, no matter what. But you didn't fail her, Dane, any more than any of the rest of us did. Sheila was going to do things her own way, no matter what."

He nodded after a moment and turned for the house.

Kelsey followed him in.

Once they were inside, Dane double-locked the doors. He walked toward the kitchen. "I need an aspirin. You want one?"

She shook her head. "I'm all right." She hesitated. "I think I'm going to take a long bath and lie down. Is that all right?"

He nodded. "I'm going to call and make sure they've got a man stationed at the duplex. I want to talk to Jorge again, too, see if Marisa did go to the police."

Kelsey nodded and went up the stairs, feeling drained. She ran hot water into the tub, then found herself digging through his toiletries, wondering if she would find bath beads and glad when she didn't. She didn't want to think that Dane had downplayed his recent relationship with Sheila.

He did have shampoo. She poured some into the tub to make bubbles. Then she leaned back in the water, letting the heat warm her. But when she closed her eyes, she kept seeing the photograph of Sheila. The medical examiner's office had tried, she was certain, not to make the picture any more shocking than it had to be, but they hadn't been able to hide the remnants of the tie around her neck. It hadn't been removed yet—the forensic investigators hadn't finished with her.

Something about the picture, besides the awful image of what had once been the face of a beautiful woman, was disturbing. It had teased at Kelsey all afternoon, but for the life of her, she couldn't figure out what it was.

Dane tapped softly at the door. "I'm taking the diary downstairs to read. All right?"

"Sure."

"You all right?"

"Yeah." She was quiet for a moment. "At least we know."

He was silent. "At least we know," he repeated.

He left, and Kelsey settled back in the tub. Her head was pounding. For the longest time she just lay there, listening to the pounding. She decided it was her pulse.

The water grew cold, and she got out of the tub. She found clean underwear in her bag and slipped into one of Dane's T-shirts, which, despite her height, fell comfortably to mid-thigh. She wanted to lie down and let sleep dull the image of her friend that persisted in remaining in her mind's eye.

She lay down and closed her eyes, but when she did, she saw Sheila.

She sat up and noticed that Dane had taken the diary but not the pile of papers. Maybe there was something she had missed.

She lifted the pile of papers and started going through them again. She came to the drawing Sheila had done as an adult. Then she drew out the one she had done as a child. She frowned. They were poor drawings, of course. Sheila had never had the least interest in art; she had always been impatient whenever Kelsey had wanted to stop and sketch a scene.

She looked from one picture to the other. The female in both drawings was obviously Sheila. She had put the little mole on her left cheek in both drawings. But the man appeared different. In the second drawing he seemed straighter and heavier. Not fat, just heavier. As she puzzled over the pictures, she leaned forward. Her motion sent the pile of papers flying, dropping from her lap to the floor in disarray.

Softly cursing herself, she rose, then got down on her knees. The pictures had scattered on the floor, and some had slid beneath the bed. As she collected them, she hit one of the floorboards. To her astonishment, it moved.

Her first thought was that she needed to tell Dane he had a faulty floorboard. Then curiosity got the best of her. As she pressed it, she saw that it could be removed. Dane must keep his private papers here. Or personal objects. Or...

It was none of her business.

A strange feeling settled over her, and she warned herself that this might be like opening Pandora's box.

She couldn't stop herself. She pulled up the floorboard.

Shock, like being squeezed by icy fingers, settled over her.

Then fear and amazement set in. She wasn't just seeing Sheila's face in death in her mind's eye, she was seeing it in Polaroid color.

The first article in the space beneath the floorboard was a picture of Sheila. When life had just left her. Sheila's eyes were still open. Her lips were blue...her face tinged with blue.

And she was on the beach. Dane's beach. A corner of the dock could be seen at the edge of the picture.

Even if the picture hadn't shown her on Dane's beach, it would still have pointed clearly to Dane as the murderer. She knew what had been bothering her about the picture she had seen at the morgue.

She had recognized the remnants of fabric around Sheila's neck. The tie. It was Dane's tie. She knew it because she had given it to him for Christmas years ago. She had given one to Joe, as well. It was a hand-painted tie. There were sea creatures moving through a background of blues and grays. The ties had been special. She had labored over them for a very long time. Seeing it now, before the water and the muck had conspired to hide the pattern, it was obvious. So obvious.

Sheila. Dead. On Dane's beach. Strangled with Dane's tie.

Horror...fear...constricted her throat and every muscle for untold moments. She tried desperately to get her mind to function. She couldn't panic.

She had to get out.

She remembered the day she had first talked to Dane. How he had told her to go home.

*What an idiot she was!* The signs had all been there. Sheila had left the Sea Shanty with Dane. Sheila had slept with Dane the last night she'd been seen. Sheila's earring had been on Dane's floor.

Dane had killed Sheila.

And she, Kelsey, like a fool, hadn't wanted to believe it. He had been so convincing. He had gone to the strip clubs looking for suspects. He had pursued Andy Latham. Of course he had. He was going to see that the murders were pinned on Latham....

She forced herself to rise. She looked across the bed where he had left the .38 special that morning.

The gun was gone.

She picked up the receiver in the bedroom, then replaced it as carefully as her shaking fingers would allow. Dane was on the phone.

She looked around the room. He was a private investigator. There had to be another weapon around somewhere. She looked under the bed, then went through several of his drawers. She saw that she had left the board up and panicked anew, so she ran back and replaced the picture and the board.

She couldn't stop shaking. And she wasn't reasoning any-where near as well as she should have been.

The picture was replaced. The board was replaced. There was no weapon to be found. He would come up the stairs at any minute.

She would never be able to hide the fact that she knew he was a murderer. A sick murderer. He had taken a picture of his vic-tim as a trophy.

She started for the door. She needed her purse and her cell phone. He was probably at the dining-room table, where he had set up his home office. That meant she had to go out the front door without being noticed. She could do it.

She was in a T-shirt, barefoot. No time to change, but she did need her shoes. Sandals, but better than nothing. The ground was strewn with crushed shells and pebbles. She would never make it barefoot. She slipped on her sandals and hurried to the door. Her purse was downstairs. She had left it on the table.

The table where Dane was undoubtedly working.

Her phone was in her purse. She needed her phone. No, she needed to get the hell out of there. She knew the way off the is-land. And she could run. She couldn't keep up with Cindy at the gym, but she was fit enough, and terror would give her wings.

Kelsey left the bedroom and moved to the top of the stairs. He wasn't on the stairway, at least. She started down, praying the old wood wouldn't creak.

At the foot of the stairs, she paused. Then she crept silently toward the rear, desperate to see where Dane was and what he was doing. If only he were in the kitchen, she could slip into the dining room and grab her purse.

She looked cautiously into the dining room. Dane was at the table, drumming the surface of it as he spoke on the phone in a low tone.

She saw her purse, just inches from his hand. His own cell phone was sitting right in front of him.

She bit her lip and backed away. She had to get off the island.

Kelsey turned and headed for the front door. As silently as she could, she turned the bolts. They seemed to snap open as loudly as a clash of cymbals, but she knew the sound was only in her mind. She opened the door, then closed it carefully, praying he wouldn't know she was gone until she was far from Hurricane Bay.

Dane heard the deep sigh on the other end of the phone line. Gary Hansen spoke patiently despite the sound.

"No, we haven't caught up with Andy Latham yet. Dane, everyone is looking for him. We've called the cops out in Collier County, as well. I talked to Jesse Crane, and his boys are looking in the Everglades. Trust me, every law-enforcement officer in the state is looking for Latham. We've got people working the airports, the train stations and the bus terminals, as well as the highways. They've set up a road block on US1 so that he can't get on to the mainland—unless he's already run that far already. If so, he can't get back on. Not with a car. And it's one damned long walk. Dane, do me a favor. Don't call every half hour. I'll call you. If you feel you have to call me, make it at least an hour between calls."

"You definitely have a man at the duplex?" Dane asked.

"I swear it, on my mother's grave, my father's grave...on the grave of every ancestor I've got. I'm responsible for the safety of the people out here. Don't you think this is driving me insane?"

Dane ran his fingers through his hair. "Yeah, Gary, sorry. It's just that...well, shit. I feel like he's out there, like he sees us but we can't see him."

"You're in your house, right?"

"Yup."

"Locked up tight, right?"

"Yup."

"You've got a gun, right?"

"On me, yup."

"And Kelsey's with you, and I have a guy at the duplex. Shit, Dane, go to bed. Get some sleep. They'll find him."

"All right."

Dane hung up. Sheila's diary sat in front of him. It told him so much.

It told him nothing he needed to know.

He rose. Here he was, being an ass again. Kelsey was up there, and she was devastated. Holding it together, but devastated. It wasn't a time for hot passion; it was a time to hold on to each other.

He walked through the house to the stairway and slowly made his way up to the bedroom.

It was empty.

"Kelsey?"

He walked to the bathroom door and looked in. No sign of her. Frowning, he went back to the bedroom.

"Kelsey?"

No answer. He ran downstairs, calling her name, tearing through every room. He went back upstairs, looking around.

Then he saw the pictures scattered on the floor. By the board.

He groaned aloud. She knew. She had to know. He should have told her from the beginning. He couldn't have told her from the beginning. And now...

He tore back downstairs. Her purse was on the dining-room table, so she didn't have a cell phone. She was hoofing it off of the island, certain she had been staying with a psychotic killer. The back door was still locked from the inside.

The front door had been opened.

And quietly closed when she left the house.

Dane tore out the front.

"Kelsey!" He shouted her name against the wind and the rain.

No reply.

Why would she answer him? In her mind, he was a homicidal maniac.

He had to find her. Not just because of what she thought. But because he had that feeling again. That feeling that they were being watched.

The cops hadn't been able to find Andy Latham. Which meant Latham was out there. Somewhere.

And so was Kelsey.

Kelsey ran down the road, cursing as the rain started again and the wind picked up, the trees dipping low. The private gravel road spat tiny rocks at her, and she nearly tripped over tenacious roots as she raced along. She could hear herself breathe. The pounding that had been her pulse seemed amplified. She had to keep looking back. She was afraid that if Dane was after her, she wouldn't be able to hear him. All that she would hear would be that pounding.

So far so good.

Then...

She could hear him. From a distance. He was shouting her name.

He had discovered that she was missing. And he would know. He would know what she had found.

She doubled her efforts, ruing the wind that whipped around her. She swore as the raindrops began to fall harder.

If she missed the fragile connection to the mainland, she would be swimming her way to safety. Something she could do, if she had to. But it was so dark, and the rain...

The rain was coming down so hard it hurt her flesh as she ran.

Suddenly she saw lights ahead of her. Strange lights. She blinked against the rain. They couldn't be Dane's Jeep lights, because the Jeep had been at the house, and these lights were coming from the mainland.

She kept running, waving her arms madly, wondering if the driver could see her.

The vehicle stopped. The lights were blinding. She shielded her eyes, ready to run to the driver's side for help. She blinked and saw through the rain. Saw who it was.

Andy Latham.

She stopped dead in her tracks, fear chilling her flesh with far greater speed than the rain.

But then she realized that she didn't have to be afraid of Andy Latham. Dane had murdered Sheila.

"Andy!" she said.

"Hey there, little girl. What are you doing out here? No matter. It's sure mighty fine to see you in that wet T-shirt. They say you're with some snooty ad agency up in Miami, but my, my, you could make some real money with that body. Oh, yeah. What are you doing running around in the rain?"

"Andy, I need to get off the island." Even though she was desperate, he still made her skin crawl. The rain was coming down in sheets now; she had to shout above it.

"Step right in, little lady."

"You can drop me at the highway," she told him. Despite knowing what she did about Dane, she was filled with apprehension, but it was too late to escape now. Andy was out of the truck. He had her arm.

He was wearing gloves.

He might be thin, but he was strong. He was dragging her, rather than walking her, around to the passenger side of his truck.

"You know, Andy, I think I'll just go ahead and walk," she said.

"In this rain? No way, Kelsey." There was a drawn out hiss as he said her name.

"Andy, let me go. I'll walk."

"There's thunder and lightning."

"I like the rain. I'm sorry for bothering you. Let me go. I'll just walk."

"No."

He had the car door open. She tried to wrench free, but his grip was unbelievably powerful. She reached out, clawing at his hand to get him to release her. She shrieked as she drew blood.

He reached into the car for something. In the rain, she couldn't see what.

Then it came crashing down on her head and it no longer mattered, as the gray light and rain faded away.

Dane took the Jeep, knowing that Kelsey would have to stick to the road if she wanted to get off the island.

The rain became blinding as he drove. He hunched forward in the seat, his bright lights on, trying to see ahead.

No sign of Kelsey, but...

He jerked the Jeep to a halt. Even in the rain, he could see the way the foliage was crushed. He hopped out, heedless of the rain, and walked to the left side of the road. Something had been in there. Though the rain was lashing the ground and making thick puddles of muck, he could see the tire tracks. A large vehicle had been parked in the bushes.

A truck.

Latham's truck.

Latham had been here now, right now, when Kelsey had suddenly run. How had he known she would run?

He hadn't. But he had been watching them. He had been watching them at the Sea Shanty, and he had known they were heading out to Hurricane Bay, so he had come here to wait. Maybe the rain even inspired his need to hunt, to kill. How the hell had he eluded the police?

It didn't matter. All that mattered was that he'd been here. And he had Kelsey.

Dane ran back to the Jeep for his floodlight. He was going to have to follow on foot. He would never be able to follow the tire tracks if he didn't.

Kelsey felt a rocking. She was lying on something soft but...smelly.

Her head hurt like hell. She wanted to touch it, but some instinct kept her from doing so, just in case she was being watched. She opened her eyes slowly and carefully. She swallowed back the scream of pure panic that came to her throat.

She was on a boat. A fishing boat.

She was lying on a bunk in a cabin. A small, tight, claustrophobic cabin. The bunk took up almost all the available space. She could hear movement on deck.

She gritted her teeth, trying to stop the rocking in her head and figure out if Latham was trying to move his boat out into high seas or if he had done so already.

She couldn't let him get out to sea. The wind was so high...the rocking would be worse if they were far out.

She tried to rise. Her head was spinning. As she sat up, she noticed the rack on the cabin wall, within arm's reach of the bunk.

It held a row of ties.

Silk ties, cotton ties, linen ties, black, patterned...even a cartoon tie.

Fear shot through her like a bolt of lightning. Andy Latham was the Necktie Strangler. Then what was the picture beneath Dane's floorboard?

She couldn't worry about that now. She had to find the strength to get off the boat. Where? Into the sea, into the mangroves...even though she probably didn't have the strength to swim two strokes.

She would find it.

She shimmied to the end of the bunk and rose. The sleeping quarters led out to a small galley and salon. Tight, utilitarian, nothing more. She was dizzy. She brought her fingers to her head, and when she drew them away, they were red with blood. He had struck her hard.

She made it to her feet, though the room spun crazily. Some instinct for survival kept her from passing out.

Kelsey braced herself against the walls as she made her way out of the bedroom. Latham was still topside, cursing as he hauled in his anchor. Where the hell were they? She bit her bottom lip, fighting nausea and dizziness. She made it through the salon to the few steps that led topside. The rain had slackened to where she could see him. His back was to her.

Kelsey rushed from the door to the port side of the boat. Latham heard her just as she reached the edge and dived in.

The sea was dark. Pitch-dark, and cold from the rain and the thunderous sky above. Kelsey shot away from the boat. She surfaced, trying to look around. She could see mangroves around her. And a broken down old dock. Beside it, an overgrown path. She knew where they were. They were near the mainland, just before the road that led to Dane's...in good weather. The road would be flooding now.

She began to swim. If she could reach the trees and crawl ashore, she could elude Latham. If she could just...

A hand wound around her ankle. Pulled her under. She was choking. She kicked, scratched, pummeled....

He wouldn't let her up.

She wasn't going to be strangled. She was going to drown.

Gloved fingers threaded through her hair and hauled her up. She took a desperate breath. Latham was swimming strongly, dragging her with him. She renewed her fight for freedom. His hand rammed through the water, catching her jaw.

For a moment she saw stars in the sea.

He had her. He was shoving her up. Up, over the bow. He was crawling up beside her.

She fell to the deck. Desperate, she made herself rise. She lunged for the side again. Latham captured her around the middle. He swore, ignoring the nails that tore into his flesh, heedless of the fact that he smashed her against the door as he pushed and shoved her back down the few steps to the salon. She began to scream.

Despite her efforts, he got her back into the tiny sleeping quarters, where he threw her on the bunk and reached for a tie.

Kelsey rose, screaming. He shoved her back.

"Kelsey...prim, proper Kelsey. I've always liked to play. But with you...we'll have to play after. And you won't know then. You won't care. You'll smile...and you'll like me then. Of course, you won't be able to whisper any sweet nothings in my ear, but—"

She rose in a whirlwind of motion, slamming both her fists into his face. He fell back, but she was trapped by his body, which was blocking the door. She tried to squeeze past him, and she nearly succeeded.

But then the cartoon tie came flipping around her neck, jerking her back.

Dane ran through the rain, following the tracks with desperation spurring his footsteps. He could barely see to follow, but he was grateful that Latham couldn't be that far ahead of him. The rain hadn't yet washed away the deep grooves the truck was leaving in the road.

He raced across the dirt and gravel path that would soon be under water and was back on the main island of Key Largo. After a hundred feet, the tire tracks suddenly twisted hard to the right. Dane followed.

Years ago there had been a road here. Now the movement of the vehicle had crushed through the dense brush, leaving a trail that was easy to follow. But how long since Latham had come through here?

The rain had slackened, but it was still coming down.

Dane suddenly knew where he was going. There had been a dock here once. A private home that had fallen in to decay over the years. The state owned the land but hadn't decided what to do with it yet.

But a beat-up old fishing boat could have been brought in and tied to what was left of the dock.

His heart pounding, he prayed that it would still be there.

That he was in time...

He burst through the last of the brush.

The boat wasn't at the dock.

He stared in gut-wrenching dismay.

Then he saw the boat, out on the water. He ran to the mangrove-tangled shoreline and crashed through the water until he could swim. He kept an eye on the boat, damning the waves that seemed to force him back with every stroke.

Kelsey fought. Even with the tie around her neck, she fought, bucking against Latham, desperate to kick, to claw.

They would know. At least they would know for sure. She had scratched him and scratched him. She had drawn blood. They would find his flesh and blood beneath her fingernails...when they fished her body from the water. If they were in time, before the fish...

No...

She grasped at the tie around her neck. Latham jerked and struggled, trying to get her flat on the bed, determined to get her beneath him.

"No, you aren't like Sheila, are you? Heard today that she was dead, the little slut. Came to the end she should have come to. She was a born slut, you know. Like her mother. Cheating bitch. She didn't care what I did with her daughter, but then, the daughter didn't mind. Mother, daughter. You don't know what fun can be, do you, little girl?" Latham demanded. He was panting between his words. "Can't answer, can you? Got no breath. You go ahead. You struggle. I like it. I like that look in your eyes."

She kicked him. She had no breath and the room was spinning, but she kicked him. For an instant he lost his grip.

She desperately gulped in air.

He fell on her again. He had both ends of the tie, and he wound them tighter and tighter and tighter....

She would fight, fight, fight....

The cabin was growing dark.

Light, and life, were fading.

Something huge and wet hurled itself onto the bed. The constriction around her neck slackened instantly.

She gulped in air again, coughing as if she would never stop. Bodies slammed against her. She pressed against the cabin wall, still coughing. Her mind was numb. She was aware only of the bodies at first, flailing and thrashing around her. The boat was rocking madly in the high seas brought on by the storm.

Then Latham was jerked up. There was a tie around his neck.

Kelsey saw his eyes as he was jerked backward out of the cabin.

She crawled to the foot of the bed, then slid off it, using the wall for balance as she got to her feet. Dane was there. Dane had come to rescue her from Latham. They were still struggling, though Dane had the tie. He was dragging Latham away from her as Latham's fingers tried to ease the hold of the tie around his own neck. It must have loosened, because he got free and turned, heading up the steps. Dane was right on him.

Kelsey staggered after them. They were on deck together. Dane had the tie around Latham's neck again.

A huge wave struck, and the two men went crashing over the side.

Kelsey's cry was drowned out by the thunder that cracked almost immediately after the vivid flash of lightning that lit the sky.

She made her way to the port side, looking down at a dark sea.

"Dane!"

The wind whipped away her voice.

She saw a head, bobbing to the surface. A hand, reaching out...

Dane's hand?

Or Latham's?

She bent down, reaching over. Strong fingers grasped hers.

She pulled.

A body began to rise. Two hands gripped the hull of the boat.

She caught hold of them both as Dane Whitelaw struggled up and over the rail. Together, they crashed to the deck.

# CHAPTER 18

Andy Latham's body washed up on shore three days later.

By then Kelsey had been out of the hospital a full twenty-four hours herself, and when the group met at the Sea Shanty, it was to celebrate rather than to mourn.

Dane had spent as much time with the police as she had healing, so once they were together, everyone started asking him questions, trying to get him to put the pieces together.

Cindy said, "My God...this is still so scary. So when we were kids, Latham was abusing his stepdaughter, and as the years went by, he started killing?"

"Unfortunately we'll never know for sure what happened," Dane told her. "I admit, when I reached the boat, I wanted to kill him. But I wouldn't have—except that it turned into a life or death struggle."

"Why would you have wanted to keep him alive?" Nate asked.

"Because he could have answered questions for us. No one knows when he started killing. There could be more victims in the waterways, in the swamps. We'll never know. And there are so many missing women out there. Families who will live with the dread all their lives but never have any kind of closure. He probably started off abusing Sheila, and then the violence escalated when she got older and broke free. No wife, no kid...and he probably always frequented strip joints and cruised the streets looking for prostitutes. Hector Hernandez believes he may be responsible for a number of unsolved rapes. And then he probably went from rape to murder."

"And he was watching us, all of us, before he attacked Kelsey," Cindy said. "It's possible that he walloped me with his crowbar that night, then ran off when he realized Nate and Larry were so close."

"Maybe. And maybe you just ran into the storm shutter."

"How did you know it was Latham so quickly, even before the police had him down as a suspect?"

"I knew it was someone who knew me," Dane said.

He looked across the table at Kelsey. She flushed. "He tried to frame Dane. Before he killed Sheila, he broke into Dane's house. He knew that Sheila had been there, so he went into Dane's place when he was at the Sea Shanty one day. He took one of Dane's ties, and he strangled Sheila with it. He watched Dane's schedule, and he saw Sheila when she left Dane's. Then he waited for Dane to leave again the next day, posed her on the beach and took a picture before disposing of her body."

"Then he left me to sweat, wondering where the next piece of evidence against me would turn up. The picture was left beneath my door," Dane said. "I didn't dare take it to the police. I couldn't afford to be arrested when I knew the real killer was still out there."

"Wow," Larry said. "So you knew she was dead all along."

"Yes. I'm sorry. I couldn't trust anyone."

"Have the police seen all this yet?" Nate asked.

"I've told Hector Hernandez," Dane said. "Problem is...the picture is gone."

Kelsey cleared her throat, staring at Cindy. "That's how I

wound up with Latham. I found the picture under Dane's floor-board. He had it hidden. I was there and I stumbled on it. I could swear I put it back, but...anyway, we're searching for it. God knows, I was in such a panic, I might have held on to it and lost it somewhere while I was running. But it doesn't matter. Latham's not going to hurt anyone again, and that's what counts."

Dane said, "That's right. It's over. Thank God, it's over."

"And you're really all right, Kelsey?" Larry asked anxiously.

She nodded. "I'm fine." The bruises around her neck were going to stay a while, but that didn't matter. She was alive.

In fact, she was far more alive than she had been in years. She was home. And she was with Dane.

"We'll all think about Sheila, though, for years to come," she said.

"The only solace is that..." Nate paused, looking for the right words. "Well, like we said before. She was at peace. Sheila wasn't just running. She was miserable. She had been miserable for years. She didn't know how to live anymore. Latham didn't just kill her when he strangled her. He killed her over the years. He killed her when she was a kid, bit by bit."

"Well," Kelsey told him, "we're going to try to do something for her. I was her beneficiary—a lawyer contacted me today. According to the terms of her mother's will, Latham only received money from the trust fund while Sheila was alive. At Sheila's death, the bulk sum came to me. So Dane and I have discussed it, and we thought the best thing to do was donate the money to an agency in Miami that cares for abused wives, children and runaways. We thought the best memorial to her would be to try to see that what happened to her never happens to another child."

"Bravo!" Cindy said. "What a great idea."

"Curious, though," Nate murmured.

"What's that?" Larry asked.

"That Latham killed Sheila. She was his meal ticket."

"I thought of that," Dane said. "I didn't realize it at the time, but that might have been part of the reason he was after Kelsey."

"Who would have thought Latham was smart enough to pull off everything he did?" Cindy murmured.

Larry shrugged and looked at Kelsey. "I take it you've decided that you're going to need more than a week's vacation time?"

Kelsey smiled ruefully. "I sent in my resignation, Larry."

"What?" Larry said, astounded. Then he looked from Kelsey to Dane and back again.

"Oh."

"I'm going to paint down here for a while," she said.

"Sure," Nate teased. "Paint. That's what they call it these days?"

They all laughed. "Seriously, I haven't done any real artwork since I took the job in the art department," she said ruefully.

"Shall I guess that you're not going to stay at the duplex?" Cindy asked.

"She'll be living at Hurricane Bay," Dane said.

"Congratulations," Nate said. He lifted his glass and smiled at Kelsey. "Really. Congratulations. It took you two long enough to admit you want to be together."

"Thank you, Nate," Kelsey told him sincerely.

"It better be one good wedding—when you get around to it," Cindy said, adding the last hastily.

"Of course we plan on it being one good wedding," Kelsey said.

"You're not going to elope or anything?" Nate demanded.

She shook her head, smiling at Dane. She was amazed that she could have lost an old friend and so recently have been near death herself, yet know such a strange, poignant sense of happiness. Sheila had done her the greatest favor in the end. She had brought her home. And to Dane.

She looked from Dane to Nate. "Actually we're going to go up and see my parents, and tell them, then come back and get married down here. And guess what else? My mom is pregnant. So Dane and I are going to go see them, then we'll arrange the wedding."

"Wow," Cindy said. "Your mom is pregnant?"

"Uh-huh. I'm going to have a baby brother."

"Wow," Cindy said again.

"That's great. Really great," Nate said.

"A toast," Cindy said. "To life."

"And friendship," Nate said.

"Hear, hear," Larry agreed.

They ate dinner together and were pleased when Jorge joined them. Marisa was with him, having given up her job at the club to work as a chef on Jorge's boat.

Kelsey was certain there was something going on there, as well.

It was late when they returned to Hurricane Bay. Dane locked the doors carefully, as he had done every night since Kelsey had been attacked.

Since he'd picked her up from the hospital, he had been treating her like glass. "Want me to run a bath for you? Need a cold compress for your neck?"

She shook her head, smiling. "I need you."

"Kelsey, he hurt you pretty badly. It's pretty late. You probably want to go to sleep."

"What I want to do is make love."

He eyed her for a long moment. "Careful," he said softly. "You know I'm easy."

"And good. Don't forget good."

"Naturally. So be careful what you ask for."

Kelsey wrapped her arms around his neck and kissed his lips. "I want good. Damn good," she told him.

Later she realized that he was still awake, staring up at the ceiling. "What's the matter?" she asked him.

"Something is still bugging me," he said.

"What?"

"What Nate said. That it was weird, Latham killing Sheila. She was his meal ticket."

"That is strange. Know what else?" Kelsey said. "It's hard for me to remember, because I'd been knocked on the head and I was busy trying to get away, but when Latham talked about Sheila, it was as if he hadn't killed her."

Dane rolled onto his elbow, staring at her in the moonlight.

"What?" he demanded.

"Hey, you sound like the police. I can't remember exactly what he said. Something about he knew that she was dead and that she had gotten what she deserved."

Dane lay back down. She knew he was staring at the ceiling again.

Kelsey looked over at him. "Dane, he was the Necktie Strangler. We know it, the police know it. Maybe, in his warped mind, he didn't want to believe he killed Sheila. Maybe he didn't even plan to kill her."

"How do you not plan to kill someone—and have a stolen tie to strangle her with?" he asked quietly. "There's something else," he added.

"What?"

"The fish."

"The fish?"

He nodded in the shadows. "Andy Latham came over here the day of the barbecue with all those fish, convinced we were dumping dead fish on his property. Those fish had to come from somewhere."

"We're in the Keys. They could have come from anywhere."

"I know, but it's almost as if the fish were put there to make sure Latham would come after us. Or me. It's as if someone was trying to make sure Andy Latham would make himself a suspect."

"Then again," Kelsey said slowly, "maybe he caught the fish, then forgot about them until they rotted. He might have reached a point where reality and his psychosis were all mixed up in his mind."

"The whole thing still bothers me," Dane said. "Shit," he muttered. "I can't sleep. I'll go downstairs so you can get some rest."

She was immediately wide-awake.

"Don't you dare leave me. I'm not sleepy right now myself. And I can think of a perfect way to get some exercise and then relax."

"Kelsey, you're hurt. Are you sure twice is okay?"

"I never feel better than when I'm with you," she told him.

He wrapped her in his arms.

The call came early. Dane had just come downstairs, and Kelsey had made coffee. She had been staring out the window, basking in the sunshine.

"I love Hurricane Bay," she told him.

"Great," he teased, walking to where she stood and slipping his arms around her waist. "You're going to marry me for my island."

She laughed. "I love Hurricane Bay because it's an extension of you."

He wasn't able to reply, because that was when the phone rang.

He picked it up. Jesse Crane was on the line.

"Hey, Jesse," Dane said.

"Dane, let's have coffee."

"Jesse, you know I'm always ready to meet you. But I just woke up, and...why don't you come out here?"

"Dane," Jesse repeated firmly, "I need to meet you for coffee. Alone. I'm halfway there. I'll see you at the coffee shop at the base of the island."

Dane frowned. Apparently Jesse didn't want to spell anything out, but Dane could tell from his tone that it was important that they meet.

"All right."

He hung up. Kelsey was looking at him. "Who was that?"

"Jesse. Seems he needs to see me."

"Is he coming here? I'd love to see Jesse."

"No, I've got to go meet him. I'll be right back, though."

She smiled. "I'm not an invalid, Dane. I still have a little cut on my head and some bruises, but I'm fine. Take your time."

He still wasn't happy leaving her. Ever since the attack...

"I'll be right back."

He started out. Kelsey followed him to the porch.

"You know where the gun is. Under the bed, my side," he told her.

"I know where the gun is," she assured him.

He was still disgruntled, but he didn't ask her to come with him. Jesse had wanted to talk alone.

He wasn't going far, and he would be right back. He kissed her briefly, then left.

Kelsey walked out on the dock with her coffee. She loved to sit there, dangling her feet in the water the way she had years ago, as a child.

She found her eyes wandering to the beach. She bit her lip, recalling the photo of Sheila, posed there. The memory would haunt her for a long time. But she did love the property. Hurricane Bay hadn't caused the misery and horror—a man had done that.

On a whim, she went back into the house and picked up Sheila's diary and the papers she had gathered. She wished Sheila had said something more in the diary. It was still disturbing, no matter what she had said to Dane, to ponder exactly why Latham would have killed Sheila when she was his source of income.

She started scouring the pages again, noting a few she had skimmed over.

*Shopping with Cindy. Midget. I called her Midget today. She got mad. It was her nickname when we were kids.*

*I told her Midget wasn't bad. After all, the guys all called me Boobs. And they did it in public.*

*She isn't mad at me anymore.*

*I wonder if Kels would be pissed if I called her Bubble Butt today. I think I'm the one who made up that name. Had to have something that went with Boobs.*

*Then there was He-Man. We liked to call Dane that. He even got the good name.*

The entry ended. A few pages later, Sheila wrote:

*Another day at the bar. I called Nate Liver Lips. He laughed and asked me if I'd heard from Web. I said yes, of course.*

*He loves me too much. Even outright cruelty doesn't seem to get through to him.*

"He loved you too much, Sheila. If only you had been able to love him."

She glanced at the stack of papers again. The two pictures still bothered her. The man in the second drawing wasn't Andy Latham. She was certain of it.

And it wasn't Dane. The man in the drawing had dark hair. She frowned, studying the picture. She turned it and looked at it from every angle. Sheila had scrawled some kind of a border around the drawing. She tried to follow it. Was it just a border? It had the look of elongated writing.

She was so engrossed that she didn't hear the footsteps behind her. She jumped, dropping the diary, when she saw the shadow looming over her on the water.

Jesse was there when Dane arrived.

He must have driven like the wind.

Dane slid into the booth across from him. The waitress knew him and brought coffee right away.

"That's it, Sally, thanks," Jesse said.

Dane arched a brow. "This must be important."

"It is. They're going to reopen Sheila's case."

"What? Why?"

"Do you remember me telling you that there was something about the bodies that the police didn't tell anyone? Like a signature?"

Dane frowned. "Yes."

"The first two girls had the middle toe of the left foot removed."

"And Sheila's toe was there?"

Jesse nodded. "I wanted you to know right away. Because you're going to be in for another round of questioning. And I had to come here because...well, just in case any lines were being tapped or anything like that."

Dane felt a chill creep into him.

He jerked out of his seat. "I've got to go, Jesse. Kelsey's alone."

"Hey there," Larry said. "I just came to say goodbye. I'm heading back. We can't all retire and live the good life in the Keys, you know."

"Oh, Larry." She rose, giving him a hug. She stepped back. He was dressed for the office in a neatly pressed suit, silk shirt and tie. She smoothed the shirt. "I'm going to miss you. I'm going to miss working with you. But you'll be back. I'll see you again soon."

"What were you reading so intently?" he asked her.

"Oh, that. Sheila's diary. And some drawings of hers. I'm just...well, I don't know. I'm trying to make it all jell."

"Make what jell?"

"What Nate said yesterday. That it didn't figure for Latham to have killed Sheila, since she was his meal ticket."

"He was psychotic," Larry said.

"I know, but how do you explain the whole fish thing?"

"The fish thing?"

"The fish that Latham dumped here, remember, claiming we had dumped them on his property?"

"He was psychotic," Larry repeated.

"I suppose. We'll never know all the answers."

"Find anything in the diary? Or in those papers?"

"No." She laughed suddenly. "Sheila made me think of old times, though. She talks about us using our old nicknames." She made a face. "Remember, I was Bubble Butt. And you were Web. Weekend Boy. So you still have to be Web, all right? Come down often."

Larry stared at the diary.

"Want some coffee?" she asked him.

"Sure. Where's Dane? I thought I passed him out on the highway when I was coming here."

"Out. He went to see Jesse."

"Oh. Sure, I'd love coffee."

He followed her into the house. She walked straight to the kitchen, setting the diary and papers on the counter. "You know," she told him, "there's something else that's bothering me. Really bothering me," she said, pouring coffee from the pot. "When Latham was attacking me, he talked as if he hadn't killed Sheila. And did Latham really have the brains to take that photo and stick it under Dane's door? To break in and get a tie, then bide his time and watch the house?"

She looked up. Larry looked pale.

"Are you all right?"

"Fine."

She set a cup of coffee in front of him on the counter. She ran her fingers over the drawing, twisting it again to better see the strange border.

"It *is* writing, I think," she said.

"What is that?"

"A drawing Sheila made. Looks like a guy trying to hurt a woman. And you know, she had told Dane she was afraid. Larry, you're sweating. Are you okay?"

"It's a little warm. The suit, you know."

She took out the milk and sugar, and turned back. Larry was

taking off his tie. As she walked back, she saw the paper from a different angle.

"Loosen your shirt collar, too, Larry," she said absently. Then she stood very still.

The first part of the border was definitely a letter. A *W* that swept over a third of the bottom of the page. She twisted the page around and saw that she had been right. Sheila had created a border out of letters. The first was a *W.* The second was hardly recognizable because it was so elongated in script. It was an *E.*

"Larry. Look at this. She was writing something to go with the picture."

She twisted the picture again. The last letter was a *B.* WEB. Weekend Boy.

She had written down Larry's nickname.

She looked up, instinct creating a warning chill within her. Larry didn't just look pale. He looked sick. She noticed the tie in his hand. The way he was knotting it.

The milk fell to the floor.

Larry stared at her, shaking his head. "I didn't want to do this, Kels. Really I didn't."

"Larry...no."

*Why the hell hadn't Sheila just told her she was afraid of Larry? Because she worked with him, because she'd taken his side, and if she'd just had a chance to spend time alone with Sheila, her friend would have told her all the little reasons why.*

"You know, Kels. I know that you know. I went through the house. I read the diary. There wasn't anything in it that pointed to me. I even went through those papers. I thought that...I thought that was one of Sheila's kid drawings. I never would have realized she was spelling my nickname. Not if you hadn't pointed it out. You never let go, Kelsey. You're like a determined little terrier. I should have realized that. Even without that drawing, you probably would have figured it out eventually.

Found out how often I had been down here and seen Sheila. It's a good thing I came by."

"If I figured it out, Dane will, too."

He shook his head. "No. They'll think Dane did it. Naturally I'll get rid of that paper. And everything else points to Dane. Sheila slept with him the night I caught up with her, you know. I knew she would. And I knew when Dane would leave the house, so I knew when to bring her here and take the picture. And since he's already told them about the photograph, all I have to do is make sure they find it."

"Larry...why?" she whispered.

"Jesus, Kels, how can you ask that? I loved her, and she treated me like shit. She humiliated me. I was the only guy she wouldn't sleep with. And then there was Dane. He-Man, while I was Web. All my damned life. I couldn't stand it anymore. I had to kill her, so I did. And I planned it so it would look like the Necktie Strangler. Oh, Latham really was the Necktie Strangler. I thought he might be. He was such a sicko. But that didn't matter. I knew if I killed Sheila on Dane's property and took the picture, he'd have to go after the killer, and I knew I could count on him to find him. And he did. But...well, I didn't think Latham would talk to you while he was trying to do the deed. And I sure as hell didn't know about the trust fund—Sheila never told me anything. You can't imagine how I hated her."

"You're not going to kill me, Larry."

"I'm sorry, Kels. Honestly. As much as he's been a thorn in my side my whole life, I didn't really even mean to make Dane pay. But the way it's worked out...well, he's going to have to take the fall. For Sheila, and for you."

She shook her head. "No, Larry, come on, think about it. If you plead temporary insanity and tell the jury about your marriage, I'm sure they'll understand. If you kill me as well...Larry, don't be an idiot. Someone will figure it out. Dane will be back." She was trying to speak rationally. Trying to find an escape route as she spoke. She glanced at where he stood, and at the back door. "You're not wearing gloves," she pointed out. She was shaking inside, a continual "No!" wailing through her head.

Dane would be back.

But maybe he and Jesse had a lot to talk about.

It didn't matter. She wasn't going to let Larry kill her.

"No, I don't have gloves. I really don't want to do this, Kelsey. But this time I'll take the weapon with me," he said softly.

"Your tire tracks will be out there."

"So? I came to say goodbye. And then I found you. I'll call 911 right away."

Kelsey was still incredulous. She had worked with Larry for years. She had sympathized with him at his divorce.

She had slept alone with him in the other room in Sheila's house.

He took a step toward her.

Kelsey was terrified, but she'd fought for her life once already. She wasn't going to give it up now.

"Kels..." he said very softly, "I'll try not to hurt you."

She backed up against the counter. He followed.

She reached behind her, grabbed the coffeepot and brought it crashing against his head. He screamed as the glass and scalding liquid seared his flesh.

Kelsey shoved him hard. Then she began to run.

Dane burst into the house just in time for Kelsey to race into his arms.

Larry was flying after her.

Dane caught Kelsey and moved her aside, ready to meet her attacker.

To his amazement, Larry stopped and stared at him from a distance. Coffee stained his clothes, and there was a gash on the side of his head.

"So, you killed Sheila," Dane said softly.

"No...you killed her. That's the way it will look."

Dane pulled out his cell phone, staring at Larry.

Larry pulled a small gun from his pocket. "Don't! You're not the only one who knows how to use a firearm, Dane. Like this little piece? So small. It's usually a woman's gun. Fits into even a small handbag. But at close range...Dane, you're not dealing with Latham here. I'm not a madman. I just did what I had to do. Drop that cell phone. I'll hit you dead on in the chest if I fire now. And I will do it," he warned. Dane hesitated, slowly lowering the cell phone.

"They'll definitely catch you if you shoot us," he said.

"Let's go outside," Larry said.

Dane's eyes met Kelsey's. She stared at him and knew that he was silently telling her to listen...to buy time.

"All right," Dane said. "We'll go outside since you like to murder people on my beach."

"I'll shoot you right here, if need be. I know what you're doing, of course. Every second gives you a ray of hope, right, Dane?"

"Every second. But I know that you want every second, too. You're trying to figure out a way to kill us without getting caught. But you've blown it this time. Your prints are all over the gun. The cops aren't idiots."

"I can wipe off prints."

"They'll trace it."

"Don't be ridiculous. I bought this gun from Izzy Garcia. It can't be traced back to anyone. Let's go outside."

"Come on, Kelsey, let's walk outside," Dane said.

He prodded Kelsey before him. He followed her, and Larry followed him. Nervously.

"You know, Larry," Dane said, "you always were jealous of my beach. My property. My home. And, of course, my friendship with Sheila."

"Fuck you," Larry said angrily.

And in that moment he followed too closely.

Dane balked at the steps, slamming his body backward. Larry staggered. Dane turned, grasping him. He pinched his fingers into Larry's wrist, knowing the pain would cause Larry to lose his hold on the gun.

But it went off anyway, and Dane knew he'd been hit. In the leg. He could only pray that it had missed the artery.

Still, he forced his weight down on top of Larry's. He heard something crack. A bone. Larry's, thank God, not his.

But Larry was still struggling, reaching for the gun.

He didn't make it.

Kelsey dived in like a hawk. Suddenly the gun was in her hands, pointing down at Larry.

"One move and I shoot you dead! No, first I'll go for your kneecaps. For Sheila. But trust me, I *will* shoot," she said, and she meant it.

Dane knew he was losing blood. A lot of it.

"911, Kels, 911," he managed to say.

He was trying to remain conscious. He thought he must be insane. He could hear a siren. And then someone running.

Jesse. Jesse had followed him back to Hurricane Bay.

"I've got Larry covered, Kelsey," Jesse said. "Hurry up—call an ambulance. Fast."

Things hazed in and out. An ambulance came...and then a helicopter. Dane was being taken to the trauma center at Jackson Memorial in Miami.

He knew he was going in for surgery, knew he was being given blood.

And he knew when Kelsey was beside him, whispering to him.

"Don't you die on me, Dane. I love you. I need you. Oh God, Dane, we've both failed in many ways. But you never failed me. Don't you see? You never failed me."

He managed to open his eyes, though the sedation was stealing away what remained of his consciousness.

"I never will, Kelsey," he promised. Big words.

His eyes closed, and he was wheeled into surgery.

# EPILOGUE

The wedding was at Hurricane Bay in November, when summer's edge had cooled but the days were still gloriously warm and the night blissfully touched with the soft breezes of fall.

The groom still limped.

The bride was beautiful, and, despite the limp, the groom was incredibly handsome.

Nate was best man; Cindy was maid of honor.

Kelsey's father gave her away with the greatest pleasure.

After the ceremony, the bride spent her time moving between her guests and her mother—and her new baby brother. Joshua Michael Cunningham was just a month old, but big and beautiful, and the bride's mother was so flushed and happy, she might have been the bride herself.

The partying afterward went on and on. It was midnight when the guests at last dispersed. Most of them. Kelsey's parents were staying. They had at last gone up to the master bedroom, where both Kelsey and Dane had insisted they stay with their newborn.

Kelsey and Dane planned to stay in his old room, down on the first floor.

Dane slipped his arms around Kelsey as she disposed of the finery she was wearing.

"This may be weird," he said.

"What?"

"Having your folks in the house. And we don't leave for the north and our honeymoon until tomorrow."

She turned to him. "But it's our wedding night."

He sighed. "I'm not as good when I have to be really quiet."

She laughed. "It seems like tonight, of all nights, you should get a chance to be really, really good."

"All right," he said. "I've got it."

"Oh?"

"There's a really beautiful boat docked out there."

Kelsey smiled. "I knew you wouldn't fail me," she said softly.

"As long as we live," he said softly. "I'll do my best to never fail you—in any way."

She stood on her toes and kissed him.

And whispered her reply.

Hand in hand they walked toward the boat. Then ran.

It was a calm night at Hurricane Bay. Even so, the old boat rocked beneath the moonlight.